WAVE
OF
TERROR

OTHER TITLES BY JON JEFFERSON

WRITING AS JEFFERSON BASS (IN COLLABORATION WITH FORENSIC ANTHROPOLOGIST DR. BILL BASS)

Carved in Bone
Flesh and Bone
The Devil's Bones
Bones of Betrayal
The Bone Thief
The Bone Yard
Madonna and Corpse
The Inquisitor's Key
Jordan's Stormy Banks
Cut to the Bone
The Breaking Point
Without Mercy

WRITING AS JON JEFFERSON AND DR. BILL BASS

Death's Acre: Inside the Legendary Forensic Lab the Body Farm Where the Dead Do Tell Tales
Beyond the Body Farm
Identity Crisis

WAVE
OF
TERROR

JON JEFFERSON

THOMAS & MERCER

Published by Thomas & Mercer, Seattle

www.apub.com

Amazon, the Amazon logo, and Thomas & Mercer are trademarks of Amazon.com, Inc., or its affiliates.

ISBN-13: 9781542049870
ISBN-10: 1542049873

Cover design by Jae Song

Printed in the United States of America

For The Amazing Jane.
And for the millions of other smart, strong, courageous women
doing heroic work around the world.

PROLOGUE

Taburiente Volcano
La Palma, Canary Islands—250 miles off the northwest coast of
Africa

Megan O'Malley's head whipped around, her red hair swirling and her brain reeling as she tried to make sense of what she'd just glimpsed out the car window. Was it a hallucination? An artifact of jet lag and fatigue and altitude-induced oxygen deprivation? It most certainly couldn't be what it appeared to be, because what it *appeared* to be—in the fraction of the second that she'd seen it—was the Eye of God: an immense, unfathomable eye of blue, set in a vast, stony brow.

O'Malley hit the brakes, and the rental car, a tiny Toyota Yaris, slithered to a stop on the shoulder of the road, a cracking two-lane snaking along the rim of an immense, cratered volcano. The car bucked and the engine died. *The clutch,* she reminded herself. *Don't forget the clutch.* The rental car had a manual transmission, and she hadn't driven a stick in years.

The shoulder was narrow and the road treacherous; if she'd skidded a few feet farther off the pavement, the car would have gone careening down the mountainside. Beyond the shoulder, the slope angled a thousand feet and then dropped away altogether, sheering off into a cliff. Far below the edge was an unbroken sea of clouds, surrounding the shattered volcanic cone like a fleecy Christmas-tree skirt. A mile below the cloud tops lay the Atlantic, a fact she knew because she had landed at the coast three hours before and had been shifting and twisting upward ever since. The view was stunning, but what the hell had she just glimpsed out her window?

Granted, she was here—"here" being the rim of an ancient volcano on La Palma, home to one of the world's best observatory complexes—to investigate a celestial mystery. But the mystery she'd come to investigate—to *solve*—had nothing to do with God and everything to do with science. An astronomer and a planet hunter, she had come from Baltimore to Spain's Canary Islands on a quest for Planet Nine, a huge, as-yet-unseen orb circling the sun somewhere in the outer dark, far beyond the known planets.

Her celestial search couldn't begin until nightfall. Meanwhile, the unsettling something she had seen—the Eye of God, she seemed to have named it—required further research. As a scientist, she had a duty, or at least a compulsion, to seek an explanation.

Even without the Eye, the setting would have seemed strange and forbidding. The combination of elements—craggy lava around her, white and silver telescope domes looming above her, and the sea of clouds below—gave the place a stark, otherworldly look, as if she had teleported to some scientific outpost on Mars.

O'Malley parked on the shoulder, the car's engine ticking with heat, and wondered if she'd really seen the Eye or had simply imagined it. She rolled down her window—a manual crank (Christ, how long since she'd used one of those?)—and leaned out, scanning the terrain behind and above. All she saw was a brown mountainside strewn with brown rocks ranging in size from eggs to elephants. Baffled, she jammed the gearshift into "Reverse." The gears gnashed, and the clutch caught with a series of whiplash-inducing jerks. She lurched backward for fifty yards and stopped, this time remembering to depress the clutch, then scanned the slope to her left once more. Nothing. *Bloody hell,* she thought. *I know I didn't make that up.*

She eased out the clutch again, more smoothly this time. Backing up another two hundred yards—back to the curve she had rounded just before she and the Eye had swapped glances—she stopped again, then began creeping forward, retracing her earlier approach, this time at a snail's pace.

Nothing. Nothing. Nothing. Then, suddenly, there it was, staring at her once more. She stomped the brake, and the car shuddered to a stop, the engine bucking and stalling again. "The *clutch*, O'Malley, the *clutch*," she scolded. She leaped out, her "nerd purse"—the waist pack containing her wallet, passport, and iPhone—snagging on the seat belt. After disentangling herself, she hipped the door shut and turned to glare at the mountainside. Nothing but rock glared back. In the space of three seconds and ten feet, the Eye had winked shut again.

She walked slowly up the road, scrutinizing the slope, her gaze as focused as a laser. As she walked, buffeted by a rising afternoon wind, she heard a soft, high-pitched moan, a keening sound that made the hairs on her arms and neck prickle. And it was precisely then, mid-prickle, that she found herself staring anew into the Eye of God.

But this time, the Eye was not vacant and bottomless; this time the Almighty's Eye contained—or, rather, reflected—an immense square *building*, centered precisely in the pupil. O'Malley whirled and looked behind her, though she knew perfectly well that behind her lay nothing but open air and, far below, the sea of clouds concealing the Atlantic.

She turned back toward the Eye to see if it was still there, still open. It was, and she began picking her way up the rocky slope, dodging the ankle breakers underfoot. Every few steps she stopped to glance over her shoulder, as if a building might materialize in midair. And why not, after all, given how suddenly and inexplicably the Eye itself had appeared?

Abruptly she stopped in her tracks and laughed, one quick, barking "Ha!" She, of all people—Megan O'Malley, rising star of the Johns Hopkins astronomy department—should know a telescope mirror when she saw it, even an outrageously oversize mirror sitting buck naked on a mountainside.

The mirror wasn't actually round, she saw now. It was octagonal—a concave, fifty-foot STOP sign—pieced together from hundreds of small, square mirrors, their surfaces polished and silvered to perfection, their edges butted together as tightly as bathroom tiles. And the immense "building" reflected at the center of the mirror was actually a suitcase-size metal box—an electronic detector—suspended in front of the mirror, at its focal point.

The detector was magnified a thousandfold by the gigantic mirror, and as O'Malley entered the field of view, she, too, was magnified a thousandfold. Her head appeared the size of a Mount Rushmore president's; the pores of her nose gaped like potholes in a battered Baltimore street; her chin sported a rogue whisker as thick as a tree trunk. *Christ,* she thought, *like I need the world's biggest makeup mirror to see my flaws.* She already saw her imperfections at high magnification, unceasingly and unrelentingly. What was it David had said years before, when he'd leaped from the roller-coaster car of their brief marriage? "If you liked yourself even half as much as I did, we could've been epic." David was a bit of a wimp—more sensitive than any woman O'Malley knew, or at least more sensitive than any woman she *liked*—but he was right about the ruthlessness of her self-critical gaze; she saw that flaw, too, of course, as clearly as she now beheld the whisker in her chin, seemingly thick enough to call out for a chain saw. "A pause for reflection," she announced wryly, and then—holding her vast head motionless in the mirror—she plucked the giant whisker with gargantuan fingers, giving the world's biggest wince as her mammoth mouth squawked *"Ow."*

Now that the Eye had morphed—from cosmic miracle to tool of the trade—her logic circuits rebooted. Even aside from its immensity, the Eye was unlike any telescope she had ever seen. It was a reflecting telescope, obviously, but there was virtually nothing to it except for the huge, segmented mirror, plus one slender, curved arm supporting the detector at the focal point. Framing either side of the mirror, so delicate as to be nearly invisible, was a web of cables, trusses, and pulleys—the motorized mechanism used to control the mirror's movements, angling it toward this exploding supernova or that imploding galaxy.

The wind gusted and the eerie, ethereal moan intensified, and O'Malley realized that the haunting music came from the telescope's cables, singing in the wind like the rigging of a ship. As she walked around, studying the setup, she noticed another mirror—an identical twin—perched on the hillside a hundred yards away. She smiled. God, it seemed, was no one-eyed Cyclops after all; God had binocular vision. And God's binocular vision, she deduced, was X-ray vision: these must be MAGIC-I and MAGIC-II, the observatory's pair of X-ray telescopes, designed to study not stars and planets but pulses and bursts of invisible energy from deep in the cosmos.

As she drew near the instrument's base, she spotted an information plaque, from which she learned that the telescopes had a tragic history. When MAGIC-II was finished—the very night before the ribbon-cutting ceremony, in fact—the astrophysicist who had designed the instruments fell to his death from a scaffold, where he'd been putting on the finishing touches in the darkness. Perhaps the haunting sound was more than just wind and wires after all; maybe the massive telescopes were lamenting their dead creator. Or perhaps he himself was shrieking, his falling scream forever caught in the wires.

Glancing westward, O'Malley noticed the sun sinking toward the ocean of clouds, and she realized she'd better hurry if she wanted to get checked in, unpacked, and acquainted with her assigned telescope before dark. She turned downslope and began picking her way back toward the Toyota.

Just then another car topped the grade and rounded the crater's rim. The driver glanced up at O'Malley, and then the woman's head jerked and her mouth gaped as she, too, beheld the Eye in astonished confusion.

Fresh from the disorienting sight herself, O'Malley smiled. But her amusement was short-lived. "Hey," she yelled as the car hurtled directly toward her own. "Look *out!* Look—" Metal crunched and plastic shattered as the new arrival rear-ended O'Malley's car full tilt, without so much as a token tap on the brakes. The tiny Yaris lurched and, with a metallic snap, jumped out of gear. As O'Malley watched in frozen horror, her car ricocheted forward, rolling along the road's narrow shoulder and then angling off the edge and jouncing down the volcano's flank—moving slowly at first, then faster and faster, like some bad-karma illustration of Newton's law of gravity. It sailed off the cliff and cartwheeled into the sea of clouds, taking with it O'Malley's clothes, her books, her laptop—everything except the few essentials zipped into the pack that was clipped to her waist. After a long, quiet pause—even the wind and the eerie moaning seemed to stop to listen—she heard a distant but telltale *sploosh!*

O'Malley stared at the tiny hole the car had punched in the vapor. "Well, shit," she said, turning to address the all-seeing, unblinking Eye of God. "I guess I should've gotten the comprehensive coverage after all."

I: THE DRAGON BOWL

CHAPTER 1

Isaac Newton Telescope
Observatorio del Roque de los Muchachos
La Palma

Nice butt, thought O'Malley as the Spaniard sauntered away, his snug, faded jeans luminous in the glow from the telescope's control console.

The Spaniard—Iñigo Rodriguez—was O'Malley's liaison at the observatory: her host, guide, mentor, telescope technician, and new fantasy object, all rolled into one.

Iñigo turned and looked back over his shoulder. The shoulder, out-lined beneath a tight sweater, was also nice—muscled, but not so big as to be beefy. His hair, black and wavy, fell almost to the knitted collar. "If you have a problem, just call me."

"I will, thanks" was what she said. But what she thought was *My problem is it's been forever since I've gotten laid. Can you help me with that, Señor Iñigo?* Suddenly she had a naughty thought. *Or should I say . . . Señor In-ya-go?* She sighed and rolled her eyes. *Focus, O'Malley.*

She redirected her attention to the control console of the instrument, the Isaac Newton Telescope. The INT was much older and far smaller than MAGIC, the immense pair of exposed X-ray telescopes perched on the slope a half mile away. With a diameter of eight feet, the

INT's concave mirror was modest by twenty-first-century standards—a fraction the size of the biggest optical telescopes here on La Palma or at the world's other top observatories. Still, if Galileo could discover the moons of Jupiter with a handheld spyglass, she could make *her* astronomical mark with the INT. *If* she looked in the right place, and *if* the planets—the known ones and the unknown—aligned for her.

She entered a set of coordinates into the control console, pivoting the telescope toward a cluster of stars directly overhead. As of yet, no one had succeeded in spotting O'Malley's quarry, provisionally named Planet Nine; its existence had only recently been inferred from slight irregularities in the orbits of the other outer planets. Jupiter, Saturn, Uranus, and Neptune all wobbled slightly, as if something—something distant but massive—was tugging on them from the outer dark. Whoever first found and photographed that something would have naming rights, as well as a lasting place in astronomical history, so O'Malley was doubly eager to be that person.

She pulled an oversize, borrowed jacket around her shoulders—a guilty loan from the woman who had sent her car off the cliff. The woman had also given her a ride the rest of the way to the observatory, where she, too, was heading: not an astronomer, she'd explained, but a friend of an astronomer. O'Malley had accepted the coat with more grace and gratitude than she had accepted the woman's apology. It was a challenge to be gracious when all of her warm clothes, toiletries, and even her precious laptop lay submerged beneath the sea cliff.

Zipping the coat against the chill, she turned to the telescope's control panel. She was here; that was what mattered. The quest, the prospect of being the one to find Planet Nine, was enough to make up for the loss. Almost.

But her excitement didn't last long. Ninety minutes later, the rush—even the memory of the rush—evaporated. "Shit," O'Malley said to herself, or to the telescope, or to the heavens. It had taken a solid hour to get the telescope trained on the speck of sky she was searching.

Then, just when she'd locked onto it and programmed in a series of overlapping time exposures with the telescope's camera, something had jarred the scope, jolting its gaze toward an entirely different speck of sky somewhere to the south. Now she'd have to start all over again. "Shit," she repeated. "Shit shit *shit*." An hour's work—an hour's telescope time, of which she had precious little—down the drain, all because of . . . what? Grit in the telescope's bearings? A slamming door somewhere in the observatory? A powerful thunderclap? *No, not thunder,* she thought. *I'd've heard thunder. Besides, the sky's clear as a bell.*

It was entirely possible that this new, randomly revealed sliver of sky was full of signs and wonders—incipient supernovae, binary stars, the birth of new galaxies—spectacular stellar phenomena, far grander than the dark sphere whose cold and lonely existence she was hoping to confirm. But planet hunting was what she was here for; it was *all* she was here for; it was what she'd spent the past year preparing for and proposing and pleading for the chance to do.

"Iñigo?" She called into the darkness and waited for a response, but got none. "Iñigo!" Where the hell was the handsome tech? Earlier, when she'd checked in to her cubicle-size room in the Residencia, he'd been impossible to shake, despite multiple hints. He'd hovered, making small talk—chatting about the island, the observatory, the World Cup—when all she'd wanted to do was shower and wash her underwear—the only pair she had now, the pair she'd been wearing for thirty hours straight. Was that too much to ask? Ten minutes of hot water and five minutes with the blow-dryer? And now, when she actually needed him, he was nowhere to be found. "Iñigo, *help!*"

A dim rectangle of red appeared on the dome's far side—the doorway to the lounge, a room illuminated by a dim red bulb so as not to wreck the astronomers' night vision—and then winked shut. But in the moment it was open, O'Malley glimpsed Iñigo's silhouette and that of another figure. A woman's figure. The woman, she was sure, who had hit her car. *Dammit,* she thought at the woman. *Just because you were distracted by the prospect of nookie?*

Iñigo was zipping a jacket as he arrived at the control console; underneath the jacket, he appeared to be shirtless. "Is there a problem?"

"A huge problem," O'Malley said, biting back a snarky comment. "I just spent an hour getting locked in on my reference stars, and the second I finished, the telescope jumped." She held up a hand and shook it violently to demonstrate. Iñigo looked puzzled, or maybe skeptical, so she elaborated. "The image shifted. The scope moved. Jumped. Jerked. I completely lost my fix." She repeated the hand gesture to make sure he understood how abrupt the movement had been. "There must be something wrong with the drive mechanism."

Iñigo shook his head slowly, looking distressed to be contradicting her. "No, I don't think so. The telescope is perfect. As solid and steady as the earth. It moves"—he held up a hand and swept it in a fluid arc—"like the moon and the stars."

O'Malley noticed two things: first, that Iñigo spoke and gestured more like a poet and a dancer than a technician, and second, that his jacket was half-open, and his chiseled chest made it difficult to concentrate.

She realized that he was looking at her, waiting for a response to a question or comment she had failed to hear. "Sorry, what?"

"Let me see," he repeated. "Show me the picture."

Together they huddled over the console, whose array of screens and dials and controls resembled those of an airliner or a nuclear power plant. The largest screen showed what the telescope was "seeing" in real time—a modern, computer-age substitute for an eyepiece, which the INT did not actually possess. Eyepieces were obsolete, except on small, amateur telescopes; many of the astronomers O'Malley knew had never even looked through an eyepiece, and some dealt exclusively with numbers rather than images. O'Malley was good with data, but she still loved seeing stars and planets; the beauty of the night sky was what had attracted her to astronomy in the first place and what kept her enthralled still.

Beside the main monitor was a smaller screen showing thumbnails of time-exposure photographs the telescope had taken. She clicked on the first image to enlarge it. The screen filled with pinpoints of light. "You see," said Iñigo. "Perfect. As steady as the earth itself."

O'Malley opened the next picture, which, instead of precise pinpoints, showed jerky, zigzagging tracks of light. "This one's not perfect; this one's not steady. This one is useless, Iñigo. Maybe there's sand in the tracking mechanism. Or maybe one of the gears has a chipped tooth."

Iñigo frowned. "No, I do not think so. I have seen this before," he mused, tapping the screen.

"It's a chronic problem? Jesus, why hasn't it been fixed? People come from all over the world to use this instrument. I'm missing a week of teaching, and I'm spending ten thousand dollars of my budget on three nights of telescope time here. It's a huge waste if the telescope doesn't work right."

"Ah, forgive me," he said gently. "I am explaining badly. I have seen this before—just one time. We could not understand it; we could not explain it. We took the telescope apart to find what was wrong. No success. Finally, we learn the answer. A *terremoto*, an earthquake. Very small, but magnified many times by the instrument. If the island shakes, the telescope shakes. So, you see? As solid as the earth." He smiled, and O'Malley felt herself redden. She told herself the flush stemmed from embarrassment over her accusatory behavior—that it had nothing to do with the man's warm smile, the charming gap between his two front teeth, the chiseled chest.

"Iñigo?" The call came from the direction of the lounge. In the faint red light spilling through the doorway, O'Malley glimpsed the woman's silhouette once more.

Iñigo gave O'Malley a sheepish shrug. "Try again," he suggested. "I think you will not have the problem now." He smiled once more, with a slight nod that might have been a hint of a bow, then turned and walked away. O'Malley sighed. *Cute butt, dammit,* she thought again as he sauntered toward the lounge—toward the dark-eyed, dark-haired, long-legged woman for whom the earth seemed likely to move in a more pleasing way than it had moved for O'Malley.

Two hours later, the telescope jerked again. "*Damm*it," said O'Malley when she checked the image and saw the zigzag star tracks again. "Fucking *hell*." She had only two more nights of telescope time here, and if tonight was any indication, she was wasting her time and her research funding.

She turned toward the lounge to call for Iñigo, but then she thought better of it—she'd be interrupting his lovefest again; besides, he'd already made it clear that he was unable to solve her problem. Not tonight, anyhow. She stared at the screen, stewing. One by one she scrolled through her images again, staring at them, searching them: not for Planet Nine—even if it was there, in one of her images, there'd be no way to see it—but for . . . what? What *might* she see, if she looked at the images in just the right way? She let her gaze soften and drift sideways, hoping to sneak up on whatever was just out of view.

Her gaze softened further, her head moved closer to the screen, and before she knew it, she was facedown on the console, snoring softly.

She was climbing a high, narrow scaffold. As she ascended, she saw that it actually wasn't a scaffold; it was the open steel framework of an immense reflecting telescope: the skeleton of a vast tube, without an outer skin. When she reached the top—the telescope's open end—she hoisted herself up and stood, balancing on a narrow, curving beam of steel. Overhead, the Milky

Way flowed across the sky, its stars so abundant in the high, clear air of La Palma that it seemed a solid river of light rather than billions of individual specks.

O'Malley narrowed her gaze, ignoring the sky-spanning splendor, and focused intently on one small region: the region, blacker and closer than the backdrop of stars, where she suspected a dark, frozen world lurked, unseen and yet powerful, exerting its influence on every other planet, including Earth. "Where are you?" she whispered to it. "Show me. I'm here to find you."

As if in answer, she felt a slight buzzing sensation—some force field from afar. "Show me," she repeated, and the sensation strengthened, became a shiver and then a shudder.

But the vibration was not originating from the sky overhead. It was coming from beneath her feet, and as it intensified, the telescope's steel framework began to shake. O'Malley teetered on the narrow beam, her arms flailing for balance. And then she fell, tumbling headfirst into the telescope, her open, screaming mouth magnified a thousandfold by the immense object that she recognized, in her final instant, as the unfathomable Eye of God.

CHAPTER 2

Fort Wadsworth
Staten Island, New York

Dawtry took a step closer to the edge of the crumbling stone parapet and squinted across the Narrows. Seven miles north, lower Manhattan's temples to the gods of commerce and capitalism glinted in the morning sun. The light ricocheted off the blue-gray glass of One World Trade Center—"Freedom Tower," Dawtry sometimes called it aloud, though his private, unspoken name for it was "Tombstone Tower"—shattering into millions of sparkling shards on the mile-wide strait that formed the gateway to New York Harbor. Then Dawtry—FBI Special Agent Christopher "Chip" Dawtry—swiveled his gaze upward, scanning the long, dark underbelly of the suspension bridge that loomed above him.

Dawtry's vantage point, an archaic artillery battery, had been built during the Civil War to repel Confederate ships that never came. With its massive arches of rough brick and stone, the fort would not have looked out of place in ancient Rome. High above, fifty thousand under-dressed runners were jumping and jogging in place, their breaths fogging the November morning as they waited for the crack of a gunshot.

"We need you to call it," a voice murmured in Dawtry's earpiece. "Green or red? Go or no go?"

"One minute," Dawtry muttered into his mic. "I just need one last look." Pacing the parapet, he felt himself shiver. Perhaps the shiver was a gesture of solidarity with the huddled masses suspended above him—*Huddled masses yearning to run free,* he thought, the riff inspired by the Statue of Liberty, a few miles to his left. Or perhaps the chill was closer to the bone: the shadow of Richard's death, which still fell across him whenever he glimpsed the skyline of the financial district. Whatever the reason, Dawtry felt a vague sense of unease—a deep reluctance to green-light the start of the race—but he could see nothing to justify delaying further.

"We've got fifty thousand people lined up to cross that bridge, Agent Dawtry," the voice urged. "They've come from all fifty states and more than a hundred countries to run this marathon. Do we say *go,* or do we tell 'em the FBI says to get the hell out of here? Make the call, man."

"I said sixty seconds," snapped Dawtry, jogging to the corner of the parapet. A stone's throw away, the south tower of the Verrazano-Narrows Bridge reared from the water and rose seven hundred feet above him. His breath coming faster than the brief jog accounted for, he took one final look at the bridge tower, his view magnified and sharpened by the augmented-reality goggles he wore: sleek, Star Trek–looking glasses whose AR capabilities he'd been tasked with evaluating—and today, of all the high-stress days. The reasons for the urgency weren't entirely clear to him. What *was* clear, though, was the view through the lenses. The view was glare-free, contrast enhanced, and high resolution, with a distance scale superimposed on the imagery and a magnification of up to thirty times normal. Magnification sufficient, at this moment, to reveal dozens of streams of urine sparkling in the morning sun, as waiting male runners relieved themselves over the railing one last time before the race began. "Nice," Dawtry muttered, grateful that the wind wasn't blowing in his direction.

The FBI had gone to extraordinary lengths to ensure the safety of the runners and spectators throughout the twenty-six-mile course. The 2013 Boston Marathon bombing, together with a continuing spate of ISIS-inspired attacks around the world, had made the New York City Marathon's organizers understandably skittish. Thousands of NYPD officers and New York State Police had been posted all along the race's five-borough route; in addition, the Bureau had detailed hundreds of special agents from the New York City Field Office, the Counterterrorism Division, and even the Weapons of Mass Destruction Directorate. With dotted-line responsibilities to both Counterterrorism and WMD, Dawtry was the Bureau's logical point man to give the go-ahead—which also meant that he'd be the fall guy if anything went wrong.

He had chosen his own observation point—almost directly beneath the race's starting point—through a grim combination of imaginary empathy and cold-blooded calculus: if *he* were a terrorist trying to kill the most people and inflict the deepest, most impressive wound possible, what would he do? The answer had come to him with swift and terrible certainty: *Hit the bridge at the start, when it's got fifty thousand people on it—and a shitload of cameras streaming it around the world.*

As the sun inched upward, the shadow of the bridge tower fell across the fort like some dark portent, at least to Dawtry's worried mind. Setting off bombs simultaneously at each end, when both decks of the roadway were packed with runners, would surely cause a deadly stampede toward the center, one that could crush hundreds or even thousands of people. The real prize, though, would be to bring down the bridge completely, like the World Trade Center towers. *It would be a stunning coup,* Dawtry thought: toppling America's biggest bridge *and* killing fifty thousand people. He flashed to the climactic scene from Richard's favorite World War II movie, *The Bridge on the River Kwai*—a scene in which US commandos blow up a strategic Japanese bridge, while a misguided British colonel tries to stop them. "Madness,"

Dawtry quoted, swept up in the conflation of the movie scene, the augmented reality of the goggles, and the insidious combination of his own imagination and memory.

Zooming out, Dawtry gave the belly of the bridge a last look, as if one more glance could possibly show him something new. As if he hadn't already studied the structure a hundred times or more over the past three days, not just in the daylight but at night by floodlight and infrared light and dream light—nightmare light. His gut felt queasy, but Dawtry reminded himself—or prayed—that the nausea was owing only to the greasy eggs he'd eaten at 4:00 a.m. He gave the sky a quick scan, making sure no airliners were banking toward the bridge. He thought of Richard again, wondered for the thousandth time if his brother had seen the plane before it hit.

"Time's up," the serpent whispered in his ear again. "Call it."

Dawtry grimaced. Ignoring the vague inner voice shouting *wait*, he said, "Green light," his voice projecting more confidence than he felt. "Let 'em go."

Five seconds later, he heard a faint pop high overhead, then a chorus of cheers and whoops and boat whistles, followed by the siren of the lead motorcycle. Underneath those sounds, almost imperceptible at first, came a muffled but steadily rising rumble: the rumble of a hundred thousand feet, each pair marking a slightly different cadence, but combining to create a deep, almost visceral vibration.

Now zooming in on the bridge's upper deck, Dawtry glimpsed a line of bobbing heads near the rail—elite runners, already streaking toward the center of the main span, which was the one-mile mark. He checked his stopwatch, which he'd instinctively started when he'd heard the pop of the starting gun. A five-minute first mile: amazing, considering that the whole mile was one long climb—up the ramp and up the sloping deck to the center of the bridge, the roadway's highest point. Dawtry felt himself beginning to relax now, his jangled nerves and queasy stomach gradually settling. He glanced to his right, where a

Bureau sharpshooter—a guy he didn't know, from the Hostage Rescue Team—scanned the bridge and the shoreline over the scope of his sniper's rifle. Dawtry tried to recall the guy's name—Walton? Dalton? "Looks like a fast start," Dawtry said, just for something to say.

"Weather's perfect for a marathon," replied the sniper. "Low fifties—supposed to stay that way for the next couple hours. By then, the top runners'll be in Central Park, sprinting for the finish line."

They watched the leaders disappear down the far side, moving even faster on mile two, aided by the downhill slope as they descended toward Brooklyn. By now the entire span was jammed, the runners packed tight, their shoulders practically touching, their legs churning inches apart. "Wonder which weighs more," Walton/Dalton mused, "the usual traffic, or all these people jammed together, fifteen or twenty of 'em in the space one car takes up."

"Well," Dawtry mused, "fifty thousand runners averaging, say, a hundred fifty pounds apiece. That's, what, seven, eight million pounds? The bridge's decking itself weighs a hundred million pounds, say the engineering specs. So the weight of the runners is trivial. A fly on an elephant."

"A hundred million pounds?" said Walton/Dalton. "Hanging from just four cables?" Dawtry gave a goggled nod. "Imagine if one of those cables snapped." The sniper paused. "Imagine if all *four* snapped."

"Cut it out, man," said Dawtry. "Don't jinx it."

"Snapped," the guy repeated. "Or got cut."

"*Stop.*"

"I saw a cool YouTube video the other day. Showed an old suspension bridge over the Ohio River being demolished," he went on, now ignoring the race and looking straight at Dawtry instead. "The demo contractor used explosive charges to cut the main cables, and the whole damn thing just folded in on itself and plopped into the river." The guy's mouth was twitching in a slight, smug smile, and Dawtry's blood turned icy. "Can't help wondering, what if something went wrong with the cables up there right now?"

"You're not from Hostage Rescue," said Dawtry, a terrible realization dawning. "Who the fuck are you?" He reached for his sidearm, and the guy's smile got bigger and smugger.

"Look up there," he told Dawtry. "About ten feet from the end of that nearest cable." He pointed with the barrel of the rifle. "See that thing that looks like an angle bracket running around the cable? You can zoom in pretty tight with those goggles. Magnification of what, twenty?"

"Thirty," said Dawtry, all life drained from his voice now.

"Oh, right. Thirty. Zoom in on that angle bracket thing, tell me what it looks like at thirty X."

Dawtry zoomed in with the goggles, full tight. "Looks like it's got an electrical wire connected to it," he heard himself say, as if in a bad dream. "Looks like I've fucked up big-time."

"Sure does," the guy agreed. "'Cause that thing that looks to you like an angle bracket? To a demo expert, it looks like a shaped charge—a cutting charge—circling that cable. The other cable, too. Both ends of both cables. You might want to zoom out wide, Agent Dawtry, so you can see the whole bridge, 'cause those charges are fixin' to blow." The guy checked his watch. "Right . . . about . . . *now!*"

And at that moment, as Dawtry watched, paralyzed, a cluster of quick, bright halos encircled the ends of the suspension cables—*A burning ring of fire,* Dawtry thought—and then the high-tech lenses of the AR goggles filled with the sight and sound of the taut cables snapping, thrashing like dragons' tails. The massive bridge towers shrieked and groaned, leaning slowly inward, and then began to topple toward one another like seven-hundred-foot redwoods. As they fell, the entire span of the bridge plunged down, down, down toward the slate-gray water of the Narrows, taking fifty thousand runners with it.

The roadway's impact launched a geyser a hundred feet high and more than a mile long, stretching from Staten Island all the way to Brooklyn. As the spray subsided, Dawtry saw a fifty-foot wave hurtling toward the old fort. "*Damn* you," he said, cursing not the messenger of doom who had foretold the collapse, nor the wave that was about to kill him—he surely deserved death—but cursing himself, in the final instant before the wave's impact.

But there was no impact. Dawtry saw the wave rear above him. He saw the wave begin to crash down upon him. But he felt nothing.

He staggered forward, having instinctively leaned to brace against an impact that did not come. He would have tumbled right off the parapet if a strong hand hadn't gripped his arm and dragged him upright.

Dazed and disoriented, Dawtry ripped off the goggles and stared wildly around him, gaping in disbelief: gaping at the calm, sparkling water of the Narrows; gaping at the crisp shadows of lofty girders and taut cables above him; gaping at the graceful bridge soaring—still soaring!—high overhead, rumbling with the footfalls of tens of thousands of runners and joggers. "What the fuck is going on? Can you please tell me what's *real* here? 'Cause I sure as hell don't know." It was as if he'd been transplanted into the sci-fi movie *Vanilla Sky*, the boundaries between virtual reality and actual reality and nightmare utterly erased.

The guy was grinning like a Cheshire cat now, but the grin faded slightly when Dawtry raised his weapon. "Who are you?" demanded Dawtry. "You're not FBI."

The guy's hands were up, his fingers spread in a *stay cool* sort of gesture. "You're right, I'm not FBI. I'm DOD."

"*Defense?* What branch?"

"Duh. DARPA, 'course."

Something finally clicked in Dawtry's rational brain, which was beginning to reboot. DARPA—the Defense Advanced Research Projects Agency—was the Pentagon's geek squad. The military's science lab. The multibillion-dollar R & D department of the mightiest fighting force on the planet. Walton/Dalton nodded at the look of recognition in Dawtry's eyes. "We're the only ones with the know-how and the computing power to do this."

"By 'this' . . ." Dawtry waved his goggle-clutching hand in a vague gesture that took in the bridge, the AR headset, and his own very confused self.

"By 'this' I mean a computer simulation that takes multichannel, real-time inputs—video input of what you're seeing, three-D sensors that track your position and movements and your directional gaze— and then modifies the display and the audio track, superimposing computer-generated images and sound. All within a fraction of a second."

Dawtry felt himself playing multiple games of catch-up. His heart was still pounding, he remained disoriented, and he felt furious and humiliated that he'd failed to see the explosives—or, rather, the "explosives"—girdling the suspension cables. He channeled his turbulent feelings at the DARPA guy, whose name he still couldn't quite recall. "And what dimwit had the bright idea of using this high-tech shit for some sort of sadistic prank, anyhow?"

Dalton or Walton—no, *Carlton* (why the hell couldn't Dawtry remember *Carlton?*)—flashed him another grin. "*You* did, Special Agent Dawtry. Not the specific scenario, of course—I'll take some credit for that. Seeing that suspension bridge demolition on YouTube really did inspire me. But the basic concept? Using AR goggles to piggyback a simulated mass-casualty attack on a real-world event? Lifted straight from a memo you sent to your director last year."

"Son of a bitch," Dawtry said, suddenly remembering.

"Your director liked the idea. Reached out to DARPA, asked us to implement it. So who better to be the first guinea pig than you?"

Dawtry winced. "Me and my big mouth. I guess it's back to Buffalo for me now, since I flunked my own damn test."

Carlton shook his head. "It wasn't *you* on trial here, man. It was the *technology*—the training methodology you suggested. Judging by your reaction—our telemetry says your heart rate shot up to one sixty, and your blood pressure to two twenty over one ten—I'd say the experiment was a home run. A lot more convincing and intense than I expected, frankly." After a moment, with a sly grin, he added, "DARPA and the Bureau weren't the only ones watching this."

"What are you talking about?"

"The CIA asked for a feed, too, though their interest is a bit more personal. Or should I say *personnel.*"

"I'm not following you."

"You didn't hear it from me, but rumor has it the Agency's looking for a new FBI liaison."

Dawtry frowned, but he also felt a buzz of excitement. "But what about Coutant? He's been our Langley interface for years."

Carlton shrugged. "Maybe he's retiring. Or maybe they just want fresh blood. And maybe you're it."

Dawtry's *hmm* was casual and ambiguous. But if people at the CIA were tracking his heart rate and blood pressure at this moment, the numbers would have sent a decidedly unmixed message about his reaction to the prospect of having his finger on the pulse of America's domestic and global counterterrorism efforts: *Hell, yeah!*

CHAPTER 3

Observatorio del Roque de los Muchachos
Day two

The Residencia, where visiting astronomers stayed on La Palma, was a long, low structure of concrete and glass. The building included a kitchen that served three meals a day, as well as administrative offices and a small library that was stocked with a Babel of books and three computers. O'Malley was working at one of the computers; more accurately, she was attempting to work, or pretending to work, but what she was actually doing was stewing.

She was stewing at the computer for two reasons. Reason Number One was the loss of her own computer, a loss she had felt keenly all day long. Reason Number Two was the crap weather that had blanketed the island in order to make her life a living hell. Outside, the sun had just gone down; she knew this because she knew, to the second, what time the sun set on La Palma today: at 17:37:28 UTC, Greenwich Mean Time (which astronomers around the world used), or at 18:37:28—just after 6:30 p.m.—local time. But despite the westward-facing windows lining the wall of the narrow Residencia, and despite her obsessive staring out those windows, O'Malley had not actually witnessed the setting of the sun. All she had witnessed was a steady deepening of the gloom inside the dense fog shrouding the mountain. Fog, she realized, was a relative term in this case: down at sea level, the island's coastline might well be in the clear; even now, some of the locals might be looking up, watching the clouds scudding thousands of feet overhead. But from where O'Malley stood—or, rather, sat and stewed—the clouds obscured and obfuscated and enveloped.

Her foggy funk was interrupted by the speakerphone on the desk beside her. "*Doctora* O'Malley? You are there?" She recognized the voice as that of Antonio, the receptionist in the lobby of the Residencia.

She picked up the handset. "Hello? Yes, this is O'Malley. Antonio?"

"*Doctora*, Iñigo calls to ask if you come to the telescope soon?"

"Why? What for? There's nothing to see—we're completely in the clouds."

"Wait just one moment, please." O'Malley heard a click, then silence. After a pause, she heard another click. "Excuse me, *Doctora*. Iñigo says the liquid nitrogen in the camera needs to be replenished. Did you forget this?"

Damn, she thought. "No," she said—a small lie. She checked her watch; she had nearly an hour until the coolant had to be replenished to protect the camera. *Hold your horses, Iñigo*, she thought. "Please tell him I'm coming." She hung up the phone and scurried to her room for the borrowed coat. She would definitely need it; the windchill was already edging toward freezing. Sixty seconds later, she jogged through the lobby.

"*Doctora!*" Antonio called to her from behind the counter. He held up a set of keys and jingled them. "You are forgetting the keys. The observatory car."

"I think I'll walk."

"But it's cold, and your telescope is two kilometers away!"

"That's okay—I need the exercise. If Iñigo calls again, tell him I'll be there in twenty minutes." And with that, she waved and blew through the double set of glass doors and out into the fog. The clouds. The suspended aqueous aerosol that was a galaxy-size pain in her astronomical ass. She jogged, partly to hurry, partly to generate heat, partly to vent frustration.

Five minutes later, she was regretting her rashness in turning down the car; ten minutes later, she was gasping for breath, her heart pounding from the exertion of running. *Man,* she thought, *they aren't kidding when they say the air's thin at seven thousand feet. You could go down in history as the first astronomer to die at the Roque de los Muchachos.* Then she felt a stab of shame at her insensitivity, recalling the German scientist who had fallen to his death from MAGIC-II.

The road to the Isaac Newton Telescope wound upward past MAGIC, and although she couldn't see it through the fog, she could *hear* it again, the wind—or the ghost of the dead German—moaning in the taut steel cables.

O'Malley paused to listen and to catch her breath. The air was thick with water vapor, but it remained thin on oxygen—20 percent thinner than the air back home in Baltimore, she knew. When she resumed moving, it was at a walk, not a run. Why take chances, with the altitude *or* the route? The two-lane road ended at the rim of the caldera, and in the pea-soup fog it would be easy to miss the turnoff to the telescope and stumble off the edge.

Half an hour after dashing out of the Residencia, O'Malley arrived at the INT building, which was barely visible in the dark and the mist. She entered by the basement door, then trudged up the metal staircase to the third floor, where the telescope was.

The interior of the dome was dark and cold. The darkness was to preserve the night vision of the astronomers. The cold was simply an occupational hazard: the metal dome was uninsulated, so the telescope would adjust to the outdoor air temperature, minimizing distortion from thermal air currents. Even in summer, the nighttime temperatures at this altitude dropped into the fifties or forties; in winter, it could go well below zero.

By the faint glow of the red work lights, O'Malley located the dewar of liquid nitrogen—a short, squat tank the size of a wastepaper basket, mounted on wheels—and rolled it from the edge of the dome onto the telescope floor. As she approached the base of the instrument, she was surprised to see a figure huddled there. "Hello?" she called.

"Ah, Meh-ghan, you are here," said Iñigo. "I was getting worried."

"It took me longer than I thought. Sorry. I forgot I wasn't running on flat ground. At sea level."

"No problem. I am glad to see you."

O'Malley peered more closely into the gloom and saw another short, fat tank of liquid nitrogen. "Iñigo, why are you refilling the coolant? Didn't Antonio tell you I was coming?"

His white teeth flashed, and O'Malley felt her night vision—or was it her clearheadedness?—diminish a bit. "Well, I was here, with nothing to do. And I didn't want your work to be delayed."

"What work? We're totally socked in. Unless you're a meteorological magician, there's no work for me to do."

He looked thoughtful. "For you," he said, "I will try to make magic. Come with me." He held out a hand; after a moment's hesitation, she took it. His hand was large and strong, and warmer than she had expected. He led her to a doorway that was tucked into the low, curving wall that supported the dome. SALIDA DE EMERGENCIA, read a faintly glowing red sign: EMERGENCY EXIT. Iñigo paused, his free hand on the crash bar. "First," he said, "you must close your eyes."

"Close my eyes? Why?"

"Because a security light comes on for a moment when I open the door."

"Got it." O'Malley squeezed her eyes shut tight. Human eyes took half an hour to adapt fully to night, and a stray flash of light would reset her eyes to their daytime setting, requiring another thirty minutes to resensitize to the darkness. Remarkable, really: at night, the human eye was a million times more sensitive to light than in bright sunlight. Remarkable, too, she realized, how much more sensitive her fingers were when her eyes were closed. "Okay," she managed to say. "My eyes are closed."

She heard a thunk and a rasp as Iñigo pushed the crash bar and opened the door, then felt a tug on her hand. "It's safe," he said. "The floor is smooth. Come with me."

"Can I open my eyes now?"

"Not yet. Almost."

She let him lead her, stepping gingerly. He stopped, then guided her hand to a cold metal railing, which she gripped, first with one hand, then with the other. "Okay. Now you can open your eyes."

When she did, she gasped, releasing the railing and bringing both hands to her mouth. "My God, it's *incredible!*" She was standing upon a sea of clouds whose wispy tops swirled and eddied around her very ankles. Overhead, the Milky Way arched from horizon to horizon; below, the clouds glowed by the light of the stars. O'Malley felt her throat tighten and her eyes brim with tears. To find herself poised here, exactly on the surface of the clouds, even the roof hidden from view, astonished her. "Incredible," she whispered. "It's like I'm standing on the sky. So beautiful."

"Yes," Iñigo said. "*Muy bonita.* Very beautiful." His voice was close, his lips almost touching her ear, and she realized that he was not looking at the clouds; he was looking at her.

Uh-oh, she thought, her knees going weak. *Girlfriend, get a grip.* She reached for the railing to steady herself; in her mind's eye, she pictured herself tumbling forward and spinning downward through the clouds, just as her car had done.

"Would you like to dance on the sky?" he murmured, swaying his body against hers. O'Malley felt his breath on her neck, then felt his lips grazing her neck, kissing her neck. She drew in another breath and released the railing with one hand, turning toward him. As she did, she heard alarms shrieking in her head. She batted them away, closing her eyes and parting her lips. His face came closer. His lips brushed hers and—

"Iñigo, wait," she said. "Stop. Something's wrong!" The alarms were not shrieking inside her head; the alarms were shrieking inside the telescope dome. "What's that alarm?"

29

He blinked, as if awakening, and his gaze shifted to the open door. *"Mierda,"* he swore. "The smoke detector. I left something cooking in the kitchen." He turned back toward her with a smile. "It's okay, I'm sure. I'll go see about it in a minute." He leaned in again, trying to take up where they'd left off.

But the spell was broken. O'Malley turned away and headed toward the open door, toward the looming telescope, toward coolheaded professionalism and her search for Planet Nine. "I should get to work," she called over her shoulder, hoping her voice was steadier than her knees. "And you should go put out the fire in the kitchen."

"Mierda," he said again.

She paused in the doorway and turned back toward him. "But thank you for fixing the weather. And for helping me walk on the sky."

Unbelievable, O'Malley thought. *Un. Fucking. Believable.* She stared at the latest photo. Like the others, it was worthless: the stars, which should have dotted the image with crisp, steady pinpoints, instead traced jagged, spiky tracks across the sky—a thousand tiny bolts of lightning, zigzagging in unison. *Worthless. Utterly worthless.*

She checked the clock above the console: half past midnight, La Palma time. In Baltimore it would be five hours earlier—seven thirty—and California was three time zones west of that. *Four thirty, Berkeley time. Perfect.*

She found the telephone on the console—Antonio had shown her how to dial international calls, which, luckily, were a courtesy the observatory extended to visiting astronomers. She punched in the US prefix and then a number she'd known by heart for a decade. After three rings, the call was answered. *"Hola,"* said a man's voice. *"Laboratorio de sismología."* The voice was right, but the language was wrong, and the accent was even more wrong: a cartoon caricature of Spanish, with a topspin of Southern-boy redneck. O'Malley cringed and pulled the handset away from her ear briefly before responding.

"David, is that you?"

"O'Malley? Is that *you*?"

"Why the hell are you answering the phone in that atrocious Spanish?"

"Why the hell are you calling from Spain? I saw 'Spain' on the caller ID, so I thought I'd *hablo* in a friendly manner."

"Never. Do it. Again. You'll cause an international incident. I'm in the Canary Islands. Spanish, but not in Spain. Somewhere off the coast of Morocco."

"Sounds exotic. Like a line from a movie script. 'Meanwhile, somewhere off the coast of Morocco . . .' You on vacay?"

"Work. There's a big observatory complex here. I'm looking for Planet Nine."

"We already *have* Planet Nine, Megan. It's called Pluto."

"Not anymore."

"It's gone? Or it's no longer called Pluto?"

"Neither. It's no longer called a planet. It got demoted. Pluto's now classed as a dwarf planet."

"That seems politically incorrect," he said. "Insensitive, too. You're looking for a bigger, better planet to take its place?"

"Yep. Way bigger. Way out there, a long ways past Pluto."

"If you're the one who finds it, you get to name it, right? Isn't that how it works in astronomy?"

"Theoretically. But I'm not gonna be the one to find it."

"But if you do, you'll name it after me, right?"

"Sure. I'll call it 'My Favorite Ex-Husband.' Catchy, huh?" It was an old joke between them. O'Malley liked the term's versatile ambiguity: David was her only ex-husband, she still liked him, and she was glad to be out of their brief, almost comically bad marriage—a union that had seemed like a good idea for one drunken night in Las Vegas. Most of the time, she said the term with fondness; only occasionally did a note of sarcasm sneak in. "But as I say, the way it's going, I've got no chance of finding it. Which is why I'm calling you."

"To beg me to fly over and console you?"

"Ha. Dream on, Dr. Quake. Here's the thing. I've got three nights on this instrument here—the Isaac Newton Telescope—and tonight's my second night. Last night was a total loss, and tonight's the same damn thing, all over again. I spend an hour getting the telescope lined up on the patch of sky I'm searching, and then *bam*, something jolts the telescope and ruins my photo."

"A wayward seagull? A drunken Spaniard? A drunken *you*?"

"Very funny. No, it's vibrations. The telescope engineer swears it's not in the machinery. He says it's seismic."

"Wouldn't be surprised. That whole island chain is young and active. Full of volcanoes and fault lines. Wouldn't take much in the way of moving and shaking to cause a serious seismic shitstorm." In the background, O'Malley heard the clatter of computer keys. "Hmm. *Hmm.*"

"What does 'hmm' mean?" O'Malley said. "Is that like when the doctor says 'uh-oh'?"

"It means 'hmm.' You say it's happened, like, in the past few hours?"

"Like, in the past ten minutes. Like, ninety minutes before that. And ninety minutes before *that*."

"Hmm."

"Stop saying that and tell me what you're *seeing*."

"So, I'm looking at the GSN now . . ."

O'Malley smiled, pleased that she remembered. The GSN was the Global Seismographic Network, a web of sensors all over the world.

"Is there a station on La Palma?"

"Not on La Palma," he said, "but close. On Tenerife, eighty miles east."

"And you see data from the past few hours?"

"I can see data from the past few seconds. It's real-time monitoring. Uploaded automatically from every seismic station. When did you say these jolts happened?"

"The last one was, let's see . . . seven minutes ago. The one before that, ninety-five minutes ago. The one before that—"

"Can't you be specific, O'Malley?"

"Sorry, yeah, I can pin it down more exactly," she began. "The photos are time-stamped. The latest exposure started—"

"Kidding, *kidding*. Okay, here's what I'm seeing. Nothing."

"In what sense do you mean 'nothing'?"

"In the sense of 'zero, zip, nada.' Nothing's happening, Megan."

"David, the telescope trembled like a wino with the shakes. Something's definitely happening. A *lot* of somethings—almost all my images are ruined."

"Well then, there you go. It's your equipment that's the problem. With a capital *P* that rhymes with *T* that stands for scope."

"But it's *not*. I talked to Iñigo, the engineer; he swears it's not the mechanism. Iñigo says the earth shakes sometimes."

"Clearly this Iñigo is an intuitive seismological genius. Why'd you bother calling me, when you've got Iñigo?"

"Don't be a dick, David."

"I'm not being a dick. I'm just telling you: nothing's happening. Nothing seismic. Nothing big enough to register, anyhow. Could be very localized. Road construction. Dumpsters being thrown to the ground by garbage trucks."

"In the middle of the night? At an *observatory*? Where people tiptoe around in the dark in their *socks*?"

"What can I tell you, Megan? Either something's wrong with the telescope, or *somebody's* not tiptoeing."

Three hours and a dozen ruined photographs later, Iñigo came into the control room. "So, everything is good tonight?"

"No," she said bleakly, pointing at the thumbnails of the ruined photos. "Everything is *not* good. Everything is shitty. I'm going to contact the Astronomical Institute—the island's governor, too—and ask them to investigate and fix this."

He looked shocked—or was it angry?—so she hastened to assure him. "Look, I'm not blaming you, but my whole trip has been wasted. If this happens to other astronomers, the observatory's reputation will be ruined."

Iñigo offered a conciliatory smile. "I'm very sorry for the problem," he said. "Is very bad luck for you. But please don't let the whole trip go to waste. I have a bottle of wine in my apartment. Let's go drink some wine, eat some grapes and cheese, listen to music. Dance a little. You seem like a good dancer, Megan. You like to dance, yes?" He cocked his head, still smiling.

She shook her head. "No. I mean, yes, I do, but I . . . Iñigo, I can't go there. I'm too upset." She waved her hand at the control console and the ruined images. "You say the telescope's not the problem. My ex-husband—a seismologist—says the seismology's not the problem."

Iñigo's eyebrows shot up. "You have called him about this?"

"Yes. He says there's no seismic activity on the island. So if it's not a seismic problem or a mechanical problem, then what the fuck *is* it? And why do men keep treating me like I'm stupid?"

Iñigo sighed. "I don't think you're stupid, Megan. I think you're very smart. And I think—no, I promise—that tonight is the last night you will have this problem."

With that, he held up both hands—a cease-fire signal—and backed away, leaving O'Malley to wonder what the hell *that* was supposed to mean, and why she felt such a volatile mixture of lust and caution in his presence.

She watched dawn break on a monitor in the telescope control room. The stars faded as the sky lightened, imperceptibly at first, then distinctly. "Oh *God*," she groaned. She had stayed at the telescope all night—a slow learner, a glutton for punishment—hoping against hope to collect at least a few images. *A total waste,* she thought again as she scrolled through the ruined photos. Maybe she should have taken Iñigo up on the hookup offer—at least she'd have had the brief but pleasant consolation of getting laid.

Tonight would be her final chance to salvage something—anything—from the telescope. Or from Iñigo. He had fled the scene after her curt rejection, though, so perhaps Iñigo was not on offer for tonight.

She trudged back to the Residencia—fortunately the walk was downhill, but unfortunately the morning was cold and windy—and staggered into the lobby. Inside, she nearly collided with a startled Japanese man who was wheeling an enormous suitcase toward the door. She mumbled an apology and turned toward the hallway that led to her room. "Good morning, *Doctora*," called Antonio from behind the counter.

Christ, is he on duty 24/7? she wondered. "Good morning, Antonio," she managed.

"A good night of observing?"

"A terrible night," she said.

"No! Oh, *Doctora*, this makes me very sad."

"Me, too, Antonio. Maybe tonight will be better."

He frowned, then shook his head sorrowfully. "I am afraid not," he said. "You have not heard?"

"Heard what?"

"The weather. Tonight, the wind is *muy fuerte*. Very strong. Eighty kilometers per hour." O'Malley did the conversion: fifty miles an hour. "Are you sure?"

"Gusts—that is the word, I think?—gusts of one hundred kilometers per hour! Tonight, the telescopes cannot operate. The domes must remain closed."

O'Malley wanted to scream. She wanted to sob. She wanted to get the bloody hell out of La Palma. Right *now*. Actually, she wanted never to have come to La Palma in the first place, but given that undoing the past wasn't an option, cutting her losses and getting out as soon as possible seemed the best she could manage. "Antonio, is anyone going into town today? To Santa Cruz?"

"Santa Cruz?"

"Yes. I need to leave."

He squinted at her, puzzled, then looked down and consulted the papers on his desk. "But, no, *Doctora*, you are staying until tomorrow."

"I can't," she said. "I need to leave now. Please. Anyone?"

He frowned, then shrugged and consulted the schedule again. "The only one is Shinji Yamamoto. But he just left."

When he heard the bang, Shinji Yamamoto naturally assumed that he had backed into something—another car? a light pole?—but when he cast an alarmed look in the rearview mirror, he saw not a crumpled fender or a bent pole; he saw a crazy woman frantically pounding the trunk of his car with both hands.

Before he could put the transmission in "Drive" and make his getaway, the woman ran to his window. "Please," she said. "I need a ride to Santa Cruz." He stared. "Santa Cruz," she repeated, clasping her hands in a pleading gesture. *"Please."*

Measured against the yardstick of O'Malley's Japanese, Shinji Yamamoto's English was good. But measured against the two hours it took to descend the mountain and reach the airport in Santa Cruz—a destination O'Malley communicated by pantomiming an airplane in flight—his command of the language was sadly lacking. They shared five awkward minutes of halting conversation: "Which telescope?" "Isaac Newton." "Ah, Isaac Newton! Very famous astronomer. You look for comet?" "No, Planet Nine." "Ah, you look Planet Nine! Very good! I study red shift."

"Red shift—oh yes, that's very interesting." O'Malley had a sudden thought. "Did you have any problem with the telescope?"

"Problem? What problem?"

"Did your telescope shake? Move?" His brow furrowed, so O'Malley resorted again to gestures. She held up both hands, her fingers curled around an imaginary spyglass, and then shook her hands rapidly. "My telescope," she said. "Also yours?"

"Ah," he said, nodding. "Yes, sometimes. But for me, small problem. Most data, very good. I don't use bad data. But only small amount."

"You are very lucky," O'Malley said. "All of my data—all my photographs—are bad. I can't use."

"Oh, that is very shame." He looked genuinely sorry.

Very shame indeed, O'Malley thought bitterly. Then: *Iñigo was right—it's not the scope; it's the island.* Then: *But David swears it's not the island. Is he lying, or just incompetent?* Then: *Fuck my life.*

Their shared vocabulary and cross-cultural interests exhausted, she and Shinji lapsed into silence, and soon O'Malley slumped against her door and napped, sleeping by fits and starts amid the road's careening curves and Shinji's jerky braking. Finally, the ride smoothed out, and she began sinking into a deeper sleep. That was when Shinji shook her awake. "Airport," he said.

CHAPTER 4

CIA Headquarters
Langley, Virginia

Dawtry emerged from the glass atrium into a courtyard containing a garden, well tended, though its grass and trees were already dressed for winter.

He had been invited to Langley to give a presentation; that, at least, was the pretext. The unspoken agenda, though, was that he was here to audition for a spot as the FBI's liaison to the Central Intelligence Agency—a possibility he found both exciting and intimidating.

"You might find this interesting," said Dawtry's host, Jim Vreeland, detouring to a large copper sculpture at one corner of the garden. Perhaps eight feet tall by a dozen feet long, affixed at one end to an upright log of stone or petrified wood, the sculpture resembled a metallic flag waving in some unseen breeze. An inscribed, encrypted flag: the entire piece was covered—no, was pierced all the way through—with capital letters, hundreds or even thousands of them, seemingly chosen and arranged in utterly random order, with no spaces or punctuation between them.

"So this is *Kryptos*," Dawtry said.

"This is *Kryptos*," said Vreeland. "My daily dose of humility."

Dawtry chuckled. The sculpture was the most famous unsolved cipher on earth, and it probably drove Vreeland nuts to see it every time he crossed the courtyard. Vreeland currently ran the CIA's counterterrorism section, but for years before that, he'd headed cryptography. Vreeland and dozens of other CIA code breakers had long struggled to decode the message carved into the piece. The sculpture was an homage, a challenge, and possibly also a taunt to the spy agency that had commissioned it. "Hang on," Dawtry said. "I think I've got it. It says, 'What the hell took you so long?'"

"So you Feebies really *are* smarter than we are," said Vreeland. He smiled as he said it, but Dawtry thought he sensed an edge to the joke.

He led Dawtry across the courtyard, through a low, arched concourse that resembled an airline terminal, and then outside again. They approached what appeared to be an immense igloo, fitted with glass doors on one side. *The Bubble,* thought Dawtry. *Holy cow—I'm talking in the Bubble.*

He had expected to be speaking in a conference room, briefing a handful of intelligence analysts—a dozen, tops. Instead, here he was in the main, iconic auditorium at CIA Headquarters. Vreeland led him through the glass doors and into the Bubble. Heads turned—many, many heads: every one of the four hundred seats was taken, and more people ringed the perimeter, slouching against the curved walls.

They were there, hundreds of CIA spies and analysts, to hear him talk about his own career in spying, of sorts: a series of FBI stings, directed by Dawtry, which had foiled more than a dozen terrorist plots on US soil during the previous five years. The plots ranged from relatively modest plans to shoot up military recruiting centers to ambitious efforts to destroy large, important targets, including JFK International Airport, the Sears Tower, the Brooklyn Bridge, Times Square, and even the US Capitol. The key to stopping them had been undercover agents who had gotten close to the would-be terrorists, in many cases infiltrating groups and providing disabled assault rifles and fake explosives.

Dawtry ended his presentation with a montage of images that reminded the CIA analysts of things they already knew but probably wouldn't mind knowing *he* knew—images illustrating the urgent stakes, the high-value targets, and the powerful ideologies in play: The collapsing World Trade Center towers. The smoldering Pentagon. Osama bin Laden. The White House. Nuclear power plants. The Golden Gate Bridge. Masked ISIS fighters waving guns and swords. "Although we have not—so far—seen another attack as deadly as 9/11," he concluded, "no one knows better than this roomful of people that these are perilous times. As perilous as any we've ever faced, with enemies as elusive and insidious as any we've ever fought." He paused for effect. "Intelligence is the front line in the battle to protect America. Thank you for fighting the good fight."

Dawtry nodded and stepped back from the podium, and the agents—the aloof, brainy agents and analysts for whom he'd just auditioned—responded with enthusiastic applause.

Whew, he thought. *I'm not dead yet.*

But the presentation, he knew, was the easy part of the audition. He suspected that the next step, his actual job interview with Vreeland and a handful of higher-ups, might be more akin to a round of waterboarding.

CHAPTER 5

Santa Cruz de la Palma Airport
Day three

"I'm *very* sorry," the lovely young ticket agent told O'Malley. "We have seats on the eight a.m. flight tomorrow morning, but no seats available today."

O'Malley groaned. What had she been thinking? Why hadn't she called? *If I'd called, I'd've missed my ride,* she reminded herself. Then: *So? Fat lot of good the ride did you. If you'd missed the ride, you might be getting laid tonight. Dumb-ass.* "Is there another airline that could take me to Tenerife? Or Madrid?"

"I'm afraid not."

"Is there any other way to get off the island?"

"Well," the woman said, "there's a ferry to Tenerife. But it only runs once a day, and unfortunately you've just missed it."

"Thank you," O'Malley mumbled and walked away. *Get used to disappointment,* she thought bitterly—a line of *Princess Bride* dialogue she often quoted, though usually as a good-natured joke.

It was 10:00 a.m., and she had twenty-four hours to kill. *Might as well kill it by playing tourist,* she decided. She headed for the terminal's exit, walked out, and caught a cab. *"Al centro, por favor,"* she told the driver. He nodded and headed briskly for town. As she settled back into the leather, O'Malley felt fatigued and frustrated, but she felt something else, too, something unfamiliar: she felt unencumbered—by luggage, by appointments or deadlines, by expectations of productivity or accomplishment. When the taxi entered the city center, she drank in the sights. Santa Cruz had an old-world ambience: narrow, mazy streets flanked by stuccoed buildings in tropical hues of white, blue, salmon, and gold. Some of them featured balconies supported by stout, dark beams—beams that might have been carved in the days of Christopher Columbus and Sir Francis Drake and Henry the Navigator.

The car stopped at a crosswalk where the road intersected a pedestrian street thronging with tourists. "Here," she said. *"Aquí, aquí."* The meter read 15.50. O'Malley opened her wallet, snatched out a crisp twenty-euro note, and thrust it at the driver. *"Gracias, señor,"* she said, springing from the car and closing the door just as the light changed.

She headed down the pedestrian street lined with boutiques and bars, and spotted—actually, smelled first, then spotted—a coffee shop set in an ancient courtyard lush with palm trees and flowering bushes. She knocked back a double espresso and a savory pastry and, thus fortified, sallied forth to explore. This was not the region of the cosmos she had traveled to La Palma to explore, but at the moment, it was the one she was able to explore. The streets were narrow and mazy; O'Malley was careful to check the names of street signs, which were embedded in the walls of buildings at each corner. She smiled at one street name in particular, which she translated as "Virgin of the Light." *Beats "Seventeenth Street" by a mile,* she thought.

A zig and a zag beyond Virgin of the Light Street, a weathered stone plaque caught her eye. Beneath an image of a royal crown and a string of Roman numerals—MDCCCLXXXI, which O'Malley translated as 1881—were the words REAL SOCIEDAD COSMOLÓGICA. *I'll be damned,* O'Malley thought. *Out of all the gin joints in all the world, I stumble onto the one devoted to the origin and nature of the cosmos.* A carved scene depicted Saint George slaying a dragon. The dragon of ignorance, perhaps? Beside the plaque was an ornate wooden door—an open wooden door—and O'Malley felt the urge to step inside and see if any vestige of the Royal Cosmological Society remained.

As it happened, every vestige of the Cosmological Society remained, though more as museum or recital hall than as center of scientific inquiry. A bulletin board in a small entrance hall featured posters promoting upcoming concerts and art lectures. VISIT THE LIBRARY, suggested a sign in English, its hand-drawn arrow pointing up a narrow flight of wooden stairs. O'Malley took the sign's suggestion and creaked up the stairs. She emerged into a high-ceiling, raftered room paneled in dark wood. Tall, wide windows at the far end offered a panoramic view of the harbor, where a cruise ship was just then docking, its arrival announced by a long blast of its deep horn.

Bookcases lined most of the library's walnut walls, with the exception of a large, framed relief map, which was dated 1877. The most prominent feature of the yellowing map, apart from the immense volcanic caldera, which the observatory now inhabited, and the island's high north-south ridgeline, was an improbably straight line—solid at each end, dashed in the center—transecting the ridge from east to west. Thin, spidery script identified the line as a *túnel de agua*: water tunnel. A typed and fading card tucked behind a corner of the glass informed O'Malley in both Spanish and English that the tunnel project was designed to transport water from the abundant streams of the east to the dry slopes of the west. Construction began in 1867 with teams digging from both sides, aiming to meet in the middle, but work ceased ten years later, when insurmountable problems—financial, engineering, and geological—forced the abandonment of the project. She felt a flash of schadenfreude—a moment of misery-loves-company comfort—in knowing that her cosmic quest was not the first scientific undertaking to be foiled by the island's difficult and unpredictable nature.

Scanning the bookshelves, she saw a wildly varied collection of leather-bound books, many of them in English: *Don Quixote. David Copperfield. United States Laws.* A small, slim volume titled *Brown's Madeira, Canary Islands, and Azores,* by A. Samler Brown, intrigued her, so she extricated it from between two tall, thick tomes. The book's subtitle filled half the cover: *A Practical and Complete Guide for the Use of Tourists and Invalids, with Twenty Coloured Maps and Plans and Numerous Sectional and Other Diagrams.*

The book's opening pages were crammed, magazine-style, with advertisements touting steamship lines, hotels, travel agents, photographers, wine merchants, bankers, and dentists—even suppliers of "chemical manure," whatever that was. Tucked amid the ads, she found the copyright information (seventh edition, London, 1903) and table of contents. The book appeared to be equal parts travel guide, textbook, and encyclopedia, with sections on history, geography, geology, meteorology, industry, agriculture, and commerce. Much to her surprise, O'Malley found herself mesmerized by an account of the cochineal boom of the mid-1800s: a sort of agricultural and entomological gold rush, one fueled by cochineal bugs, cactus-loving insects that yielded blood-red dye when dried and ground into powder. In the 1830s the Canaries had gone crazy for cochineal and carmine. Investors and small-scale farmers planted cactus on every acre of flat ground, and once the flat acreage was claimed, they terraced and planted dizzyingly steep slopes, too. Land prices soared, but mortgages were easy to get, given the high profit margins. Production skyrocketed, from a mere eight pounds of cochineal in 1831 to more than six hundred thousand pounds in 1869. Canarians made money hand over fist. "The landed gentry ordered expensive furniture, silver-mounted saddlery and other costly goods from Europe," Brown wrote, "or spent their time in general dissipation."

Eventually, inevitably, the bubble burst, as a result of the invention of synthetic dyes, which were cheaper and easier to produce.

"Retribution was swift, sudden, and universal," Brown wrote. The cochineal market imploded. Landowners went bankrupt. *So did water tunnel investors,* O'Malley intuited, casting another glance at the yellowed map on the wall.

Her excursion into La Palma's boom-and-bust past was interrupted by the sound of knuckles rapping on wood. "*Excuse* me," said a voice in Spanish-accented English. O'Malley whirled and saw a frowning woman at the top of the stairs. "This room is closed."

O'Malley flushed. "But the sign downstairs says 'visit the library.' I thought it was open."

"No. Closed," said the woman. "You cannot be here."

"Sorry. I didn't know." She pushed back from the table, closed the book, and descended the stairs in embarrassed exile from the Sociedad Cosmológica. But the bright, beckoning day made it impossible to remain gloomy, so she cast about for her next adventure.

She found it a few blocks away, down on the waterfront near the cruise ship dock. A storefront car rental agency—*not* the agency whose car O'Malley had lost—was offering vehicles for just five euros a day. *Five bucks? How can they do that?* she wondered. She tugged open the door and walked inside. It wasn't only the bargain—wasn't even *mainly* the bargain—that enticed her. What enticed her was the giant poster in the window: an aerial view of spectacular volcanic craters lined up one after another along a ridgeline trail. What was it David had called the Canaries—very young and active, full of volcanoes and fault lines? Judging by the acnelike swellings and pockmarks shown in the photo, the Canaries were in the throes of geologic puberty. "Hike the World Famous Ruta de los Volcanes!" the poster urged. "30 minutes by car!"

The five-euro rate was a bait-and-switch scam, she soon learned—*that* car had already been rented, the clerk told her regretfully. The only car available would cost thirty euros—but O'Malley didn't actually mind. Fifteen minutes later, she was behind the wheel of another Toyota Yaris, pulling onto the waterfront highway.

This time, she had sprung—an additional ten euros—for the comprehensive insurance.

One hour after renting the car, O'Malley eased to a stop in a gravel parking lot in a spectacular pine forest. The hilly highway had taken her through two tunnels, one of them quite long, boring straight through the heart of the island's mountain range; apparently twentieth-century highway tunnels were easier to complete than nineteenth-century water tunnels. Smoke wafted from barbecue grills, and children played on monkey bars and swings at a wooded park tucked just below the island's ridgeline. Refugio El Pilar, the park was named. "Refuge of the Pillar"—a reference to some Catholic miracle or other, she suspected, perhaps one wrought by the Virgin of the Light.

She locked the car and found the trail, which began on the far side of the playground. The path ascended steeply, winding up through widely spaced pines, some of them towering a hundred feet or higher. After two miles of climbing, the trail leveled off, undulating along the mountain's western flank, occasionally crossing a saddle. At one point she glanced to her left and saw what appeared to be a pair of stone walls, set six feet apart, angling up the mountainside in perfect parallel. *Virgin of the Masonry,* she thought, smiling at the irreverence. She was hungry, she realized, and decided to eat her lunch—bread and cheese she'd bought at a roadside grocery on the outskirts of Santa Cruz—sitting on one of the walls. The warmth of the sunny ledge was like a bath for her aching thighs. The parallel rock walls weren't actually walls, she noticed; rather, they were a neat fissure in the mountainside, angling uphill for as far as she could see.

She was three bites into the cheese—a good smoked Gouda—when she caught a flicker of movement to her left. She turned to look, and as she watched, a lizard skittered toward her, pausing occasionally to rear up, raising its front legs like cactus arms, splaying the digits wide. She stared, mesmerized by the odd display, which the lizard repeated several times as it skittered closer. Did lizards have scent organs on the feet—was he stopping to sniff the cheese? Or was the odd, yogalike pose meant to be intimidating? O'Malley wasn't intimidated; she was amused—at first. Then she noticed other flickers of movement, other lizards, skittering toward her: a few at first, then a dozen, then a hundred or more. She shooed them, stamping her feet, and they backed away, but after a few seconds they resumed their advance. "Scram," she said. "Scoot!" She scooped sand with one hand and flung it at them. They flinched and dodged, but still they advanced, pausing and rearing up, their ranks steadily growing, their leaders almost upon her. O'Malley bit off a final chunk of cheese, then mumbled, "Fine—take the damn cheese." She flung it away and scurried back to the trail, glancing behind her occasionally to make sure she wasn't being followed by the swarming reptiles.

Another half hour of brisk hiking brought her above the tree line and onto bare rock, stark and windswept. One blasted, stunted tree, no taller than O'Malley, huddled beside the trail, the wind seething through its shuddering branches. The sound was as haunting as the MAGIC telescope's moaning wires, but more ominous, somehow: more a hiss than a song. Still, stubbornly, she pressed on. She topped a slight rise, then nearly tumbled head over heels. Directly ahead the earth dropped away, opening into a deep crater with steep, sloping sides made of small black cinders. Instinctively she backed away from the edge. She had intended to hike another mile of the trail, to see the next two craters, but this crater, and the suddenness with which it had opened directly at her feet, unsettled her. The wind was growing fiercer, too. What had Antonio said the forecast predicted? "Gusts of a hundred!" He was talking kilometers—one hundred of which translated to "only" sixty miles an hour—but a gust that strong would be more than enough, she reckoned, to blow her off the trail and over the edge.

She turned back, her pace and her pulse fast, until she was safely below the tree line once more. There, sheltered from the wind, back among the pines, she finally felt herself relaxing.

Ahead, a clearing caught her eye, and she stepped off the trail, over an ankle-high border of stones, for a closer look. The clearing wasn't actually a clearing but instead a flat layer of exposed stone, the plane of its surface dotted with a few wobbly-looking cairns, waist high, and thousands of fist-size rocks. "How cool is *that*," she said as she took in the pattern: laid out on the smooth slab was a labyrinth—a perfect spiral, fifty feet in diameter, outlined by individual stones. "Incredibly, magically cool!"

She found the spiral's opening and stepped into it, winding her way toward the center—walking at first, then running, her arms stretched out like wings. By the time she reached the middle, she was dizzy from exertion, exuberance, and the ever-tightening turn. Panting and laughing, she sat down at the very center. Then she lay back, her right arm crooked beneath her head. The sun angling onto her face was warm and comforting, like balm to her jangled spirits. She closed her eyes, her left hand resting on her belly, rising and falling as her breathing slowed and deepened, and she felt herself drifting—spiraling—into sleep.

She woke with a gasp, her skin soaked with a sudden bloom of sweat. She lay motionless, stone-still on the rock, her eyes scanning the surroundings to see what had awakened her. Another dream of falling? An onslaught of lizards? She saw only blue sky, pine trees angling upward, the stacked cairns and spiraling labyrinth. No lizards. *What a wuss,* she scolded herself. She drew a deep breath, puffed it out, sucked in another.

Just as she was about to exhale again, she felt it: the ground beneath her was pulsing. Almost imperceptibly, but undeniably, the earth was trembling. The instant the movement registered, she recognized it: she had felt that same trembling a few moments before, in her sleep. It had been enough to wake her then; it was enough to send shivers down her spine now. Suddenly, with a clatter, one of the rickety cairns collapsed.

She scrambled to her feet, her gaze darting from the fallen marker to the center of the spiral, as if that were the epicenter of the quake. Then she began to run. She ran all the way back to the car, her feet churning in a headlong descent that was never more than a hairsbreadth from a fall.

"Bullshit," she snapped into the phone. "The ground was shaking, David. Swear to God. It shook hard enough to wake me up, and then it shook again."

"I don't know what to tell you, Megan," said her ex. She had called him as soon as she'd gotten back to Santa Cruz and found a hotel for the night. "I'm looking at the data. *Nothing happened.* I see quakes today in Montenegro and the Caribbean and all around the Pacific Rim, but nothing within a thousand miles of La Palma."

"Dammit, David, you're pissing me off."

"Story of my life, babe. I know you're telling your truth, but I'm sitting here in Berkeley, looking at readings from a hundred fifty seismometers, all of 'em telling *their* truth. I'm a datahead, Megs. If I throw out the data, I got nothing. And the data says all's quiet on the western front in La Palma."

"There's something going on here, David. I don't know what, but I know that much. It fucked with my work, and now it's fucking with my mind. If you can't help me, I'll just have to . . . well, hell, I don't know what, but I have to do something."

"You could consider letting it go," he said. "You could stop picking at it."

"I can't stop picking at it, David. I'm no good at that. Never was, never will be."

"Ha—tell me something I don't know, honey." He paused. "You could put a few dragon bowls around the island. See if they know something the seismic stations don't."

"Dragon bowls? What the hell's a dragon bowl?"

"World's first seismoscope," he said. "Very cool, actually. Invented almost two thousand years ago in China. By a guy named Chang Heng. A regular Renaissance man, but fifteen centuries before the Renaissance. He was an inventor. A poet. An artist. Oh, and an astronomer, of course. Like all the cool kids."

"Of course." O'Malley almost allowed herself a smile. Despite the divorce, and despite her frustration, part of her could still appreciate David's smarts and humor. "How come it's called a dragon bowl?"

"Ah, glasshopper, risten and rearn," he said. His fake Chinese accent was even worse than his Spanish one.

"Stop talking like that, or I'm hanging up now."

"Promises, promises. The dragon bowl was six feet across, and—"

"Six feet?" she interrupted. "That's not a bowl—that's a bathtub."

He sighed. "Honey, I *love* it when you play Story Helper."

"All right, all right, this is me shutting up. I'm all ears. Tell me about this six-foot bowl."

"So, first, it doesn't look like a bowl. More like a giant water heater. Or a Bronze Age R2-D2."

"R2-D2? The *Star Wars* robot?"

"Correct you are. Tell you I will, if listen you can. It was a big copper cylinder, six feet wide, ten feet high, with a dome on top. It had eight dragons mounted around the outside—"

"Hence the name?"

"Hence the name. Each dragon faced a different compass direction. Inside the mouth of each dragon was a ball, and—"

"A ball? What kind of ball?"

"Aarrgghh. A *round* ball. A ball carved from the finest jade. A ball made from a golden turd shat out by the Buddha. A *ball*. Christ, O'Malley, I know *toddlers* who listen better than you do."

"I don't doubt it. But can those sheeplike toddlers tell you the airspeed velocity of an unladen swallow?"

He took the bait, as she knew he would. "African or European swallow?" It was an old, comfortable routine for them, racing through entire scenes of dialogue from *Monty Python and the Holy Grail* or their other shared favorite, *The Princess Bride*. But before she could volley back the next line—"I don't know that!"—he cut her off. "*Any*how, the cool thing, the brilliant thing, about the dragon bowl was this. There was a pendulum inside, hanging down from the center of the dome. If an earthquake hit, the pendulum would skew sideways."

"Equal and opposite reaction?"

"Law of inertia, actually. Technically, the pendulum itself would hang motionless, while the *bowl* moved. When it did, the pendulum would touch a lever on one side of the bowl—a trigger mechanism—opening the mouth of the nearest dragon. *Ptui*—the dragon would spit out the ball."

"Sounds like that kid's game, whatchamacallit. Mousetrap. That, or a Rube Goldberg invention."

"A bit. So the ball would drop out of the dragon's mouth and plop into the open mouth of a frog sitting underneath."

"A frog? A *live* frog?"

David groaned. "Yes," he snarked. "A highly trained, exceedingly patient frog. *No*, doofus, a *copper* frog. Part of the gizmo. Eight dragons, eight balls, eight frogs, their eight mouths open wide in perpetual readiness to swallow a ball."

"Ah so. And did it work, whatshisname's handy-dandy Rube Goldberg Earthquake Detector?"

"I'm glad you asked. When our hero, Chang Heng, presented it to the emperor, people thought he'd lost his marbles."

"So *that's* where the balls came from!"

"God, you never give up, do you? Anyhow, the gizmo sat there, gathering dust in the imperial palace, for two years. Then one day— *ptui*—one of the dragons spit out a ball. People made fun all over again, because nobody'd felt the slightest tremor. Two days later, though, a messenger came riding in, hell for leather, from three hundred miles away. There'd been a massive earthquake, in *exactly* the direction the dragon bowl pointed. Heng's genius was vindicated."

"How nice for him," said O'Malley. "The dragon bowl sounds like just the ticket. How many of these things do I need? And can I buy 'em online? And is Amazon doing drone deliveries to La Palma?"

"You could get by with two, but three would triangulate—get it, *tri*-angulate?—with better accuracy. But, no, you can't get them from Amazon. Not even from eBay. There's only a handful of these things in the whole world. All replicas. All in museums. And only one of them actually works. The others are just for show."

"Well that sucks. You got me all worked up for nothing. Just like when we were married."

"Ouch," he said. "A low blow."

"Sorry. I've had a terrible, horrible, no-good, very bad week, David."

"Take two aspirin and the first flight home. But no need to call me in the morning. And now I gotta go—seriously. *Bye.*" He hung up before she had a chance to protest.

She stewed for five minutes, mad and hurt and confused about what to do next. Something was percolating its way up from her subconscious, but she had no idea what. Suddenly she muttered, "Eureka!" and hit "Redial."

David didn't pick up until the sixth ring. "Now what?"

"I've been thinking about the dragon bowl," she said.

"Swell."

"I just had an epiphany."

"Make it stop," he groaned. "I knew I should've dumped this to voicemail."

"You said the dragon would spit out the ball when the bowl got jolted sideways by an earthquake, right?"

"Right."

"So basically it was a primitive accelerometer?"

"Basically. *Very* primitive."

"Indicating the direction of the quake."

"Right-ee-o. Do you actually have a point, or are you just trying to prove that you were paying attention?"

"My point, Seismo-Genius, is that I *had* a dragon bowl on La Palma," she said, her excitement rising.

"Come again?"

"My telescope. It was the world's biggest dragon bowl."

"Uh . . . not for the first time, I'm not quite following you, Megs."

"Don't you see? It skewed toward the origin of the vibrations. Skewed? Slewed?"

"Either," he said. "Okay, maybe it did. A tiny bit."

"A tiny bit that was amplified a huge amount by the telescope's magnification."

"Hmm. Interesting idea."

"Work with me on this," she said. "Seismometers pick up tiny movements in the ground and then amplify them, right?"

"Yeah. Electronically."

"Electronically, optically—what's the diff?" She was speaking in rapid, excited bursts now. "If I magnified my images from La Palma, I could see which way the stars shift. The tracks—"

"Tracks?"

"Star tracks. Trails of light. Like tiny comet tails. They'd point directly toward the quakes."

"They would," he said slowly. "*If* there were any quakes. But there *weren't*. You don't believe me, see for yourself. Earthquake.USGS.gov."

"David, I'm telling you—"

"*Stop,*" he said. "I've got a grant application to submit by midnight, a journal article due tomorrow, and my tenure review is next week. I don't have time for this."

"But David—"

"Stop picking at it. Good*bye*."

CHAPTER 6

Baltimore, Maryland
Twenty-four hours later

O'Malley shrugged off her jet lag and shrugged on her backpack, then hoisted her bicycle over her shoulder and descended the stairs from her third-floor apartment. It was a pain to lug the bike up and down the steps, but theft was rampant in the neighborhoods around Johns Hopkins, and her bike—a featherweight $5,000 machine (*three hundred bucks a pound,* she sometimes marveled)—would be a prize to any thief who knew beans about bikes. Besides, with its carbon-fiber frame and lustrous aluminum components, the machine was as beautiful as it was functional, and O'Malley had made it the centerpiece of her interior-decorating plan. When it wasn't transporting her, the bike perched on the living room fireplace mantel, gleaming beneath halogen accent lights.

Wrestling the balky door at the bottom of the stairs, she felt as if she'd been overserved the night before—the week before—and indeed she had. But it was an excess of frustration and an overdose of fatigue, not a surfeit of partying, that had her dragging ass. The two-mile ride to campus would help.

Gripping the hand brakes, she clipped her left foot onto the pedal and, in one smooth, familiar motion, released the brakes and swung her right leg over the bar. Turning onto Roland Avenue, she stood on the pedals, sprinting to pick up speed, then leaned into the turn onto University Parkway. From here, University swooped downhill for nearly a mile, the lanes divided by an oak-studded median. The grade was steep enough for serious speed—O'Malley had once clocked herself at forty miles an hour—and curvy enough to send her adrenaline spiking.

When she reached the bridge at the base of the hill, she rose to a crouch, letting her knees absorb the jolt of the expansion joints. On the far side of the short span, she leaned sharply into a right turn onto San Martin Drive, a winding road bordered on one side by woods and the creek, and on the other by the Georgian brick buildings of the main Johns Hopkins campus—including O'Malley's building, where more than a hundred physicists and astronomers pondered problems and explored realms beyond all explaining to most people. *A critical mass of brainpower,* she thought at times. *The world's highest concentration of nerds,* she thought at others.

The place where my career's going to hell if I can't explain why I've got nothing to show for my ten-thousand-dollar junket to La Palma, she amended as she walked in the door, her bike slung over her shoulder.

Her call went straight to David's voicemail. She tried three more times, over the course of half an hour, with the same result. Finally, in desperation, she tracked down the main number for UC Berkeley's Seismology Center and called it. When the secretary answered, O'Malley said, "Hello, I'm trying to reach Dr. David Solomon about an urgent matter. Is he in?"

"Let me check," said the secretary. "May I tell him who's calling?"

"Just tell him I'm with the National Science Foundation. It's about his grant."

"One moment, please." O'Malley was put on hold.

It was a very brief hold. Five seconds later, David picked up the call. "Hello, this is Dr. Solomon," he said, sounding serious and dignified.

"I lied—it's me," she said. "Don't be mad."

"Christ," he said. "You beat everything, you know that?"

"Listen," she pleaded, "this is important. You agreed that if there was a quake on La Palma while I was taking photographs with the telescope, and if the star tracks shifted in a discernible straight line . . ."

"In theory, it *could*," he said, "*if* there were a quake. Which there wasn't. But if there had been, it would give you a vector—a compass direction toward the source of the event—but not a distance."

"Ha," she said, her voice triumphant. "I *knew* it!"

"Megan, slow down. You'd have to measure—"

"I already did. I enlarged my images and plotted the direction. The quakes came from the south. Compass heading of one hundred seventy-three degrees. Every single time."

"Megan, listen to me. There were. No. Quakes."

"David, I'm looking at seventeen images, all of them skewed the same way. Tiny, zigzag jolts, less than a second long. *Lots* of them."

"Wait, *wait*," he said. "Short pulses? How short?"

"Very short. A fraction of a second. Maybe a microsecond."

"You've just proved my case. Those are not earthquakes, Megan."

"David—"

"Megan, would you for once in your life just shut up and *listen* to me? Earthquakes are not short pulses. Earthquakes are long, slow events—multiple seconds, sometimes even minutes in duration. It's the *earth* quaking; get it? That doesn't happen in a microsecond. *If* you're seeing some sort of events in those photos—which I'm still not convinced you are—they're for damned sure not earthquakes. Maybe— *maybe*—construction. Roadwork. Blasting a highway cut through the mountains. Short pulses are a signature of dynamiting. 'Ripple shots,' they're called. A wave of sequential explosions, microseconds apart, to break up rock." She could hear his keyboard clattering. "I'm looking at La Palma on Google Earth. Zooming in on the caldera . . . I see the observatory complex on the north rim . . . a heading of one hundred seventy-three degrees from there runs right through the center of the caldera." He paused. "God, that's one humongous hole in the ground. Could there be a construction project happening in the caldera?"

"You think somebody's building luxury condos inside an old volcano? Give me a break, David."

"No, smart-ass, I think maybe somebody's building a visitor center. The caldera's part of a national park, according to Google Earth."

"Yeah, but that doesn't—"

"I'm looking closer at the caldera itself. There's an overlook and parking area near the south rim, across from the observatory. Maybe they're building an interpretive center. Blasting a shelf in the rock, or holes for foundation footers."

"At night? Why would they be dynamiting a cliff in the middle of the night, David?"

"I don't *know*," he said. "I don't have a fucking clue. Ask *them*. Ask anybody but me."

"David, something weird and scary is happening on La Palma. You yourself said that the island's a seismic shitstorm waiting to happen."

"That's not—"

"There's more," she interrupted. "The quake I felt the last day I was there. I *felt* it, David. That means it wasn't some tiny microblast—"

"Ripple shot," he corrected.

"Ripple shot, whatever you call it. It lasted twenty, thirty seconds. That whole island was shaking, hard enough to topple a stack of rocks. A USGS website—the United States Geological Survey—"

"I *know* what the damn USGS is," he snapped.

"The USGS says if you can feel a quake, it's gotta be magnitude three or higher. You need to take another look at the seismic data, David."

"No, I don't, Megan, 'cause I already did. *This* is what I need to do." She heard a click. The line went dead. David—her favorite ex-husband, or, rather, her *former* favorite ex-husband—had hung up on her. Again.

She felt better after venting about David to Gracie—her former roommate and best friend, now a middle school science teacher in Delaware—and then sublimating, churning out thirty brisk miles on the bike. Her thighs protesting, O'Malley staggered up her staircase and showered. But in the shower, a place where she often thought through problems, her frustrations came back. Then an idea came to her, and she threw on jeans and a sweater and climbed into her Prius for a trip to Baltimore's Middle Harbor.

Going against the rush-hour traffic on the Jones Falls Expressway, she made it to the waterfront in only fifteen minutes, arriving just at sunset. She spied an open parking spot at the corner of Thames and South Ann Streets—a stroke of luck, given that the Middle Harbor tended to be crawling with tourists, especially on an unseasonably warm evening like this one—and nosed the car into it.

The sidewalk tables outside the bars along the north side of Thames Street were jammed with happy-hour drinkers lingering over their brews as the sunset faded and the first stars appeared. *The last of the Lite,* punned O'Malley, eyeing a can of low-carb beer.

She walked west for a block—past the Cat's Eye Pub and an ice-cream shop and the Oyster House—then crossed South Broadway and entered Broadway Square, a brick-paved park with a dozen or so trees and a few benches, some occupied by homeless people. It was there, opposite the hot dog stand, that she found Herman.

Even though darkness was just now falling, he was already peering through the eycpiccc of a stubby, tripod-mounted telescope—an eight-inch Schmidt-Cassegrain reflector, O'Malley happened to know, whose eighty-inch light path sped neatly back and forth three times within the length of its twenty-inch tube. It was a portable, or at least luggable, version of the vastly bigger instrument she had gone to La Palma to use. A sign taped to the instrument proclaimed HERMAN HEYN, BALTIMORE'S STREET-CORNER ASTRONOMER—HAV-A-LOOK! Positioned between the legs of the tripod was an upside-down cowboy hat containing a few one-dollar bills and a sprinkling of change. A man wearing faded jeans, a sweatshirt, and a dark-blue beret bent over the lower end of the tube, peering through an eyepiece.

O'Malley looked in the direction the telescope was pointing. In the west, just above the rooftops, Venus blazed in the indigo twilight, as bright as a helicopter searchlight. O'Malley dug deep into her memory for a line from Shakespeare. "O, she doth teach the torches to burn bright," she quoted. The image was Romeo's description of Juliet, but it fit the planet perfectly. "It seems she hangs upon the cheek of night . . ."

"Like a rich jewel in an Ethiope's ear," finished the man, still peering through the lens. O'Malley clapped with delight, and the man straightened. His eyes were edged with crow's-feet, and the huge smile he gave O'Malley was surely deepening them. "Dr. O'Malley, what a nice surprise!"

"Good to see you, Herman." She reached out and hugged him. "But you gotta stop that 'Doctor' nonsense."

"Not a chance." His grin widened. "Proudest moment of my life, when you told me I was the one who inspired you to become an astronomer."

O'Malley smiled. "God's truth. You changed my life. Twenty years ago, but I remember like it was yesterday. Standing on a stool—is that the very same stool?" She pointed to a battered, shoebox-size wooden stool tucked beside the cowboy hat, and he nodded. "Standing on that stool, looking through the eyepiece, and seeing Saturn, this gorgeous Christmas tree ornament glowing in the sky, with honest-to-god *rings* around it. It seemed too beautiful to be real."

He chuckled. "I must have done a really good job of focusing that night. The sharper the image, the faker it looks. How are you? What are you doing these days?"

"I'm good. Mostly." She gave a half nod, half shrug. "Still at Hopkins. Still looking for Planet Nine."

"Well, if anybody can find it, it's you," said the aging astronomer. "I wish I could help, but you've got heavy artillery, and all I have is this tiny peashooter." He eyed her closely. "Why do you say 'mostly'? What's wrong?"

"I'm hitting a wall, Herman," she said. "Beating my head against it."

He raised his eyebrows. "So just quit."

"Quit? My job at Hopkins?"

"Goodness no. Quit beating your head against the wall. Climb over it instead. Or take it down, brick by brick by brick."

It was 3:00 a.m., and O'Malley sat hunched over the desk in her living room, a hundred or more mouse clicks down a dizzying maze of online rabbit holes—holes her new lightning-fast laptop allowed her to descend with head-spinning swiftness.

After hearing the details of her frustrations with La Palma and David, Herman had repeated his advice—"climb over the wall, or take it apart"—but instead of doing either of those, she seemed instead to be burrowing deep beneath it, and she was starting to wonder if she'd ever find her way back to the surface. At the moment, it seemed more likely that the wall itself, plus the shaky ground it stood on, would collapse and bury her alive.

Her dive down the rabbit hole had started innocently enough, with a few Google searches about seismic activity and earthquakes. David had been right about one thing, she quickly learned: the short, pulsing shocks that had jolted her telescope almost certainly came from small, controlled explosions. She had gleaned that insight from an article in a geology journal, illustrated with seismograms comparing the brief, uniform jolts of dynamite ripple shots with the slower, more random rumblings of natural earthquakes. But the insight raised more questions than it answered: Who was blasting on La Palma—in the middle of the night—and why? And what was the connection, if any, between the explosions and the tremor that had awakened her from her nap beside the volcano trail?

Next, she began picking in earnest at that tremor. She revisited the USGS website, the one explaining how to estimate the intensity of an earthquake's shaking. According to the website, earthquakes were harder to detect outdoors than indoors—surprising but reasonable, she concluded, since trees and dirt weren't as prone to rattling as, say, pictures on a wall or dishes on a shelf. To be felt outdoors, a quake needed a Richter-scale magnitude of 4 to 5—not a small number. And to be awakened from a sound sleep, she reasoned, she must surely have felt a jolt of at least that scale. And yet . . . and yet David insisted that there had been no recent seismic activity on La Palma. He had even sent her a series of email attachments after their last call—no message, just attachments—showing readings from the seismic station on Tenerife, one island away from La Palma. The seismograms, which plotted activity for the prior seven days—including the day O'Malley had been awakened from her labyrinthine nap—showed no activity. "But the Earth *does* move," O'Malley muttered, quoting Galileo's famous response to the Vatican inquisitors who had challenged his assertion that the Sun, not the Earth, was the center of the solar system.

She glared accusingly at the seismograms David had sent, zeroing in on the day and time she had been jolted awake. The graphs—three sets of squiggly lines, not just one, representing three different frequencies—reminded O'Malley of audio waveforms, like the squiggly soundtrack animation in the Disney classic *Fantasia*. If the small squiggles she was looking at had actually been sound waves, they'd have been whispers, she concluded—and if they'd been EKGs from a hospital patient, that patient would be in serious need of speedy CPR . . . or perhaps leisurely transport to the morgue. "I don't get it," she muttered. "Either I'm insane or the data's off."

Having no objective way to evaluate her sanity, she decided to drill down into the data. What David had sent were only screenshots. O'Malley sought out the database itself. On one of the images, she found the website address and entered it into her browser bar. The address took her to the data archive for the GSN, the Global Seismographic Network—specifically, to the data recorded by the seismic station on Tenerife, eighty miles from La Palma. Scanning the search options, she was pleased to see that by simply entering a calendar date, she could see a plot showing seismic readings for the entire twenty-four-hour period. She began by studying the day she'd been hiking the volcano trail, focusing intently on the time when she estimated her nap had been interrupted. Not surprisingly, the plot in the data archive matched the screenshot David had sent, with three plots for each date, showing three different data channels. O'Malley pored over them, memorizing every small squiggle in the black lines. She stared until her vision grew blurry, and when she closed her eyes, the same lines—this time in white, on a black background—were etched on the inside of her eyelids.

After committing the pattern to memory, she began scrolling backward, day by day: "T minus one," she said as she clicked backward to the prior day. She called off the numbers for each day: "T minus two. T minus three . . ." The patterns varied, but only slightly, from day to day, and by the time she had scrolled through an entire month's worth of plots, O'Malley was back to questioning her sanity, or at least her methodology. She was looking for something, but she didn't know *what*, so how on earth would she recognize it if she found it?

"Christ, O'Malley, pay attention," she scolded herself. Somehow, in trying to scroll farther backward, to begin looking at the prior month's data, she had accidentally returned to her starting position, day "T," the day of her hike. She recognized that day's three plots as easily as she'd have recognized the Big Dipper, the Little Dipper, and Orion in the night sky. "Once more with feeling," she said. "T minus thirty." She clicked on the calendar icon, and the screen refreshed.

The hairs on her arms and neck stood up, as if an electric current were passing through her body. She stared at the date she had entered—it was indeed "T minus thirty"—and then stared at the three waveforms on the screen. They were identical—absolutely, utterly 100 percent identical—to the waveforms from the day she had been shaken awake. Just to be sure, she opened another window on her computer screen and called up the day of her hike. Her eyes darted back and forth from one to the other. The correspondence was perfect. Her pulse racing and her adrenaline surging, O'Malley called up the plots for day T–1, November 13, and in the other window, day T–31, October 14. "Jesus God," she whispered. These, too, mirrored one another exactly, squiggle for squiggle. Her cursor now moving faster and faster, she scrolled back, in parallel, through a second month's worth of data, and by the time she finished, she knew, beyond any shred of doubt, that the archive had been altered. Somehow, someone had gone into the database and pasted in fake readings for the Canary Islands' seismic station—at least two months' worth of copied data, pasted in. But *why*? The answer was both obvious and troubling: to conceal whatever seismic events were actually occurring.

But it was when she Googled "La Palma earthquake" that the rabbit hole turned truly deep and dark, a new shaft opening beneath her feet like a trapdoor into a bottomless pit. The top hit on the list had an odd, ominous title: "La Palma Mega Tsunami." The next hit included an even more explicit summary: "Scientists warn of massive tidal wave from Canary Island volcano." She clicked on the link. The article was written by a British science writer. Its opening made O'Malley gasp:

> A wave higher than Nelson's Column and travelling faster than a jet aircraft will devastate the eastern seaboard of America and inundate much of southern Britain, say scientists who have analysed the effects of a future volcanic eruption in the Canary Islands. A massive slab of rock twice the volume of the Isle of Man would break away from the island of La Palma and smash into the Atlantic Ocean to cause a tsunami—a monster wave—bigger than any recorded.

The story, which appeared in several British newspapers in 2001, cited an article in a respected seismology journal. O'Malley clicked on a link to the article and found herself reading a scholarly piece filled with maps and tables. Scanning rapidly, she read that the scientists' computer modeling predicted that the wave could be up to 100 meters high—330 feet—when it hit the nearby coast of Africa. Even after traveling all the way across the Atlantic, the scientists said it could still strike America with a height of 50 meters, or 165 feet.

The articles were slightly misleading in one detail: strictly speaking, the tidal wave wouldn't be caused by a volcanic eruption but by a massive landslide—a slide that could be triggered by an eruption. La Palma's volcanic ridge, running north to south—the very ridge O'Malley herself had hiked on just two days before—formed the island's rocky backbone. According to the scientists quoted in the article, a long, deep fault line bisected that ridge. If an eruption or earthquake should cause the fault to fail suddenly and catastrophically, an immense portion of the island—"twice the volume of the Isle of Man," as the journalist put it—could slide swiftly into the sea, triggering a tsunami of unprecedented height and destructiveness. The wave would spread like a ripple from a stone tossed into a pond—only in this case, the stone could be the size of two hundred thousand Great Pyramids, and the ripple could be higher than Niagara Falls. And according to the scientists, it wasn't a question of whether the event would happen; the only question was when.

O'Malley clicked on link after link related to "La Palma Mega Tsunami," and clicked on those links' secondary links, and *those* links' links. She read dozens of the articles, mainstream and scientific. Some articles vehemently denounced the theory as far-fetched and alarmist; others, though, considered it plausible or at least possible. As she thought about La Palma's seismic and volcanic instability, she grasped why David had initially said the word "shitstorm," even though he'd later tried to unsay it, or at least downplay it.

Then came the video: a computer animation made by the tsunami modelers to show how the disaster could unfold. O'Malley watched it with a combination of scientific detachment and morbid horror. The video was no Hollywood special-effects spectacle; the video was simply a color-coded animation, not unlike weather radar images of a storm's movement and intensity. In this case, though, the storm was the wave—the tsunami—radiating outward from the island of La Palma. The animation used different colors to represent different heights, graphing predicted "runup heights" at various points where the wave would strike coastlines. As the animation played, O'Malley found herself mesmerized by the blooming colors: Yellow. Orange. Red. Crimson—no, carmine. Fuchsia. Violet. Blue. It was as if some exotic, rainbow-hued flower were unfurling in the waters of the Atlantic. *A corpse flower,* she thought abruptly. *When it blooms, we die.*

She replayed the video again and again, hitting the "Pause" button to study the wave's height at major cities. The Canaries themselves, being closest, were hardest hit, of course, with runup heights of four hundred meters or more—a wave as high as the Empire State Building.

For cities and towns along the islands' coastlines, destruction would be swift and total. What was it A. Samler Brown had written about the bursting of the cochineal bubble? "Retribution was swift, sudden, and terrible"? Something like that. According to the animation's model, the northwest coast of Africa would be hit by a wave potentially as high as the Brooklyn Bridge. Spain and Portugal, forty to sixty meters, perhaps the height of a fifteen- to twenty-story building. France and the UK, twenty or thirty meters high—up to a hundred feet. "North America gets ~30 m runup," read the caption on a freeze-frame image in the animation. "A bit less to the south and a bit more to the north."

O'Malley read that line aloud—"a *bit* less to the south, a *bit* more to the north"—stunned by its offhandedness about the prospective devastation.

The Bahamas, Bermuda, and Puerto Rico would be hit by 100 to 130 feet of runup, while the Lesser Antilles—the Virgin Islands, Antigua, Trinidad and Tobago, Aruba, and other specks she couldn't name—might get 160 feet. Brazil's northern coast would be slammed by a runup of up to 125 feet.

The wave's impact, explained a website created by one of the scientists modeling the disaster, would be similar to that of the 2011 tsunami that had devastated Japan, with one key difference: a La Palma mega tsunami could affect one hundred times more coastline. "On the bright side," the scientist offered, "there is no evidence that this will happen anytime soon . . . and with the odds of a collapse at just a few percent each century . . . don't rush to sell your seaside condominium." This final pearl of real estate wisdom was juxtaposed on a photoshopped image of a hundred-foot wave smashing into Florida's Space Coast. The incongruity—the upbeat, chummy advice superimposed on the bleak image—drew a bark of outraged, appalled laughter from O'Malley.

Eventually she broke free from obsessively watching the animated disaster and—a scientist herself, after all—moved on to gathering contextual data. She took terse, elliptical notes from a Wikipedia article on tsunamis: "Before 1900, only 44 recorded tsunamis," she wrote, after counting down the list. "Since 1900, another 38." A moment later, "Deadliest modern tsunami was 2004 Indian Ocean wave. Initial surge 108 ft. Killed 230,000!" When she read the entry about the 2011 earthquake and tsunami in Japan, she noted, "Wave 133 feet high when it hit village of Miyako!"

Eventually her Google searching and link clicking brought her to a lengthy piece in the *New Yorker*, a source to which she assigned greater credibility than many of the sensational publications trumpeting disaster. The story—titled "The Really Big One"—opened with a remarkable vignette: A group of seismologists, attending an earthquake conference in Japan in 2011, felt their hotel begin to shake. They rushed outside, some of them timing the duration of the event on their digital watches. The shaking lasted for nearly five minutes—a marathon, as earthquakes go, and therefore a sign that it was a big, bad one. But the Japan earthquake described in that opening vignette wasn't the "really big one" mentioned in the title. The really big one was an earthquake and tsunami that seismologists were predicting could strike America's Pacific coast in the near future. The quake's epicenter would not be the well-known and notorious San Andreas Fault; rather, it would occur in a lesser known but potentially far deadlier place called the Cascadia Subduction Zone, a seven-hundred-mile offshore fault running from Northern California all the way past Oregon, Washington, and Vancouver Island.

During the next fifty years, the *New Yorker* story explained, the Cascadia Subduction Zone had a one-in-three chance of producing a major quake—a magnitude 8 or even magnitude 9 monster—followed swiftly by a tsunami anywhere from twenty to one hundred feet high. That tsunami, the article said, could devastate coastal cities throughout the Pacific Northwest. "FEMA projects that thirteen thousand people will die," the article went on, "and the agency expects that it will need to provide shelter for a million displaced people." She reread the passage again; surely she had misread it? No: thirteen thousand people dead, one million people displaced. "Our operating assumption," a FEMA official was quoted as saying, "is that everything west of Interstate 5 will be toast."

O'Malley felt stunned by the article's revelations. Tsunamis were things that happened in distant, perilous parts of the world, weren't they? Japan. Indonesia. Thailand. Madagascar. But Washington? *Oregon,* for chrissakes? Her mind wandered back to a bicycle trip she'd taken the summer after her freshman year of college. She had pedaled from Portland to Astoria and then down the entire Oregon coast. Mentally she ticked off the towns she'd visited, wondering how hard they'd be hit.

Astoria? The waterfront's a goner, but some of the town's on a hill. Run for high ground. Seaside, that pretty little beach town? Kiss it goodbye. Cannon Beach, ditto—only safe place would be on top of Haystack Rock, but you'd have to be a world-class rock climber to scale it.

She raced farther down US 101, the coast highway, ticking off the doomed towns: Manzanita, Tillamook, Rockaway Beach, Lincoln City, Newport. And those were just in Oregon; she didn't even know the names of all the places in Northern California, Washington, and British Columbia that would be swept away.

O'Malley felt not just stunned but stupid, too. Why had she never heard of the Cascadia Subduction Zone, with its one-in-three chance of devastating seven hundred miles of coastline, its potential to kill thirteen thousand people and displace a million more? She also felt *betrayed,* she realized. Why wasn't the government doing more to prepare people in the Pacific Northwest to survive? She sent a text to David: Cascadia subduction zone—how come nobody's talking about this or prepping? Madness!

Then the realization hit her: The potential loss of thirteen thousand lives from a quake and tsunami in the Northwest was minor—practically trivial—compared to what could happen if the worst-case version of a La Palma tsunami hit America's Eastern Seaboard. How many Americans lived in low-lying coastal cities and towns along the Atlantic coast—twenty million? Fifty million? Good God, it was probably closer to a *hundred* million. What was FEMA doing to watch and prepare for *that* potential clusterfuck? She shot another text to David: La Palma mega tsunami—WTF? Why the hell didn't you mention that to me?

A moment later, her phone buzzed—a sound like an angry cicada that had gotten trapped on its back—delivering David's response: Didn't mention b/c I knew you'd freak out. As you're clearly doing. STOP PICKING AT IT.

She fired right back: STOP PATRONIZING ME.

She returned to the video animation, the beautiful bloom of disaster unfurling from La Palma and blossoming across the ocean to New England, New York, the mid-Atlantic coast, poor doomed Florida. And then another realization hit her. Swamped her. Damned near drowned her in dread: The ripple-shot explosions on La Palma—the ones someone had altered the GSN data to hide—had nothing to do with visitor-center construction or highway work. No, the ripple-shot explosions that had wrecked her astronomical observations had everything to do with *this*: with a landslide and a mega tsunami. Someone—some monster—was actively trying to tip the seismic scales on La Palma. Trying to trigger a massive landslide and unleash a gargantuan wave that could kill millions upon millions of people. Were the recurring explosions enough to do it? Or—she shuddered at the thought—were there more things, bigger things, in the works, too?

She felt a wave of fear—a tsunami of terror—crash into her, churn her, reduce her to blind, instinctual panic. *Dammit, O'Malley, think,* she ordered herself. *Breathe and think and do something.* But what?

Eventually she typed a web address—FBI.gov—and explored pages labeled "What We Investigate," "Submit a Tip," and, intriguingly, "Weapons of Mass Destruction." But the FBI's focus seemed to be on domestic crime and terrorism attacks "originating within the United

States," and its definition of "weapons of mass destruction" included nothing remotely resembling earthquakes and tsunamis.

Her hands shaking, O'Malley typed another Google search: "Central Intelligence Agency." "The work of a nation, the center of intelligence," read a slogan at the top of the home page. To the right of the slogan she saw a button labeled "Report Threats."

"If this ain't a threat, I'd hate to see one," she muttered.

She clicked the button, and a box of text appeared on the screen. Beneath two paragraphs of text about the agency's commitment to combating terrorism was another button labeled "To Contact the Central Intelligence Agency Click Here."

O'Malley took a deep breath—and then another, and then another. And then she clicked.

CHAPTER 7

CIA Headquarters
Langley, Virginia

Dawtry flashed a nervous smile at the seven men seated equidistantly around the mahogany conference table. "Thanks, Jim," he said after Vreeland had made brief introductions all around. Five of the seven had been at Dawtry's talk in the Bubble a few days before, and he took that as a hopeful sign, given that the talk had seemed to go well. But today the stakes were higher; today was his for-real, formal interview for the post as FBI liaison to the CIA. Vreeland had told him, sort of, not to worry, though the man's choice of words—"The job is yours to lose"—had seemed odd in the moment, and had been gnawing at Dawtry's confidence ever since.

"I'm honored to be here," he began, "and I'm excited by the idea of working directly with you and your colleagues." Several of his listeners gave slight nods—acknowledgment, or perhaps even slight encouragement? "So, since we've all got clearances, I'd love to hear your candid thoughts on the big-picture challenges and threats on the horizon. Jim?" He looked first to Vreeland, seated at the opposite end of the table.

Vreeland paused before speaking. "Actually, we had something different in mind," he said. "We hear ourselves talk all the time. We'd much rather hear *you*. We've just been reading some of your internal memos about counterterrorism, and we're eager to hear more of your thoughts. See if we're on the same page." He smiled, and the smile's thinness—as thin as a blade—sent a chill down Dawtry's spine.

Shit, he thought. *Which memos? Is something I wrote about the CIA about to bite me in the ass?* He felt a sudden trickle of sweat under his arms. Was it possible they'd gotten their hands on the "CIA blind spots" memo he'd sent his boss, by way of explaining why he'd like to serve as the Bureau's interagency liaison? If so, they'd be furious. *Please, God, no,* he prayed. "Yes, of course," he said, hoping his voice didn't betray his rising anxiety. If he was lucky, they were simply reacting to some lesser faux pas. Perhaps he had merely overstepped by not hanging back and letting Vreeland launch the discussion. "Where would you like me to start?"

"Wherever you like. What do *you* see as—how did you put it?—the big-picture challenges and threats on the horizon?"

Smooth move, Chip, Dawtry thought. *Nowhere to run, nowhere to hide.* He cleared his throat, then forced another smile. "Well, obviously, you guys are the experts, so I might be out of my depth here, but I've been thinking about history lately." The CIA traditionally recruited from Ivy League schools and their secret societies—Skull and Bones, Quill and Dagger, Scroll and Key—and Dawtry hoped that this tradition might translate into a former history major or two at the table, liberal arts guys who would understand and appreciate a bit of historical contextualizing. "What was it Churchill said? 'Those who fail to learn from history are doomed to repeat it'? I've been wondering if we've failed to learn from some important events in recent history."

"Santayana," Vreeland said.

"Excuse me?"

"Churchill didn't say that." Vreeland's voice seemed a degree cooler. "It's widely misattributed. It was the philosopher Santayana who said it. By the way, you're misquoting as well as misattributing." He smirked. "I double-majored—history *and* philosophy." Dawtry heard a few chuckles, and he glanced around nervously. What he saw, in every set of eyes now, was avid, predatory cunning.

"But I digress," Vreeland added genially. "What lessons of history have we failed to learn?" His colleagues—the other wolves in his pack—leaned forward.

Dawtry swallowed hard. "Consider the World Trade Center towers. Look, I'm not here to point fingers—at your agency or at mine—but in hindsight, obviously, we failed to connect the dots. And failed to communicate effectively. Which is why this interagency liaison position was created after 9/11. That was a huge step in the right direction."

"Yes, thank heavens for it," said Vreeland. "However else would we learn from history, with all the blind spots that interfere with our ability to read, and to see the big picture?"

Dawtry's armpits were pouring sweat now. *That's it,* he thought. *They've read the memo, and I'm cooked.* "Well. Anyhow," he stumbled on, "I've been looking back at 9/11, and also looking at our current intelligence gathering." As if to compensate for his swampy underarms, his mouth was as dry as Death Valley. "I'm wondering if we're not spending so much time and so many resources examining trees that we're losing sight of the forest." He paused, hoping for a question, but when one came, he wished it hadn't.

"What a delightful bonus," said the man on Vreeland's left, who happened to be Vreeland's division chief. "History *and* forestry. Speaking as one of the benighted scrutinizers of bark and branches, I would love to be enlightened as to the nature of the forest. What do you see from your lofty perch?"

Dawtry reddened. "That was a poor choice of metaphor," he said. "Forgive me. What I mean . . . what concerns me . . . is that we—and by 'we,' I mean our nation's leaders, our policy makers, even our citizens—we seem to be acting as if the new norm of terrorism is now the *only* norm."

"The new norm?" The question, accompanied by raised eyebrows, came from Vreeland.

Dawtry nodded. "The lone wolf. The small cell. The microattack. A jihadist drives a car into a crowd, mows down a dozen people. A neo-Nazi opens fire in a black church in Charleston. A shooter sets up a sniper's nest on the thirty-second floor of a Vegas hotel. More and more, we're focusing our resources on finding and stopping these low-level attacks."

"And in your view, that's unnecessary." It was a statement, not a question, from the man seated on Vreeland's right. He was thin and hawkish, his cheekbones sharp as blades, his steel-rimmed glasses glinting with reflections that hid his eyes.

"No. *No.* Preventing lone-wolf attacks is *necessary*, to the degree that we can do it. But it's not *sufficient.* Let me go back to the World Trade Center."

"Really?" Vreeland's voice dripped sarcasm. "Your vision of the future is rooted in the year 2001?"

Dawtry could feel his bridge burning behind him—and ahead of him. And beneath his feet as well. *What the hell,* he thought. *I've already screwed the pooch here. Might as well speak my piece.* "Actually, a lot earlier than that. It's also important to remember 1993—the *first* World Trade Center bombing. A truck filled with explosives, parked in the underground garage. The plan was to topple the North Tower like a tree—smash it into the South Tower to bring down both. Obviously—luckily—it didn't work, but it would have, if the truck had been parked closer to the foundation wall." The faces around the table were stony. "The blast caused heavy damage to the garage, but it killed only six people. Things go fairly quiet for seven years—mostly microattacks, right? But then in 2000, *bam*, another audacious attack, this time on the USS *Cole*—an American *warship*, for God's sake. Ballsy, but only a warm-up. Eleven months later, down come the twin towers, a global symbol of American hubris. That event changed the world, maybe as powerfully as

Hiroshima and Nagasaki did. It revealed that the American homeland was vulnerable to attacks. To *mass-casualty* attacks." Dawtry held out both hands, palms upturned. "How many people died on September 11?" He looked around for an answer, but no one responded. They weren't giving him a thing. "Three thousand. That's a lot—it's three thousand too many. But because they died in a single attack—a dramatic, iconic, and *telegenic* attack, shown again and again around the world, the reaction was extraordinary. We were terrified. We went to war in Iraq and Afghanistan. We dialed back on civil liberties. We started conducting mass surveillance of our own citizens. We ignored the Geneva Conventions against torture and unlawful confinement."

Vreeland cocked his head. "I understand your brother died in one of the towers." Dawtry felt his face flush. "Terrible, of course," Vreeland added coolly. "But I wonder if that skews your thinking. Makes you prone to apocalyptic fears."

You bastard, Dawtry thought. "Of *course* it skews my thinking," he said. "But just because I'm paranoid, that doesn't mean they're not out to get us in big, dramatic ways."

"Help me understand this," said Vreeland's boss. "We took out Osama bin Laden in 2011. We've conducted hundreds of drone strikes—in Afghanistan, Pakistan, Yemen, Syria, Somalia, Iraq—and killed thousands of jihadists. Al-Qaeda is dead on the table, and ISIS is on the run. What is it you think we're missing?"

"I'm not so sure al-Qaeda's dead," Dawtry shot back. "Maybe they're just deep underground. What about bin Laden's second-in-command, al-Zawahiri? We've still never gotten him. We've been after him ever since 9/11, and he's still on the loose. And bin Laden's son is now grown and calling for more attacks. But let's not get stuck on Qaeda. My point is, we've stopped looking for the next 'spectacular' attack. The next out-of-the-box, pie-in-the-sky, world-changing attack."

"And where do you suggest we look for that?" asked Vreeland.

Dawtry shrugged. "That's the puzzle, right? The black swan. The operation so audacious and outlandish it's inconceivable . . . until it's already happened. Until we're picking up the bodies." He drew a deep breath to steady himself. It didn't work. "The terrorists have already weaponized vehicles and airliners and even skyscrapers. We know they're interested in weaponizing nuclear power plants. What's next— DC's public water supply? The Superdome during the Super Bowl? The Verrazano-Narrows Bridge during the New York City marathon? Or something even worse—unthinkably worse—than any of those scenarios? We've got to start thinking like they do, only better. We've got to put more resources into finding and stopping the Next Big Thing."

"Of course," said Vreeland drily. "I'll ask NASA to check the dark side of the moon Monday morning, in case SPECTRE has installed a giant rocket thruster there, to crash the moon into Manhattan." His comment was rewarded with smirks all around the table. Vreeland glanced around, evidently gratified by the reaction. Then he placed both palms on the table and stood up. "Gentlemen, I believe that pretty well covers it. Thank you for the history lesson, Special Agent Dawtry. We'll be in touch."

Dawtry nodded. He mumbled his thanks and made his way out of the building and across the courtyard, past the *Kryptos* sculpture, and out to the visitor parking lot, where his black Tahoe sat ready to take him away from the new job he wouldn't be getting. It had been his to lose, and he'd lost it.

As he approached the guard booth at the exit, still in a fog of dejection, Dawtry glimpsed movement to his left. He hit the brakes just in time to avoid slamming into a bicycle that hurtled off the curb and landed directly in his path. The cyclist had not even glanced to check for traffic. Dawtry gave the horn a peevish toot; in response, the cyclist took his hands off the handlebars, sat bolt upright, and raised both middle fingers high in the air. "Yeah, thanks for the signal, asshole," Dawtry muttered. He was about to gun the throttle and intercept the guy to discuss cycling safety and etiquette when he noticed an odd, shiny reflection. In lieu of a helmet, the cyclist's head appeared to be crowned with the world's largest Hershey's Kiss: a ten-inch silver dome whose top swirled upward into a graceful tapering tip. Looking closer, Dawtry glimpsed a miniature fencelike structure encircling the rim, constructed of three-inch spikes linked by wire mesh.

Huh, Dawtry thought, shifting his transmission into "Park." He got out, approached the door of the guard shack, and tapped the glass. One of the two guards turned and gave Dawtry an annoyed look before opening the door. "Can I help you?"

"Radiohead," said Dawtry, pointing. "The guy on the bike who nearly T-boned me. Not one of yours, I'm guessing?"

The guard shook his head. "Not hardly. But not for lack of trying. We see him every Friday, rain or shine. Four o'clock on the dot."

"Impressively methodical. What does he want?"

"Dunno," said the guard. "He's not authorized to tell me. Says he has a top-secret message for the director's ears only."

Dawtry gave a slight smile. "Maybe he does."

The guard grunted. "The director actually came out here one Friday. He'd heard stories about this guy, so one Friday, at five to four, the director shows up and waits."

"Yeah, right."

"Gospel truth. Captain Tinfoil pedals up five minutes later, and the director steps outside—which I *strongly* advised him not to do, by the way. 'Hello,' he says. 'I hear you have an important message for me.' Captain Tinfoil looks him up and down, then yells, 'Guard. *Guard!*' I hustle out, my service weapon drawn, 'cause I don't like how this is going down. 'This man is an imposter,' says Captain Tinfoil. 'Arrest him immediately!' So I step up to the director, grab him by the elbow, and say, 'Sir, you need to come with me. And don't give me any trouble.' I start hauling him inside, and at the door, I turn around and give Captain Tinfoil a salute with my weapon. He returns the salute, then pedals away until the next Friday."

Dawtry furrowed his brow skeptically. "You wouldn't be shitting a gullible G-man here, would you?"

The guard laid a hand on his heart. "Swear to God. You don't believe me, ask him yourself."

"Who, the director?"

The guard snorted and shook his head, then pointed. "The guy pedaling onto the GW Parkway right now. If you miss him, you can find him later at the group home near the zoo."

Dawtry had no clue where the group home was, but he knew exactly where the zoo was: a quarter mile up Connecticut from his own condo. He and Radiohead were practically neighbors. "You actually know where he lives?"

"Woodley House. Room 202." Dawtry raised an eyebrow; the guard shrugged nonchalantly. "We have a few skills."

"You track all the loonies?"

"Nah, just the ones that stand out," the guard said. "Though you can't always judge a book by its cover."

"What do you mean?"

"Crazy comes in all shapes and sizes," the guard said. "Ten minutes ago, we had another one. Looked like a soccer mom who just took the wrong exit. Well dressed, good-looking. Driving a Prius with a peace sign and a faded Hillary Clinton bumper sticker." The guard chuckled. "I guess that should've been my first clue."

The car, the peace sign, or the Hillary sticker? wondered Dawtry. "What brought her here, besides the hybrid?"

"The moon and the stars."

"Come again?"

"She's an astrologer."

"Astrologer?"

"Age of Aquarius, all that shit. Apparently, our national horoscope is headed for the crapper. She lost me pretty quick, but long story short, she studies the stars, and she's figured out that the terrorists can control the forces of nature now. Earthquakes, volcanoes, the ocean. They're about to turn Kansas into beachfront property."

Dawtry smiled. "I guess you and I should start buying up cow pastures."

"I guess so." The guard held up a finger—*hang on a sec*—and reached behind him, into the booth. He thrust a large manila envelope at Dawtry. "Here. She left this. Says it explains everything."

Dawtry frowned at the envelope. "I can't take that."

"Sure you can," said the guard. "I saw your title on the visitor list. You're a counterterrorism guy. Weapons of mass destruction. Earthquakes and volcanic eruptions—that's about as mass as destruction gets."

"But she brought it here. She gave it to you. It's CIA material." A horn beeped; Dawtry saw three cars backed up behind him and more on the way. "Looks like quitting time," he said. "Guess I better get out of the way."

He clambered back into the Tahoe. Just as he began tugging the door shut, something spun past his face, a corner tickling the tip of his nose, as the manila envelope whirled into the vehicle. It thwacked against the passenger door, then slid to the floor on the far side of the seat.

"It's Bureau material now," the guard said, grinning. "Have a great weekend." He stepped back, waving Dawtry forward through the gate, off the property, and away from the scene where his career had self-destructed.

The exit road curved away from the wooded campus and spat Dawtry onto the GW Parkway. As he merged, joining the torrent of traffic that flowed in parallel with the Potomac, he kept one eye peeled for a cyclist wearing a shiny, spiky helmet. Consequently, he paid no attention to the car parked on the road's shoulder. It was only after he was well past it that its details registered on his distracted mind: the car had been a metallic-green Prius with a Hillary bumper sticker and a peace sign, and sitting behind the wheel had been a woman. A good-looking, well-dressed woman who might have been a soccer mom and who also, he realized belatedly, might have been weeping, her face buried in her hands, slumped on the steering wheel.

Dawtry slid the plate away, pissed at himself for wasting the food. The chicken tikka masala was half-eaten, the sauce congealed; the garlic naan had gone cold and limp, the Kingfisher warm and flat. He beckoned to the server, Sanjay, and handed him a twenty, then pushed back his chair and stood.

Sanjay frowned at the uneaten meal. "Is there a problem with the food? Usually we don't even need to wash your plate when you've finished."

"No, the food was fine, Sanjay. The problem is me. I had a bad day. I'm in a foul mood."

"I am sorry to hear it. It must be a very foul mood indeed if even Indian food can't fix it."

"True." Dawtry managed a half smile at the joke. "I'll make up for it next time." He lifted a hand in a gloomy farewell and walked outside.

Connecticut Avenue was gridlocked with typical Friday evening traffic. Dawtry headed south from the restaurant, turned left onto Calvert, and headed for home, a block away. Then he stopped. "Well, *shit*," he muttered, then reversed course, back to Connecticut, and north.

He passed the Indian restaurant, passed the sushi bar, passed the Italian place and the coffee shop and a dozen other spendy establishments catering to the affluent, fortunate residents of Cleveland Park. Halfway between the Metro station and the zoo, just beyond a cheaply stuccoed apartment tower, Dawtry stopped, turning to study a low, wide town house. It was the sort of stodgy brick structure built back in the 1920s, back before Connecticut got expensive and built up.

The building was set back from the sidewalk by ten feet, with a tiny lawn—an honest-to-god little lawn—and a few scrubby bushes, plus a couple of pots of forlorn begonias on the front steps. From the outside, there was nothing to indicate the nature of the place or its residents, but the address and the architecture matched what Dawtry had found on Google.

He climbed the steps. The solid front door—painted white, protected by a glass-paneled storm door—was framed by narrow panes of glass spilling warm golden light. The night was turning cold, and the panes were fogged with condensation. Dawtry leaned to his left and risked a peek inside, but the condensation, plus a set of sheers, screened the entry hall from his prying eyes. *What the hell am I doing here?* he wondered. Then he rang the doorbell.

He listened for footsteps, but the cacophonous traffic on Connecticut would have drowned out even gunfire. After a few moments, a shadow flitted across the sheers, and then the peephole in the door—glowing like a cat's-eye—winked dark for a count of five, then brightened again.

A dead bolt rattled and the heavy door opened a foot. A woman somewhere north of middle age, gray hair pulled back in a bun, peered around the edge. "Yes?"

"Sorry to bother you, ma'am," said Dawtry.

What?" she shouted over the din. She looked Dawtry up and down, assessing the potential threat, then said, "Oh, just a minute. Hold on." She fumbled with the lock on the storm door, then opened it. "Yes?"

"Sorry to bother you," he began again. "I understand this is a group home, is that right?"

Her eyes narrowed warily. "How can I help you?"

"I believe you have a resident, a gentleman, who has—how to put this?—interesting taste in hats."

She closed her eyes and heaved a visible sigh. "Oh Lord. Is Benny in trouble again? What's he done now?"

"No, ma'am, he's not in trouble. Not at all. I apologize for worrying you. I just . . . I ran into him today, you might say, and I was . . . interested. I wondered if I might talk to him."

She studied him again: the short, neat haircut, the starched dress shirt, the cinched tie, the long overcoat. "You're from the CIA," she announced, her voice flat and weary.

"No, ma'am, I'm not."

"It's Friday," she went on, ignoring his response. "He was there again, wasn't he?" She glanced behind her. Dawtry followed her gaze and saw two women peering from the far end of the hall. The gray-haired woman stepped onto the porch, closing the storm door behind her. "Look, I know he can be a pest, but he really is harmless. I wish you people could get that through your heads." Her voice was both challenging and pleading.

"I believe you. And I'm not from the CIA. Really. But I was there today—that's where I saw him. Benny and I both had . . . imperfect experiences at Langley this afternoon."

"*You* don't look crazy."

He smiled. "Are you supposed to say that? Are you even *allowed* to say that?"

"Mister, I run a group home for people with mental illness. If anybody's allowed to say it, it's me. I know crazy. And you ain't crazy."

He shrugged. "Tell that to the guys at the Agency." The woman had folded her arms, hugging herself, and Dawtry noticed her starting to shiver. "I'm Chip Dawtry, by the way. And you're freezing. I'm sorry—I didn't mean to drag you out in the cold. Would it be possible for me to see him?"

"Why? You want to ask him questions about the conspiracy?" He shook his head. "If you get him agitated, Mr. Dawtry, it's not helpful—not for him, not for the other residents, and certainly not for me."

"I don't want to get him agitated. I don't want to ask him questions."

"Then what *do* you want?"

Dawtry shrugged. He held out his hands, empty and upturned. "I don't know, exactly. I imagine it's not easy being him—getting turned away and made fun of. I guess I just want to be, I don't know, a decent human being to him. Play checkers, talk bikes, whatever."

She gave him the gimlet eye. "So you want to be Benny's *friend*, is that it? You're gonna come over and spread some happiness every Friday now, help make up for his screwed-up brain and his lousy life? Or is this just a one-night stand to make you feel better about something?"

Dawtry blinked, stung. "I . . . you know what? You're right. I hadn't thought about it that way. Good night, ma'am. Sorry to bother you." He spun on his heel and trotted down the steps.

"Chess," she called after him.

He stopped, looked over his shoulder. "Excuse me?"

"Not checkers, chess. Do you play?"

He blinked. "Well, I used to. But it's been a while."

"Come inside. But take off that tie. And do something to your hair."

"What's wrong with my hair?"

"Nothing. That's what's wrong with it. Makes you look like a federal agent."

Dawtry laughed. "I *am* a federal agent." He reached up with both hands and rubbed his head. He felt the gel let go, felt the neatly combed strands part company. "Better?"

"Not much, but it's a start. Come on in."

"Benny?" Three men were in the living room watching the Weather Channel, where an attractive young woman was gesturing at a cold front. None of the men reacted. *"Excuse me, Benny."* One of them—the oldest, who looked to be an old fifty or a young sixty—tore his gaze from the screen and looked toward the doorway. "Benny," said Margaret—she had told Dawtry her name after inviting him in—"could you come here, please?"

Benny looked from Margaret to Dawtry, then back at Margaret, then got off the sofa and came to the doorway. Margaret beckoned them into the hall. "Benny, this is Chip."

"Hi, Benny." Dawtry extended a hand, which Benny ignored, so after an awkward moment, he withdrew it and gave a *no problem* sort of shrug.

"Benny, Chip plays chess." She paused to let that sink in. "I know you've missed playing chess since Marcus left. Would you like to play chess with Chip?"

Benny looked at him, his face neutral.

"No pressure," Dawtry said. "Totally up to you. I should warn you I'm pretty rusty. But I used to be decent. My friends in Chess Club called me Kamikaze Chip. If you're interested in a match, I'll try to keep up."

Benny glanced back at the TV, as if deciding between the chess-playing stranger and the cute weathergirl. Then he looked at Dawtry again. "Okay." He turned and headed across the entry hall, through another doorway, and flipped on a light. This room, the building's other front room, was lined with bookshelves; in the center sat a square wooden table, surrounded by four wingback armchairs.

Dawtry shot a questioning glance at Margaret. She raised one eyebrow and one shoulder. "Be careful what you wish for," she said sotto voce, then—louder—"Benny, the chess set is on the top shelf. No, the far end. The other side of Scrabble."

Benny found the chess set and slid it from the shelf. Even from the doorway, Dawtry felt a pang of nostalgia. It was exactly the kind of set Richard had given him for Christmas the year Dawtry had turned twelve and fallen in love with the game. The board was a shallow wooden box, hinged along one side and folded in half like a tall book, its "covers" inlaid with veneer squares of birch and walnut, light and dark. Benny brought the board to the table and then sat down, unlatched the metal clasp, and folded back the top half of the board. The hollow, felt-lined interior was filled with the chessmen. Benny began removing the pieces in order of rank, alternating between white and black, segregating them into the two armies: white king, black king; white queen, black queen; and so on, methodically down the hierarchy. Dawtry slid into the opposite seat and began scooping out pawns.

"You can have white," Benny said. "Since you haven't played in a while."

"Thanks," said Dawtry. It was a courtesy—white got first move, a strategic advantage. "Probably won't make any difference, though."

He was right. It didn't affect the outcome.

"Checkmate," Benny said. Again.

Benny had beaten him three times straight. The first match had taken barely ten minutes, the board still full of pieces. The second match took twice as long, and cost each of them quite a few men, though Dawtry's losses—including both bishops, a rook, and his queen—were worse than Benny's, which tended to be smaller, strategic sacrifices. The third match, however, was hard fought, the board gradually emptying; for a few promising moments midgame, Dawtry even managed to put Benny on the defensive, but then he'd made a mistake, and Benny had regained control.

Dawtry took a breath and blew it out. "Man, that was a good one." He checked his watch: nine o'clock. "I should go. I'm beat, in more ways than one." He stood up. "That was great, Benny. Thanks." He reached across the table. Benny gave him an odd, lingering look, then took his hand and shook it.

"I recognize you, you know."

"You do?"

"Sure. I saw you leaving the CIA today. You almost ran over me."

Dawtry paused. Should he deny it? *No. Tell the truth.* "Sorry. I didn't mean to. You almost T-boned me."

To Dawtry's surprise, Benny laughed. "Yeah. I was trying to."

"You were *trying* to? Why?"

"I dunno. Just mad, I guess. They never listen to me. It's frustrating."

"They didn't listen to me, either, Benny. It *is* frustrating."

Benny smiled. "I could tell you weren't one of them."

"How?"

He shrugged. "I just could. You're FBI, right?"

Dawtry gave a sheepish laugh. "That obvious, huh?"

Benny nodded. "You'd be pretty good at chess, if you played more often."

"You mean like more than once a decade?"

"Yeah. It comes back pretty quick. You nearly had me that last match. You've got a good head for strategy."

Dawtry smiled. "I learned a lot from my big brother. We played all the time when I was a kid. I miss playing with him."

"I'm sorry," Benny said, as if he had somehow intuited the details of Richard's death. "Your main problem is you overthink things. You'd've won if you hadn't second-guessed yourself. You should trust your instincts more."

True that, Dawtry thought, *and not just in chess.*

Benny hesitated, looking self-conscious for the first time all evening. "You can come back and play again sometime." He looked away.

"Yeah?"

"Yeah. If you want to." Benny looked him in the eye again. "No pressure. But why the hell not? I could teach you some things."

"No shoptalk? Just chess?"

"Just chess."

Much to his surprise, Dawtry felt a slow smile spreading across his face. "Sure, Benny. Why the hell not?"

CHAPTER 8

Baltimore

O'Malley poured the last of the scotch into her glass and took a long pull. Then she muttered, "Oh, fuck it," and dialed the number she had managed to find via Google. She counted eight rings, thinking, *Christ, don't the Brits believe in voicemail?* She was about to hang up when she heard a groggy, plummy, pissed-off voice say, "Yes? Who the devil is this?"

"Oh," she said, bolting upright in surprise. "Dr. Boyd? I thought for sure I'd get your voicemail."

"No such luck, I'm afraid," said the man. "What you've *gotten* is me out of bed. It's midnight here, you know."

"I'm so sorry," she said. "Really I am."

"Yes, well, that makes two of us," he said. "You sound American, and you have an American phone number. Are you calling me from the States, or are you having a midnight stroll here in London?"

"I'm in Baltimore, Maryland. I apologize for disturbing you. My name is Megan O'Malley. I'm an astronomer at Johns Hopkins University, and I'm calling because I've just read your paper about La Palma."

"Oh good God. Well, thank you, Professor O'Malley," said Boyd drily. "I'll look forward to reading *your* work soon—and awakening *you* to let you know. Do tell me when to call so as to be certain of rousing you."

"Look, I'm really sorry, but I'm also very worried, Dr. Boyd. I was just on La Palma—at the observatory—and there's a *lot* of seismic activity on the island. Some of it small, some of it strong. I think bad things are happening."

She heard a sigh from clear across the Atlantic. "Ms. O'Malley, I appreciate your concern, but I make a point of checking the Global Seismographic Network on a daily basis. I assure you there is *not* a lot of seismic activity happening on La Palma. Now, if you'll excuse me, I'd like to get back to sleep, if I'm able."

Before O'Malley could respond, the line went dead. "Shit," she said. She punched the "Call" button again. This time it was answered on the fourth ring.

"Professor O'Malley," Boyd said, his voice icy. "Do not call me again or I will contact your department chair."

"Wait," she said—no, shouted. "The GSN data—it's bogus. The readings are supposedly uploaded in real time from the seismic stations, but the numbers are fake. Cut and pasted. The network's been hacked." Boyd groaned. "It's *true*," she said. "The seismograms have been altered to hide the quakes."

"Good night, goodbye, and good luck with your psychiatric issues." The line went dead again.

"Fuck," O'Malley said. "Fuck fuck *fuck*." She slammed her palm on the table so hard that her glass lifted off by a quarter of an inch, launching a small geyser of scotch that spattered her sweater and jeans. "Goddammit," she muttered, though there was no heat to the curse this time. She felt defeated, deflated, and decidedly depressed. "TGIF. These geologists are fuckheads."

She knocked back the rest of the drink—two fingers in one long pull—and took the empty bottle out the kitchen door toward the recycle bin on the back stairs. Standing on the darkened porch in the twilight, she leaned forward so she could see a narrow band of sky bounded by the porch roof and the treetops. She caught a glimpse of Orion, the hunter, the three bright stars of his belt angling downward. She moved this way and that, trying to make out the rest of the constellation—his shield, his club, his dog—but suddenly she was blinded by a dazzling light: a police helicopter zoomed overhead, its searchlight pointing directly into her eyes. "Ow, son of a bitch," she said.

She considered hurling the scotch bottle toward the chopper to vent her frustration: sending the container spinning, then listening for the smash when it hit. The back porch was forty feet off the ground. *Distance equals one-half acceleration times time squared,* she boozily prompted herself—a high school physics formula she still used with some regularity. *So it'll hit in one point five seconds, maybe one point six. Ignoring the effect of air resistance. Which is negligible, since it's not a swallow.*

She hefted the bottle, gave a dry-run snap of the wrist. She could clean up the glass tomorrow, in the daylight, if she woke up feeling guilty about it. O'Malley drew back her arm and aimed for a gap in the trees behind the parking lot.

A noise, loud and unexpected and nearby, caused her to freeze, the bottle cocked behind her ear. It sounded as if someone had stumbled and fallen on the wooden staircase a flight or two below her. "Hello?" she called. Silence. She hurried inside and locked the door, weaving slightly from the liquor. Her heart pounding, she almost failed to notice the ringing of her phone.

CHAPTER 9

Washington, DC

Dawtry half hiked, half crawled up the embankment from Rock Creek, his pride stinging as much as his palms and his left knee did.

After two sleepless nights, most of which he had spent replaying his CIA debacle, Dawtry had pulled up his socks, laced up his running shoes, and headed for a Sunday trail run in Rock Creek Park. It was his favorite route, a ten-mile loop that took him all the way to the northern end of the park and back. Heading north, he always chose the high ground: the Western Ridge Trail, thick with towering oaks, tulip poplars, and hemlocks. Returning south, he followed Rock Creek, imagining himself gliding home effortlessly, fluidly, as if the stream itself were bearing him down toward the Potomac.

But instead of flowing and gliding, this time Dawtry had stumbled and tumbled. Two miles into the ten, he caught a toe on a root and face-planted, hard. His palms and knee took the brunt of the fall, leaving behind three patches of bloody skin on the rocky ground.

It took him an hour to limp back to his starting point, and another five minutes to climb the steep makeshift path to the back of his building. He hobbled into the parking garage and pressed the elevator's call button, then—just as the doors opened—he remembered that in his car's glove box was a first-aid kit containing a cold pack, disinfectant, and, most helpfully, lidocaine spray. After fishing his key fob out of his zippered pocket, he unlocked the vehicle and opened the passenger door.

A fat manila envelope fell from the car and tumbled to the concrete, a sharp corner nicking the raw patch on his knee on its way down. *"Oww."* Dawtry stared at the envelope, briefly puzzled, then remembered: the crazy astrologer had left it with the guard at the CIA, and the guard had tossed it at Dawtry. "Great, thanks," Dawtry said, his sarcasm directed in equal parts at the crazy lady, the smirking guard, and the envelope itself. Bending down—no easy task, given how his knee was seizing up—he picked up the envelope and tucked it beneath an arm, then retrieved the first-aid kit from the glove box. He locked the car, limped to the elevator, and headed upstairs.

His first move, once inside, was to toss the fat envelope into the recycle bin. His second was to start the bathwater—he craved the lidocaine, but he wanted to soak for a few minutes first. His third move was to pour himself a double shot of tequila and wash down three ibuprofen caplets with a big swig. "Wowzer," he muttered, his whole body shuddering from the burn of the liquor. Move number four was to peer guiltily into the recycle bin and then retrieve the manila envelope—not because he was curious but because he was still, at heart, a Boy Scout. There might be things in the envelope that wouldn't recycle well: Glossy paper. Binder clips. Anthrax powder.

He didn't actually think a Hillary-voting, Prius-driving peacenik was likely to be spreading anthrax; still, when he opened the envelope's metal clasp and peered in, his threat sensors automatically switched on. Instead of reaching inside to retrieve the contents, he held the envelope over the kitchen table and angled it so that the sheaf of papers would slide out without being touched.

Dawtry had no idea what he'd been expecting to see, but he damn sure hadn't expected to see a piece of Johns Hopkins University letterhead. The paper was crisp and expensive—hell, it probably contained more linen fibers than all of Dawtry's shirts put together—and the university's name was printed in big blue letters beneath a fancy coat-of-arms-looking shield. Below the university's name, in smaller blue letters, was "Krieger School of Arts & Sciences," and below that—smaller yet, but still legible and impressive—"Department of Physics & Astronomy."

Physics? Astronomy? That wasn't what the guard had said. "Age of Aquarius and all that shit" was what the guy had said. Dawtry glanced at the signature: Megan P. O'Malley, PhD, Assistant Professor of Astronomy. Maybe she really was a wacko—professors surely weren't immune to mental illness—but the letter didn't look like a loony's handiwork; it certainly hadn't been assembled from words and letters scissored from magazines.

He began to read. Except for the handwritten signature at the bottom, it was formatted as a memo:

To: Central Intelligence Agency

From: Prof. Megan O'Malley, PhD, Johns Hopkins University

Subject: Geoterrorism—A Potentially Catastrophic Threat Targeting US Eastern Seaboard
Recently, during astronomical observations in the Canary Islands—Spanish territory off the coast of Morocco—I became aware of frequent seismic activity on the island of La Palma. This seismic activity was manifested in vibrations sufficiently strong to jar the telescope I was using (the Isaac Newton Telescope) and distort the astronomical photographs I was taking

(please see Attachments 1–4, time exposures affected by the abrupt telescope movement).

Upon further investigation, including discussions with a Berkeley seismologist, I learned that the vibrations I observed—which were brief, discrete, and uniform pulses—were almost certainly anthropogenic, or man-made: the seismic signature of "ripple-shot" blasting (see Attachment 5, a seismograph recorded near a highway construction project where ripple shots were used to blast through a mountainside). Natural seismic activity, by contrast, is characterized by gradual, irregular, and sustained vibrations (Attachments 6–8, seismograms from recent earthquakes in Oklahoma).

Investigating still further, I discovered that a geologic fault line exists on La Palma, and that an earthquake could cause this fault line to slip catastrophically, triggering a massive landslide and—as a consequence—unleashing an immense tsunami. This tsunami, which could strike America's eastern seaboard with potential wave "runup" heights of up to 100 feet, could endanger millions of people (Attachment 9, Boyd et al., "The La Palma Cumbre Vieja: Modeling a Potential Mega Tsunami," *Journal of Seismology*).

Last but not least—most disturbing of all, in fact: In seeking to understand the extent and magnitude of anthropogenic seismic activity on La Palma, I have discovered that the Global Seismographic Network (GSN) database appears to have been altered, with data sets replicated multiple times, by copying and pasting, in what appears to be an attempt to mask explosions and seismic activity. The inference of the altered data seems clear: the clandestine explosions

appear to be intended to trigger—and to *weaponize*—
a catastrophic geologic event.

As a scientist, I am compelled to seek rational
explanations for observed phenomena. As an American
citizen, I am terrified by the explanation that best fits
the facts. I encourage you—I implore you—to investigate and take whatever action is needed to protect
countless American lives from the dangers posed by
these clandestine actions on La Palma.

I would appreciate the opportunity to review my
research and findings in more detail with the appropriate person(s) at your agency.

Yours truly,

Megan O'Malley, PhD

Dawtry had been standing up when he began reading. As soon
as he read the subject line, he rolled his eyes, but he kept reading. At
some point, he must have sat down, for when he finished reading, he
found himself in a chair, his left elbow leaning on the table, his head
propped on his thumb and fingers. The letter had been paper-clipped
to the stack of attachments. Dawtry unclipped it, set it to one side, and
began rereading, this time scanning each attachment as it was referenced
in the letter.

Soon his heart was pounding, and he felt himself sweating pro-
fusely, in a way that had nothing to do with the swig of tequila he had
knocked back before opening the envelope.

As he reread, he sought the loopiness in the letter, the madness in
the memo, but he could not discern any. It was possible—it seemed
unlikely, but it was certainly possible—that the woman had faked the
photographs and seismograms and even the scientific journal article.
But if she'd faked them, she'd done a damned good job of it.

A business card had been tucked under the paper clip. Dawtry now inspected it. Professor O'Malley's campus address and Hopkins phone number were printed on the card in neat, small type. Her cell number had been added in pen. He reached for his phone and was preparing to dial when the phone buzzed in his hand. Startled, he dropped it. The phone clattered to the table, where it continued to buzz and twitch. "Calvert Woodley," read the display—the name of Dawtry's condo building. Why on earth was the building's management calling him on a Sunday afternoon? Was he behind on his monthly maintenance dues? He didn't think so, but it didn't matter—not compared with what he was dealing with. Dawtry rejected the call and began dialing Professor O'Malley's number. He would call her office first, as a matter of protocol, then—when he got her voicemail, as he surely would on a Sunday—he'd phone her cell.

He was halfway through the number when his phone buzzed again. "Calvert Woodley."

"Christ," he muttered, but this time he took the call. "Hello," he snapped.

"Mr. Dawtry?"

"Yes. Who's this?"

"It's Rick Stone, the building engineer."

"The building engineer?" The man might as well have said he was the Russian tsar. "What's going on?"

"You're in 2A, right?"

"Yes, why? Is there some problem? Is the building on fire or something?"

"Uh, no. The problem isn't fire. It's water. Have you noticed any sort of problem with your plumbing—a leaking toilet? Your dishwasher? Reason I ask is the woman in 1A—Mrs. Harbison? She called to say that water is pouring through her bathroom ceiling."

The bathtub! He'd completely forgotten that the bathtub taps were wide-open. To make matters worse, the tub's overflow drain was sealed with duct tape, which Dawtry had put there so the tub could be filled all the way to the rim. *Above* the rim, he realized with a sinking feeling.

An hour later—an hour spent mopping and toweling up water, removing and hiding the soggy and incriminating duct tape, groveling to his neighbor and the building engineer—Dawtry finally got back to phoning O'Malley. The office number rolled to voicemail, as he'd expected. "Professor O'Malley, my name is Christopher Dawtry," he said. "I'm calling because I'm very interested in the information packet you delivered Friday afternoon." He thought it best not to be specific in the message, in case the message were intercepted; she would surely know what "information packet" he meant. "I'll try your cell, too. Please call me at my office or on my cell at your earliest opportunity." He gave both his numbers, then repeated his name, then repeated both numbers.

Next, he dialed her cell, hoping for better luck. "Hi, this is Megan," she said cheerily.

"Professor O'Malley," he began eagerly, but immediately he was interrupted: "I'm sorry I missed your call. Leave your name and number, and I'll call you back."

"Crap," he muttered. Disappointed, he left the same message he had left on her office voicemail, then disconnected and glared at the phone, as if the device itself were to blame for his inability to reach her.

He looked out the kitchen window. To his surprise he saw that it was late afternoon, nearly sundown; the trees out back were already shadowed by the building, with the exception of one lone oak. It towered over the north end of Calvert Street bridge, its limbs stripped bare, its crooked branches reaching skyward like tortured fingers supplicating a pale, empty sky.

Dawtry glanced down at the papers spread across the kitchen table. What was it Benny had said after their third chess game? "Trust your instincts"? "Don't second-guess yourself"? If he'd trusted his instincts the morning of the New York City Marathon, he wouldn't have made the wrong call—wouldn't have given the all-clear signal when he'd felt a sense of doubt. Ultimately, given that the bridge collapse was just a simulation, his second-guessing hadn't done any harm, except to his ego. Still, he couldn't help thinking, *What if it'd been the real deal?*

Dawtry stacked the papers neatly, slid them back into the envelope, and fastened the clasp. Then he opened his laptop and searched for Megan O'Malley's home address.

Without taking time to shower, he changed, trading his running clothes for his work uniform—a starched white shirt, a gray suit and tie, and a shoulder holster with his nine-millimeter Glock—and headed out the door toward the parking garage, toward Baltimore, and toward Megan O'Malley.

He recognized her building from the street view that Google Maps had offered. The building looked respectable—elegant, even, in a faded, past-its-prime sort of way—and its proximity to the Johns Hopkins campus seemed a further argument for Professor O'Malley's sanity, or at least the pragmatic common sense of keeping her commute minimal. He turned off Roland Avenue and into the narrow driveway, parking beside a small No Parking sign that had been jammed into the grass beside an irresistibly wide patch of asphalt.

Three walls of apartments flanked a center courtyard, with a doorway and a stairwell in each wall. According to the address Dawtry had found, she lived in 3A. He went to the nearest door and entered. At the base of the stairs were three mailboxes: 1C, 2C, and 3C. Dawtry crossed the courtyard and entered the opposite stairwell, where he found 1A, 2A, and 3A. "O'Malley," said a handwritten label on 3A. He smiled and started up the stairs, then thought better of it. He went back outside to the courtyard and looked up. The bank of windows on the top floor was dark, at least on this side. He walked out to the street; from there, he could see a balcony and, deeply set beneath the overhanging roof, more windows, also dark.

Damn, he thought. He crossed the yard, past the corner of the building, and checked the windows on the south side. No joy. He picked his way through the narrow side yard, using his phone as a flashlight, and emerged, brushing stray twigs and leaves from his hair, into a small parking lot behind the building. He glanced at the handful of cars—two rusting Hondas, a silver Mazda, and a red BMW, but no peacemongering Prius.

Three wooden staircases zigzagged up the back of the building, echoing—in exposed and flammable symmetry—the three enclosed stairwells at the front. Dawtry took the one that served the A units, treading softly and hoping he wouldn't cause a 9-1-1 call or catch a bullet. When he reached the third-floor landing, he felt a jolt of dread. He found himself looking at a dark, chaotic scene through a doorway that stood wide-open, its frame splintered by a crowbar or a powerful kick. Even by the dim light from Roland Avenue, some of which filtered through the apartment's front windows and across the books and papers strewn across the living room floor, it was instantly clear:

Megan O'Malley's apartment had been ransacked.

Dawtry's boss, Acting Assistant Director Andrew Christenberry, was not a happy man. In fact, Christenberry could have cheered up by an order of magnitude and still have fallen short of being a happy man. "What the hell are you doing, Dawtry?" he barked after Dawtry had summarized the situation and conveyed his concerns.

"Well, at the moment, I'm standing on the balcony of Professor O'Malley's apartment. I've taken a quick look around—enough to see that it's been tossed—but I don't want to disturb the scene before the forensic guys get here."

"What forensic guys?"

"*Our* forensic guys. That's why I called you, sir—to request authorization for an evidence team."

"I'll ask you again. What are you *doing?*"

"I'm not sure I understand your question, sir."

"Clearly not. Two days ago you destroyed a decade's worth of constructive engagement between the Bureau and the CIA—do you know that they're considering abolishing the liaison position altogether, thanks to the way you insulted them? And now you're chasing bogeymen dreamed up by some crazy astrologer?"

"Astronomer."

"What?"

"She's an astronomer, sir. An actual scientist. With a PhD."

"So the hell what? Half the academics I know are fruitcakes, and the fancier the pedigree, the nuttier the professor. Our job is law enforcement, not psychiatric services or home security."

"I'm not trying to play social worker or rent-a-cop, sir. I'm just asking for authorization to bring in a forensic team to Professor O'Malley's apartment."

"Hell, no, you can't bring in a forensic team," Christenberry snapped. "We have no jurisdiction, no investigation, and no reason to start one. You don't even know if a crime has been committed. *Maybe* breaking and entering, *maybe* burglary, but maybe not—maybe this woman just flipped out after she got the cold shoulder from the CIA, or just had a fight with her boyfriend, and threw some shit around to blow off steam. For all you know, she's gone to Vegas for the weekend, or she's at her boyfriend's having fabulous makeup sex. Or maybe she's checked in to a psych ward. We don't know, and we don't need to know. Not our problem. Not our business."

"With all due respect, sir, I think it *is* our business, or *could* be. The back door was forced, and the files have been ransacked. It wasn't a burglary—there's a fancy bicycle sitting here, worth a couple thousand bucks, minimum."

"Nobody ever said burglars were geniuses."

"Sir, if she's right, we're talking about a matter of urgent national security. A plot to launch a mass-casualty attack on a scale that's unprecedented. Unimaginable, almost."

"Jesus, Dawtry, do you have any idea how crazy you sound?" Dawtry heard a heavy sigh, and when Christenberry resumed speaking, his voice was softer. "Chip, I know it sucks—it'll always suck—but your brother's gone. You can't bring him back by spinning out disaster scenarios and obsessing on how to stop them."

"Obsessing?" Had Vreeland planted that word—that dismissal—in Christenberry's mind? "Sir, I know it's a stretch," Dawtry persisted, "but I've read Professor O'Malley's report carefully, and she makes a credible case, at least for considering the possibility. The tsunami theory she cites is controversial, but the geologist who did the modeling is legit."

"How do you know that? Do you have a geology doctorate I don't know about?"

"No, sir, I don't. But he's got a lot of publications, and the journal that published the modeling is reputable. I haven't had a chance to look into the seismic data O'Malley says has been hacked, but I'll get on that first thing tomorrow."

"No, you won't."

"Sir?"

"First thing tomorrow, you'll hand me a report—a very detailed report—about the errors in judgment you showed at Langley on Friday. You'll also draft, for my review and approval, a letter to Jim Vreeland apologizing for your unprofessional behavior and your egregious misunderstanding of national security priorities. Is that clear?"

Dawtry grimaced. "And should I also write, five hundred times, 'I will not think for myself without permission'?" That was what he *wanted* to say, at any rate. But what he actually said was "Yes, sir. Very clear."

"And Dawtry? Drop this—let it go—and get the fuck out of that woman's apartment before you get arrested. Or shot."

"Yes, sir."

Christenberry hung up. "Well, shit," Dawtry said. He heaved a long sigh, then headed through the balcony door and into the living room. He resisted, once more, the urge to flip on the lights; if someone was watching the apartment, Dawtry didn't want to be seen. And his boss certainly didn't want him to be seen.

But he didn't—couldn't—resist the urge to look around, given that there was no risk of complicating the work of a forensic team. He switched on his phone's flashlight, cupping one hand around the end of the phone to narrow the beam and shield it from view. The living room was big and sparely furnished: A futon, which served as a sofa. A ladder-back rocking chair, its rockers long and steeply curved, for serious rocking. A long, narrow table nested beneath the front windows, its glossy red surface bare except for a printer and a wireless router. The table was supported by two file cabinets whose drawers were open and empty, the contents—mostly manuscripts and article reprints and letters and large, glossy photographs of the night sky—strewn across the floor. His eye was caught by a newspaper page, and Dawtry knelt to examine it. The story, which covered most of the page, had run in the *Baltimore Sun*'s features section three years before. It was headlined "Starstruck"; the subhead read "Planet-hunting Hopkins astronomer caught astronomy bug from Baltimore's street-corner astronomer." The story was accompanied by a large color photograph. At the center stood a fat blue telescope on an aluminum tripod. **HAV-A-LOOK**, urged a sign taped to the stubby tube. On one side stood a white-bearded man wearing glasses, a blue beret, and a proud smile. On the other side, looking up from the telescope's eyepiece, was a woman identified by the caption as "Astronomy professor Megan O'Malley."

The CIA guard had gotten O'Malley's profession wrong, but he'd gotten two other details right: she was indeed well dressed, and she was quite good-looking. Her eyes looked lively and intelligent, with no sign of madness in them. Not as of three years ago, anyhow.

From his kneeling position, Dawtry noticed something he hadn't seen before. Tucked beneath the red desktop, between the file cabinets and shoved back against the radiator that was ticking with heat, were two wire-mesh wastebaskets. He took a pen from his pocket, hooked the rim of one, and slid it toward him. It contained an assortment of discarded tissues, chewing gum packages, protein bar wrappers, and other detritus that seemed uninteresting and uninformative.

The second basket appeared to be dedicated to recyclable paper. Through the mesh, he made out mountains of mail—catalogs, fundraising letters, sales circulars. On top of the mountain was a wadded-up Post-it note. After a moment's hesitation, Dawtry picked it up and unwadded it. It contained a cryptic notation, 80YD, followed by a long string of numbers, fifteen in all—too many to be a MasterCard number, too few to be an American Express number. As for 80YD, it looked like an airline ticket confirmation code or some secret cipher, and Dawtry had never been good at cracking codes, even ones far simpler than the CIA's *Kryptos* puzzle.

Then it hit him and he laughed. The string of numbers—which began with 01144—was an international long-distance number for someone' in the United Kingdom. Someone whose name was not 80YD, but BOYD. "Boyd. Charles Boyd," he intoned in his best Sean Connery James Bond voice.

Dawtry counted eight rings. He was on the point of giving up when he heard a plummy, pissed-off voice say, "Why does every person in the American colonies feel compelled to call me at bloody midnight?"

"Hello, is this Charles Boyd? The geologist?"

"Who's calling?" He didn't say he was Boyd, but he didn't say he wasn't. A good sign.

"My name is Dawtry. Chip Dawtry. I work for the US government. I'm a special agent with the FBI—that's the Federal Bureau of Investigation."

"I know what the FBI is," the man snapped. "Why is the FBI calling me—and why at midnight?"

"I'm calling to ask about your La Palma tsunami modeling. This *is* Professor Boyd, isn't it?"

"What about it? And, yes, I am Charles Boyd. *That* Charles Boyd."

"I'm wondering if you keep track of seismic activity on La Palma."

"Well," Boyd said slowly, "I do have an ongoing interest in it."

"But do you track the activity? Recent activity, in particular."

"I have looked at recent data, yes."

"Data in the Global Seismographic Network?"

"Data from a variety of sources. Do get to the point, please."

Boyd was hedging. Dawtry pressed. "Are you familiar with recent data in the Global Seismographic Network pertaining to La Palma?"

There was a long pause before Boyd answered. "Yes, I am."

"And in your opinion, sir, is that data accurate, or has that data been altered?"

This time there was no hesitation, and the tone was suspicious—accusatory, even. "Wherever did you get that idea?"

"I got it from a scientist at Johns Hopkins University, here in the States."

"What scientist? What's his name?"

"*Her* name, actually," corrected Dawtry, wondering if Boyd was trying to trip him up with the pronoun. "Her name is Megan O'Malley. Has Professor O'Malley been in touch with you?"

"Listen here," said Boyd. "You might very well be who you say you are, but I have no way of knowing that. And I've never heard of you, which makes me disinclined to continue this discussion."

"I got your name from Professor O'Malley," Dawtry persisted. "She put together a packet of information that came to me. Your article was part of it. So were the photos she took at the observatory in La Palma. And the GSN data. I haven't been able to reach her, so she doesn't know my name and doesn't know I'm investigating this." He cringed when he said the word "investigating," as if Christenberry might somehow be listening in.

"I see," said Boyd.

Another evasion, thought Dawtry.

"Tell me your name again?"

"Dawtry. Special Agent Chip Dawtry."

"Quite so. Tell me, Special Agent Dawtry. This packet of information that 'came to you'—where did it come from?"

"I told you. From Professor O'Malley."

"Ah, forgive me. I should have framed the question more precisely. Where did Professor O'Malley take the information in the first place, before it came into your possession?"

He knows, thought Dawtry, his adrenaline spiking. *He knows she went to the CIA. They're in touch!* But on the heels of his excitement came caution. *But is he on her side? Or is he on the other side—whatever side that is?* "Trust your instincts," Benny had said. "Don't second-guess yourself." Dawtry winced and prayed and said slowly, "To be honest, Dr. Boyd, I don't know all the places she might have sent similar packets. All I know is that she took this one—the one I have—to the Central Intelligence Agency. I was at CIA Headquarters Friday afternoon when she delivered it. She gave it to a guard at the gate. He thought she was crazy, and he fobbed it off on me. That's the truth. You've got to believe me."

"As a matter of fact, I do believe you."

"Oh." Dawtry was brought up short by Boyd's sudden shift in tone. "And has Professor O'Malley indeed contacted you?"

"She has. Not long after she was turned away by the CIA."

"And do you share her concerns?"

"If you've read a single academic journal article, Agent Dawtry—including mine—you are familiar with the academician's mantra: 'Further research is required.' And to be honest, I was dubious and dismissive when she first called me—in fact, I hung up on her. But then I looked at the seismic data, and I found that she was right. The GSN database *has* been falsified. So I called her back. And, yes, in my opinion, Professor O'Malley makes a plausible and troubling case."

The words electrified Dawtry. "Thank you, sir. Thank you for your candor. I have another important question."

"And what would that be?" His tone had grown more guarded again.

"When did you last talk with her?"

"I told you—Friday. Night before last. Why?"

"Frankly, sir, I'm very concerned for her safety."

"What makes you say that?" The guardedness was gone, replaced by alarm.

"Her apartment has been broken into and searched. The back door was forced open. Her files were strewn all over the floor. It didn't appear to be a burglary—more like someone was looking for information. Or looking for her."

"Dear Lord," Boyd said. "When were you there?"

"I'm there right now. The place is a wreck. I don't know when the break-in happened. And I don't know where she is."

"I do," Boyd said. "She's on her way back to La Palma."

"*What?* Why?"

"She's determined to get to the bottom of the blasting."

"Christ," Dawtry muttered. "Do you know where she's staying?"

"Hotel San Telmo."

Dawtry heard a sudden gasp on the other end of the line, followed by a low groan. He went on high alert—was Boyd at risk, too? "Professor Boyd? Is something wrong?"

Boyd grunted. "Just . . . *nnnhh* . . . some discomfort. I had my appendix taken out a few days ago. The incision is still causing a bit of pain."

"I hope you feel better soon. Meanwhile, if you're in touch with Professor O'Malley, please tell her to be very careful."

"I will."

"And tell her I'm on my way."

"On your way where?"

"To La Palma." His words astonished him. How the hell could he go to La Palma, when his boss had ordered him, in no uncertain terms, to have nothing to do with O'Malley? But then he remembered what had happened when he'd ignored his instincts the morning of the marathon. He'd probably be fired if he went—but given his CIA screwup, he might be fired anyhow, or at the very least marginalized, relegated to the Bureau's most bureaucratic bush leagues. So what did he have to lose by going? *Why the hell not?* he thought, unconsciously echoing his parting exchange with Benny.

"When is your flight?" said Boyd.

"I have no idea," said Dawtry. "But not soon enough."

II: THE MURDEROUS INNOCENCE OF THE SEA

CHAPTER 10

La Palma

O'Malley froze, straining beneath the weight of the seismometer and the heavy car battery. Fifty feet down the slope, the mountainside sheered off into a fourteen-hundred-foot cliff. Fifty feet up the slope stood the man with the gun, its laser sight marking her chest with a bright dot of red light.

Twenty-four hours earlier

"Ladies and gentlemen." The pilot had already made the announcement in Spanish, and O'Malley had caught one worrisome word that required no translation: *turbulencia.* "We are beginning our descent to Tenerife," he continued. "Please tighten your seat belt, as we are expecting a little bit of turbulence on the way down."

The words still hanging in the air, the plane made a stomach-churning drop, and several passengers shrieked. And so it began, a thudding, thumping roller-coaster ride down, the likes of which O'Malley had never experienced before. *A "little bit of turbulence" my ass,* she thought, her knuckles white from the force of her grip on the armrests. *Like the Pope is "a little bit Catholic."* The plane was shrouded in clouds now, and threads of rain raced horizontally across her window.

Just as she was sure she would need to release her grip and make a grab for the barf bag that was tucked into the seat back, the turbulence slackened and the clouds thinned. She looked out the window and gasped: a mountain peak—sharp and forested and no more than a few hundred feet off the wingtip—ghosted past. A moment later the plane whumped onto the runway, eliciting a chorus of screams. Then, when it was clear that they had survived and would all live to tell the tale, the screams turned to whoops, whistles, and applause.

Tenerife, alas, was not O'Malley's final destination. Rather, Tenerife was the place where she would board yet another plane, this one a twin-engine puddle jumper, for a thirty-minute hop to La Palma. Inside the terminal, checking a bank of monitors, she saw her flight number flashing ominously, accompanied by the word *retrasado*: "delayed." In fact, every outbound flight was flashing, and while several others were also *retrasado*, most were *cancelado*. Looking out through the airport's rain-lashed windows, seeing the palm trees thrash in the wind, she didn't know whether to pity those whose flights were *cancelado* or to envy them with every fiber of her fearful being.

For the next six hours, as scheduled departure times came and went with no improvement in the weather, she alternated between pity and envy as flight after flight was canceled. Soon, only one flight remained—O'Malley's. By 9:00 p.m., airport ticket agents and baggage handlers were leaving. Shops and car rental counters were going dark. Cleaning crews began mopping the floors.

Then—against all odds—came an announcement, followed by a flurry of activity. Through the wall of sodden windows in the boarding area, O'Malley saw a green-and-white shuttle bus labeled with the island-hopping airline's name—Binter Canarias—pull to the curb and open its doors. All around her, bleary-eyed passengers clambered out of chairs and off the floor where they had taken up residence, packing knapsacks and scooping up carry-ons. She cast a disbelieving glance at the monitor and saw that the flight number had ceased to blink. It glowed serenely, as if there had never really been any doubt. *"Embarque,"* the status now read.

O'Malley watched as her fellow travelers rushed the glass doors. "Holy crap, we're boarding," she said out loud. "We're actually boarding. Thank you, Jesus." Hoisting her bag and staggering toward the scrum, she added, "God help us."

They boarded the bus beneath a large, protective awning, but as the bus trundled toward the waiting plane, the vehicle was buffeted by wind and driving rain. And by the time O'Malley staggered up the exposed staircase to the plane's boarding door, she—like every other passenger—was soaked to the skin. *This is insane,* she thought. *What the hell are you doing here?*

She almost turned and got off—did turn, in fact, but she didn't get off, because the flight attendant had just wrestled the aircraft door shut, and when she saw O'Malley standing there, preparing to bolt, she shook her head and flashed a tight smile that conveyed a clear warning: *Don't even think about it.*

"Ladies and gentlemen, the aircraft door has been closed," the flight attendant announced over the howling wind and roaring propellers. "Please take your seats, fasten your seat belts, and enjoy our brief, thirty-minute flight."

Enjoy? thought O'Malley. *Yeah, right.* She sank into her seat, water pooling at her feet and elbows, and prepared to die.

But somewhere between the plane's slewing takeoff from Tenerife and its quick landing in La Palma, a meteorological miracle occurred. The sky opened, the wind calmed, and O'Malley stepped off the plane and into a soft, clear night. The temperature must have been nearly seventy; overhead, the Milky Way splashed the sky from horizon to horizon. In spite of her exhaustion, and perhaps also because of it,

111

O'Malley—the last passenger, from the last seat, of the last flight of the night—stared up at the stars and laughed.

She awakened slowly. At first she thought it might be night still, but then she noticed narrow streaks of light slipping past the edges of heavy drapes.

She had arrived at the Hotel San Telmo at 11:00 p.m., just as the proprietor—a thirtysomething man with a German accent (or Danish or Dutch, definitely not Spanish)—was locking up for the night. "Oh, you made it," he said. "I thought you do not come."

After checking her in and giving her a key, he had pointed to a stairwell off the lobby, then to a mini fridge, its top doubling as a table for bags of chips, apples, and bananas. "Please to help yourself."

"Thank God. I'm starving."

"Well, good night," he'd said, eager to be done. "Welcome, and have a good sleep."

O'Malley had thanked him and headed downstairs, snagging a bottle of white wine and a bag of potato chips on the way. She descended three flights of stairs before she found her room. *Christ, I'm in the sub-basement,* she grumbled inwardly, but when she entered her room, she noticed a patio outside, complete with an arbor, flowering vines, and a large fountain, all artfully notched into what was clearly a steeply sloping site.

After plopping down in a chair beneath the arbor, she had wolfed the chips, washing them down with two glasses of wine. Then she tumbled into bed and slept dreamlessly.

Seeing the light spilling around the curtains now, she checked her watch and was astonished to discover that she had slept for nearly ten hours.

She dressed and raced upstairs, arriving just as her host—Gerhardt?—was gathering up the remnants of the breakfast buffet. "I'm sorry," she said, "I just woke up. Am I too late to eat?"

She detected a flicker of annoyance in his eyes, but he shrugged. "No, it's okay." He set down the granola and yogurt, and O'Malley snagged the one clean bowl that remained.

"Thank you," she said. "I don't suppose a package has arrived for me yet? I'm expecting one today by air express."

"No, it's too early for that. It will come late this afternoon—if the weather doesn't turn bad."

She was disappointed by this news. Her hands were tied until the shipment of instruments arrived: three portable seismometers, powered by batteries and equipped with a satellite data uplink. The gear had been ordered by Charles Boyd, the British geologist, who—after his initial skepticism and curt hang-up—had completely changed his tone. When he'd called her back, to say that she was absolutely right about the faked GSN data, he'd promised to help in any way he could. She had asked him—begged him—to travel to La Palma and set up the seismometers himself, but Boyd was recovering from an appendectomy and wouldn't be able to travel for weeks. So, instead, he'd arranged to overnight the seismometers to her, along with instructions for positioning them at three distant points on the island, to optimize their ability to triangulate any seismic activity, natural or man-made.

Disappointed to learn that she couldn't spend the day unpacking the instruments and familiarizing herself with them, O'Malley decided that the best use of her time would be to procure the batteries she needed—three large 12-volt batteries, the kind used in cars. She rose from the table and spotted whatshisname—Werner?—behind the counter, feeding a document into a copier. "Excuse me," she said. "I'm wondering if you can tell me where to buy something."

"Yes? What do you need to buy?"

"A car battery."

His brows furrowed. "You rented a car at the airport, yes? From Cicar?"

"Yes."

"Just call them. They will come fix it for you."

O'Malley smiled sheepishly. "It's not for the rental car. I need to buy a battery—actually, I need to buy three batteries for . . . something else." He looked puzzled and possibly suspicious. "I'm a scientist. I need them to power some instruments for an experiment."

"What kind of experiment?"

"I'm an astronomer," she said. Technically, it was a true statement, but it looked like a lie, walked like a lie, and quacked like a lie. Still, he seemed to accept it.

"Let me make a few calls," he said. He reached under the counter and took out a phone directory, then flipped to the back. After perusing the listings, he picked up the phone and dialed a call, then began speaking in rapid, German-accented Spanish. He listened, replied, listened again, then grunted. *"Un momento,"* he said into the phone, then covered the mouthpiece with his hand and caught O'Malley's gaze. "He says they can have them here on Wednesday."

"Wednesday?"

He nodded.

"That's the day after tomorrow!"

"They have to make a special order."

"But I need them today," she said. "Tomorrow at the latest."

He shrugged: *not possible.*

"Ask him if there's any place else I can get them faster."

He frowned, but he relayed the request. A lengthy discussion ensued. Finally, he covered the mouthpiece again. "He says any place you go will have to order, same as him, if you want new batteries."

O'Malley frowned.

"But if used batteries are okay, he knows a place. A recycling place."

"Recycling?"

He shrugged. "A junkyard."

The junkyard, Reciclajes Pérez, was a few miles north of the city, perched atop the junction of a steep ravine and an even steeper sea cliff. The view seemed more suited to a five-star hotel than a chop shop.

The owner, Señor Pérez, met her in the office. He assured her that he had three batteries in excellent condition. "These cars were almost new when they wrecked," he said. "The batteries are primo."

He led her out of the building—a prefabricated warehouse–looking structure where curious workers wielding wrenches and cutting torches paused to stared at her—and toward the back of the salvage yard, where a dozen or so mangled cars waited to be dismantled. He pointed at three vehicles in quick succession, then led her to the first one. The battery was in plain view, the car lacking a hood; either the wreck had ripped it off or the part had already been sold. He nodded at the battery. "Is good," he said. He reached into a large pocket of his cargo pants and took out a small instrument, which O'Malley recognized as an old-fashioned analog voltage meter. Setting the dial to "12V," he pressed the metal tip of a red wire to one of the battery's terminal posts—the one marked "+"—and the tip of a black wire to the "–" post. A needle on the meter jumped wildly, then steadied a hair above the "12."

O'Malley flashed him a thumbs-up. "Great. I'll take it."

The second car had been T-boned, its right side pushed two feet in. O'Malley hoped no one had been riding in the passenger seat at the time, but she resisted the urge to look for blood. The hood was still attached, crumpled along the right edge and bulging upward at the center. Pérez popped the latch and pulled upward on the front, but the side snagged. He swore softy in Spanish, then climbed onto the car, placing one foot on the front bumper and one foot on the left quarter panel, above the wheel. He squatted, gripped the hood with both hands, and yanked hard, grunting with the effort. Metal rasped and shrieked, and Pérez nearly tumbled backward when it came free. He blew out a

115

breath, wiped his hands, and checked the voltage. This one registered slightly less than twelve volts; not perfect, but good enough, O'Malley figured. Hoped, anyhow.

The third car had burned. Its windows had shattered from the heat, and the interior had been reduced to blackened seat springs and sooty floor pans and door panels. Miraculously, the hood latch still worked, but when Pérez touched the voltmeter's leads to the battery posts, the needle remained at zero. Frowning, he scraped the tops of the posts with the leads and tried again. Again, the needle declined to move. He scowled, then looked at O'Malley and shook his head.

She grimaced, then nodded toward the remaining cars on the lot. "*Más?* More?"

Again he shook his head. "*Eso es todo.* That is all." He waved a hand toward the other mangled carcasses and flipped his fingers upward dismissively. "No good."

O'Malley sighed. Was there another junkyard anywhere nearby? *Más junkyardes*—would that be anywhere near correct, or at least halfway comprehensible? If she couldn't scavenge another battery, could Boyd work with data from only two seismometers? Two wouldn't be as precise as three, but might two suffice, in a pinch? She held up a finger to put Pérez on pause, then fished out her phone and called Boyd.

The call rolled immediately to his voicemail. As she began mentally composing a message—urgent but not hysterical, that was the balance she hoped to strike—a horn blared just beyond the junkyard gate. A moment later the gate slid open and a tow truck entered. It was hauling an answer to prayer: a freshly totaled Fiat, the radiator still spewing steam. As the wreck eased to a stop directly in front of them, steam wafted out of the engine compartment and into the sunlight, surrounding the dearly departed like a halo.

The workers at Señor Pérez's junkyard did not share O'Malley's sense of urgency; on the contrary, judging by the glacial pace at which they extracted the batteries from the wrecks, they seemed to feel obliged to counter O'Malley's urgency, so as to keep the universe in balance. By the time she paid the bill and drove south along the coast, back toward Santa Cruz, the sun had already dropped behind the massive flank of the Taburiente volcano, and darkness was falling.

On the bright side, by the time she returned to Santa Cruz, and to the San Telmo, the package of seismometers had arrived. She lugged the box downstairs and tore into it. The seismometers were, as Boyd had promised, very compact—cylinders roughly twice the size of a coffee can, with a carrying handle built into the top—but heavy, fifteen or twenty pounds apiece. The voltage step-down converters, which were needed to keep the car batteries from frying the seismometers' circuits, were not much bigger than a pack of gum. The combination of massive batteries and low-power demands would keep the instruments running for several months—not quite as long as solar panels or the electricity grid, but plenty of time for O'Malley and Boyd to see if the GSN data was still being hacked. And plenty of time to triangulate explosions and seismic activity, if they were still occurring.

O'Malley was impatient to hit the road and place the instruments, but given the remote, rugged locations she and Boyd had agreed on— the southern tip of the island, the northwest coast, and the northeast coast—she knew it would be foolhardy to attempt the task at night.

To make the hours until dawn pass more quickly, O'Malley popped a sleeping pill—she always traveled with a few Ambien, mainly to help her sleep on overseas flights or red-eyes. Twenty minutes later, she felt herself spiraling downward into a deep and dreamless sleep.

She woke at six: well before daylight, but not too early to load up and take the coast road southward, down toward the tip of the island.

She retrieved the car and double-parked in front of the hotel, her flashers asking permission or forgiveness or simply ninety seconds of patience. Hurrying inside, she dashed down the stairs and then lumbered back up, fifty pounds of boxed gear stacked like Christmas presents in her arms.

She loaded the boxes into the car, switched off the flashers, and made her getaway without delaying a single car. Half a block later she turned downhill, zigzagged down to the harbor and the coast road, and turned south.

If she had been a minute slower at the hotel—if she had paused to pee, or had walked down the three flights of stairs rather than having sprinted—she would have emerged from the door just as a black Audi had pulled up and double-parked, and two men got out and approached the hotel's entrance.

"Grove of trees, my ass," O'Malley muttered. The countryside outside Fuencaliente, the island's southernmost town, was practically devoid of individual trees, let alone the "dense grove" where Boyd had suggested she hide the seismometer. The contrast between the lush, heavily forested northern end of the island and the scrubby, desertlike south was striking. Up north, the slopes were steep and cut by deep, jungly gorges, like the mountains of Peru; here, the terrain was more like southern California's: variations on tan and brown, punctuated by green, flatlobed cacti. She delighted in the cacti, not simply (or even mainly) because they brightened the monochrome landscape but also because they reminded her of A. Samler Brown's engaging account of the island's cochineal boom-and-bust cycle a century and a half before. If she hadn't been on a mission, she would have stopped to inspect the underside of the cactus pads in search of tiny crimson beetles.

On the western side of Fuencaliente—just as she was starting to despair of finding a place to put the seismometer—she saw it: beside the road, practically *in* the road, was an outcropping of stone, which had been hollowed out and fashioned into a religious shrine. On the slope above the shrine was a clump of pine trees, four in number, stunted and twisted but better than any other trees she'd seen in an hour. "Any port in a storm," she said. "Thank you, Jesus." She parked on the shoulder just beyond the shrine and got out. After checking to be sure no cars were coming from either direction, she opened the back of the SUV— she had requested a four-wheel-drive vehicle this time, knowing she might be on dirt roads. She set a battery and a seismometer on the ground, tucked a voltage regulator in a pocket, and closed the hatch.

Back at the junkyard, Señor Pérez had rigged a makeshift carry-ing strap for each battery, a sling made from multiple wrappings of duct tape. O'Malley picked up the seismometer with her left hand and hoisted the battery with her right, grunting slightly with the effort. It was a load, especially uphill on rocky ground, but luckily the trees weren't far off the road.

She placed the battery and seismometer on a scrap of level ground between the trees. Kneeling beside them, her face low, she was pleased to see that the curve of the hillside and the jumble of rocks concealed the rig completely from the view of passing motorists. She had tucked the setup instructions for the instrument into a back pocket of her jeans, and she took them out now and reread them. The procedure was bless-edly straightforward: She clipped the leads of the voltage regulator to the posts of the battery, then connected the leads of the seismometer to the regulator. Next, she pressed and held the instrument's power but-ton until the digital display came on. Once it did, the instrument itself led her through a menu of options, including the "call home" setting.

It was only then that she remembered Boyd's admonition. She pulled out her cell phone and checked for a signal. Three bars: plenty. She entered the number Boyd had given her for the data calls, then pressed "Test." The display pulsed for an agonizing minute, then announced "Connection Successful." O'Malley blinked in surprise, double-checked the readout to make sure she hadn't imagined it, then rocked back onto her heels. "*Hell*, yeah," she crowed. "Thank you, Jesus!" Her face opened into a broad, cheek-stretching smile. "One down, two to go." At this rate, she'd be done by lunchtime.

Her self-congratulation had been a bit premature, she discovered at site number two. As the SUV did a bump-and-grind routine on a rocky jeep road, jouncing toward the remote northwest park Boyd had suggested, O'Malley checked her cell phone obsessively. The Brit had said that a signal might be spotty in this area, but as it turned out, Boyd had a gift for understatement: spotty would have been a major upgrade. Whenever the road approached trees, the signal vanished, possibly because the trees tended to favor low spots where moisture would collect. And whenever a lone bar of signal flickered onto her display— invariably on a high, exposed patch of rock—trees and other sources of concealment were nowhere to be found.

O'Malley spent an hour fruitlessly seeking a signal in the coastal park before conceding defeat. She backtracked to the highway, then back toward the village of Puntagordo, glancing at her phone between jolts of the vehicle. As she approached the town, she got a solid, steady signal bar, then two. When a third bar appeared, she cheered up. Now she faced a different problem, though: how to conceal the instrument amid the houses, barns, and sheds peppering the hillside.

She had already passed the house before its details registered on her conscious mind. It had been a house, once upon a time, but now it was a ruin. The stone walls were still standing, for the most part, but the roof had collapsed completely, so long ago that trees had taken up residence inside the house, their tops now higher than the walls.

Rusting iron bars covered the door opening, as if to protect the trees from burglars. There was no guarantee, of course, that the ruin would remain undisturbed—for all she knew, a salvage crew might show up tomorrow morning to recycle the stones for another structure—but she didn't have time to be choosy. *The perfect spot? No,* she concluded as she turned around and parked nearby. *But the good-enough spot.*

The vegetation was thick, and O'Malley had to force her way along the wall, branches clawing at her jeans and jacket. When she came to a window opening—the glass in shards, the framing long since rotted—she heaved the battery over the sill and leaned down, letting her feet rise off the ground and using her body as a counterweight as she lowered the heavy object. Then she repeated the maneuver with the seismometer before clambering up, over, and down.

The floor was strewn with dead leaves and branches. She cleared a spot for the rig and ran through the setup routine, this time without needing to consult the instructions. When the test transmission went through, O'Malley skipped the smug "Hell, yeah" and went straight to "Thank you, Jesus." This time it came out sounding more weary than triumphant.

When she got back to the SUV, she checked her reflection in the glass of a window. She looked dirty and bedraggled—and she wished she felt as good as she looked. "Two down, one to go," she muttered as she started the engine, put the SUV into gear, and eased out the clutch. "Third time's the charm."

CHAPTER 11

As he stepped off the plane into La Palma's soft afternoon sun, Special Agent Chip Dawtry was a man with a dilemma. Actually, he was a man with three dilemmas.

Dilemma #1 was Megan O'Malley, who was somewhere on the island—but where? He had tried phoning and emailing her at various points during his journey, to no avail. He had also tried repeatedly to reach her at the Hotel San Telmo, where Boyd had said she was staying. She never answered the phone in her room, and when Dawtry called back and quizzed the German-sounding guy at the front desk, he came up empty-handed. The guy said he hadn't seen her at breakfast, or at all today, for that matter. He added something that made Dawtry's blood run cold. "She is very popular, Ms. O'Malley. Two other men are very eager to find her." Dawtry asked for details, but the German was vague. Men in their thirties, dark hair, dark beards, very tan. Driving an Audi—he did remember that much. "A good German car," the desk clerk had added. *Crap,* thought Dawtry. *I've got to find her before they do.* He had no indication who "they" might be—jihadists of some stripe, he assumed, possibly al-Qaeda—but if they were intent on triggering a mass-fatality disaster and suspected O'Malley was onto them, they would surely not hesitate to capture or kill her.

Dilemma #2 was Boyd. Like O'Malley, the geologist seemed to be missing in action. Dawtry's calls and emails to Boyd, too, had gone unanswered. They'd had the one conversation—the one that had prompted Dawtry's impulsive dash to the airport—but no contact since. Dawtry might have suspected there was a problem with his phone if not for a mountain of evidence to the contrary: a flurry of calls and emails from Dilemma #3.

Dilemma #3 was Acting Assistant Director Christenberry, who would certainly fire Dawtry as soon as he realized the full measure of Dawtry's insubordination.

Christenberry's messages had begun reasonably enough: Waiting for your draft report, read the first subject line. Also your draft letter of apology to Vreeland, read the second. Why the delay in getting these to me? read the third. Where ARE you? demanded the fourth.

Upon landing in Madrid, Dawtry had sent a brief, vague response:

Had to leave on short notice for urgent personal matter. Sorry not to give you a heads-up.

En route from Madrid to Tenerife, he had received several more queries, which began with What sort of urgent personal matter? and Are you okay? but then swiftly spiraled up, alternating between cold fury and thermonuclear rage.

Dawtry did not reply. For one thing, nothing he could say would make matters better, only worse. For another, he'd had to sprint, literally, to catch the puddle jumper to La Palma. The doors of the shuttle bus were closing as he dashed into the gate area, waving frantically, barely managing to catch the eye of the driver.

He spent the thirty-minute hop from Tenerife to La Palma composing and then trashing a series of emails to Christenberry. Their tone ranged between sheepish apology and abject groveling. Finally, he settled on a vague nine-word message:

Sorry to be out of touch. Will explain soonest.

He saved it in his "Drafts" folder, for sending upon his arrival in La Palma. It wouldn't solve the Christenberry Dilemma; it would merely postpone the reckoning—a reckoning that was likely to end his career. But until he knew more, postponing was the best he could do.

As the plane descended, he surveyed the island, whose roughly triangular shape he had already committed to memory from his study of the map. From the tapered southern tip it rose, gradually at first and then more sharply, the slope pocked with volcanic craters and cones. A high ridge formed the island's north-south spine, and with each mile to the north, the flanks of the ridge grew steeper, wilder, and greener— more vertiginous, beauteous, and dangerous.

The twin-engine plane turned parallel to the ridgeline and dropped, slewing in a wicked crosswind. As a former military pilot, Dawtry knew that crosswinds could be tricky, especially in the vicinity of changing terrain. Fortunately, these pilots flew this approach multiple times a day. *Hell,* Dawtry told himself, *they can probably nail this landing in their sleep.* The wings rocked and wagged as the plane neared the ground, causing him to clench the armrests, but the plane leveled just before touching down. It was only when he exhaled that he realized he'd been holding his breath.

The plane trundled to a stop beside La Palma's small terminal, and Dawtry switched on his phone, gritted his teeth, and prepared to hit "Send." But before he had a chance, his screen flashed with an incoming email alert. The message's sender was identified as CharlesABoyd@ seismo.co.uk. Update—urgent, the subject line read. His pulse quickening, Dawtry opened the message. Just out of hospital, the message read.

Severe septic shock—emergency surgery to remove a sponge left in abdomen by inept surgeon.

O'Malley is placing three seismometers at locations on attached map. Has already placed sensor #1. Data uploading. Three explosions and two quakes recorded since noon today, mag 2.7 and 3.2, originating due north of town of Fuencaliente. Sensors 2 & 3 should pinpoint location shortly, if seismic activity continues. Meanwhile, GSN shows ZERO activity. Data is being masked in real time! V. sophisticated—and v. worrisome!

Dawtry read the message three times. Then he forwarded it to Acting Assistant Director Christenberry, with a brief note of intro:

See below from Prof. Charles Boyd, British seismologist. Fire me if you want or need to—I realize I've disobeyed an order, and I'm acting totally on my own—but I am on La Palma, looking for Prof. O'Malley. Have strong reason to believe she is in imminent danger. More soon.

He hit "Send," then called up the La Palma map Boyd had sent, with pins marking the three locations where she was placing seismometers. She wouldn't be at the first location, obviously, but was she en route to the second, or already heading to the third?

He zoomed in, checking the roads, then surveyed the afternoon sky. It was three thirty, and already the November sun was dropping toward the island's ridgeline. A highway tunnel seemed to cut directly through the island's north-south ridgeline, which he estimated meant he could reach the west coast in an hour, but from there it appeared to be another half hour, maybe twice that, up a hairpin highway to the second seismometer location. He might—*might*—make it there before dark, but if he didn't happen to catch her there, he had absolutely no

Jon Jefferson

hope of reaching the third location before dark. Dawtry was a good driver at high speed—he'd had pursuit training at the Academy—but the only rental car option available was a Toyota Yaris, not a Formula One racer. "Shit," he said. *Fucking scientists. When the hell are they going to quit stalling and invent the damned transporter beam?*

CHAPTER 12

The road from Puntagordo climbed steeply, corkscrewing up the northwest flank of the shattered volcano. After a few miles it brought O'Malley to a Y, and to an unexpected choice. To the left, the road leveled out—as level as roads could get on the north end of the island—and wound across the flank toward Barlovento, where she planned to place the third monitor. To the right, the road snaked upward to the Roque de los Muchachos. To the observatory complex on the caldera's rim.

She stopped to consider the options that presented themselves. Taking the fork to Barlovento meant staying on task, completing her mission as quickly as possible. Taking the fork to the observatory meant a short detour, a brief break, before getting back to it. She checked her watch; it was not even one o'clock yet. Thanks to her early start, she still had plenty of time. *I could grab a sandwich at the Residencia. I could take a shower—sweet Jesus, I could take a shower!* She spun the wheel to the right and began to climb.

Thirty minutes later, she pulled in to the parking lot. The receptionist, Antonio, whom she remembered from her prior visit, did not seem to recognize her. *No wonder,* she thought, seeing the dirty, bedraggled woman reflected in a mirror behind the counter. *I look like a homeless person.* "*Hola*, Antonio," she said. "Megan O'Malley. From Johns Hopkins University. It's nice to see you again."

The man's brow furrowed as he processed the information and then struggled to reconcile it with the grimy woman standing in front of him. Finally, recognition dawned in his eyes—recognition that appeared mixed, not surprisingly, with puzzlement and concern. "Ah, *Doctora* O'Malley. Welcome back." He hesitated, then glanced down. O'Malley heard papers shuffling, saw Antonio's eyes darting down to make swift scans of the pages. "Forgive me, *Doctora*. I forgot that you were coming."

O'Malley smiled and shook her head. "No, no, it's not your fault, Antonio. It's a surprise visit. No one knows I'm here."

The poor man looked more confused than ever. "A surprise?"

"I'm not here to use the telescope," she explained. "I came back to La Palma as a tourist."

"Ah, yes?" He took the liberty of staring at her with frank, appraising curiosity. He pointed toward her left ear. "You have been hiking?"

O'Malley reached up and finger-combed her hair, retrieving a twig. She laughed self-consciously. "Yes, I have been hiking." She leaned forward, elbows on the counter. "I'm wondering if I could ask a big favor. Two favors, actually."

"Favors? Sure, what favors?"

"First, I'm starving. I'd love to get a sandwich."

"Of course, *Doctora*. *Mi casa es su casa.* You remember where is the café?" He pointed down the hallway behind her.

"Yes, I remember. But even if I didn't, I could follow my nose. I can smell it from here, and it's making me even hungrier." She hesitated. "The other favor might be more complicated."

"Yes?"

"Yes. I'm wondering if I could take a shower."

He blinked. "A shower?"

"Yes." She gave him a self-deprecating smile and waved one hand at her head, then extended the gesture to encompass all of herself. "I fell down in the woods. As you can see, I'm very dirty. And I pulled a muscle in my back. So I would love to take a hot shower." It came out sounding pushier than she liked. "But only if you have a room that's empty, of course."

"*Doctora*, it's no problem—we do have a room. Of course you may take a shower. And you may stay here tonight if you want to. It would be our pleasure to accommodate you."

"You're very kind, Antonio, but I can't stay. A sandwich and a shower would be *fabuloso*, though."

He swiveled and took a key from a pigeonhole on the back wall, then laid it on the counter. "Room seventeen. Our finest accommodation. The . . . how do you say it? Penthouse?"

O'Malley laughed. "Will I find roses and champagne waiting for me?"

"Of course, *Doctora*."

O'Malley took the key and gave a slight bow. "Thank you, Antonio. I'll see you on my way out."

He returned the bow. As she turned to go, Antonio glanced down, reaching for the phone.

O'Malley was eager for the food but downright desperate for the shower. She headed straight upstairs for the "penthouse," which was like every other room in the Residencia: small and spare, but offering a stunning view of the sea. She spent a nanosecond admiring the panorama, then stepped into the bathroom, turned on the shower, and peeled off her clothes. As soon as she glimpsed steam, she stepped into the spray. "Oh my God," she moaned. "Oh."

She spent a while luxuriating under the water, then soaped up her body and shampooed her hair and slowly rinsed. Then she luxuriated awhile longer. Eventually, reluctantly, she turned off the water and toweled off, wishing she had brought a change of clothes. As she was pulling up her muddy pants, she heard a knock on the door. "Oh crap," she muttered. She grabbed her sweater—no time for the bra—and tugged it over her head as she walked into the bedroom. "Yes?"

She half expected to hear someone say, "Housekeeping."

But this was not a hotel. Instead, she heard the doorknob rattle and saw the door swing open and gaped as a man—a handsome Spaniard—stepped into the room.

"Iñigo—Jesus!" She yanked the sweater down, hoping she hadn't just flashed her tits at him. "What are you doing here?"

The question she was really asking was, *What the hell are you doing in my room?* The question he chose to answer was, *How did you know I was hoping to see you?*

"Antonio told me you were here. A wonderful surprise! You came back to see me?"

"Not exactly. I came back because I'm still trying to figure out the problem I had with the telescope."

His brow furrowed; then he nodded. "You are very persistent." He flashed her a disarming smile. "When Antonio told me you had returned, I looked for you in the café, but you were not there. Obviously. Because you were right here." He stepped toward her. "I am happy to see you, Meh-ghan. Welcome!" He took another step, reached out, and enfolded her in a hug.

O'Malley was angry at being walked in on, half-dressed and dripping wet. Christ, what if she'd still been in the shower—would he have come in anyway? Walked into the bathroom? She was embarrassed that so little fabric separated them. And she was acutely conscious that in spite of her anger and embarrassment, her nipples were hardening against his chest.

She worked a hand between them and pushed away slightly, but still he held her.

"Why did you leave so suddenly last time?"

O'Malley didn't answer.

"Anyway, I am happy to see you," he repeated. He pressed against her, and she noticed that her nipples were not the only things growing hard. "I have missed you very much."

"Oh, please," she said, realizing too late that her sarcastic words might be open to a different and problematic interpretation.

His hands slid around to her sides. "I cannot stop thinking of you. I wrote you a hundred emails."

"No, you didn't."

"I did. But I was afraid to send them. Is true, Meh-ghan."

She felt a stronger throbbing against her belly. *Oh God,* she thought, then—to her dismay—she heard the words again, whispered aloud this time. "Oh God."

Reaching up, he cradled her face in his hands and leaned down, his eyes locked on hers. O'Malley felt her breath catch as his mouth met hers, and her knees buckled. With a soft moan she sank against him, and when she did, she felt a more insistent throbbing, now against her, against her thigh. No, not a throbbing, exactly. A pulsing. An oddly incongruous, almost mechanical buzzing: the buzzing of her cell phone vibrating in her hip pocket. She broke off the kiss—difficult to do, for multiple reasons—and pushed back from him again. "My phone," she gasped.

"Sshh," he whispered. "It can wait."

"No, it can't." Regretfully she extricated herself from his embrace and pulled her phone from her pocket. "Oh, fuck. I have to go," she said, as she realized the implications of the message on the display: not an incoming call or text, but a low-battery alert. Maps and signal-seeking were both huge battery sucks, she knew, and if her phone died, she wouldn't be able to locate a spot with a good signal for the third seismometer.

"Meh-ghan, Meh-ghan," he pleaded. "Don't go. Stay here tonight. With me. I beg you."

"I can't."

"Why not? What's so important?"

"I can't tell you," she said. "But it is."

"Don't go."

"I have to. Believe me, I'm sorry."

He turned away and sighed heavily, then leaned on the windowsill and hung his head. "You break my heart."

"Iñigo, please," she began, but he held up a hand and waved her off. Dismissed her.

"Just go," he said, spinning on his heel and striding toward the door. "Goodbye." Without looking back, he opened the door and walked away, leaving her stunned.

O'Malley was surprised and angry to feel tears on her cheeks. "Damn you," she muttered—a curse that encompassed Iñigo, herself, her dying cell phone, and the obsessive fool's errand that had brought her back to La Palma. Stomping into the bathroom, she tugged on her socks and boots and glared at her bra. "Oh, fuck it," she said, snatching it off the towel bar and stuffing it into a pocket.

Checking the paper map the car rental agency had provided, O'Malley noticed a shortcut she could take to Barlovento. The shortcut meant she wouldn't have to backtrack all the way down to the fork in the road—the fateful, ill-chosen fork that had brought her up to the rim of the caldera. Up to the brink of torrid sex with Iñigo.

Spilled milk, she told herself, stopping to inspect a narrow side road branching—"twigging" might have been a more accurate word—from the highway. High above to the right, perched on the rim of the volcano, she saw several of the observatory's gleaming white telescope domes. To her left was a ribbon of pavement, one lane wide and badly cracked. It angled across a stretch of rocky, treeless terrain—the one flat spot on the entire island, in O'Malley's limited experience—and then dropped over an edge and down into a sea of clouds, which had apparently coalesced during her stop at the Residencia.

O'Malley eyed the road doubtfully. Was this really her road? Was this really a road at all? A small, weathered sign, labeled with an arrow and the word "Gallegos," seemed to confirm that it was. She didn't like the look of it, but at this point, she doubted that she had enough daylight and battery power to backtrack to the bigger, better route that she had impulsively rejected for the sake of a hot shower and a steamy kiss. "Okay, here goes nothing," she muttered, activating the four-wheel drive and then easing out the clutch with considerable unease.

As she neared the edge of the relatively flat stretch, the cracks in the asphalt grew bigger and more numerous, and soon the road was more crack than pavement. As the road dropped over the edge, all pretense of paving vanished: the single lane became a pair of ruts, rocky and twisting, snaking down a grade steeper than any O'Malley had ever driven on. "Holy shit," she muttered, hitting the brakes.

Nothing happened.

Actually, something happened, but it was the opposite of what O'Malley had intended. The pedal turned mushy under her foot and sank to the floor. She pumped the pedal, but still it refused to hold pressure. Her brakes had failed completely. "What the . . . ?" she muttered. They'd been working fine before her stop at the observatory. Had something broken since? *No*, she realized with terrible clarity, *they've been sabotaged.*

The road was worsening and the vehicle was gathering speed, bucking like a furious rodeo bull. She gripped the wheel tightly, not just to steer—an increasingly difficult proposition—but also to keep from being flung around like a rag doll. In desperation she floored the clutch and shoved the gearshift from second gear toward first. The transmission fought back, the gears gnashing—O'Malley imagined the metal teeth snapping off in rapid sequence like machine-gun fire—but she had no choice, so she slammed it again, harder. This time the transmission snarled all the way into first, and she popped the clutch and lurched hard, slowing with whiplash-inducing force.

In first, the engine whined like a jet turbine, the tachometer edging up toward its red line, but at least she was still in control, sort of, and still on the road, such as it was.

O'Malley was getting lightheaded, and she realized she was hyperventilating—her brain, like the engine, close to redlining—and she fought to slow her breathing. She forced herself to breathe in through her nose, which made her feel as if she was suffocating, then blew out slowly through pursed lips. *Again,* she commanded herself. *And again.*

It worked, until she looked ahead and saw the road vanish. Fifty yards ahead the mountainside ended abruptly; beyond and below was an unbroken sea of clouds. "No no *no*," she moaned. She flashed back to her first day on La Palma, a seeming lifetime ago, and to the little Toyota tumbling down into the clouds. The crucial difference, the lethal difference, was that this time she was inside the doomed vehicle. Should she bail out? *Could* she bail out? She had to try.

She fumbled for the seat belt release, but her fingers encountered an obstacle before they found the seat belt button—a shape that felt familiar and somehow helpful. Still staring ahead at the fast-approaching edge of the abyss, O'Malley analyzed the tactile data, and when she grasped the meaning, she grasped the thing itself—it was the parking-brake lever—and yanked with all her strength. The SUV bucked and lurched, the engine stalled, and O'Malley slithered to a stop in a cloud of dust and a miniature avalanche of loose stones, twenty feet before a sharp turn that surfed the very edge of the precipice.

She was alive. Saved by the parking brake, she was alive. And she was sobbing, her head on the steering wheel.

But not for long. O'Malley reached again for the seat belt release, almost as frantically as before. This time she found it and punched it. When the belt retracted, she flung open the door, staggered out, and vomited, though there was nothing much in her stomach to lose. *Well,* she consoled herself once the heaves had ceased, *I guess it's a good thing I didn't have that sandwich.*

As she contemplated her options, she realized that they weren't good. She was on a narrow, knife-edge ridge, with no room to turn around. In reverse, her driving was marginal even at best—even on pavement in her Prius, which was equipped with a backup camera. Here, it would be suicidal to backtrack. Yet going forward, around the bend, and along the ledge seemed the height of lunacy.

But going forward was the only way to place the third sensor. She *had* to find a way forward. Could she abandon the SUV and walk to the third location, carrying the sensor and the battery? Realistically, she doubted it; the location was a good ten miles away—no, a *bad* ten miles—maybe more. And the sun would be setting within an hour or so.

Think, O'Malley, think, she ordered herself. She had stopped the runaway SUV once, she reminded herself. Could she stop it again, or slow it enough, to make the sharp turn up ahead? She walked down and studied the terrain up close. Up close, it wasn't quite as tight a turn, or as narrow a ledge, as it appeared from above. And the ledge itself wasn't that long—less than fifty yards. If she could manage to stop just before the turn, then restart slowly, she might make it.

Suddenly she laughed. "Well, *duh,*" she said out loud. Of *course* she could manage to stop before the turn: all she had to do was switch off the ignition with the transmission in first, and she'd jerk to a halt immediately. *Or,* she realized, *if I put it in second or third but leave the ignition off, the engine's compression will work like a brake, and I'll crawl like a snail. Piece of cake!*

It was not a piece of cake; it was a harrowing, hair-raising, white-knuckle thrill ride. But she hung on, working the transmission and the hand brake in tense tandem to slow her through the turn. She crept along the ledge, hugging the rock wall to her left as closely as possible—so closely, in fact, she knocked off the driver's side mirror, but she judged the loss minor, considering the alternatives. And then she had made it—across the ledge! Gradually the track widened and smoothed, and in less than a mile she was back on pavement, honest-to-god pavement, and approaching her final destination outside the town of Barlovento.

After a couple of false starts, which took her down dead-end alleys and driveways, she found the dirt road she had spotted on Google Earth the night she and Boyd had selected the seismometer locations. The road zigzagged and switchbacked its way toward the high cliff on the island's northeast coast. O'Malley's phone was nearly dead—"3%," read the blinking battery-charge indicator—and she jolted along the road as fast as she dared, alternating between taps on the gas pedal, yanks on the brake lever, and strategic switchings-off of the ignition. By now the makeshift combination of workarounds was nearly second nature. With a bit more practice, she might even be able to manage the maze of city streets back in Santa Cruz.

The cell signal was better here than at the prior location, bouncing back and forth between one steady bar and two flickering bars. She came to a place where the road crossed a small, wooded ravine that cut through a tight switchback. She risked another obsessive glance at her phone. Two steady bars. *Jackpot!*

At the top of the ravine, she eased the vehicle onto the narrow shoulder and parked, being careful to angle the wheels up the slope and give the parking brake a hard yank. As she opened the door, it was caught and nearly yanked from her grasp by the wind whipping off the ocean and up the face of the nearby cliffs. O'Malley forced it shut, then popped the rear hatch and leaned into the cargo space. "Third time's the charm," she muttered again, hoisting the last of the three seismometers and its battery.

From behind her, against the wind, she heard a voice. "I think it would work better on the edge of the cliff."

O'Malley whirled. Twenty feet away she saw a man—Iñigo!—standing beside a jeep whose arrival she had not heard.

"*Dammit*, Iñigo, you scared me! What the hell are you doing here?"

He shrugged. "I followed you."

"You *followed* me? Why?"

He didn't answer.

"Are you stalking me? Because I didn't have sex with you?"

He smiled slightly. "No, of course not. Not because of that."

"Then why? Why on earth would you follow me?"

"Because I was worried about you."

"Worried about me?" O'Malley snorted. "I'm just fine. You don't need to worry about me."

"Yes, I do, Meh-ghan. What you are doing is very worrisome."

"What I'm *doing*?" O'Malley felt her nerve endings go on high alert. For the first time, she sensed that something besides macho swagger lay beneath his concern. "What am I *doing*, Iñigo?"

"You are making a lot of noise. You are asking questions and poking around. You are meddling in something that is none of your business." He reached a hand behind his back, and when it reappeared, it was holding a pistol, and the pistol was pointing at her. The blinding light of a laser pointer—a laser sight—flickered briefly across her face, and then the small circle of light, bright as carmine dye or heart's blood, settled onto her chest.

CHAPTER 13

Frozen in space and time, the seismometer in one hand, the car battery in the other, and the red dot of the laser sight on her chest, O'Malley felt a seismic shift within her mind. A whole series of tumblers clicked into place, and a realization hit her with swift, sickening clarity. Iñigo's lack of concern about the malfunctioning telescope and his teasing deflections—even his romantic advances—made sudden, sinister sense. "You're part of it. My God, Iñigo, you're *part* of it."

He cocked his head, waiting, not denying.

"The fault line, the explosions—you're the one trying to trigger a landslide."

"Me personally? No. I am not setting off the explosions. I myself will not cause the landslide. But I am aware of what is happening, and I do have a part to play."

"What part is that, Iñigo?"

"At the moment, unfortunately, my part is to stop you from calling more attention to our project."

"Who is 'we'? Stop me how?" He did not answer.

Another realization: "My brakes—they didn't fail. You sabotaged them, or had somebody sabotage them, just now at the observatory. You tried to kill me in a car accident!"

He shrugged.

"For God's sake, *why?*"

"As I said, you are causing problems."

She shook her head. "Not 'why are you trying to kill me?' Why are you *doing* all this? You and whoever you're working for? You're trying to trigger a huge mass disaster—you know that, right?" He didn't respond, but she saw a glint of confirmation in his eyes. "Are you insane? Or do you have some terrible hatred of Americans?"

He scratched his cheek with the muzzle of the pistol. "Individually, no. But collectively?" His eyes hardened. "When I was three years old, my father was killed. By your government. My mother lost her mind with grief. I was sent to an orphanage. I swore an oath that when I grew up, I would do everything in my power to avenge my father's death and my mother's suffering."

"I . . . Iñigo, that's terrible. But *this*—trying to kill millions of innocent people?"

"Innocent people?" His eyes narrowed. "America is the biggest bully on the planet. You're running low on oil? Just invade a Middle Eastern country. You don't like a nation's leader? Just stage a coup." He made a face of disgust. "Don't talk to me about innocent people."

O'Malley felt her anger rising. "So because your father was killed when you were three, you think it's okay to kill thousands—*many* thousands—of American three-year-olds?"

He waved the gun as if shooing a fly, as if shooing her arguments. "Your disapproval is irrelevant. The world will soon start to run out of food and water. Only the strongest will survive."

"Do you want to be remembered as the world's worst mass murderer?"

He smiled. "No one will remember me or blame me. The world will remember and blame radical Islam. And radical Islam will feed on that hatred. Grow stronger from it." He swung the pistol, pointing it toward the edge of the cliff. "Take the seismometer over there."

"No."

Jon Jefferson

"No? You want me to shoot you?"

"No, asshole, I *don't* want you to shoot me. I want you to put the gun away, get in your car, and get the fuck *away* from me."

He shook his head slowly. "I cannot do that." He pointed the gun at her again. "Take the seismometer over there."

"No."

He muttered what she assumed was a curse; then he stepped toward her and grabbed one of her arms and jerked hard. The pull spun her, so that she was facing away from him and toward the edge of the cliff, some fifty yards away. Pressing the pistol against her back, he began pushing her toward the edge.

Do something, O'Malley, she shrieked at herself, but her mind—so often brimming with ideas and plans and scenarios—had gone as dark as a black hole.

Three feet from the edge, he halted. "Here," he said, releasing her arm. "Put it down here."

She stared over the edge. Far, far below, breakers smashed and foamed on the rocks. The wind swept up, cold and damp and strong— almost, she suspected, strong enough to catch her in midair and blow her back up. Almost, but not quite. How long, she wondered absurdly, would it take her to fall that far? *Too long,* she thought. *And not nearly long enough. How high had Google Earth told her this cliff was? A thousand feet? No: fourteen hundred. Fourteen hundred friggin' feet. Feet.* The word "feet" gave her the glimmer of an idea. Desperate, maybe even dumb, but an idea.

Slowly she turned to face him. "Okay," she said. "I'm putting it down now." As she said the word "now," she slammed the car battery and twenty-pound seismometer downward, with all her strength, onto his feet.

Iñigo howled in pain, then sank to his knees. As he did, the hand with the gun swung toward her. She grabbed it and he bellowed again, the sound more animal than human, as she twisted the gun and his

140

index finger splintered. But her grip on the gun was only partial, and as she tore it from his hand, it slid from her own as well, and went flying, cartwheeling, over the edge and into the void.

She kicked at him, but he managed to block the kick, and she fell, twisting and scrabbling away even before she hit the ground. She got to her feet, but the fall had sprained her ankle, and as she staggered away, her steps were agonizingly slow—and utterly agonizing.

She limped along the edge of the cliff, needing to steer a wide berth around him before angling uphill to her car. She glanced back, praying that Iñigo was still crumpled on the ground, but he was on his feet, and despite whatever damage she'd done—surely some of the bones in his feet were broken?—he was chasing her. And he was gaining on her.

"No!" she yelled. The wind tore the word away and—as if somehow fed by it—grew louder. Louder and more powerful, with a pulsing force she could feel throughout her body. The pulsing intensified, and suddenly O'Malley jerked to a stop as a spinning rotor, and then a gleaming helicopter, ascended from below the rim of the cliff. The helicopter wheeled, turning directly toward her. She whirled, gasping as pain shot through her ankle, and staggered up the slope. There was no point in trying to get away, she realized: the only question was whether it would be Iñigo or the helicopter that reached her first. But damned if she'd give up without a fight.

She looked back just in time to see the helicopter wheel again—this time toward Iñigo—and tilt forward, the leading edge of the rotor angling downward, only a few feet off the ground. Iñigo froze, raised his arms to cover his face, and reflexively dodged. The aircraft moved toward him, and he scurried away. Suddenly he stumbled, arms flailing, and seemed to hang suspended for an instant. Then he toppled backward and disappeared over the edge. The helicopter hung motionless, as if the aircraft itself were surprised by this sudden turn of events.

O'Malley gasped in surprise and horror. She felt on the verge of vomiting once more, but she forced back the nausea and began staggering toward her car again, her breath ragged and heaving.

The thrum of the blades increased, the rotor wash buffeting her as the helicopter skimmed overhead, spun to face her, and landed directly between her and the car. O'Malley stumbled; she fell to her knees, breaking her fall with her hands, and found herself unable to rise.

The helicopter's engine spooled down and the blades slowed. The cockpit door opened and the pilot emerged, his eyes hidden behind sunglasses. O'Malley remained on all fours, shaking her head slowly, her pain and fear and fury overtaking her in ragged rasps as the man approached. He stopped a few feet away, and suddenly, as if she had entered the eye of a hurricane, she felt a strange stillness, along with a pang of sorrow. *Let it be quick,* she prayed, bowing her head. *Please let it be quick.*

"Dr. O'Malley? Megan? Are you hurt?"

Her head jerked up. The voice: it sounded American, and it sounded kind.

"I'm Special Agent Dawtry," the man went on. "FBI." He knelt in front of her, his brow furrowed with concern. "Are you hurt?"

O'Malley tried to speak but couldn't. She managed to shake her head before breaking into deep, racking sobs. "It's okay," she heard him say, and she felt his arms encircle her. "It's okay," he repeated. "You're safe." She sagged against him, her breath still coming in ragged gasps. "Take your time," he said. She nodded. She drew a deep, shuddering breath and held it, then blew it out slowly between pursed lips. She repeated the procedure, and then—after a third cycle, steady this time—she pulled away and stared at him.

"Where the hell did *you* come from?" Before he could answer, she added, "And what the hell *took* you so long?"

A peal of laughter burst from him, and O'Malley laughed, too, then found herself crying again. "Goddammit," she said. "I *hate* to cry." She wiped her face with her sleeve, blowing her nose messily in the crook of her elbow. "Yuck."

"Can you stand up?" She nodded, and he got to his feet, offering her a hand to haul her up—he was strong, this G-man. But when she put weight on her right foot, she gasped. "What's wrong?"

"I sprained my ankle. Nothing to worry about." She tried a step, and pain knifed through her. *"Oww."*

"Here, lean on me. Let's get you to the car." He put one arm behind her back and held her waist, taking hold of her upper arm with his free hand. She reached up and held his shoulder, and they hobbled up the hillside in a clumsy parody of a three-legged race. "We should probably wrap that and put an ice pack on it."

"How?"

"There's probably a first-aid kit in the helicopter." He gave a small laugh. "As if a first-aid kit would do anything if you crashed."

"Agent Dawtry—"

"Chip, by the way."

Under the circumstances, she couldn't quite make the shift to a first name. It wasn't even an actual name; it was a *nickname*, a kid's name. "I appreciate your concern. I especially appreciate the rescue. But . . . don't you need to see about . . . *him*?" She nodded toward the edge of the cliff.

He gave a slight grimace. "Nothing to see—not from up here—except maybe a smear on the rocks."

"Jesus. Poor Iñigo. I mean, he was trying to kill me, but still—"

"Wait." He stopped, squeezing her arm.

"Oww."

"You *knew* that guy?"

"Yeah. He was a colleague."

"A *colleague*? I do not think that word means what you think it means." O'Malley blinked. Was this FBI agent actually quoting dialogue from *The Princess Bride*, or was the choice of words pure coincidence? He shook his head. "Murder isn't an act of collegiality."

"We worked together," she said. "Only briefly. He's a telescope operator—a staff astronomer, basically—at the observatory."

O'Malley could see him processing this, his eyes flitting back and forth, his brows knitted. "I don't get it. Why would another astronomer try to kill you? Did you steal his discovery or something?"

"Agent Dawtry—"

"Chip."

"He's part of it, Chip. They're trying to set off a giant landslide. You probably think I'm crazy, but—"

He shook his head slightly. She thought she saw a smile in his eyes and the corners of his mouth. "Dr. O'Malley, would I be here if I thought you were crazy?"

Now it was her turn to smile, for a nanosecond or so. "Good point," she conceded. "Okay, *Chip*, if you don't think I'm nuts, quit calling me Dr. O'Malley."

"Deal, *Megan*. But I still don't get it. You said 'they.' You said, 'They're trying to set off a landslide.' Who are 'they'—the observatory? A bunch of sociopathic astronomers?"

She couldn't help laughing at the absurdity of the idea. "No, not the observatory. I don't *know* who. I just know that Iñigo's involved because he hates America. *Hated* America. He blamed the US government for his father's death."

Dawtry drew back slightly and looked at her, his gaze intensifying. "His father was killed in a war? Where? When?"

"I don't know. He didn't say. All he told me was that the US killed his father, his mother went crazy from grief, and he—Iñigo—grew up in an orphanage. He's spent his whole life seeking vengeance."

"Wow," he said. "Weird. Just like Iñigo Montoya in *The Princess Bride*."

She raised her eyebrows—he *was* a fan—and then nodded. "I hadn't thought of that. Coincidence? The name, I mean? Two vengeful Spaniards named Iñigo?"

"Maybe, maybe not," he said. "And maybe Iñigo's not his real name."

"Why would he use a fake name?"

"Gee, I dunno," he said. "Maybe to conceal his true identity while he slaughters millions of innocent people? Do you think he was telling the truth about why he was doing it?"

"It *sounded* true," she said. "He was about to kill me, so why bother lying? I got the feeling he thought I deserved to know why I was about to die. That, or he wanted to brag. Or maybe twist the knife a little."

"Or maybe *D*, all of the above. You think you can walk?"

"Yeah, I think so."

He released her arm, but when he did, her right leg buckled, so he caught her and resumed serving as her crutch. "What else did he tell you?"

She tried to replay their last conversation—his last confession, as it turned out—but she had trouble retrieving the transcript. "He said that the world would condemn radical Islam. And that the condemnation would help radical Islam grow stronger." She frowned. "But I didn't get the feeling that he's actually a jihadist himself. More like he was helping them because of his grudge. But I have no idea how he connected with them."

He scowled. "Easy to do, these days. ISIS and al-Qaeda have gotten very savvy at finding and recruiting people with chips on their shoulders." Either the wind was picking up or O'Malley was bordering on shock; she was now shivering. "You're cold?"

She nodded, her teeth beginning to chatter.

"Okay, let's get you to the car and turn on the heat, and then we'll take care of that ankle." They continued their three-legged hobble.

She stopped abruptly. "Don't we need to call 9-1-1—or whatever the Spanish version is—before we do anything else?" He didn't answer, and she thought perhaps he hadn't heard her. "Chip?" His name still felt strange and oddly, embarrassingly intimate.

"Let me think about that," he said. After detouring around the helicopter, they reached her SUV. The rear hatch was still open, and he helped her turn and ease down onto the shelf of the cargo space. Dawtry turned away, staring for a while into the distance—at the vast ocean, or at the edge of the cliff, or at something visible only in his mind's eye—and then shook his head and turned back to her. "I don't think we can call the police."

"What? A man is *dead.*" The way she said it, it sounded less like a fact than an accusation.

"I *know* he's dead. You think I'll forget the look on his face when he started to fall?"

She saw real pain in his eyes, and she wished she could take back her words, or at least change their tone. "I'm sorry. I'm not criticizing, just . . . I think we have to call the police."

He frowned. "Normally, I'd be the last person on earth to say this, but I think it's better to leave the police out of it. For one thing, I disobeyed an order to come here and find you, and it'd put the Bureau, not to mention me, in a bad spot to file a report. For another, if we get tangled in red tape, we lose our chance to find the bad guys and stop them."

She looked away and chewed her lip, thinking, then turned back to him. "So if we don't call the police, what *do* we do?"

He locked eyes with her. "Nothing. We get the hell out of Dodge. We pretend we weren't here."

She gaped, dumbfounded.

"Megan, this guy wasn't some loco nutcase, some lone wolf. He's part of something big, right? There are more people involved—maybe lots more—and we don't know who they are or where they are." He turned and scanned the rutted, serpentine road, as if a convoy of killers might be careering toward them even as he spoke. "We can't trust anybody here. Including the police."

His paranoia, if that's what it was, was contagious. Her eyes searched his face. "You never answered my question," she said, feeling a surge of dread.

"Huh?" He looked puzzled, or possibly concerned about her clarity of mind. "Yeah, I did. I said that what we do is get out of here and keep our mouths shut."

"Not that question," she said. Without moving her body, O'Malley slid her right hand in a small arc, feeling for something. Her fingers found what they were seeking: the tire iron that had been clattering constantly during her drive. Her fingers curled around the cold steel shaft, and her grip steadily tightened. "My first question."

"What first question? What are you talking about?"

"I asked how you found me."

His eyes narrowed slightly. "I work for the FBI, remember? We know how to find people." He gave a laugh—a smug laugh, it seemed to O'Malley. Then he turned and studied the road again. "Looks like nobody's spotted us," he went on, and O'Malley felt her throat tighten with fear.

He's part of it, too, she realized. *It's now or never. Him or me.* She pushed herself to stand. Pain shot through her ankle again, and she gritted her teeth to keep from crying out. Luckily, foolishly, he still had his back to her. O'Malley drew back in a windup, as if for a tennis serve, then realized that she couldn't swing the tire iron overhead without snagging it on the top of the SUV's opening; she'd have to swing it sideways. A forehand, then, not an overhead smash.

"Professor Boyd," he said, as her arm began to swing. "We should call him. Let him know you're okay. See what the seismometers are saying." But she was too late to hear his words, to hear their reassuring tone, to glimpse the open smile as he began turning toward her again.

Given a few minutes—and a calculator and a few bits of data—O'Malley could have computed the force with which the tire iron was about to strike the FBI agent's skull. But she didn't have a few minutes, or even a few seconds, and she certainly didn't have the strength to override the momentum that her fear and adrenaline had imparted to the heavy tool. Newton's first law: a body in motion tends to remain in motion unless acted upon by an outside force . . .

What O'Malley had—all that she had—was a nanosecond. It wasn't much, but it would have to do.

She let go. Just. Let. Go.

Released from the gravitational pull of her grip, the tire iron instantly attained escape velocity. Rocketing past Dawtry's head, it spun away like some lopsided, one-way boomerang, sailing clear over the helicopter, clear off the edge of the cliff, and dropping from sight.

"I can't believe you tried to brain me," Dawtry said again, O'Malley's foot in one hand and a small spool of elastic bandage in the other.

"I *started* to brain you," O'Malley pointed out. "Then I realized my error, and I stopped."

With a dubious grunt, he finished wrapping her swollen ankle. "Lucky for me I said 'Boyd' just in the nick. The magic word that saved my skull. We both owe Boyd big-time. If he hadn't given me the GPS coordinates for the seismometer locations, I wouldn't have found you until too late. It would be you, not Iñigo, spattered on the rocks down there."

"Ugh." She shuddered. "Okay, so now we hightail it out of here. Where to? What's next?"

Dawtry frowned. "Hang on. I'll be right back." Leaving her perched in the open back of the SUV, he jogged past the helicopter and continued to the edge of the cliff. Perilously close to the brink, he leaned over the precipice to study the rocks below.

O'Malley's heart raced. *Don't you dare fall off,* she telegraphed to him. After a moment, he turned and picked up the battery and the seismometer—*The instruments of my deliverance,* she thought—and then trudged up the slope. To her surprise, he stopped at the helicopter and set them in the cockpit before rejoining her.

"Hey," she called, "what are you doing?"

"We can't leave these here. I'll fly offshore a ways, drop 'em in the ocean."

"What? No!" He gave her a quizzical look; she responded by holding out her hands, palms up. "We need the data!"

"Let me get this straight," he said. "In spite of everything that's happened, you're still hell-bent on this triangulation project?"

"*Because* of everything that's happened," she said. "Don't you see? If we don't set up this third gizmo, we miss our chance. Waste the opportunity."

He stared at her; O'Malley couldn't quite read the look. Was it admiration or exasperation?

After a moment, he said, "We shouldn't set it up here. We have to put it somewhere else, where it won't be found."

She nodded. "I passed another spot a couple miles up the road. Not quite as good, because it's farther inland, but probably fine.

Dawtry retrieved the rig from the chopper and set it in the back of the SUV, then helped O'Malley hobble to the passenger seat. Then he got behind the wheel and reached for the key. "What the hell?"

"What?"

"The brake pedal—it goes all the way to the floor."

"Oh, I forgot to warn you about that. Iñigo sabotaged the brakes. You have to use the hand brake. And the transmission. Cut the ignition, if you have to stop on a dime."

He turned toward her. "You've been driving these mountain roads with no brakes?"

"Just for the last twenty miles." He stared, and she told him about her stop at the observatory and her encounter there with Iñigo, skipping over the part about their brief make-out session. "He tried to talk me out of poking around in this. I figured he just thought I was crazy, or a pain in the ass. Me and my big mouth—spilling the beans to one of the bad guys."

"Hey, look on the bright side," he said. "You got us a huge clue—and lived to tell the tale."

She flushed. His use of the word "us" gave her a rush of validation. First Boyd, now Dawtry: she was finally being taken seriously.

It took Dawtry a while to get the hang of using the hand brake instead of the pedal, but after a few nail-biting, careening turns, he mastered it. O'Malley guided him to a secluded ravine a few miles away, and with her calling instructions from the car, Dawtry placed the seismometer and powered it up. "It's alive," he said. "Transmitting data."

He hurried back to the car, and they shared a celebratory high five. She began writing an email to Boyd, to confirm that all three rigs were up and running, but halfway through the first line, she groaned. "Well, shoot."

"What's wrong?"

"My phone just died. I left the charger at the hotel this morning."

"I'll tell him," Dawtry said. He dictated an email, so she could hear the message, and hit "Send."

"So," she said. "*Now* what?"

He frowned. "It's complicated. We've got two vehicles. I have to return the helicopter before dark, but you're in no shape to drive. I guess we have to leave the car."

"We can't," she said. "Remember? We have to pretend we weren't here. I can drive."

"Bullshit," he said. "You can't even walk."

"I don't have to walk. All I have to do is put a little pressure on the gas pedal. And, hey, silver lining—I don't even have to step on the brake!" He shot her a dubious look. "Really," she insisted, "I'll be fine. If it'll make you feel better, you can tail me all the way back to Santa Cruz." Without warning, he pulled over and parked, although they were still a half mile from the helicopter. "Why are you stopping here?" she asked.

"Prove it," he said. "Show me you're able to drive."

"God, you're as stubborn as I am," she muttered. "Okay, I'll show you."

He got out and came around to her door, then helped her limp to the driver's side and get in.

She drove slowly, wincing whenever they came to an upgrade that required pressure on the gas pedal, but when she stopped beside the helicopter and shot him a challenging look, he shrugged. "Okay, you pass," he said. "I wouldn't send you on a trip across the US, but you only need to make it back to Santa Cruz, which is pretty close."

"Want me to pick you up at the airport?"

"Sure," he said, but then he shook his head. "On second thought, maybe that's not such a great idea."

"How come?"

"Might be better if we meet up someplace touristy, so we blend in." She gave him a quizzical look. "Like I said, we don't know who the other bad guys are, or where. And so far, there's nothing here that connects you to me." O'Malley glanced toward the precipice where she had fought with Iñigo. Dawtry followed her gaze and grimaced. "Well, nothing they know about yet. Keeping quiet about it buys us a little time."

She turned back toward him. "So is this goodbye? You fly off into the sunset, and I never see you again?"

He snorted. "Are you kidding? Somebody has to keep a close eye on you."

"But didn't you just say we shouldn't be seen together?"

"I didn't say we shouldn't be seen together. I just said you shouldn't fetch me from the airport." He looked thoughtful for a moment; then a slow smile spread across his face. "I'm here as a tourist. No reason I couldn't go to some touristy restaurant and strike up a conversation with a good-looking fellow tourist."

She nodded slowly. "There's a Cuban place, Habana, in the center of town. Looks touristy. Maybe even fun."

"See you there. Act like you don't know me."

She narrowed her eyes but grinned, too. "You're sneaky. Probably a good quality in a spy."

"I'm not a spy," he said. "I'm a federal agent. Or a former federal agent. Who just happens to be doing clandestine stuff. In a foreign country."

"Like I said. A spy."

He shrugged and gave a nod that might have been a slight bow. "As you wish."

CHAPTER 14

Again, O'Malley scanned the people crowding the bar at Habana. Again, she failed to spot Dawtry, and her anxiety ratcheted up another notch. Had something gone wrong? Several times on her zigzag trip back to Santa Cruz, she had glanced up and seen the helicopter. Mostly, it had meandered just off the coast, with occasional detours inland, up this or that dizzying ravine. When O'Malley had turned off the coast highway and entered the labyrinthine streets of Santa Cruz, the chopper had leveled off and made a beeline for the airport.

But that had been nearly an hour ago, she saw when she checked her watch for the umpteenth time. The airport was close—five miles? ten, tops—so it shouldn't have taken an hour to land, turn in the keys (*do helicopters have keys?*), and catch a cab back to town.

Had he crashed? *Oh God, please not,* she thought; then she shook her head at her obsessiveness and foolishness. From what little she'd seen, he was a damned good pilot—could every FBI agent fly a helicopter? Was that part of the training? She wished she'd been able to hitch a ride back to town with him, riding shotgun five hundred feet above the spectacular scenery, instead of creeping along the asphalt, juggling the gearshift, the hand brake, and the infernal gas pedal, which sparked a volley of pained profanity every time she pressed it.

By now she was feeling better. A quick change of clothes at the hotel had helped reboot her mood, the ibuprofen was easing the pain, and the mojito—her second—was helping her not give a particular shit about the ache anymore, anyhow. "Buy you another?" murmured an unfamiliar voice in her ear. O'Malley jumped. She swiveled and saw a florid, beefy-faced fellow—a Brit? Australian?—leering at her. "Uh, no, thank you," she said, and turned back toward the bar.

"Fancy a bit of convo?" She shook her head, but he wedged himself into the infinitesimal gap between her and the next patron. She felt something pressing against her side, and she glanced down and was horrified to see that it was the man's belly.

O'Malley held up a hand. "No, really. I'm not looking for company."

"But you found some anyway, didn't you, love?" The man laughed— a bleary, beery laugh—and she realized that he was drunk in addition to being rude and revolting. "If you want to win friends and influence people, there's nothing like a firm bum in tight white jeans."

O'Malley felt jostled by more contact, then felt a squeeze, and she realized that the man had put his hand on her. He was touching—no, *squeezing*—her ass! *"Hey,"* she yelled, winding up to slap the shit out of him.

Strong fingers suddenly caught her wrist, holding her arm. *"Honey,"* she heard Dawtry call over the din. "So sorry to keep you waiting. I thought I'd never find a parking place." Still holding her right wrist, he wrapped his other arm around her left shoulder in an affection- ate and casually possessive gesture, then leaned forward and kissed the back of her head. "Hello, mate," he said to O'Malley's unwanted suitor. "Thanks for watching out for the wife. Can I buy you—" But Dawtry's offer was choked off by his sudden fit of coughing—racking, consump- tive coughs, which nearly doubled him over. He lurched sideways, put one hand on O'Malley's back, and reached with his other hand for the drunken Brit's shoulder to steady himself. "Sorry," he wheezed, then launched into another coughing fit. "Coming down—*rrrhhhnnn*—with some damned bug. Screw those mosquitoes, right, mate?" He set about snorting and clearing his throat with such force that O'Malley half expected him to hock an oyster onto the bar.

The beefy man stared. He seemed to be contemplating taking a swing at Dawtry, but another round of wheezing seemed to settle the matter. The Brit slouched away, crimson-faced, muttering words that sounded like "bloody Yanks" and "quarantine." Dawtry coughed a few more times, driving another person from the bar, then straightened up and turned to O'Malley. "You okay?"

She stared. "*I'm* fine. But you? You sound like you're dying."

He winked. "I'm not dead yet," he said in a broad British accent.

"What?"

"I said, 'I'm not dead yet.' It's crowded and loud in here—we should go someplace quiet, where we can hear each other."

"I heard you," she shouted. "But, mister, you got some 'splainin' to do."

He leaned closer to her, so he could speak in a normal tone. "I just didn't want you to start a bar brawl," he said. "We're blending in, remember?"

"I don't mean 'splainin' about keeping the peace," she said. "I mean 'splainin' about the quotes."

"What quotes?"

"The movie quotes. A while ago, you said, 'As you wish' and 'I don't think that word means what you think it means.' Dialogue from *The Princess Bride*. Just now you said, 'I'm not dead yet.' *Monty Python and the Holy Grail*. So start 'splainin'. Have you been stickin' your nose in my DVD drawers?" Was it her imagination, or was she starting to slur her words—and were those words veering toward inappropriate innuendo?

He laughed. "Those were my big brother's favorite movies. Those, and that Christmas movie about the kid who wants the BB gun."

She slapped Dawtry playfully on the chest. "You'll shoot your eye out, kid!" His chest felt solid, and she felt a powerful urge to thump it again. *Shit, O'Malley, you're looped,* she thought. *Two mojitos on an empty stomach. Poor planning.*

He leaned back and seemed to study her face. Could he tell she was wasted? Apparently, because he said, "Let's go get some food." He flagged down the bartender and gave the man a twenty-euro note, gesturing at O'Malley's empty glasses. The man nodded and half-heartedly offered to bring change, but Dawtry waved off the offer. "Can you walk?" he asked O'Malley.

"I'm not actuarially looped," she protested.

"Actuarially?"

"I'm not," she insisted, her voice indignant.

"I was asking about your ankle," he said, "not impugning your sobriety."

"Impugning? *Impugning?* Ooh-la-lah, Agent Fancy-Pants." She made a swishy, flipping motion with her hand. "Say, cowboy, do they teach you those big vo-*caballero* words at the FBI Academy?" She leaned close and added, in a confiding murmur, "I can walk just fine. I brought an umbrero from the hotel. It keeps off the rain, but works like a cane." She giggled. "Oooh, I made a rhyme! I'm a poet, but you didn't know it."

"I still don't," he said drily. "Where is this camouflaged crutch?"

"This what?"

"The umbrero—where is it?"

"I don't know," she said. "*But* I do know that my favorite color is blue. And I know that to maintain airspeed velocity, a swallow has to flap its wings forty-three times a second."

"African or European swallow?" She blinked, but before she could answer, he added, "Truly, you have a dizzying intellect."

God, he's smart, she thought dizzily.

CHAPTER 15

Dawtry spotted the umbrella—the "umbrero"—leaning against the wall just inside the doorway, but he shepherded O'Malley outside without pausing to snag it. For one thing, he had his hands full with her; the weak ankle and the strong cocktails had undermined her ability to ambulate, and Dawtry couldn't handle anything extra. For another, there was the risk that she would insist on carrying the umbrella herself, and he could envision all sorts of problems with that scenario, including (but not limited to) her inadvertent skewering of some unlucky passerby's eyeball. *You'll skewer an eye out, kid,* he thought.

Directly across from Habana, Dawtry noticed another restaurant, La Placeta. It had a cluster of outdoor tables, as well as indoor dining on two levels. It was close and easy, but it looked fancy—the customers appeared affluent, and therefore unlikely to take kindly to a couple that included a slightly wasted woman. Besides, he reasoned, a walk might help O'Malley sober up.

"Where's your car?" he asked O'Malley.

"At the airport."

"The *airport*? Why did you park at the airport?"

"So I could get on a plane, silly. Can't *drive* here from Baltimore. We're on an island."

Dawtry closed his eyes briefly and prayed for patience. "Not your own car, Megan. The rental car, here in La Palma. The SUV with the bad brakes and busted mirror. I flew the helicopter back to the airport, and—"

"I *saw* you," she said, nodding. "You're an amazing pilot. Is that what makes you a special agent?"

He smiled in spite of himself. "No. Only extra special agents can fly." Her eyes widened. "I'm kidding. I learned to fly in the army. I was a helicopter instructor for a while, until I decided to join the Bureau."

"So you're a G-Man *and* a GI. What else?"

"That's about it. Anyhow, we need to find your car. Your rental car—that white SUV."

"That white SUV—what a piece of shit," she said. "The damn brakes don't even work."

He laughed. "Yeah, it's a total piece of shit. But where did you *park* the piece of shit, Megan? Somewhere near the restaurant?"

"What restaurant?"

He pointed over his shoulder. "This one. Habana. Where you had the swell mojitos."

"The mojitos *were* swell," she agreed. "But the clientele sucked. Some guy actually grabbed my ass in there, can you believe it?"

Why, yes, Dawtry thought, but instead said, "Inconceivable," shaking his head. "So, the piece-of-shit rental car, Megan. Where did you park it?"

"Oh, that. I got really lucky. I found a parking place *right by* the hotel. It was a pain in the ass to get into, though—I had to back into it. Uphill. With a stick, and a clutch, and no brakes. Did I tell you I've got no brakes? None."

"You did. That rental car of yours is a piece of shit."

"A *total* piece of shit! Don't get me started. The gas pedal? It's almost as bad as the brakes. The gas pedal is an implement of torture.

Implement? Instrument? Point is, it hurts like a son of a bitch to press on the gas pedal."

"I had a rental car like that once," he said. "Hey, do you remember where the parking place is? Or the hotel?"

"Sure. That way." She pointed to the right. "It gets kinda mazy, though. I always get a little turned around. Virgin Something-or-other Street."

Great, Dawtry thought. *That really narrows it down, in a Catholic country.* "How about the hotel, Megan—what's the name of the hotel?"

"San Something-or-other," she said. "They name everything after saints and virgins. This place is lousy with saints and virgins." She stopped suddenly, jerking his arm to make him stop, too. "Did you know, by the way, that Saint Anthony is the patron saint of *lost* shit?"

"Uh, no, I don't think I did."

"It's true. Now *that's* a useful saint, 'cause I'm always losing my shit. Literarily *and* metamorphically." She laughed. "Ha—I even lost my faith. But I don't think even Saint Ant'ny can find that for me."

"Mmm," Dawtry grunted. He had taken out his phone and opened a map of Santa Cruz. Their location showed as a blue dot—a comfortingly familiar anchor, given the uncertainty swirling around them. He typed in "Hotel San" and hit "Search," not expecting much. To his surprise and relief, the map showed him a Hotel San Telmo—quite nearby, and just off a street whose name—Virgen de la Luz—seemed to translate as "Virgin of Light."

"San Telmo?" he asked.

"No, Ant'ny," she said. "I'm talking about Saint Ant'ny. You don't pay very good attention for a super-duper FBI guy."

"I mean your hotel, Megan. Are you staying in the Hotel San Telmo?"

"I told you that already," she said. "You're not listening."

"Sorry," he said. He pointed to the right, in the direction that both the map and O'Malley had indicated. "So, let's head toward the hotel and look for a good place to eat."

"Wow," she told him, "that was tasty. What an amazing find."

He smiled and nodded, pleased that she liked it as much as he did. *Good finding, Dawtry,* he told himself. *You're a regular Saint Anthony.*

From the Cuban place, they had made their way, slowly and unsteadily, toward O'Malley's hotel. The route had initially taken them along a pedestrian street, filled with tourists and expensive shops. After several blocks, though, the map steered them uphill, away from the crowds. They had passed her rental car, tucked into a tight spot on a narrow, hilly street—she *had* done a good job of parking, Dawtry saw—and crossed a charming square. The square was fronted by a school, some of whose students, perhaps—boys aged eight or ten—practiced skateboard tricks, their parents chatting in clumps on the school's steps. The streets here were nearly empty, and the conversations were all in Spanish. At the far side of the square, O'Malley had pointed at a stylish restaurant that had tables on the square—Cinnamon Bar, it was called, and a quick phone search told Dawtry that it got good reviews. Approaching, however, they'd been engulfed in cigarette smoke, and they'd turned away, grimacing and disappointed. It was then that Dawtry had spotted another place—this place—directly across the street. The sign proclaimed it to be a pizzeria, and the inside was tiny and uninspiring, but the patio—half-hidden to one side, screened by a wall of lush planters—turned out to be charming, with two quiet couples and one chattering family dining beneath fairy lights.

"Yes, tasty indeed," he agreed, raising his glass—they were both drinking sparkling water—and clinking it against hers. Happily, the pizzeria's menu had proved to be far more diverse than the name had suggested. O'Malley was finishing off a plate of cannelloni, smooth but tangy, judging from the bite she had shared with him. For his part, Dawtry had polished off a platter of seafood paella, and he'd never tasted better, with the *possible* exception of the black squid ink paella at Jaleo, a DC tapas restaurant a few blocks from the FBI building.

Dawtry watched as she used a hunk of bread to mop the last of the sauce from her plate. The food, the walk, and the passage of an hour appeared to have sobered her up completely. That was good, as they both needed to be clearheaded. "So, Megan," he began, then paused. Her name sounded oddly out of place now, as he set down his fork and took up his profession. "First off, I'm sorry nobody took you seriously at first."

She smiled slightly—a wry, sad smile, it struck him—and shook her head. "Doesn't matter. It does sound crazy. The only one that stings is David, my seismologist ex. I really hoped Dave would believe me." She grimaced. "David used to say that my tombstone will read, 'Couldn't stop picking at it.' Anyhow, what matters is you believed me—you came through for me—when I needed you."

He grunted. "Better late than never, I guess. So, can we try to rewind? Can you back up, tell me how it all started? And how we got to"—he looked around, as if reminding himself where he was, and shrugged—"*here?*"

And so she did.

Dawtry interrupted her story often, mainly to drill down into details, but partly to prolong the pleasure of the conversation as well.

He excused himself from the table twice: once to go to the bathroom, once to send a terse memo to his boss.

> Have found O'Malley, just in time to keep her from being shot. Assailant now dead. He confirmed to O'M that plot is serious. Prof. Charles Boyd, in London confirms that global seismographic

network (GSN) is being hacked to conceal plot. Boyd is now receiving genuine data from seismometers O'M has installed here. Suggest you follow up with Boyd to confirm and get latest info. Also suggest looping in CIA, if they haven't stopped taking our calls. Maybe British intelligence, too, since Boyd's a Brit. National security and millions of lives at stake. A clear and present danger.

Dawtry added Boyd's email address and phone number at the bottom of the message before hitting "Send."

Both times he left the table, Dawtry took the precaution of stepping into the street and scanning both directions, as well as peering over the edge of the patio and checking the street below—Virgin of Light—which ran parallel to San Telmo. No one seemed to be looking for them, at least not yet, but he knew that whatever head start they had gained by not reporting Iñigo's death was bound to evaporate. *Later, please,* he prayed, *not sooner.*

O'Malley had hesitated whenever she mentioned Iñigo, and Dawtry sensed that she was uneasy. Initially he attributed her discomfort to the strong emotions stirred up by the man's attempt to kill her, or by the distress of seeing him fall to his death. Gradually, though, a realization dawned: *She's embarrassed about something.* His FBI training told him to bear down, to confront or coerce her into revealing whatever it was she was withholding. But another voice—the same voice that had finally sent him looking for her at Johns Hopkins—told him to trust her, to give her space and time around whatever it was she was reluctant to disclose.

"I knew something wasn't right," she was saying, "but he kept reassuring me. Downplaying my worries. Teasing me." She looked away, chewing her lower lip, then turned back and looked Dawtry frankly in the eyes. "I let him distract me," she said. Even by the faint glow from the table's candle and the overhead fairy lights, he could see her flush. "He made a pass at me, and I . . . I fell for it. What a chump, right? I let him play me like a fish."

Dawtry half frowned, inclining his head to one side. "Easy to see it that way in hindsight," he said. "But at the time? How were you to know? Are you supposed to be suspicious of every guy who finds you attractive?" He opened his mouth to continue, then closed it and felt himself turn crimson. "No judgment here, Megan. I think you've been perceptive, persistent, and very, very brave. I admire the hell out of you."

She drew back, staring, as if surprised by his words or uncertain of his sincerity. She looked away once more, and when she faced him again, he saw tears rolling down her cheeks. "Do you mean that?" Dawtry started to smile, but the smile froze when she added, "Or are you just playing me, too?"

He blinked, surprised and stung by the implied accusation. "*What?* Oh, wait, I see. 'Fool me once, shame on you; fool me twice, shame on me'?" She neither confirmed nor denied his analysis. "Fair enough. But, no, I'm not playing you, Megan."

"Then I'm sorry," she said. "And thank you."

"It's okay. And you're welcome." But still it stung; when he'd finally pulled the plug on his two-year relationship with Gina—a woman he'd really liked but not truly loved—she'd accused him of playing her, so O'Malley's echoing of it touched a nerve. "It's late," he said, scanning the now-empty patio, "and you must be exhausted. You should get some sleep. First thing in the morning, we've got to get you out of here."

"But my flight's not till Thursday."

He snorted. "Jesus, Megan. Everything's changed. Whoever Iñigo was working with has got to be looking for him. For you, too." He told her about the break-in at her apartment, but when he saw her alarmed expression, he decided not to mention the two men who had inquired about her at the hotel. "Besides," he added gently, "the seismometers are up and running. We're done—you did it. So let's get while the getting's good."

Halfway down the third flight of stairs, Dawtry muttered, "Sheesh, where did they put you, O'Malley—in the wine cellar? The bomb shelter? The catacombs?"

"I was lucky to get anything," she said. "They book up months in advance. Only reason I got it was because they had a cancellation."

"Hmm," he grunted as he fumbled for a light switch in the hallway. "You sure the *hotel* isn't playing you?" He was taking a risk with the joke, he knew, but O'Malley had shown herself to be smart and funny, with a strong streak of self-irony.

"Smart-ass," she said, but her tone sounded amused and approving. *Whew,* he thought.

She put her key in the lock and twisted, but before she could open the door, Dawtry held up a hand, then pointed to himself. "Me first," he mouthed.

"Where's your gun?" she mouthed back, pantomiming a pistol and a quizzical expression.

"DC," he mouthed, but her lipreading wasn't up to the challenge. "DC," he whispered. "Not allowed on international flights." He pushed her aside gently.

Then his gentleness ended. Dawtry kicked open the door with enough force to shake the wall, enough force to stun anyone lurking behind it, enough force to dent the steel and bruise his heel. Reaching inside the room, he felt for the light, switched it on, and bobbed his head into the doorway and swiftly back out again. Having glimpsed no one, he risked a longer look, and, satisfied that he was not about to be shot, he stepped into the room, motioning for O'Malley to wait in the hallway.

Methodically, he cleared the room, lifting the lid on an immense blanket chest (*Room for two,* he thought, relieved to find it empty), peering under the bed (many dust bunnies, one crusty earplug), opening and closing the floor-length drapes, inspecting the interior of the wardrobe. Next, he checked the bathroom, where his laserlike gaze was drawn, briefly but appreciatively, to a lace thong dangling from the showerhead. He did not linger but hurried back to the doorway and motioned her inside, hoping that his face looked cool, professional, and not nearly as red as it suddenly felt.

He closed and bolted the door behind her, then nodded at the laptop perched on the small desk. "You want to see how soon we can blow this pop stand?"

"Okay. Sure." She flipped up the screen, and the Apple logo glowed in the lid and the display lit up. Using the track pad, she moved the cursor and clicked. Dawtry came closer and stood behind her, watching over her shoulder as she scrolled down a page. "Earliest is at eight."

"Eight? That sucks."

"Would you prefer ten?"

"No," he said, "I'd prefer six, but what I'd like most is midnight tonight."

"Toto, we're not in Kansas anymore," she said.

"Obviously. Okay, if eight's the best we can do, let's do it. Can you change your ticket online?"

"I don't know. Let me look."

"Here," he said, reaching over her shoulder and tapping the screen. "Change Flight."

"Hey," she squawked, "it's not a touch screen. Look, you left a fingerprint."

"Look on the bright side. You can get the cops to run it—make sure I'm who I say I am."

She swatted his arm. "So. Not. Funny." She clicked on the now-smudged link, then signed on, typing her name and a ticket number.

"You know your ticket number by heart?" Dawtry was amazed and also appalled—it seemed a waste of good brain space.

"I'm good with numbers," she said. "Besides, that one's easy—it's the first seven prime numbers, in order."

He leaned closer and studied the sequence: 1357111317, which, indeed, could be read as 1, 3, 5, 7, 11, 13, 17. "I'll be damned," he said. "You're right."

"Thanks for the validation." She highlighted the 8:00 a.m. departure and clicked "Select this flight." After a moment, a message appeared on the screen. "Unable to complete your request online," it read. "Shit," said O'Malley. "Want me to try the ten o'clock?"

Dawtry spun through several possible scenarios, and he didn't like most of them. Maybe there was simply a glitch in the online booking system, but maybe there were no seats available. Or, worse, maybe O'Malley was on a watch list. *Christ, is the local government in on this?* "Nah, never mind for now," he said, as casually as he could. "The flight's only nine hours from now. Such short notice, we probably have to change it in person, at the airport. Let's just get up early so we've got plenty of time."

She shrugged. "That's fine. I don't have much packing to do."

Dawtry couldn't help thinking of the thong dangling from the showerhead. *You could pack that in your pocket,* he thought. *With room to spare.* But discretion being the better part of valor, he simply said, "That's handy."

She turned in the chair. "What about you?"

"What about me?"

"How long will it take you to get ready?"

"I'm ready now." He extended his arms, as if presenting himself for inspection.

"But what about your clothes?"

"I'm wearing 'em."

"I mean the rest of them. The stuff in your room."

"What room?"

Her eyes narrowed. "Wait. Are you telling me that you came here—across the ocean—with no place to stay and only the clothes on your back?"

"I was in a hurry," he said. "If I'd gone home to pack, I would've missed the last flight of the night—and you would've missed, oh, I don't know, the rest of your *life*." Her eyes widened. "As it was, they had to hold the plane at the gate for twenty minutes. Man, *everybody* on board was giving me the stink eye."

"No kidding?"

"No kidding. They were pissed."

"No, I mean the plane—they actually held the plane for you?"

He shrugged, then grinned. "National security hath its privileges." He hesitated. "So," he finally said, "I guess we'd better get some rest."

He could see the wheels turning behind her eyes. "Okay. Sure. Where will you . . . go?"

"I'm not going anywhere."

"Excuse me?"

"Megan. I came here to protect you. To bring you home safe. One person already tried to kill you today. I can't leave you alone."

"But . . ." Her eyes scanned the room. "I'm really not comfortable with this."

"*You're* not comfortable? I'm the one who'll be sleeping on the floor." He slid his lower jaw to one side, pressed the tip of his tongue into the pit of an upper molar—a stress response he seemed to have first developed the day of the New York City Marathon. "You still think I'm playing you, O'Malley? Take it up with my boss. If he hasn't already fired me, he'll be glad to have one more reason to." Dawtry rooted in his pocket, extricated his phone, and jabbed at the keys. "Shit," he said. "I've had better signal in a submarine than I do down here. Do *you* have signal?"

"Let me check." She fished out her phone and frowned. "I forgot. It's dead."

"Great," he said. He heaved a sigh. "Okay, let's go."

"Go where?"

He headed toward the door. "Upstairs. Outside. Someplace where my phone'll work. So I can call. And you can talk to my boss."

"You're limping."

"What?" He turned toward her, self-conscious, careful of his posture.

"You hurt your foot kicking the door. You're limping."

"No, I'm not," he said, reverting to his Monty Python accent. "It's only a flesh wound."

Apparently, movie dialogue was the key to her heart, or at least the key to her trust. Her face, which had turned stony when the subject of sleeping arrangements came up, relaxed and opened. She smiled and shook her head. "Hell," she said. "Never mind. If I can't trust you, there's nobody left to trust." She plugged her phone into a charger on the desk. "Besides, if we leave the room, you'll have to kick the door again when we come back, right?"

"I will," he said cheerfully. "It's what I do. I kick doors. Back at headquarters? Everybody calls me Door-Kicker Chip."

"Well, Door-Kicker, one more kick like the last one, and we'll have no hope of outrunning the bad guys, 'cause neither one of us will be able to walk."

"Did I mention I'm a hell of a crawler? I hold the all-time FBI record for the hundred-meter crawl. Twenty-nine point three seconds."

She snorted. "Stop, already. I'm trying to trust you, but the pathological lies don't make it easy."

"Oops. Bad strategy on my part, I now see." Dawtry reached toward the desk and plucked a coin—a two-euro piece—from a saucer where O'Malley had dumped her pocket change the night before. "I like these," he said. "The two-color effect? It's like a penny wrapped in a quarter, inside a nickel." He flipped the coin, caught it, and slapped it onto the desktop. "Call it."

She narrowed her eyes at him. "I need to know what I'm calling it for. What do I stand to win?"

He raised his eyebrows appreciatively. "*No Country for Old Men*— good job." For a nerdy scientist, she knew a lot of movie lines. "You stand to win everything. Now call it."

She lifted her chin, slightly but defiantly. "Heads."

He uncovered the coin slowly. "Well done," he said. "You get the mattress. I'll take the floor."

An hour later, another sigh wafted down toward the floor, accompanied by the militant rustle of sheets and blankets and shifting pillows. "Hey," she said softly. "Are you awake?"

"Of course I'm awake. Who could sleep through all that racket you're making up there?"

"Sorry," she said. "I thought maybe you were. You've been so still and quiet. You haven't moved once."

"Not much point in thrashing on a tile floor. It's already as comfortable as it's ever gonna get."

"This is stupid," she said. "You might as well get in the bed."

"No, no—I'm fine down here." He paused. "I have friends who'll argue the merits of carpet or linoleum or hardwood. But me? I'm a tile man from way back."

"Oh good grief," she said. "Just come on. If you were going to ravish me, you'd have done it already."

"You're a quick study, Megan; I don't care what anybody says."

"Shut up and get off the floor before I change my mind." He hauled himself up and sat on the edge of the bed. "But don't get any ideas."

"What kind of ideas?"

"You know very well what kind of ideas."

He did, but he knew better than to go down that road. "I'm on duty here. No hanky-panky while on duty. FBI regs."

"Seriously?"

"Absolutely. Section 438, Part 17, Subsection B-3."

"Bullshitter."

"Okay, it might not be in B-3. It might be A-9. But no hanky-panky. We can hang a blanket from the ceiling, if it'll ease your mind. Like Clark Gable did to protect Claudette Colbert's virtue in that old road-trip comedy. I forget the name. She was a rich runaway bride. He was a tabloid journalist chasing a story."

"Inconceivable," she said. "*It Happened One Night*. He called the blanket 'the walls of Jericho.' I need you to tell me the truth. You aren't really a federal agent, are you? You're a movie critic."

"Actuarially speaking," he said, "I *am* a federal agent. You show me your telescope, I'll show you my badge."

"Stop."

"Yes, ma'am." He smoothed the covers and stretched out on top of them, at the edge of the mattress, several respectful inches away from her. "Good night, ma'am."

"Good night, John Boy."

A sleepless hour later, he heard her turn toward him.

"Chip?"

"Yes, miss?"

"Are you awake?"

"No, miss. I talk in my sleep. Done it my whole life. Gets me into trouble sometimes."

"Chip?"

"Yes, miss?"

"Where are your people?"

"Well," he said slowly, "most of them are back at headquarters, trying to figure out what's going on and who's behind it. Some are headed this way, though. I hope."

"Oh. Oh my. Well, that's good to hear." She was silent for a moment, but only a moment. "Chip?"

"Still right here, miss," he said. "Ain't much of any place else I could be." If she caught the *African Queen* reference, she didn't let on, and he felt irrationally disappointed by that.

"I didn't mean your colleagues. I meant your family."

"Ah. My mistake." His eyes scanned the ceiling, as if it might be etched with a map and a family tree. "My parents live in Charleston. I've got a sister in Savannah. Two nephews in New York." He hesitated.

"Didn't you say you have an older brother, too?"

"Had. I had an older brother. In New York. He, uh . . . he died when the North Tower came down on 9/11."

He heard a soft gasp and felt her hand on his arm. "My God, I'm so sorry."

"Yeah. Me, too. They say . . ." He stopped, took a deep breath, blew it out. "They say he helped a lot of other people get out. He went back to look for stragglers, and then . . . He's the reason I do what I do. He's the reason I got out of the army and went into counterterrorism. He's the reason I took you seriously."

"Thank you." She squeezed his arm. She hesitated. "Anybody else? A wife? Girlfriend? Boyfriend?" She felt herself blushing at the nosy question.

He shook his head. "No, no, and no. I've had a couple close calls with marriage—one woman wanted me more than I wanted her, the other wanted me less than I wanted her—but nobody at the moment."

She nodded, unreasonably relieved at this information. "Have you told your parents and sisters to get out? To go somewhere? You know, just in case the tsunami really does happen?"

"I can't, Megan."

She sat up and turned toward him, sitting cross-legged. She was wearing only a T-shirt, and he was grateful that her legs remained discreetly under the covers. "Why not?"

"I'd be disclosing national-security information."

"But *I* know, and *I* don't have a security clearance."

"Yeah, that's why we'll have to reprogram your memory when we get back to the States."

"I'm serious. You wouldn't have to tell them why. Just tell them to go somewhere."

"Oh, right. 'Hi, Mom. Hi, Sis. I've been thinking—y'all need a vacation. Right now. In the Rockies. Until I decide you've relaxed enough.' Something like that?"

"You wouldn't have to be that obvious about it."

"You don't know my family," he said. "Takes a two-by-four upside the head to get their attention. We don't do subtle." He waited a beat. "What about you? Where are *your* people?"

She didn't answer.

"Megan?"

"I don't have any people," she said.

"Come on, everybody has people."

"My parents were killed by a drunk driver when I was twelve. I spent my adolescence in foster homes."

"Ah. I'm sorry."

"Yeah, it sucked. Still does. I was an only child, and I don't *have* a child. I do have an ex-husband, which I guess counts for something, but he's on the West Coast, so I don't need to worry about him. So in this context, at least, I have no people."

"Sorry," he said. "I didn't mean to . . . I just was wondering who you might be worrying about."

"You mean besides the fifty million people who might be killed by this thing?"

"Yeah, besides them. One death is a tragedy; fifty million is a statistic. Who said that? Hitler?"

"Stalin," she said. "The twentieth century's other great humanitarian." He saw her turn toward the window, but the light was too faint to read her features. "Grace," she said.

"Excuse me?"

"My friend Grace," she said, still looking away. "She's my people. My best friend. Gracie lives in Rehoboth Beach. She's a teacher. A poet. She and her husband tried for ten years to get pregnant. Did the whole science-project thing—five rounds of IVF. Nothing. Finally, they gave up. Six months later, *bam*—she got pregnant. Her baby's due in three weeks." He heard her swallow. "They live in this little bungalow they restored. Three blocks off the beach. According to Boyd's modeling, the wave would be twenty-six meters high when it hit Rehoboth Beach. Eighty feet." She swiveled toward him. "There. Does that count—does Gracie count—as a tragedy?"

"Yes. Of course she does."

"There's also Herman, in Baltimore. The guy who got me excited about astronomy. If the wave hit on a clear evening, he'd be down at the harbor, showing people Saturn or Venus or Jupiter through his telescope. Just sharing his love of the night sky." He heard her draw a deep, ragged breath. "I'm scared, Chip."

"I know. You'd be crazy not to be."

"Are you scared?"

"It's against the regs," he said. "And hell, yeah, I'm scared. Scared shitless." He hesitated. "My sister has two kids. A boy and a girl. I'm . . ." He had to clear his throat. "I'm their . . . uh . . . godfather."

He felt her hand tracing his arm, felt her fingers entwine with his. Then he felt her unfold and stretch out beside him, press against him, her head on his shoulder, her other hand on his chest.

Don't move, he thought. Was the thought directed at himself or at her? After a moment he realized that he was holding his breath. *Breathe, dumb-ass,* he instructed himself. He forced himself to take slow, steady breaths, even though he had started slipping into oxygen debt. Little by little, breath by breath, he made up the debt, his chest rising and falling evenly. He had synched his breathing with hers, he realized, although he hadn't done it on purpose. Once he noticed it, he liked it, and if she minded, she didn't say so.

In fact, to his astonishment, she seemed to be falling asleep. She twitched, the way a napping dog sometimes does—the way Daisy, his golden retriever, had done when Dawtry was a kid—and he smiled in the darkness. Another twitch, and she began to snore: soft snores, dainty snores, which almost made him laugh out loud. And then she shifted, burrowing against him, wrapping herself around him as if he were one of those oversize body pillows. *God help me,* Dawtry thought, careful not to move so much as a nanometer.

He suspected it was going to be a long, sleepless night, and he wished he could use his phone—the Android chess app was surprisingly good, and he was halfway through a hard-fought match with Benny and long overdue in making his next move. But for a variety of reasons, he didn't want to risk awakening O'Malley. For one thing, it had been a long time—too long—since he'd shared a bed, even chastely, with a woman, *any* woman, let alone one so smart, strong, sassy, fearless, and, frankly, sexy. There was another, more practical reason not to use his phone: even though he'd bought three spare PowerCores—external battery chargers—at the DC airport, he didn't know how long he'd be here. No, best to lie still and conserve power.

She was no longer snoring. Now, her sleep sounds were more sporadic, more random, more vulnerable, somehow, and they reminded him of his sister's children—his niece and nephew—when they were babies. She sighed. She made a faint cooing sound. She murmured a few garbled syllables into his chest.

A half-remembered poem from college found its way into Dawtry's head somehow. It was by the Irish poet Yeats, one of his favorites, and he worked to retrieve it from his memory's deep storage. Word by word, line by line, he gradually reconstructed the poem's first two stanzas. When he felt confident of them, he recited the words aloud, or, rather, a-quiet: whispering the lines like some protective spell or intercessory prayer, one that might extend to his distant niece and nephew, yes, but might somehow shield this remarkable woman breathing upon his chest as well:

> Once more the storm is howling, and half-hid
> Under this cradle-hood and coverlid
> My child sleeps on . . .

It was only when he reached the last line of the passage—as the words left his lips—that he was struck by the relevance of the final phrase. Stunned, he repeated it: "Out of the murderous innocence of the sea."

He must have said it louder the second time, because O'Malley stirred against him. "Hmm?" she murmured drowsily.

"Sshh," he soothed. "Sshh."

Three hours later, he woke with a start, his alarm chiming. He made his usual move to sit up, but he found himself hampered by something. Hampered by . . . a *woman* sprawled across his chest. Her arm encircled his neck, and a bare, muscled thigh angled across his stomach. *Holy cow,* he thought, and set about untangling himself. But where to begin? The arm would be easier to remove, he reckoned . . . but what if she slept through that maneuver, only to awaken with his hand on her thigh? *Danger, Will Robinson,* he heard a robotic inner voice warning him. Awkward, but perhaps safest, to wake her without moving her.

"Uh . . . Megan?" No response. "Hey, Megan. Time to get up." Still no response. *A good sleeper,* he thought approvingly—the woman he'd lived with once had been a restless, thrashy bedmate—but at the moment, O'Malley's comatose state was a problem. He could shout into her ear, of course, but that struck him as wrong, rude, and frightening. There would be time aplenty for fear soon, he suspected.

Dawtry's right arm lay just outside the arc of her embrace. Slowly he raised it, crooking his elbow. With exquisite care—*These things must be done del-i-cately,* he silently coached himself in a Wicked Witch of the West voice—he eased his index finger toward her head, then grazed the edge of her ear lightly. She twitched slightly, and he smiled, reminded of summer-camp shenanigans of a similar nature, although those generally involved filling the unsuspecting sleeper's hand with shaving cream or worse things before starting to tickle. He brushed her ear again, and again she twitched—harder this time—and reached up to scratch her ear, her hand almost colliding with his as he pulled it away. *Do I dare, and do I dare?* he wondered. *I do, I do. Third time's a charm.* This time, instead of the top of the ear, he touched the downy hairs just in front of it, wiggling his finger slightly. This time her whole body jerked, and Dawtry barely managed to return his arm to his side before she raised her head off his chest.

Dawtry feigned sleep. "Sweet *Jesus,* O'Malley," he heard her whisper, then felt her easing away from him—the arm from around his neck, the leg from across his belly—as slowly and surreptitiously as he had conducted the wake-up maneuver. Dawtry's alarm was still chiming, and he suspected he couldn't play possum much longer. But before he could "awaken," she got out of bed, fumbled with his phone, and silenced the alarm. Then he heard the bathroom door close, and he realized she might appreciate a minute more of privacy.

Soon the toilet flushed, the bathroom door opened with an exaggerated rattle of the knob, and O'Malley said, "Hey. Sleeping Beauty."

He grunted and shifted—*stirred but not shaken,* he thought with an inward smile—but did not yet open his eyes.

"*Yo,*" she said, louder. "*Hola. Buenos días, señor. Bonjour, monsieur. Guten Morgen, mein Herr—Achtung!*" With that, she poked him in the ribs.

He jerked. "Huh?" He stared wildly around, then sat up. "I'm awake, I'm awake. What's happening?"

"Some watchdog," she said. "Is sleeping your superpower?"

He rubbed his face briskly with both hands. "One of them. Wow— what time is it? I guess I forgot to set my alarm."

"No, you didn't. I turned it off, since you didn't show any inclination to."

"Ah. Thanks." He sat up, excused himself, and stepped into the bathroom. When he emerged, perhaps three minutes later, he was toweling his hair. O'Malley sniffed the air. "Did you just take the world's fastest shower?"

"Third fastest," he said. "I wasted precious seconds brushing my teeth."

"How did you brush your teeth? You always carry a toothbrush?"

"That's not a toothbrush in my pocket. I'm just glad to see you." She rolled her eyes and groaned. "No, of course I don't carry a toothbrush. I used yours."

"You *what?*"

"Kidding, *kidding.* But I did steal a dab of your toothpaste." He swept his tongue behind his upper lip. "Don't you hate it when your teeth start feeling all furry?"

"Ewww."

"My sentiments exactly." He glanced at his watch. "We're burning daylight here—or we will be, once the sun actually comes up—so grab your stuff and let's go take that big white bird."

❖

"Wait," Dawtry said when O'Malley fished the key fob from her pocket.

"What do you mean 'wait'?" She aimed the fob at the SUV, but he snatched the gizmo from her hand.

"I mean wait, as in 'don't *do* that,'" he said. He put the key in the lock of the driver's door and twisted. "I don't want the horn beeping and the lights flashing."

"Aren't *you* the considerate one," she said. Was there a hint of sarcasm in her voice? More than a hint, he decided.

"No," he said quietly. "I'm the one who doesn't want to call attention to us." He opened the back door and set her suitcase on the seat, then closed the door with a soft click. O'Malley reached for the handle of the driver's door. "I'll drive," he said.

"I'm fine," she said. "My ankle's a lot better today."

"I know, but why push it? Let me drive."

"You're not on the rental contract."

"Excuse me? Not on the *rental contract*?"

"Exactly."

"I drove yesterday, remember?"

"Yeah, but that was an emergency."

"And this isn't?" He held out his hands, exasperated and beseeching. "Let me get this straight. There are people trying to kill you—trying to kill *us*—and what you're worried about is the fine print on the rental contract?" She shrugged but didn't budge, so he barreled ahead. "You're turning it in with no brakes and a missing mirror, and you're concerned about an unauthorized driver?" He was on the brink of reminding her what had happened to her first rental car in the Canaries—she'd told him about its tumble into the sea—but the glint in her eyes and the set of her jaw muscles made him reconsider. Dawtry allowed himself a grunt of frustration. "You don't make anything easy, do you, O'Malley? Look, I'm not being chivalrous or chauvinist or sexist or whatever other petty thing you think I'm being. What I'm being is careful. On the chance—the tiny, tiny chance—that somebody comes after us, I need to drive." She glared. "Unless you've had training in tactical driving?"

Suddenly he saw her focus shift, and he turned to follow her gaze. A block away, a black Audi stopped at the hotel's entrance, and two men in jeans and leather jackets got out and walked to the door. "Fuck," Dawtry whispered. "The desk clerk told me two guys in an Audi were asking about you."

"What? Why didn't you tell me?"

"I didn't want you to worry. Now, it's time to worry." One of the men tugged on the lobby door, and when it didn't open, he leaned close to the glass and peered in, cupping his hands around his face to cut the glare. "Megan," Dawtry said quietly, "I need you to get in. The other side. Walk, don't run, but for God's sake do it *now*."

She did, and Dawtry slid behind the wheel and cranked the engine. The SUV's headlights switched on automatically, and Dawtry snarled. "Damned safety features," he said. "The lights, the automatic door locks—I *hate* that shit." He eased out the clutch, gradually releasing the hand brake at the same time. The vehicle was parked on a fairly steep hill, so he was forced to rev the engine, and he winced at the noise. "What are those guys doing now?"

"They're still messing with the door," O'Malley said. "I think one of them's trying to pick the lock, or jimmy it, or whatever the word is. The other one's walking back toward the car. Maybe he's getting a tool."

Dawtry was wrestling with the steering, muttering constant curses. "How'd you get into this parking space in the first place? I couldn't get a golf cart in this spot."

"There was a lot more room when I parked," she said. "That little Fiat wedged in front of us sometime later."

"That little Fiat is pissing me off."

She laid a hand on Dawtry's arm. "Crap. One of the guys is on his cell phone now. He's tapping the other one on the shoulder. Pulling him away from the door." Her grip tightened. "Now he's looking this way." She gasped. "He's pointing right at us! Hurry, Chip. *Hurry!* One of them's running this way."

The SUV lurched backward and bashed the vehicle behind them. There was a loud bang, and O'Malley shrieked. "They're shooting at us!"

"No," he said. "That was an airbag. In the car behind us."

"Gun," she said, her voice rising. "He's got a gun, Chip!"

"Get down!" Dawtry wrenched the wheel, jammed the transmission into first, and popped the clutch. Tires squealing and smoking, the SUV rocketed forward. It caught the corner of the Fiat, and bits of red and silver plastic whirled into the air and bounced off their hood and windshield. An instant later their rear windshield exploded, sending glass shrapnel ricocheting throughout the interior. O'Malley shrieked again, this time in earnest, and Dawtry yelled, "*Now* they're shooting at us. Stay down!"

He glanced in the rearview mirror just as the black car—an Audi, he guessed—hurtled toward the mangled Fiat. Dawtry careened around a corner and lost sight of their pursuers. The street stretched ahead long and straight, and he knew the lumbering SUV couldn't outrun an Audi. He had two seconds, three at the most, to dodge. Half a block ahead was a major cross street, and he considered it, but suddenly he yanked the hand brake and skidded around a closer corner—not onto a road but into a narrow, shop-lined pedestrian zone. Virtually any other time of day, he would have mowed down dozens of tourists, but at 6:00 a.m., the pavement was blessedly empty. Fifty yards in, he spun to a stop at a sidewalk café, sending a few tables and umbrellas flying, then cut the ignition to douse the lights, praying that the shrubbery-filled planters would shield them from view.

A split second later the black Audi roared past. He watched for the flash of brake lights, but there was no sign the car was slowing. Dawtry took a breath, started the engine, and headed back the way they had come. "I think maybe we just lost them," he said. "At least for now."

O'Malley's response was to bolt upright, fumble with a switch in her armrest, and vomit out the window as it slid down. "Well done," he said. "You just avoided a huge cleaning fee."

She heaved a couple more times, then slumped back in her seat. "Ugh. I hate barfing."

"But isn't it amazing how much better you feel after you've done it? Listen," he added, "I don't mean to seem, like, unsympathetic, but before you do it again, could you get directions to the airport?"

By way of answering, she tapped something into her phone. A moment later, he heard a familiar robotic voice instructing, "Proceed to the route."

He grimaced. "But how do I proceed to the route, Siri? If I knew, I wouldn't be asking for help, would I?"

"Okay," the robo-voice informed him, "I found this on the web for 'How do I proceed to the route?'"

"Go to hell, Siri!"

"Did I do something wrong?"

"Arrggh," Dawtry shouted. "Megan, help," he pleaded. "I'm headed the wrong way on a one-way street in the middle of a maze. Shut her up and tell me what to do."

She fiddled with her phone. "We need to get to the waterfront. Head downhill, then turn right."

"Hang on," he said. "Going down." Three skidding turns later, they reached the waterfront, where ancient houses and quaint restaurants huddled beneath an immense cruise ship that loomed over the wharf. "Plan B," Dawtry said. "If the flight's sold out, we could book passage on that thing."

"A cruise ship? I'd rather be shot." She tapped the screen on her phone. "There's a traffic circle coming up really soon."

"I see it."

"Take the second right. Into the tunnel."

"Roger that. We've got signage now, too," he said, nodding at a road sign bearing the outline of a plane, an arrow, and the word **AEROPUERTO**.

Suddenly, without warning, he veered onto a narrow side street. O'Malley shrieked and grabbed the oh-shit handle above her door. "What the hell?"

"Sorry," he said. "I saw the Audi tucked behind a sign at the mouth of the tunnel. They were waiting for us."

"How did they know which way we'd be going?"

"Airports and bus stations—those are always what you check first."

"What do we do?"

"Let's get out of sight. Then we'll figure something out."

He was hurtling down the side street, a narrow one-way, when he yanked the brake lever and smoked to a stop.

"Jesus, Chip, I wish you'd warn me when you're about to give me whiplash."

"Okay, then, get ready."

He slammed the stick into "Reverse," backed up, and turned, and—still in "Reverse"—careered up a crooked alley, one whose bend would shield them from view.

"I'm not loving the ride," O'Malley said, "but they did teach you to drive. I'll give 'em that."

The words were barely out of her mouth when they heard squealing tires and the roar of a revving engine screaming past.

"Son of a bitch," Dawtry said. "How the hell . . ." Suddenly he smacked his palm against his forehead. "God. I am *so stupid*. Give me your phone, Megan."

"*You've* got a phone. Plus extra battery packs. You're saving your minutes?"

"No, I'm saving our asses. These guys are tracking your phone."

"What? How can they do that?"

"It's easy—for cops, or bad guys with the right toys. StingRays, they're called. Transmitters that pretend to be cell phone towers. The

StingRay pings your phone, and your phone responds, saying, 'Here I am.' You're carrying a full-time tracking device."

"What makes you so sure it's the phone?"

"It's gotta be. Your battery died yesterday, so they couldn't see it when we came back to town. They couldn't see it last night, even though you recharged it, because we were down in that signal-proof basement. But this morning, when we surfaced, the phone popped back onto their screen. Presto, within minutes they show up at the hotel."

She rummaged in her bag for the phone; when she pulled it out, she held it at arm's length, as if it were a rattlesnake. Then she pressed and held the power key.

Dawtry shook his head. "Not good enough. Even when it's off, it's on."

"So we have to remove the battery?"

"Can't. It's an iPhone. Takes a special Apple screwdriver to open the back. Almost like cracking a safe."

"We'll just have to smash it," she said. "Or drop it in a toilet. I went swimming with my last iPhone. Drowning's a very efficient way to kill one."

"We *could* flush it," he said. "*Or . . .*" He nodded, smiling slightly. "We could use the phone to throw 'em off the scent." He pointed down the slot of the alley. Through the narrow opening at the end, the superstructure and smokestack of the cruise ship loomed. A thread of soot spooled upward from the stack, and a few straggling passengers—all-night shoreside revelers, perhaps—hurried up the gangplank. "That'd be a nice big haystack to hide a needle inside."

"But how would we get on board to hide it?"

"We wouldn't. Give me the phone."

She made to hand it to him, then suddenly snatched it back. "Not so fast. You're not doing this without me."

"Christ," he hissed. "Are we going to do this again? Have the 'no, I can drive' argument one more time?" He growled. "Fine, you win—we'll smash it. Give me one of your boots—my Merrells have rubber soles."

She glanced at his foot—she took nothing on faith—and then laid the phone on the dashboard and tugged the boot from her left foot, that one not being swollen. "Here." She handed him the boot. "You can do the honors."

"Thanks," he said. "Be right back." He snatched the phone off the dash and vaulted from the vehicle, taking her boot with him.

"Lying bastard," she yelled as he jogged, still limping slightly, toward the harbor and the towering ship.

He was gone an eternity by O'Malley's reckoning, though only twenty minutes by her watch.

"Bastard," she repeated when he reappeared.

"Sorry," he said. "I had to do it alone."

"Spill it. Was it scary?"

"Nah. I only had to dodge two bullets." Her eyes widened, and he laughed. "It was a piece of cake. There was a huge pallet of luggage getting hoisted aboard just as I got to the dock. I just lobbed the phone onto the pile. Security's nonexistent, thank goodness."

"You think they'll fall for it? The guys in the Audi?"

"I sure the hell hope so. One way to find out." He cranked the engine, eased down the alley, and threaded back to the harbor highway. He paused before turning onto it, and O'Malley grabbed his arm and pointed.

"Chip, look—there they go!"

He followed the point just in time to see the Audi racing along the wharf in the direction of the ship.

"'Bout damn time we caught a break," he said. He turned the SUV toward the airport once more. "Now let's make like a banana and split."

They plunged into the highway tunnel, a quarter-mile shaft through a mountain bordering the ocean. When they emerged, it was as if they had crossed a border. They were outside the city, the road undulating between scattered hillside houses and rocky seacoast. Three miles later, Dawtry spotted the airport's runway, a skinny strip of asphalt tucked between the highway and the ocean. He gave the rearview mirror yet another glance. "I still don't see anybody behind us, knock wood." Sixty seconds later they angled onto the exit ramp, which looped up and over the highway. "Things are looking up," he said. "Once we clear security, I think we'll be okay."

"I'm not sure we'll make it to security," she said.

"Why not?" He scanned the highway again—the high overpass offered a clear view back toward the city—but the only vehicle he saw was a battered delivery truck headed away from them. "You think they've got reinforcements waiting for us here?"

"I think the rental car people will have us arrested," she said glumly.

"The rental car people?" He guffawed. "That's hilarious!" He slowed to make the turn into the parking garage.

"What's hilarious about that? If *I* were them, *I'd* call the cops on us. Look at this!" She made a vague, sweeping gesture, one that he gathered was intended to encompass every insult and injury the vehicle had endured: the hailstonelike bits of glass littering the floorboards; the useless brake pedal; the mangled bumpers, front and rear; the shattered driver's side mirror; the flecks of vomit streaking the passenger door.

"It is a mess," he agreed. "You're right—they really might call the cops if we turned it in like this."

She furrowed her brow. "What do you mean 'if we turned it in like this'? What other way *can* we turn it in?" Instead of answering, Dawtry just smiled. "What's that shit-eating grin supposed to mean? Oh, hey, turn turn *turn!*" Her head swiveled. "Dammit, Chip, you just missed the rental car return."

"Oops!" His smile broadened, and he turned into the short-term parking section. O'Malley stared. "Wait—we're not turning the car in? Not at all?"

"What, and get arrested? Not my idea of a good time." He chose a parking spot in a dim, deserted corner and backed in, the rear bumper practically touching the wall, to conceal the shattered rear window. "There," he said. "Pretty unobtrusive, wouldn't you say?" He got out and removed her roller bag from the back seat after brushing a few bits of glass from it. He leaned his head inside. "You coming?"

"We just leave it here and fly away?"

"That's the plan."

"But once they find out . . ."

"Eye on the prize, Megan. We gotta get out of here. Once they find out, all we gotta do is pay for the damage. Which we can't do if we're dead." He closed the door, extended the roller bag's handle, and began wheeling it toward the terminal.

Behind him, he heard the passenger door open and close, then heard her hurrying—still favoring her sprained ankle—to catch up. "I used to be a decent, law-abiding citizen," she panted, "till I met you, Mr. Law Enforcement."

"Decency is highly overrated. Besides, you have the makings of a terrific scofflaw. You just need to breathe into it a little more."

"Breathe into it? You sound like a yoga teacher."

"That's good, because now that I've almost certainly been fired by the FBI, I need a fallback career."

The lovely young woman at the airline counter—was she the same woman Megan had pleaded with on her prior trip?—listened attentively, nodding sympathetically, as O'Malley explained the family emergency that required her to cut short her holiday in La Palma. "So if I could change my ticket to the eight a.m. flight today," she concluded, "that would be so helpful."

"Of course," said the young woman. She smiled—dazzling white teeth, set off by her dark hair, brown eyes, and olive complexion. "It will be my pleasure to help you with that. May I see your ticket and passport, please?"

"I don't have my ticket," O'Malley said. "I didn't have access to a printer. But I know my ticket number."

"You know the number?" The ticket agent looked very skeptical and slightly amused.

Dawtry gave O'Malley a good-natured, told-you-so nudge. She gave him a sharp, go-to-hell elbow in return.

"Yes, I know the number." O'Malley rattled off the digits.

The ticket agent keyed them in. "You are Ms. O'Malley? May I see your passport?"

O'Malley shot Dawtry a nervous look; he responded with a barely imperceptible shrug, as if to say "Can't not." Reluctantly she took out her passport, opened it, and slid it across the counter.

The young woman glanced at the photo, then at O'Malley, and flashed another blinding smile. "Just one moment, please," she said. "Let me confirm that we have a seat available." She turned and walked away, carrying O'Malley's passport, through a doorway and into a glassed-in office.

"What's she doing?" said O'Malley. "Why'd she take my passport in there? I don't like this."

"I don't, either, but let's not freak out." Dawtry leaned on the counter in what he hoped was a relaxed, casual posture as he watched what was transpiring behind the glass. The young woman handed O'Malley's passport to a fat, balding man sitting at a desk. The man's gaze flickered between the passport and the ticket agent—her face, her breasts, her hips. Next, he checked his computer screen, and then he shot a swift glance through the glass at O'Malley and Dawtry. Then—with a studied casualness that mirrored Dawtry's pose—the man made a phone call.

"Okay, panic time," said Dawtry. "We gotta get outta here." He took a quick look around, then waved to catch the attention of the man on the phone. The man looked startled. Dawtry pointed over his shoulder, to a restroom sign, then pointed at O'Malley and back at the sign once more. He ended the pantomime in a sheepish shrug—as if to say, *Women—what can you do, right?*—and took her by the elbow. "We're going to the restroom," he said. "We're relaxed. We're blending in." They strolled, with agonizing slowness, in the direction the restroom sign pointed. The moment they were out of view of the ticket counter, Dawtry scanned for an exit. "There," he said. "Fifty yards ahead, on the right. Nice and easy. We're chatting, we're relaxed, we're just a couple of happy tourists." To Dawtry's surprise, she laughed. "What's funny?"

"Nothing's funny." She was beaming at him. "I'm just a happy tourist, *honey.*"

"Ah. Excellent, *dear.*"

"I've been taking lessons from a world-class pretender."

"Thanks," he said. She was still smiling, but there was something behind the smile, or the words, or the way she said them, that unsettled him. *Leave it alone,* he warned himself. *Eyes on the prize.*

They sauntered through the exit doors, then took the stairs to the parking garage, moving faster now that they were out of the terminal.

"How did I end up on some sort of airport watch list?" she asked.

"Good question. Maybe Iñigo's friends have filed a missing-person report. Maybe they said you were the last person seen with him. Who else saw you at the observatory?"

"Antonio!" she said. "The receptionist. He's the only one. He's the one who told Iñigo I was there. You think he's in on it?"

"Could be. Could be this thing's a lot bigger, and goes a lot higher, than a handful of jihadists. We know your phone was tracked, and I bet your email was hacked. Hell, I wouldn't be surprised if these folks have been watching ever since you contacted the CIA. They sure didn't waste much time showing up at your apartment."

She shivered. "Thank God I was already gone."

He nodded. "If the authorities here are involved, they'll be looking for me soon, too. Might be already."

"What makes you say that?"

"You skedaddle out of the airport with an American guy—a guy who just happens to look like a federal agent. A guy who just happened to rent a helicopter an hour before Iñigo went missing. Doesn't take an astrophysicist to connect those dots. I'd say we're in a jam, Megan."

She frowned. "Well, you were smart not to turn in the car. We'd really be in trouble if we didn't still have it."

He shook his head. "We don't. Can't use it anymore. They'd be on us like flies on shit. The crumpled fenders and shattered windshield might as well be giant red bull's-eyes. If the guys in the Audi are in cahoots with the cops, the cops know what to look for, and they know where to look for it."

She grabbed his arm. "Then what do we do? We're trapped. We can't get on a plane—shit, we can't even get a taxi, can we?"

"Not a good idea."

"Then what, Chip?"

"Keep walking. Keep blending in, honey." He lifted his chin, using it to point toward a family coming toward them in the dim garage. A harried-looking woman was pushing a baby in a stroller; at her heels was a small dark-haired boy trundling a roll-aboard bag that was fully half his size. Somewhere in the dimness behind the mother and kids, a trunk lid slammed, and out of the shadows came a man wheeling two enormous suitcases. On his back was a pack nearly as big as the suitcases.

"*Hola*," said Dawtry pleasantly to the mother and kids. "*Buen viaje*—have a good trip." Smiling, he repeated the greeting as the dad staggered past with his burden. Dawtry turned and watched as they entered the elevator, then took O'Malley's arm and began pulling her along, almost at a trot. "Hurry," he said. "We gotta skedaddle."

"Skedaddle where? How?"

He led her to a dim stall occupied by a squared-off, rusted-out Volkswagen. The car reeked of leaking oil and half-burned gasoline, and the engine radiated heat. "Get in," he said.

"What?"

"Get *in*."

"Why?"

"*Duh*, Megan. So we can get *out* of here."

"We're stealing this car?"

"If we don't get arrested or shot while we stand here yakking about it."

"You're serious—we're stealing that poor family's car?"

"You got a better idea, I'd love to hear it." Without waiting for an answer, he opened the driver's door, knelt on the concrete, and angled his head and shoulders beneath the steering wheel, using his phone as a flashlight. A moment later the engine coughed to life. Dawtry scuttled into the driver's seat and then leaned over to open the passenger door. "You coming with, or staying to chat with our friends in the Audi?"

She got in and closed the door. "Grand theft auto," she said. Then she added, "Inconceivable."

He backed out of the parking spot and then headed for the garage exit. "Grand theft? Take a closer look at our ride. Petty larceny, tops." He looked at her and frowned.

"What?" she demanded.

"You're not exactly inconspicuous."

"Hey, I've been blending in!"

"Yeah, but they've got your passport, so they're sending out your picture. You better crawl in the back and hunker down."

"Hunker down?"

"Hunker down. A term that here means 'hunker down.' If there's an invisibility cloak back there, this'd be a swell time to put it on."

O'Malley wriggled between the seats. "Urf," she said. "It's gross back here. Smells like pee and poo and sour milk."

190

"Think of it as the sweet smell of freedom. Anything you can cover up with?"

"Gag. There's the world's nastiest blanket."

"Perfect. Make friends with it quick, 'cause I see daylight up ahead." He eased to a stop at the garage exit. "Christ, where's the ticket?"

"Look on the dashboard," O'Malley mumbled from the rear floorboard. "That's where I always leave it."

"Not there."

"Cup holder?"

"Loose change and snotty Kleenex."

"Is there a button you can push for 'lost ticket'? Or can you just crash through? Aren't those gates pretty flimsy?"

"Yeah, but it's a bad idea. They'd come running."

"Well, we can't just sit here forever."

"Whatever would I do without your incisive insights, Professor?" The glove box opened, and a small avalanche ensued. "Crap." Then: "*Aha!* Sticking out of the ashtray." Dawtry rolled down the window, then inserted the ticket into the payment machine. "Here's hoping my credit's good here. Unlike everywhere else." Ten seconds and one beep later, the arm swung upward and the car chugged forward, into the sunshine and away from the airport. "I am reminded of the words of the late, great Dr. King," Dawtry said. "Free at last, free at last. Thank God Almighty, we're free at last."

"Free to do what?"

"I'm still working on that part."

They headed south from the airport, away from Santa Cruz, on a smaller road in hopes of remaining under the radar of the police and the Audi thugs. The two-lane road was notched into the cliff, flanked on the uphill side by a massive retaining wall—the wall that supported the runway—and on the downhill side by the rocky coastline, its vistas of waters and breakers punctuated by wind turbines and airport approach-light stanchions.

South of the airport, the land grew more rolling, opening out into low hills dotted with banana plantations. At a side road, marked by a break in the stone and cinder block walls of a banana farm, Dawtry turned right, uphill. It was more a farm lane than a road—barely six feet across, with decrepit trucks and rusting farm equipment parked in the occasional wide spot. Soon the lane grew smaller and rougher, dwindling to a pair of cracked strips of pavement. "I don't like this," O'Malley said. "Last time I was on a road like this, I nearly died."

"I don't love it, either," Dawtry said, angling his phone display toward her, "but the map shows it connecting to the highway that crosses the ridge. Besides, last time you were on a road like this, it led you to me, right?"

"My point exactly," she said, but then she laughed.

At almost that exact moment, the road began to improve, and in less than a mile, it intersected an actual highway, one that switchbacked up and over the island's volcanic spine and down to the west coast. As they topped the ridge and began their descent, through towering stands of pines, O'Malley pointed to a collection of rustic facilities—a restroom and picnic pavilion and charcoal grills—to their left. "Hey, we're at Refugio El Pilar," she said.

"Huh?" He slowed the car to a crawl. "Looks nice."

"The trailhead to the volcanoes. Can we stop? Just for a minute? Long as nobody's chasing or shooting at us?"

He pulled into the parking area and they got out. The air was crisp and fragrant with pine resin and cookout smoke. She pointed. "The trail starts there, behind the picnic tables. It's truly amazing, in a forbidding sort of way, once you get up high, where the craters are."

"And that's where you were, napping in the center of the spiral labyrinth, when the quake woke you?"

She smiled. "You *do* listen to me! Yeah. That's when I knew for sure I had to keep digging into this."

"Wish we had time to hike it," he said. "Maybe we can come back someday as actual tourists. Regular, happy American tourists."

"I'd like that. If there *is* an America, and if happiness is still possible, after all this is over." Suddenly, without warning, she began to cry. "God, what if we can't stop it, Chip? What if it's already too late?" She folded against him, shuddering in his arms.

"It's not too late," he said. "As long as it hasn't happened yet, it's not too late."

"You don't know that," she whispered. "It could be past the tipping point. Like the ice sheet melting in Antarctica."

"Never give in," he said. "Never give in. Never, never, never."

"What's that from?" she said into his chest. "I know the line, but I can't remember the movie."

"Not a movie, Megan. Real life—a speech Winston Churchill gave in the fall of 1941, when Nazi Germany looked unbeatable." He gave her a squeeze. "'Never give in' was a last-minute substitute for Churchill's original line, by the way."

"Yeah? What was the original line?"

"It was 'Don't stop picking at it.'"

She balled up a fist and pounded on his rib cage. "Smart-ass," she said, half crying, half laughing. She sat up and wiped her eyes, then pulled away and locked eyes with him. "Speaking of picking at it, I need to talk to you about something."

"I hope it's about how you have the world's first portable transporter beam in your back pocket," he said.

"It's not. It's about last night."

His internal alarms began to sound. "What about it?"

"What were you saying?"

"Can you narrow that down for me?"

"After you talked about your family. After I talked about Gracie. I was falling asleep. I had my head on your shoulder. I could feel your breath on my hair, and then I heard you whispering. Were you praying?"

He didn't answer right away. "No," he said eventually. "I'm not a praying man. I must have been talking in my sleep."

"Bullshit, Chip."

"I talk in my sleep. I told you that. Always have."

"I don't believe this. You're lying to me. Why?"

"I'm not lying, Megan. I—"

"There! You just lied to me *again*! This very instant. You looked me right in the eye, and you lied to my face."

"Megan—"

"Never mind."

He groaned. "Never mind *what*, Megan?"

"Never mind *anything*. I'm sorry I asked."

She whirled and stormed away, limping but trying not to.

Dawtry caught up with her and took hold of her arm. "Megan, wait."

She shook him shook him off and kept going. "Leave me alone."

"I *can't*."

"Why? Because that would be against FBI *regs*?"

"Yes! It would!"

"You know what? I say the hell with FBI regs, and I say leave me alone." She slapped one hand across the other, as if knocking a bit of filth off her palm, and walked away, leaving him stunned and rooted to the spot.

"It was a *poem*," he shouted at her retreating form. "It was a god-damn poem."

She stopped, her back still turned . . . but she did stop. "A poem," he repeated. "Called 'A Prayer for My Daughter.' By Yeats." Damnably, Dawtry felt tears rolling down his cheeks. *Well, shit*, he thought. *I hate to cry.*

She turned toward him. "How does it go?"

"I . . . uh . . ."

She turned her head toward him. *Tell me.*

Dawtry looked up—up at the dark-green tracery of the towering trees and the azure backdrop of the sky, and he seemed almost to be falling upward, tumbling skyward. He drew a breath. "Once more the storm is howling," he began, but then faltered. He shook his head and cleared his throat. Then he closed his eyes and began again.

> Once more the storm is howling, and half-hid
> Under this cradle-hood and coverlid
> My child sleeps on.

He heard his voice strengthen as the words took him outside himself and into the poem itself.

> There is no obstacle
> But Gregory's wood and one bare hill
> Whereby the haystack- and roof-levelling wind,
> Bred on the Atlantic, can be stayed.

As he said the words, he felt the pine-scented breeze on his face. He paused, took another breath, and quoted the rest of the passage, ending—as before—with the words, "Out of the murderous innocence of the sea." He stopped, his eyes still closed. He didn't even know if she was still standing there or if she'd walked away again. Slowly, as if awakening from a deep dream, he opened his eyes.

She had not walked away; she had walked toward him. She stood two feet away, wide-eyed, her face streaked with tears. "That's lovely."

He searched her face. "There's more," he said. "That's not the end of the poem. But that's where I stopped last night."

"I know," she said. "I was listening. Don't lie to me again, Chip."

"I won't. I promise."

"Thank you." She was still just standing there, still just looking at him, the pupils of her eyes open fully—so fully that her irises were only a thin band of green and gold, like a bright ring around a dark planet or a black hole, its gravitational pull irresistible. Was it his imagination, or could he actually see the irises pulsing with each beat of her heart?

"I need to tell you something else, Megan," he said. "Since you want me to tell you the truth. I said I'm not allowed to leave you alone, and that's true. I'm not. It's my job to protect you. But that's not the only reason. I think you're amazing. You're smart, you're strong, you're brave." He shook his head. "If it weren't against regs, I'd be seriously falling for you." He blushed. "I don't mean to make you feel awkward. I'm sorry."

"Sorry? You're *sorry*? You big dummy. Do you always apologize for saying sweet things to women?"

"Generally." He sighed with relief. "Okay, you love movie dialogue. Here's a line for you. 'You make me want to be a better man.' Who said that?"

"I have no idea."

"Jack Nicholson. *As Good as It Gets.* Thing is, Megan, I actually *am* a better man with you."

She blinked. "Excuse me?"

"I said I'm a better man with you. I like that."

She stiffened. "Well, congratulations," she said. "Good for you. So that's what this is about? That's how you see me? A self-help program with tits and ass?"

"What? *Damm*it, Megan, why do you do that? Why do you seek out the flaw and focus on it, to the exclusion of everything else?" He looked up at the sky, opening and closing his fingers, then back at her again. "Here's how I see you. I see you as admirable and inspiring. I see you as a role model and a hero and somebody I want to emulate. Why do you have to twist that into something demeaning to both of us?"

He turned and walked away, although he didn't go far.
He wasn't allowed to go far.

She watched him walk away. *Way to go, O'Malley,* she thought bitterly.

In her mind's eye, she flashed back to her first day on La Palma—two weeks and a lifetime ago—when she had spotted a single chin whisker in the fifty-foot MAGIC mirror and had felt compelled to pluck it. *You really* can't *stop picking at it, can you?*

"Wait," she said. "Come back." He held up a hand and kept walking. "Please come back." He stopped and turned, staring at her, his eyes raw with hurt. "Don't," she told him. "Don't look at me. I need to say this, and I don't think I can if you're looking at me that way." He stared at the ground. "You're right, I *do* have a keen eye for the flaw," she went on. "And I *can* be relentless. I know that. It's how I was raised. My foster mother taught me well, and I was her prize pupil. But that doesn't make it right. You deserved better—*deserve* better—and I'm sorry. Ashamed, actually." She took a deep breath, blew it out. "If it's any comfort," she added, "the person I'm hardest on is me."

"Yes, I know," he said. "And, no, I take no comfort in it. Why would I want you to treat yourself badly?" He looked at her now, shaking his head. "I *hate* this. I hate being in . . . I don't know what to call it . . . in *disharmony* with you." He growled, then gave an odd, unexpected laugh. "Jesus. Truth is, if you weren't the way you are—if you *didn't* zero in on the flaw, or the inconsistency, or the seismic tremor screwing up your observations—we'd still be totally clueless about what's going on here on this pissant island off the coast of Africa. We'd be waking up one morning, next week or next month, to a hundred-foot wall of water crashing down on us."

"It could still happen," she pointed out.

"Might could," he conceded. "But thanks to you and the Acme Flaw Detector—"

"Don't forget the Amplifying Catastrophizer."

He smiled. "Thanks to you and the Acme Flaw Detector and the Amplifying Catastrophizer, we've got a chance to stop it. Are you sometimes a pain in the ass? Yeah. But are you pretty damned fabulous, too? *Hell*, yeah."

She stared at him. "Hey, Chip?"

"Yeah?"

"Come here."

"How come?"

"I just noticed another flaw. Something's wrong with your mouth."

"My mouth? What's wrong with my mouth?" They stepped toward each other. "What's wrong with my mouth?"

"It's making too much noise." She stopped six inches in front of him, scrutinizing his lips. "Hey, Chip?" He raised his eyebrows but did not speak. "I know it's against regs, but would you kiss me, please?"

A long kiss and a short mile down the road, Dawtry stopped again, this time at a switchback where an overlook offered a panoramic view of the ocean to the west and the jagged rim of the caldera to the north. More to the point, the overlook offered the first strong cell signal they'd had since fleeing the airport two hours earlier.

Dawtry scrolled quickly through his texts, voicemails, and emails. "Well, there's good news and there's bad news," he told O'Malley.

"What's the bad news?"

"Why do you want the bad news first?"

"To get it out of the way quicker," she said. "Why do you want to use up the good news first?"

"To piss you off," he joked. "Okay, the bad news is we're now both considered fugitives from justice. I told you it wouldn't take 'em long to connect the dots. We're suspects in the disappearance of Iñigo Rodriguez, a respected Spanish astronomer."

"A sleazebag, attempted murderer, and terrorist mastermind."

"My guess is that 'mastermind' gives him more credit than he's due. 'Minion-mind,' maybe."

"Okay, minion-mind," she acceded. "Is there other bad news?"

"So-so. The island's 'rumblings abdominal are clearly phenomenal.' Actually, not phenomenal but continual."

"How do you know that?"

"Professor Boyd is sending me updates from your seismometers. Continuing ripple shots and a couple of quakes, but nothing above magnitude three."

"Hmm. And the good news?"

"The good news is the CIA is now trying to take the case away from the FBI."

"How is that good news?"

"It means the CIA now considers this an urgent threat to national security."

"Well, Tippecanoe and whoop-de-do. So the hell what? Where were they when we needed them?"

"We still need them. We need everybody. But the point is, if the CIA wants to take it, the FBI will fight tooth and nail to hang on to it. Or at least to share it. That legitimates it. People *believe* us now, Megan. People will *help* us now."

"About damn time. And how do they propose to do this?"

"Well, first by sending us back into the fray."

"What? Fuck that shit! Let somebody else get into the fray for a change."

"I know, I know," he said. "Reinforcements are on the way. And they're figuring out how to get us out. In the meantime, though, we're their only eyes and ears on the ground here, so we need to gather more intelligence before we go."

"If we had a nanogram of intelligence between us, we'd already be long gone," she said. It was a cheap, throwaway line—a low-hanging-fruit pun on "intelligence"—and they both knew she didn't actually mean it. Still, the idea of putting themselves at higher risk was sobering. "So, as good news goes, that was some mighty weak sauce you just served up."

"Oh, there's much better news," he said. "I just haven't gotten to it yet."

"Then lay it on me, brother, 'cause I could sure use it. Whatcha got?"

"Well, for one thing, the National Treasury of Nigeria informs me that I'm the lucky beneficiary of a *six-million-dollar* disbursement."

She laughed in spite of herself. "Congratulations. And there's more good news?"

"There is, but I can't tell you what it is."

"Because it's top secret?"

"No, because it's super embarrassing. Let's just say that the pharmaceutical industry—technically, the dietary supplement industry—is making big strides in men's health. *Huge* ones. And wives everywhere are very, very grateful."

"Wait—you have a wife?"

"Not yet. But if I did, she'd be eternally grateful to the makers of Man of Steel."

The cell phone's map had not lied, strictly speaking: the side road Boyd had said to take was indeed there, exactly where Boyd and the map said it would be—a small road branching off from a kink in the highway and angling along the western flank of the island's backbone. But neither Boyd nor the cell phone map had mentioned that a stout steel gate barred access to the road. The gate wasn't merely closed; the gate was belligerent, adorned with KEEP OUT and DANGER signs in Spanish, English, and German, along with wordless images of menacing guard dogs.

O'Malley frowned at the gate. "You're sure this is the only way in?"

"Only way besides bushwhacking." He handed her the phone. "Here's the image Boyd sent. It's the only road that follows the mountain's flank, except for the coast highway, which is miles below this. This road heads straight to the blasting zone, according to your seismometers."

She studied the map, zooming in and out and scrolling around on the cell phone's screen. "Crap. I wish you were wrong." She brightened. "But, hey, praise me."

"Just in general, or for something specific?"

"When I told David, my ex, that the telescope was basically a giant dragon bowl? He made fun of me. But look—the seismometers show the blasting zone directly south of the observatory. *Exactly* in the direction the telescope pointed."

"I praise you. I praise the dragon bowl telescope. So MacGyver-ish of you. I love it. Wanna know what I hate?"

"What do you hate?"

"I hate it that the blasting's happening right at the center of the fault line. I hate it that these people seem to know what they're doing, and that they're totally getting away with it."

"*Have been* getting away with it," she said. "But all that's about to change."

"I like a woman with confidence." Dawtry edged the car closer to the gate, and they got out for a closer look. His first move was to check for a surveillance camera. Seeing none, he began a detailed inspection of the gate. It appeared to be of recent vintage: gleaming and free of rust, with a motorized mechanism that could be activated by either a magnetic card or a keypad. "So," he said, "I guess we won't be crashing through." Welded together from thick steel plate and square, solid bars, it looked ready, willing, and able to repel a frontal attack by a bulldozer or army tank, let alone a rusted-out, stolen Volkswagen.

"Can you hot-wire it? The way you did with the car?"

"Alas, they didn't teach us that at the Academy." He walked to the keypad and bent down to study the keys.

"You're thinking maybe somebody wrote the combination in Sharpie? Let's hope so, because it would take us forever to try every possible combination."

"I'm looking to see which keys get pushed a lot."

"Ah. Good idea," she said. "I was just about to suggest that."

"Hmm."

"'Hmm'? What's that supposed to mean?"

"It means that all the keys look untouched except for three of 'em."

"Which three?"

"The one, the nine, and the zero."

"Hmm," she agreed. "Interesting. Most keypads use at least a four-key combination. I've seen some with five or six. Seems odd to use only three different digits."

"I hear you're good with numbers, Dr. O. How many different combinations are there using only one, nine, and zero?"

She calculated for a moment. "Well, it's been a while since I had stats, but I seem to remember that the number of permutations is the factorial of n plus r minus one."

"Right," he said. "I was just about to remind you of that. Which gives us . . . ?"

"For a four-digit combination," she mused, "that would be . . . cool—only ten different possibilities!"

He was already punching numbers. "And for a six-digit combo?"

She took a bit longer this time. "Still not bad—only twenty-one possibilities. So cumulatively, that's a total of twenty-five possibilities. But a six-digit combo adds . . . let me think . . . another—"

She was interrupted by the whir of a motor and the clatter of latches releasing.

She gasped and clapped her hands together. "Holy crap, Chip, what was that, your second try?"

"I cannot tell a lie—I promised you I wouldn't. My third. Three is the number, and the number is three. Please don't think badly of me."

"That's amazing! How'd you *do* that?"

"Think like a terrorist, Megan," he said. "If you want to deal a devastating blow to America, what prior event—what prior attack—would inspire you most?"

"World Trade Center. No question." Her eyes widened. "Nine eleven!"

"See? Elementary, my dear Watson. My first try was nine, one-one, zero-one—the month, the day, the last two digits of the year. My second try was *zero*-nine, one-one, zero-one. Still no dice. Then I remembered—everybody but Americans writes the day first, not the month. So—one-one, zero-nine, zero-one. Bingo."

"So now what? We just drive right up? Act like we're invited?"

"Sure," he said. "Blend in." He waited a beat. "Actually, it'd be better to go on foot, but the blasting site is three, four miles down the road, according to Boyd's map. Long way to hoof it, there and back. I'm hoping there'll be someplace closer where we can hide the car. A side road, a shed we can tuck behind."

"What if somebody comes along in another vehicle and spots us? Only one way in, one way out, right? We're sort of trapped."

"Only if they come in the gate behind us. If they're coming from the blasting zone, we outrun 'em."

"In *this*? Zero to sixty in a day and a half? Fred Flintstone's footmobile has more get-up-and-go than this."

"Sorry. Next time I'll be sure to swipe us a Ferrari."

"Not criticizing, just nervous."

Dawtry pointed at the deep, wide tire tracks leading to and from the gate. "The good news is whatever's leaving those huge tracks doesn't have a lot of speed."

She hoisted an eyebrow at him. "The bad news?"

"It can crush us like a bug."

"Have I mentioned that your sunny optimism is what I love most about you?"

He hoisted both eyebrows at her. "So there are multiple things you love about me? Do tell, Professor. Count the ways!"

"Can't," she said. "I'm no good at numbers."

They'd gone barely a mile when Dawtry slammed on the brakes and slithered to a halt. "What the hell is *that*?" He pointed to a metal tower of red and white rising above the road a few hundred yards ahead, tilted at a forty-five-degree angle.

"It's the Eiffel Tower," said O'Malley. "Or the leaning scaffold of Pisa."

"It looks like a drilling rig," he said. "I thought we were looking for blasting, not drilling."

"Maybe it uses small explosives?"

Dawtry shook his head. "I don't think so. Just a damn big drill bit. Besides, we're still a long way from where the explosions are happening, right?"

"That's true." She shrugged, as baffled as he was.

"Let's check it out." He eased the car forward another hundred yards, then, finding a notch in the embankment where a pile of extra gravel had been bulldozed, he backed the car off the road. "You stay here," he told O'Malley.

She snorted. "Like hell." She was out of the car before he was.

He sighed and followed. "All right, but remember—we're hunting wabbits, so be vewwy, vewwy quiet."

In fact, they could have shouted or set off a car alarm without being heard over the racket of machinery: the bass thrum of a gargantuan diesel engine, the soprano wail of spinning gears and zinging cables, the clatter and clang of steel colliding with steel.

Dawtry pointed to the woods, and they headed up the slope a ways before turning parallel to the road. The going was easy, with the pines widely spaced and almost no underbrush.

As they drew near, the din grew deafening. Occasionally, the roar was punctuated by guttural, indistinct shouts. Soon O'Malley and Dawtry reached the edge of a clearing: an arc roughly the size of a baseball infield, the arc cutting deeply into the mountainside. As they watched from behind the last of the trees, a long section of pipe tilted upward from a horizontal stack of pipes, almost like a flagpole being hoisted toward vertical. Then it angled further, settling into some sort of slide or groove in the latticework. "If they're drilling," he said, "they're drilling at an angle. Any guesses why?"

Her eyes widened. "They must be drilling down toward the base of the fault line," she said. "Maybe they're making a hole for more explosives? So they can start blasting here, too? Attack the fault at multiple points?"

He shrugged, then took out his phone and began snapping pictures.

O'Malley tapped his arm and pointed slightly downhill from the rig. "Get pictures of that thing, too. What is it?"

He zoomed in as tight as the lens allowed. "Looks like a giant motor. Or maybe a pump? There's a big pipe on the downhill side. Whatever it is, I don't like the cut of its jib."

The wind, which had been blowing from the west, shifted direction slightly, blowing now from the north of the island, parallel to the ridge. With the wind at their backs, the noise from the drilling rig lessened slightly, and the stench of diesel fumes dissipated.

"So now what?" she asked. "We're still miles from the blasting zone, but I don't think we can just drive past this without being noticed, do you?"

"Not without a cloaking device." He thought for a moment. "We could just abandon the car," he said. "Walk to the blasting zone, then bushwhack downhill to the nearest village."

"Then what?"

"We look for a Lamborghini to steal."

"Ha ha."

"Seriously, maybe it makes sense to switch cars. Leave the VW as bait, as a distraction, while we make good our escape in some old Peugeot or Ford Fiesta."

She snorted. "Did you actually just say 'make good our escape'?"

"What? You'd rather make lousy our escape?"

"Amaze me you do," she said. "Okay, whatever you think. You're the secret agent."

"Special agent," he corrected. "No secret there." He pointed upslope. "I guess we gotta skirt it on the uphill side, so we don't have to cross the road in plain sight." He turned and began leading the way.

"Wait. Stop."

He looked back at her. "What? You don't like the plan after all?"

"I don't like *that*. Look!" She pointed toward the drilling rig. Two immense dogs—Rottweilers, by the look of the massive square heads and stocky black-and-tan bodies—had emerged from somewhere among the sheds and vehicles. They sniffed the breeze—the damnable north breeze—and then, barking ferociously, charged directly toward O'Malley and Dawtry.

"Jesus, Mary, and Joseph," O'Malley said. "We're screwed!"

"Run," he ordered. "Run for the car. Hard as you can. Wait—take this!" He thrust his phone at her. "If I'm not there in five minutes, go without me."

"No way—I'm not going without you."

"We don't have time to argue, Megan. If I don't make it, you gotta go without me. If they catch us both, there's nobody to stop this." She glared but took the phone. "Hit 'Redial,' it'll call my boss. Tell him what happened, and send the pictures."

"I don't even know how to start the car!"

"Touch the end of the red wire to the end of the green wire. Once the car starts, pull 'em apart. It's easy—even a PhD can do it."

"Don't you fucking dare get caught."

"Shut up and run. Fast as you can."

They took off—hurtling headlong through the woods, stumbling and lurching over rocks and roots as fast as her sprained ankle and his bruised foot would allow—a desperate dash by the halt and the lame. O'Malley caught a toe and went sprawling, catching herself an inch before her head hit a rock. Dawtry grabbed her arm, yanked her up, and gave her a push on the back to propel her forward again. Then he turned. The dogs were closing fast, their howls coming loud and frenzied.

"Chip!"

"Run, Megan! *Now!* And don't look back!"

She staggered out of the woods and slumped against the car, her breath coming in ragged gasps that quickly turned to sobs and, soon after, to retching. O'Malley had done more retching in the past three days than she'd done in the entire preceding decade. Behind her, out of sight, she heard snarling and roaring and cries of pain that might have been either human or animal, or both. "Oh God," she whispered. "Please, God. Please."

Hands shaking, she opened the driver's door and leaned in, inspecting the wires Chip had tugged free of the steering column in the airport parking garage. Two of the wires were already twisted together, but two others hung free, a half inch of bare copper exposed, so she took hold of them both, one in each hand, and brought the ends together. A spark popped and the car lurched forward a foot, nearly knocking O'Malley to the ground. "Son of a *bitch*," she swore. She reached over and yanked the emergency-brake lever up, then popped the gearshift into neutral. "Once more with feeling," she muttered, then brought the wires together again.

The car fired up again, this time without the dangerous lurch, and O'Malley stared at it, mildly astonished that it had started as easily as Chip had said it would. *Chip.* She turned back toward the woods, which had fallen silent—ominously, terrifyingly silent. "Come on," she said, crying. "Dammit, Chip, come *on.*"

But he did not come.

She checked the phone. Four minutes passed, then five. "If I'm not there in five minutes, go without me," he'd said.

She got into the driver's seat and closed the door, then pressed the clutch and put—slammed—the shifter into first gear. She rolled down the window, looking and listening. Nothing. Six minutes. "Damn you, Chip Dawtry," she said, her voice strangling in her throat. "*Damn* you."

She let out the clutch—and the car stalled, the engine dying. She pounded the steering wheel, roaring in frustration and grief, then fumbled for the wires, her vision obscured by tears. The spark was bigger this time, with a loud pop, and she felt a sharp bite on her wrist where the bare copper grazed her.

She checked the phone—*his* phone—one last time. Seven minutes. She eased forward, out of the notch and into the road, her heart a stone in her chest.

III: WAVE GOODBYE

CHAPTER 16

O'Malley had waited almost twice as long as Dawtry had told her to, and still he did not come. What was it he'd said to her? "If they catch us both, there's nobody to stop this." He was right. "God*dammm*it," she said, casting a final, bleak glance in the rearview mirror . . . and that's when she saw it: one of the huge dogs emerging from the woods, dragging one of its hind legs behind it.

And then the dog reared and stood on its hind legs—a dog that was not a dog, but was Dawtry, hunched and bloody, half walking, half hopping, one of his legs trailing.

O'Malley yanked the hand brake and put the car in neutral, then leaped out and flung herself at him. She held him and wept, then finally managed, "Thank God. Oh, thank God."

"Pray later," he said weakly. "Right now we gotta go. And guess what—you get to drive this time."

"Here, let me help you get in." She took hold of his forearm, intending to drape it over her shoulder, but he gasped with pain. She leaned away from him, still holding the arm, and looked. His sleeve was shredded, and his forearm and hand were punctured and torn, dripping with blood. "My God, Chip, we need to stop that bleeding."

"Later. Let's go. As soon as they find the dogs, they'll come gunning for us."

She moved to his other side, and he draped his undamaged right arm around her shoulder, then limped to the passenger's side and got in. O'Malley scurried to the driver's seat, released the brake, and jammed the transmission into gear. Again, she glanced at the rearview, and what she saw made her shriek. "Shit—two men! With guns!" As if to confirm her words, the rear windshield shattered, showering them with shards of glass.

"Go go *go!*" Dawtry yelled.

The wheels spun, slinging gravel as she popped the clutch. Bullets thudded and tore into the car's sheet metal, and three holes—surrounded by spiderweb fractures—appeared in the front windshield, directly below the rearview mirror.

"Bastards," O'Malley said. She power-shifted into second, the small engine screaming as she floored the gas. "Come on, baby, give me all you got."

"Keptain, I dinna think she can take much more," said Dawtry in a passable Scottish brogue. "Try third." They rounded a slight curve, and the shooting stopped. "We might have a sixty-second head start. We gotta figure out a way to slow them down."

"Crap," O'Malley said, "I forgot about the gate." The massive structure loomed a hundred yards ahead, tightly closed. "Do we have to key in the code to get out?"

"There should be a motion sensor or metal detector on this side. They only care about keeping people out, not keeping them in."

She slowed, then stopped, as they neared the gate. After what seemed an eternity, the gate clattered and began sliding open. She looked in the mirror again. "Shit shit *shit*—here they come!" Dawtry opened his door. "Wait! What are you doing? Chip? Don't you dare get out of this car."

"Gotta slow 'em down. Give me ten seconds after the gate closes. If I'm not out by then, haul ass."

"Dammit, Chip, stop *doing* this to me."

But he was already out, slamming the door and then slapping the car's flank, as if it were a horse.

O'Malley spun the wheels again, fishtailing through the gate and then slamming on the brakes, watching in terror as a pickup truck hurtled toward them, two men standing in the cargo bed, rifles propped on the roof of the cab. "Hurry up, Chip," she muttered. "Whatever you're doing, do it fast." With agonizing slowness, the gate began sliding shut. "*Hurry*, dammit," she yelled, at both the gate and Dawtry. The opening narrowed: Fifteen feet. Ten feet. Five. She could no longer see the pickup truck, but now she could hear it—or, rather, could hear bullets clanging against the steel plates of the gate.

When the gap was scarcely more than a foot wide, O'Malley saw a low form diving through it and then crumpling onto the gravel beside the car's left taillight. She scrambled out, hauled Dawtry to his feet, and helped him limp to the door and get in. Then she sprinted to the driver's side, got in, and took off down the highway, her gaze darting back and forth between the road ahead and the road behind.

"I jammed the mechanism," he panted. "They'll have to cut the chain to open it. That, or crash through with a bulldozer. Take a breath. Slow down, too—you're scaring me."

"*I'm* scaring *you*? Jesus, Chip, how are you even alive?"

"I'm not dead yet, but I've felt better."

"Your arm's a bloody mess."

"Wait'll you see my leg. My leg makes my arm look swell." He pulled up the leg of his pants—what remained of it—to show her.

O'Malley gasped. Even in the dim light in the footwell, she could see chunks of torn meat hanging from his mangled calf muscle, and she caught a glint of exposed bone on his shin. "Good God. We've got to get you to a hospital."

He shook his head. "Bad idea. The Spanish police will be watching. We're fugitives, remember?"

"What if you bleed to death? Doesn't that count as a bad idea?"

"I've got good clotting factors," he said. "My blood's practically Jell-O. I'm the world's slowest blood donor—they practically have to siphon it out of me. Isn't there a baby blanket or something in the back?"

"Yeah. Saturated in baby pee and poo and God knows what all, remember?"

"Pee's sterile. Poo, not so much, but it's good to challenge the immune system occasionally. Keeps those white blood cells on their toes."

He reclined his seat and rummaged around in the back, grunting with the pain of reaching and twisting. "Eureka," he said, extricating the blanket from the floorboard and frowning at it. "*Man*, do you reek-a." He began tearing it into strips, using his teeth to get the rips started. "Mmm. Tastes like chicken. Want some?"

"Thanks, but I can't. My nutritionist has me on an effluvia-free diet." She drove in silence for several minutes, glancing over whenever she heard a gasp or a grunt as he bandaged his ravaged leg.

When he was finished, he took a deep breath and then puffed it out in a long, show exhale. "Golly, that felt good."

"Do you need me to pull over and wrap your arm for you?"

"Nah, you just keep doing what you're doing." He began spiraling a long, stained strip around his left forearm. When he'd taken half a dozen turns around it, from elbow to wrist, he worked the free end deep beneath several layers of the wrap—"*Rrhhh!*" he growled as his fingers raked across the wounds—and then used his teeth to tug it tight. "Presto. Good as new."

"I have to know. How the hell did you get away from those dogs?"

He looked at her, then shook his head and looked away "You *don't* have to know. You don't *want* to know. And I don't want you to know."

"That bad?"

"Worse."

"I'm sorry. I won't ask you again, but if you decide you want to tell me, you can."

"I won't, but thanks." He was still staring out the window.

"What next?"

"Unfortunately, they know what we're driving now," he said. "We have a head start, but not much of one. We gotta keep moving. And we can't go someplace obvious."

"Speaking of that, I've been thinking, Chip."

"Uh-oh. I can already tell I'm not gonna like this."

"We got pictures of the drilling rig . . ."

"Oh, right. Give me the phone—I gotta send those."

"But we didn't get to the blasting site."

"I noticed that."

"We need more intel," she said. "Who are these guys? Where are they from?"

"That reminds me," he said. "I found this on the ground by the gate." He reached into a pocket and fished out a scrap of trash.

"What is it?"

"A wrapper," he said, studying the picture and text on the plastic foil. "A cookie stuffed with dates. Called maamoul. The label's in English and Arabic."

"You think the guys shooting at us were Middle Eastern?"

He shrugged. "That's my guess. I might've heard a few words of Arabic from one of the guys. But it's just a guess."

"If it *was* Arabic, does that mean it's ISIS?"

He shook his head. "Doubt it. This seems too big and sophisticated for ISIS. They're more about the small, simple attack—a single shooter, a guy with a machete, a truck plowing into a crowd."

"Who else is there?"

"If bin Laden were still alive, I'd lay this at his doorstep. Conventional wisdom says al-Qaeda's a walking corpse since he was killed. But I'm not so sure. His right-hand guy, who helped mastermind the 9/11 attacks, is still on the loose."

"Really? After all this time?"

"Really. Ayman al-Zawahiri. He's survived at least four assassination attempts. We haven't even come close in ten years. The CIA says he's irrelevant. A has-been. But British intelligence—MI6—thinks he's making a comeback. Word is he's tight with bin Laden's favorite son, so he might have serious connections and real money behind him. If any of the jihadists could pull this off, he seems like the only one. And what better way to prove that al-Qaeda's back, and badder than ever?"

"But you really think he could do it? This seems bigger and more complex—a lot more complex—than hijacking a few planes."

"I know," he said. "That's what I keep butting up against. I don't see how you hack the Global Seismographic Network, day in and day out, from the caves of Tora Bora, or wherever al-Zawahiri's hiding. You need connectivity, you need expert hackers, you probably need supercomputers."

She nodded. "Which brings me back to what I've been thinking."

"Uh-oh," he repeated.

"So, besides the guys shooting at us, who do we know, for sure, is linked to this? Or *was*, in the case of Iñigo, until you herded him off that cliff?"

"I wasn't actually trying to kill him," he said, looking distressed. "I was just trying to get between him and you."

"I'm not finger-pointing," she hurried to assure him. "I'm just saying Iñigo is still our only lead. Our best chance to find out who's behind this."

"How do we do that? We're running for our lives. Hiding from people trying their best to kill us."

"We hide in plain sight."

"Where do we do that?"

"I'm an astronomer," she said. "I hide at the observatory."

CHAPTER 17

She took the right-hand fork in the highway. It was the same fork she'd taken the day she had placed the seismometers, the day Iñigo had tried to kill her. *My God,* she thought. *Was that really only yesterday?* Slowly they corkscrewed up the northwest flank of the volcano, toward the observatory complex and the deep, dizzying caldera.

Dawtry leaned forward for a better look as the first of the massive telescope domes loomed into view on a rocky outcrop. "Cool," he said. "Very sci-fi—I feel like I'm on Mars. Is there a way to get in and out without being seen?"

She frowned. "Depends on whether anybody's watching. This is the only road up the mountain, but it's multiuse. It winds through the observatory complex, but it also leads up to a trailhead and overlook at the rim of the caldera. So there's lots of traffic during the day." She pointed to a motorized steel gate a hundred yards ahead. "At night, the road's closed, because headlights drown out the stars."

Dawtry studied the gate as they passed. "There's a video camera."

"Right," she said. "The receptionist at the Residencia opens the gate if somebody with the observatory needs to get in or out unexpectedly. The camera lets him see who's there. Keeps out the tourist riffraff."

"Are there guards patrolling the grounds?"

"Guards? *Ppffft.* None that I ever saw, anyhow. In the States, there'd be barbed-wire fences and surveillance cameras everywhere. But here? College campus meets ghost town. It's really sleepy, especially in the daytime."

He nodded. "So we could pass as tourists, heading up to see the crater, then take a detour and see if we can find out any more about Iñigo?"

"Makes sense," she agreed.

"He had an office?"

"A desk, at least, at the telescope. But he had an apartment, too. He invited me to pay him a visit." Dawtry raised his eyebrows, but she quickly shook her head, though a telltale flush crept into her cheeks. "He wanted me to come have a glass of wine, but I didn't take him up on it. Iñigo seemed like trouble."

"Iñigo? *Trouble?*" Dawtry chuckled. "I do love your gift for understatement, Professor."

A hundred yards beyond the gate, O'Malley turned onto a driveway marked by a small sign that read RESIDENCIA and, underneath, SOLO PARA EL USO DEL OBSERVATORIO: OBSERVATORY USE ONLY. Dawtry glanced around and nodded. "I see what you mean," he said. "Not what I'd call a high-security operation." He studied the Residencia, long and low, as they passed. "Looks like a Days Inn," he said.

"Similar architecture, better technology. Boatloads of bandwidth. Satellite teleconferencing uplink. It's like Mission Control on top of a volcano." Beyond the Residencia, the road curved down and around another low building. This one resembled a small condominium development, plucked from a Florida beach and transported to a barren mountainside seven thousand feet up. She drove to the last unit and parked the vehicle out of sight, just beyond the end of the building, then killed the engine. "So," she said, "What's the plan, Stan?"

"Improvise. And pray." After casting a quick look up the drive and seeing no one, he got out and headed for the front door. She hurried after him, catching up just as he turned the doorknob and pushed. "Prayers answered," he said. "I guess he left in a hurry that day."

"Yesterday," she corrected. "Twenty-four hours ago."

They stepped inside and closed the door. The blinds were open, and the interior, whose walls were white, was awash with late-afternoon light. The place was simple and sparely furnished. The ground floor had a combination living room and dining area, separated from a small kitchen by a waist-high counter. The furniture consisted of a four-chair dinette set, a love seat, an armchair, and a pedestal desk with metal drawers and a laminated wood-grain top.

Dawtry went first to the desk, which was positioned directly beneath the large front window. Outside, the mountainside sloped away steeply; a mile and a half below, the ocean glinted like pewter. "The place ain't plush," Dawtry said, "but the view rocks." A few books and a handful of memos—printed on the observatory's letterhead—covered most of the desktop. Dawtry flipped through the papers, assessing and quickly dismissing each one. He opened the desk's shallow center drawer; it held a midden of pens, pencils, and rubber erasers; a ruler, a small tape measure, a magnifying glass, and a jumble of paper clips. The side drawers were empty and dusty. "Not a hoarder, I'll give him that," Dawtry muttered, turning from the desk and heading for the kitchen.

The kitchen cabinets contained three chipped plates, two cans of soup, and a box of dried pasta. The refrigerator held a carton of orange juice, a bottle of white wine, and a can of beer, which had been opened. The freezer contained only a half-empty bottle of Smirnoff. "Man," said Dawtry, "the Donner Party had more provisions than this. He might've wined you, but he sure couldn't've dined you." He closed the freezer. "Let's look upstairs." He headed up the narrow staircase, O'Malley close on his heels.

A quick search of the small bathroom turned up nothing out of the ordinary: toothbrush, toothpaste, razor, shaving cream, Band-Aids, a comb and hairbrush, an assortment of over-the-counter medications.

The towel hanging on the hook behind the door was thin and dingy. The mirror over the sink was flecked with droplets of toothpaste, and the shower was rimmed with mildew.

The bedroom, like the living room, featured a large front window with a panoramic view of the mountainside and the ocean. The bed was a low platform with a black headboard. Beside it was a nightstand with a single drawer that contained two pornographic magazines, a box of condoms, and two empty condom wrappers. "Eww," said O'Malley. Her eyes automatically swiveled down to the wastebasket, where she saw the two used condoms, crinkled and knotted, their contents gleaming dully in the light. "Double eww," she said.

Dawtry followed her gaze. "Nice," he said, then turned and surveyed the sparsely furnished room again. "Dammit, where *is* it?" he muttered.

"Where's what?"

"His computer. Wouldn't you think we'd have seen a laptop, either on the desk or up here?"

"Hmm. Maybe it was in the jeep?"

He shook his head. "I checked the cab and the glove box. Nothing there but some tools and a first-aid kit. Oh, and a box of condoms."

"Ugh," she said. "So many condoms, so little love. I might have to start calling him Rubber Man." She pondered. "Maybe his laptop's up at the telescope dome."

"Maybe," he said. "But he came after you in the daytime, not at night. So I'm guessing this, not that, is the place he would've had his laptop. *If* he had a laptop." He walked to the closet, whose door was ajar, and inspected the clothes, the shelf, the floor. "But it's weird." He went to the dresser, quickly rummaged through the top drawer. "Have you noticed? There's not one single thing here that's personal, unless you count the books and the toiletries."

"And the condoms," she added.

"And the condoms. It's almost like he never really lived here. Or like the place has been scrubbed. Like they wanted to cover his tracks."

"Which begs the question. Who are 'they'? Who's he working for?"

Dawtry gave a shrug. He rifled through the remaining dresser drawers, frowning and muttering, then combed through the closet, his frustration visibly increasing. "There's got to be something more."

"Like what?"

He shook his head, surveying the room glumly. Then he returned to the bed. First, he peered underneath, using his phone as a flashlight. Then, one by one, he lifted the corners of the mattress. "Eureka," he said. "Like *this*." Reaching in with his free hand, he took hold of a thin, rectangular object, the size and shape of a large, thin book, and slid it out from beneath the foot of the mattress.

It was not a book; it was a large color photograph in a thin wooden frame, a diagonal crack angling across the glass. Dawtry took it to the window for more light and a better look, and O'Malley followed. The photo, wavy and washed out, showed an earnest dark-haired toddler, two or three years old, in the arms of a grinning dark-haired man.

"That's Iñigo," O'Malley said.

"Which one?"

"The man."

"You sure about that?"

"Unless he's got a twin brother," she said.

"Or unless he's a chip off the old block," said Dawtry "Look again. This picture's old—see how faded the color is?" He was studying it with such intensity that O'Malley wouldn't have been surprised to see it burst into flames. She looked over his shoulder, trying to see it through the FBI agent's eyes. The man, who looked to be around thirty, was wearing a khaki jumpsuit that contrasted almost comically with the white cowboy hat on his head. Behind the man and boy was a helicopter—a hulking, menacing shape in tan-and-brown camouflage.

"I guess you're right," she said. "That's gotta be his dad. But he looks exactly the age Iñigo was."

Dawtry had shifted his attention to the helicopter. "I think that's a Hind."

"A what?"

"A Hind. An Mi-24, I think it is."

"But what *is* it?"

"A military attack helicopter."

He turned his gaze from the photo to her face; she saw excitement in his eyes. "Iñigo told you Americans killed his father?"

"Yes. When Iñigo was three."

"Did he say where?"

"No. But you recognize the helicopter. Doesn't that tell you where it was?"

"Not really. The Hind is used all over the world. Middle East, Africa, Central Europe, South America—dozens of countries."

"So how do we narrow it down?"

"We keep looking."

"Where?"

He shrugged again. He continued staring at the photo, then—slowly and gingerly, as if the object might crumble or explode in his hands—he turned it over. "Here." The back was sealed, the cardboard taped to the wooden frame with brown packing tape. Dawtry tried to break the seal with a thumbnail, but the nail was too short and not sharp enough. He looked at O'Malley. "How are your fingernails?"

"Lousy." She held out a hand. "Down to the quick, all of 'em. I'm no good at being girlie."

"There are worse flaws." He reached behind him, opened the nightstand drawer again, rooted around, and took out a paper clip. He unbent it partway, then ran the tip of the wire around the tape, pressing it into the groove between the frame and the cardboard. When he had sliced all the way around, he used the makeshift tool to burrow beneath one corner of the cardboard, then gently pried. The cardboard stuck briefly but then let go, and Dawtry pulled it free, exposing the back of the photo itself. He stared, then said softly, almost reverentially, "Jesus H. Christ." He turned the photo so O'Malley could see it: an inscription on the back, hand lettered in ornate, exotic script. The only familiar-looking string of characters was a year, 1984.

O'Malley's brow furrowed. "What *is* that? Greek? It's Greek to me, anyhow."

"Close," he said. "Adapted from Greek, centuries ago. It's Cyrillic. I think our boy Iñigo is a Russki."

"Russian?" Again O'Malley made a sound like a puff of air from an aerosol can: *ppffft*. "No way. He went to university in Barcelona. He got his PhD in astrophysics at Oxford."

"Maybe, maybe not. From what you said, he was basically a tele-scope technician, right? Somebody who was here to help the real astron-omers—people like you. Last time I checked, Stephen Hawking wasn't doing tech support."

O'Malley groaned. "His name is Iñigo. Not Boris, not Ivan, not Dmitri. Iñigo. Iñigo Rodriguez, for chrissakes. Spanish name, Spanish guy."

"How do you know that?"

"Because he says—he said—he was a Spaniard."

"Yeah, and I say I'm a genius. Doesn't make it true. He also said he was a mild-mannered, friendly guy, right? Until he said he had to kill you, for mucking up his plot to slaughter masses."

She frowned. "Okay, maybe you've got a point."

"Yeah, and *maybe* the Pope's Catholic." He tapped the inscription. "I don't read much Russian, but this word here—the one that looks like 'Mockba'? I can read that one loud and clear. That's Cyrillic for 'Moscow,' Megan."

"You sure?"

"Sure as shooting. So you tell me, what's a nice Spanish boy doing in Moscow in 1984, sitting on the shoulder of a Soviet gunship pilot? A pilot who, oh, by the way, just happens to be his *papa*?" He laid the picture on the desk and used his phone to take a picture of the inscription. Then he flipped it over, image side up, and took a picture of the photo itself. Next, he began keying in a message.

"What are you doing?"

"I'm writing my boss and copying a few of my fans at the CIA."

"What are you telling them?"

"That the guy who tried to kill you might be a Russian agent with a Spanish cover. I'm saying his father was a Soviet pilot shot down in Afghanistan, sometime around 1985."

"Huh? Where'd you get all that?"

"From this." He nodded at the inscription. "You said he blamed the US for his dad's death. You said he was three when his dad died. Doesn't take a rocket scientist to figure out that the dad died not long after this picture was taken. And the place where Soviet helicopters were falling out of the sky in the 1980s was Afghanistan, thanks to the CIA, which was smuggling bazillions of Stinger missiles—surface-to-air missiles—to rebel warlords. The mujahideen. And teaching them how to use them."

"Oh my God," said O'Malley. "I saw that movie about the CIA in Afghanistan—what was it called? Not *Zero Dark Thirty*. The earlier one—about the congressman who funded that CIA operation?"

"*Charlie Wilson's War*. Good movie; bad foreign policy, in hindsight. We taught the Afghan rebels to fight with modern weapons. With *our* weapons. Seemed like a good idea at the time. But now . . ."

"Now *we're* the ones they're killing," she finished.

Dawtry tapped the tip of his nose—*bingo*—and did a final flurry of typing. Then he hit "Send." After the message transmitted, he took a deep breath and blew it out slowly. "This is bad, Megan. So bad. Way worse than bad."

"What do you mean?"

"I mean this isn't just al-Qaeda. This could be al-Qaeda plus *Russia*. Russia, home of Vladimir Putin, a modern-day Stalin. Putin rose through the ranks of the KGB. He's a cold-blooded thug with global ambitions." She stared at him. "If Russia pulls this off—devastates our entire Eastern Seaboard—it cripples us for years, maybe forever."

"Jesus, Chip. You really think they'd do this?"

"The brilliant part is they're hiding behind al-Qaeda. Iñigo said so himself—the world would blame radical Islamists—right?"

"My God," she whispered.

"Brilliant," he repeated. "Russia helps stab us in the heart but gets off scot-free. Al-Qaeda claims that *it* did the deed—delivered the mortal blow to the Great Satan, with the helping hand of Allah—and all the bad guys benefit."

"That's sick," she said. "But it makes a diabolical kind of sense. How the hell do we—"

Dawtry interrupted her with a raised hand. Outside, tires were screeching to a halt. "Shit," he muttered, "we've got company."

"Shit," she echoed, "we're trapped."

Dawtry spun, inspecting the bedroom, then pointed toward the bathroom. "There's a window in there. It opens onto the roof. Go!"

The window was a slider, high and narrow, but big enough, just barely. Dawtry tugged it open, popped the screen, and then interlaced his fingers to make his hands into a step for O'Malley. He boosted her up, practically tossing her through the opening, and as soon as she wriggled through, he breasted up, half vaulting out the opening and onto the roof. Then he slid the glass shut, wedged a small piece of gravel from the roof into the frame to jam the mechanism, and propped the screen back into position.

Moving at a low crouch, they scuttled along the roof, beyond the sight line of Iñigo's window. At the long building's midpoint, Dawtry nodded toward a stout drainpipe. "You okay to shinny down that?"

"Hey, I used to be a rock climber. And before that, a tomboy. I climb like a monkey. You could smear it with grease, and I'd still be fine."

He nodded. "You go first—I want to learn from a pro. Catch me if I fall, would you?"

"Ha ha."

"You think I'm kidding? My hand and my leg aren't at their best. I'm not sure how much strength I've got."

"God, I didn't even think about that. Why'd you let me put my foot in your hands?"

"Seemed better than letting you get caught or shot. Now shut up and shinny."

She was off the roof and on the ground in seconds. *Like a monkey,* he thought approvingly. His descent was just as fast but far less controlled: partway down, his mangled leg buckled and he half slid, half fell the rest of the way. Lunging forward, O'Malley managed to grab him around the waist and absorb part of his momentum. Even so, he grunted with pain when his feet hit the ground. They stood like that, her arms wrapped around him from behind, while he took several breaths. Then he turned, still in her arms. "That helped. Thank you."

She kissed him briefly. "Now what? We can't just stand here and make out."

"Too bad." He cast a quick glance around, at the rugged mountainside and the lengthening shadows. "Our options suck," he said. "The terrain's dangerous, and it'll be dark soon. I'd rather have wheels, if possible. Let's see if we can get to the car."

They crept along the back wall, then around the end of the building. When they reached the front corner, Dawtry darted his head out for an instant, then yanked back. "Bad news and good," he whispered.

"What's the bad?"

"Our car's blocked in."

"What's the good?"

"They left the keys in their truck."

"How the hell can you tell *that*?"

"With my special-agent superpowers. That, and the fact that the muffler's shot. I hear the engine running."

"Ah. So now we steal theirs?" He nodded, and she grinned. "I like it. We leave them stranded."

"And we trade up. Except for the muffler, that's a pretty good truck."

"And you think we can get in and get away before they catch us?"

"You stay here. I'll create a diversion."

"Did you just say 'create a diversion'?"

He nodded. "When you hear the diversion, run like hell for the truck. But I need to drive again."

"Can you? With your leg like that?"

"It's only a flesh wound."

"Where have you been all my life, Dialogue Man? Do be careful."

She heard the diversion—the sound of shattering glass, the sound of a rock being chucked through the bathroom window—and sprinted for the truck. As she yanked open the passenger door, she heard gunshots. *Don't you dare*, she thought, or prayed. *Don't you dare get shot, Chip Dawtry.*

A moment later, she saw him running around the corner of the building, his gait a limping, skipping stride that would have made her laugh under less perilous circumstances. Instead, she winced at the pain on his face. Leaning across the cab, she opened the door for him, and he tumbled in. She laid a hand on his arm. "Good to see you, Hopalong. Any new wounds I need to know about?"

He yanked the truck into gear. "Nah, but we gotta scoot. He'll be coming out the door"—a bullet slammed into the truck—"any second now."

The truck hurtled away from the apartments and up toward the main road. As they passed the Residencia, O'Malley caught sight of a familiar figure charging through the front door and sprinting across the parking lot, his eyes tracking them as he ran. She gasped. "My God, that's Antonio. The receptionist. He was always so nice to me. But come to think of it, he was the one who told Iñigo I was here yesterday." She turned to watch through the rear window. "He's getting into a car. He's coming after us, Chip."

They reached the main road. "Damn," Dawtry said, looking left.

"What?"

"The gate's closed. Looks like that nice man Antonio locked us in." He pointed to the right. "What's up that way?"

"The telescopes. The overlook at the rim of the caldera."

"Is there a way out?"

"Only if we sprout wings."

Dawtry spun the wheel to the right and gunned the throttle, laying down parallel tracks of rubber on the pavement. "This thing has some giddyup," he said approvingly. "How far back is he?"

"Two hundred yards? Three, tops."

He nodded grimly, his eyes scanning the road ahead. "When I say the word, open your door and jump."

"What are you talking about?"

"When I say 'jump,' you jump. Like your life depends on it. Because it does."

"What about you?"

"Do I look stupid? I'm jumping, too. Get ready."

Ahead, the mountainside seemed to drop away into nothingness, the road changing course at a switchback, ten feet short of the edge of the abyss. Dawtry checked the mirror; for the moment, a curve and an embankment hid them from Antonio's view. "Get ready," he repeated, slowing the truck and opening his door slightly. O'Malley cracked hers as well. "Haul ass for the bushes. We'll get half a second to hide. On three . . . One. Two. *Three!*"

O'Malley jumped and tucked into a roll, which took most of the impact out of her fall. She crouched on all fours and scuttled into the scrubby bushes beside the road. Suddenly she heard the truck's engine rev. Dawtry had not jumped; Dawtry was still at the wheel, accelerating toward the cliff. "Chip!" she screamed. *"No!"*

The last thing she saw was the truck reaching the curve—fast—but instead of turning, it hurtled straight ahead. It crashed through a flimsy fence, sailed over the edge, and then dropped from sight. O'Malley clapped her hands over her mouth, frozen in horror. Five seconds later, she heard a distant crash.

Her heart hammered, and she felt a surge of primal, dizzying terror course through her body. Instinctively, she began scrambling toward the edge. Just before she darted from the brush, though, a car sped past. O'Malley shrank back. The car skidded to a stop at the break in the fence, and Antonio leaped out, a gun in his hand. As O'Malley watched, her heart and breath still racing, he ran to the edge and peered over. A plume of smoke was billowing up from below, illuminated by the slanting rays of the setting sun. Antonio stared briefly; then he took out a phone, punched a button, and began talking. He nodded, gesturing excitedly with the hand holding the gun.

As the finality of the scene set in, O'Malley's legs buckled, and her knees and hands hit the ground hard. She stayed there, on all fours, trying to catch her breath, then sank to the ground and sobbed.

CHAPTER 18

"Hey, it was just a truck," came a low voice from a neighboring bush. "Next time I'll steal us that Lamborghini. Promise."

O'Malley bolted up and whirled around. "Chip! But . . . I saw you *die.*"

He spread his arms—one sleeve shredded and blood soaked, the other now dirty and torn. "I came back."

She crawled toward him and flung her arms around him, but after a moment she drew back and slammed her fist into his chest. "You scared the crap out of me."

"Ouch. Use your words, not your hammerlike fists. Well, here's hoping our friend is equally convinced. If so, we might actually make it out of here."

"When? How?"

"Soon. They're working on it—really they are. But meanwhile, let's find a better place to hide."

The sky was black and the air was frigid—the temperature had dropped thirty degrees in six hours, according to Dawtry's phone—and the wind had risen steadily. They had taken shelter in a protected niche of rock, one that retained a bit of warmth from the sun for the first few hours after sundown. Since dark, though, the rock had cooled, and instead of warming them, it gradually began to sap their heat. They huddled together—a pleasant activity, under other circumstances, but the combination of cold and danger put a damper on the romance. Dawtry briefed her on the plan but cautioned, "Remember, it's a *plan*, not a guarantee. A lot of things could derail it." Even in the darkness, he could see her face fall.

Shortly before midnight, his phone buzzed in his pocket. He pulled it out and checked the display. "What do you know," he said. "Showtime. Looks like our friends might actually come through for us."

They crept from their hiding place and picked their way across the rocky landscape at a half crouch, O'Malley pointing them toward a dark, indistinct structure. As they drew closer, a keening, moaning sound rose and grew steadily louder.

"What the hell is that?" Dawtry whispered. "It's creeping me out."

"The ghost of a dead astronomer," O'Malley said. She pointed to the MAGIC telescope and murmured the story of the astronomer's fatal fall. Then she redirected his gaze to the left. "There's where we're headed. Fifty yards. See it?"

He squinted and shook his head—he didn't—but a few steps later, he did: a smooth, dark circle in the rough tan landscape, a ten-foot "H" painted in the center: a helipad, built for ferrying astronomical gear and international dignitaries to the remote mountaintop.

She moved toward it. "Megan, wait," he hissed.

She turned back. "Why? You said midnight."

"We have to lay low till they get here. *If* they get here."

"I hate to wait. Can you tell them to hurry up?"

"My phone's dead. I didn't want to tell you, but that message a few minutes ago? Those were its dying words."

"Don't you have another one of those battery packs?"

"Nope. That was it."

"So for all your people know, we've fallen off a cliff or been shot?"
"Never give in, Megan. Never, never, never."

They huddled behind a scrubby bush, its branches hissing and shivering in the wind. In the nearby wires, the high, ethereal song continued. Then, almost imperceptibly at first, the pitch changed, complexified, as if a soprano's solo was morphing into a duet with a baritone. An immense shadow passed overhead—not so much a presence as it was a void. *A black hole,* thought O'Malley, ever the astronomer. *Or the angel of death.* Then the buffeting hit them. A vast dragonlike form, with a tapering snout and a slender tail, settled onto the helipad, its glassy eyes glowing a pale green. A rectangular opening appeared in the side of the beast, revealing a faintly lit cargo bay. Two dark figures jumped out, and O'Malley thought she glimpsed the silhouettes of assault rifles in their hands.

"*Now* it's time," Dawtry said, taking hold of her elbow and steering her toward the helicopter. When they reached the doorway, two more men in black reached out and grabbed them by the arms, hauling them inside. The two with guns—their faces smeared with charcoal—vaulted back in, and even before the door slid shut, the aircraft leaped off the pad, turned, and skimmed away from the mountaintop, dropping so fast O'Malley's stomach lurched.

They leveled off, then flew in darkness and silence for what might have been thirty minutes. Then the chopper seemed to slow, and O'Malley, craning to see out a window, glimpsed a line of green lights beneath them. The aircraft settled, rocking a bit beneath the rotor, and then lurched to a stop.

The door slid open again, and more hands helped O'Malley and Dawtry out. By then men in black fatigues, helmets, and bulky vests had already chocked the helicopter's wheels. Looking around, O'Malley saw that they had landed on what appeared to be a short runway framed by green lights. Beside them was a multistory metal building, its bands of windows glowing faintly. The windows reminded her of aquariums, but the fish swimming inside were people. O'Malley looked around, hoping to see more of their surroundings, but all she saw was utter darkness outside the narrow zone of light.

"Where are we?" she asked Dawtry. "Some military base in the desert?"

He laughed. "The desert? Not exactly."

Another uniformed man stepped from the shadows. Unlike the others, he was not wearing a helmet or fatigues but a crisp khaki uniform. He nodded at Dawtry and then saluted O'Malley. "Welcome aboard, ma'am."

"Aboard? Aboard *what*?"

He smiled. "The USS *Wasp*. Amphibious assault carrier. I'm Captain Stark."

"Jesus," said O'Malley. "I mean . . . thank you, Captain."

The bunk was narrow and the mattress was hard, but O'Malley slept like a baby. She was awakened, far sooner than she would have liked, by an insistent metallic rapping on the door.

"Hello?"

"Rise and shine," came Dawtry's voice, muffled by the metal. "We've got work to do."

She sat up, whacking her head. "*Ow.* I'm rising. Shining's a stretch. A shower and a cup of coffee would help. A plate of bacon and eggs wouldn't hurt, either."

"Then chop-chop. We're leaving in twenty minutes."

"Leaving? How? For where?" She crawled out of the bunk and headed toward the tiny shower cubicle.

"Tell you over breakfast. I'm opening the door."

"*Wait,*" she shouted, to no avail.

The door opened a crack and his hand and arm appeared, but—mercifully, since she was naked—not his head. Dangling from the hand was an olive-drab jumpsuit. "Put this on." She edged toward the door, then snatched the jumpsuit from him. He withdrew the hand. "Wait, there's more." The hand reappeared, this time clutching a pair of socks, an undershirt, and a pair of cotton briefs. "We guessed at your size," he said. "Hope everything fits. Now hurry up. I'll wait."

She hurried as best she could, cursing the shower's meager water pressure. She dried off, toweled her hair to dampness, and tugged on the jumpsuit.

"Not bad," Dawtry said when she opened the door and stepped into the passageway.

"The speed?"

"I meant the fit. But, yeah, you were pretty quick. Come on, let's eat." He turned and began walking away, moving briskly.

She hurried to catch up. "Where are we going?"

"To breakfast."

"*After* breakfast, smart-ass."

"I'll tell you over breakfast." He ducked through a bulkhead doorway and trotted up a ladderlike staircase.

She gave chase. "And you know where breakfast is?"

"I'm a special agent. I know all kinds of stuff."

He led her through a maze of narrow corridors. O'Malley picked up the scent of food; as they kept walking, the smell intensified, and by the time they entered a door marked OFFICERS' WARDROOM, she was practically floating on the tendrils of aroma like some ravenous cartoon character.

Inside the wardroom was a buffet heaped with eggs, bacon, sausage, onions, potatoes, pancakes, and syrup. "Thank you, Lord," O'Malley said.

"You're welcome," he replied, handing her a plate. "Bon appétit."

❖

"London?" O'Malley mumbled the question through a mouthful of food. "Why are we going to London?"

"To see Boyd. The geologist."

"I know who he is, thanks very much. Why are we going to see him?"

"Because he can't come to us."

"Christ, Chip, pass the pliers. It's like pulling teeth to get a real answer out of you. Why are we going to see Boyd? Why us, instead of somebody who isn't stranded on a speck of ship bobbing in the ocean a thousand miles from him?"

"Closer to two thousand," he said. "Because, unlikely as it seems, O'Malley, you and I are way ahead of everybody else on this. Even more unlikely, everybody else actually *realizes* it now."

A sailor entered the room and approached them. "Ma'am? Sir? The captain says it's time to go."

"Thanks," Dawtry said, pushing back and giving O'Malley an encouraging smile. "Ready?"

"Uh . . . I guess?" She grabbed a slice of bacon to go.

The sailor led them through another labyrinth and toward a doorway marked "Flight Deck." He stopped at a rack of equipment. "You'll need helmets," the sailor said, handing O'Malley one marked "Small."

She tugged it on. "In case we crash?"

He nodded. "At sea," he added, handing her a life vest.

"Hey, sailor," she said, "you do know how to show a girl a good time."

"This boat is huge," O'Malley said when they stepped through a bulkhead door and onto the flight deck.

"This boat is a ship," Dawtry replied. "And they've got bigger."

"It's an aircraft carrier," she said. "What's bigger than an aircraft carrier?"

235

Jon Jefferson

"A bigger aircraft carrier. This one's a 'commando carrier.' Carries helicopters, Ospreys, landing vehicles. It's designed to get marines and vehicles on the ground. The supercarriers—the ones that have catapults and runways and fighter jets—are a lot bigger."

The sailor led them forward on the deck. As they passed several helicopters. O'Malley noticed one that looked different from the others: black and menacing, all angles and facets rather than streamlined curves. She tapped Dawtry's arm and pointed. "Is that the horse we rode in on?"

"Yup."

"Even sitting still, that thing looks deadly."

"It is. Remember the raid that killed Osama bin Laden?"

"Not personally, but yeah."

"The SEALs flew to the compound in two experimental stealth helicopters. This is the one that made it back."

They kept walking. "So that's not our ride to London?"

He laughed. "If it were, we'd be swimming most of the way. Doesn't have the range. We're taking an Osprey."

"What's an Osprey?"

"*That*"—he pointed—"is an Osprey."

Ahead of them, O'Malley saw what appeared to be the bizarre, ungainly offspring of a cargo plane mated with a helicopter. A pair of stubby wings extended horizontally from a squat body. Attached to the end of each wing was an enormous engine with an immense propeller. But the engines were pointed skyward rather than forward, and the propellers, already spinning, looked like misplaced helicopter rotors.

"Can this thing actually fly?"

"Let's hope," he said. "I'm a weak swimmer."

They entered the rear of the Osprey, up a short ramp with built-in steps. The bare metal interior reminded O'Malley of a storage pod or U-Haul truck, but one that had been reinforced to contain raging rhinos or charging bulls. The passenger accommodations—folding jump

236

seats bolted along the walls—were clearly an afterthought. A crew member directed them to the forward end of the bay. Dawtry folded down a seat and sat, and O'Malley followed suit. Nylon straps hung from the seat's frame; Dawtry deftly assembled his into a harness, snugging the straps across his shoulders and hips, but O'Malley struggled to solve the puzzle of it. "It's tricky," he said. He unharnessed himself, then leaned across to help O'Malley.

He smelled of soap and aftershave, and she felt herself floating on that wave of aroma, too, though it led to a different doorway in her mind and body than the smell of eggs and bacon had.

With a whine and a thump, the loading ramp raised and sealed. Outside, the huge engines spooled up, the spinning blades thwacking and thrumming with increasing urgency. The Osprey's tail rose, then the nose. O'Malley craned to peer out a porthole in the fuselage and saw the carrier's bridge and antennas drop away. Then, as she watched in astonishment, the massive engine at the end of the stubby wing pivoted, rotating ninety degrees so that the propeller faced forward. The helicopter had transformed, in midair, into an airplane.

Six hours later, the plane transformed back into a helicopter as it slowed and descended. It landed with a slight jolt, and O'Malley looked out on a world that could not have been more different from the flight deck of the commando carrier: they were on a large, green lawn surrounded by manicured shrubbery, bare-branched trees, and—beyond, through and above the trees—the gray buildings of London.

The pilot stepped through the doorway from the cockpit. "Welcome to Regent's Park, folks. You're now free to move about the cabin and use your portable electronics. Thanks for flying with us, and please keep us in mind for your future travel needs."

CHAPTER 19

When they emerged from the bowels of the Osprey and descended the ramp at the tail—*Shat out by an Osprey,* O'Malley couldn't help thinking—four car doors opened in synchrony, and four men clambered from a pair of black sedans. All four were tall, dark-haired, and fit; all four carried themselves with the assurance of cops, former soldiers, or members of the political elite. They wore the same uniform, of sorts: knife-creased gray pants, gleaming black shoes, and thigh-length black overcoats of expensive wool. O'Malley felt absurd in her borrowed jumpsuit and bomber jacket, but she doubted that a shopping detour to Harrods was on offer, so she squared her shoulders and strode as if the military ensemble were her normal attire. *Fake it till you make it,* she coached herself.

The men met them halfway between the Osprey and a ring of Metropolitan Police cars, whose flashing blue lights defined a makeshift landing zone on the park lawn. A brief, awkward round of introductions ensued, during which O'Malley was ignored while the men shook hands and exchanged names and agency affiliations. Finally, Dawtry made a point of stepping back from the scrum, turning toward her, and saying, "And this, of course, is Dr. Megan O'Malley, to whom we owe eternal gratitude for doing our jobs for us." He gave the group a wry smile. No one smiled back.

Two of the men were Americans. One, James Howell, introduced himself as the FBI legat—"Legal attaché," he translated for O'Malley, though the translation shed little additional light to O'Malley's way of thinking. The other, Preston Kincaid, said vaguely that he was "with the US embassy," a phrase O'Malley figured meant "CIA spy." *About damned time,* she thought. *But better late than never.* The other two men were Brits, whose one-word names—Allen and Malcolm—were equally plausible as first names or last names. They offered only that they worked for "Her Majesty's government." *MI6?* she wondered. *Are they spies, too?*

The Gang of Four led O'Malley and Dawtry to the cars and offered them the back seat of one—the designated American car, apparently, since the FBI and CIA men got into the front seats. The Brits got into the other sedan and slowly led them across the damp lawn and toward a road. A few curious pedestrians gawked as the cars bumped off a curb and onto the pavement.

They crossed a bridge to exit the park, then traced an arc along a semicircular road flanked by a long, elegant row of pale stone buildings four stories high, a quarter mile of curving facade adorned with columns and balustrades. To O'Malley, it appeared as if the colonnade from St. Peter's Square had been transplanted to London, transformed from Vatican gateway to posh housing.

Dr. Charles Boyd inhabited a more modest flat a zigzag mile away. The two cars parked in a no-standing zone, and the six scofflaws got out and climbed the front steps. One of the Brits rang the bell, and they waited. And waited. "Professor Boyd," called the Brit. "Hello?"

Finally, the door was opened by a middle-aged man wearing a bathrobe, pajamas, and slippers. He didn't shake hands with the men—a smart move, O'Malley reflected, given the suture-ripping vigor with which guys like the agents tended to shake—but simply nodded and motioned them inside. His one greeting was extended to O'Malley: "Professor O'Malley, I'm so very pleased to meet you," he said, managing a strained smile and a featherlight touch of her arm. "You'll be most interested to see the data from our little seismometer project on La Palma."

Boyd led them to a dining table that was covered with papers. He looked ashen and moved slowly, but for a guy who had almost died from sepsis a few days before, he was game. "Forgive me if I sit," he said, then eased into a chair, wincing on the way down. "I'm supposed to be in bed still, but I rather thought this was worth getting up for."

He shuffled through the papers, found the one he wanted—a large map—and laid it at the center of the table. "Let's get to it straightaway, shall we?" The map showed North and South America, the Atlantic, Europe, and Africa. Amid the blue and green and desert brown of ocean and land, O'Malley saw dozens of orange circles. Some were tiny pinpoints, others the diameter of pencil erasers. "This map shows earthquakes during the past twenty-four hours," Boyd began. "The data come from the Global Seismographic Network, the GSN. As you can see, there have been dozens of them. One hundred and one, to be precise. The smallest was magnitude zero point one, in Nevada. You can't even see that dot at this scale, though if I zoomed in on the map and printed out just the western United States, you'd see it easily enough. The biggest quake"—he pointed at a large dot near the west coast of South America—"was magnitude five point four, off Ecuador, where the Nazca Plate and the South American Plate are constantly shoving at one another." He glanced around to see if there were questions; seeing none, he went on. "You Yanks might be interested to know that there were sixteen quakes in Alaska, twenty-three in California, and twelve in Oklahoma." He looked around the group. "Not a single quake showing up in the Canary Islands. Not in the GSN, that is."

He shuffled through the papers and found another page, this one a set of three squiggly line graphs. The squiggles, horizontal lines printed in red, green, and blue, looked like stock-market graphs on nightmarishly volatile days: the lines ran relatively smooth and level for an inch or so, then expanded abruptly, almost vertically, upward and down, then converged again along the central horizontal line—briefly. The wild oscillations were repeated four times; scattered between the four sustained spikes were half a dozen small ones. "These plots show the activity recorded by the three seismometers placed on La Palma by Dr. O'Malley. Same twenty-four hour period as the GSN map, very different data. As you can see, there were four significant events and six minor ones."

The men leaned in, looking at the printout. O'Malley looked at Boyd instead. "What's the scale here, Professor Boyd? How big is a 'significant' event?"

"Magnitude three or higher."

"Three?" said the CIA man, Kincaid. "That's pretty small, right, Chuck? You don't mind if I call you Chuck?"

"I *do* mind," Boyd said, "and, no, it's not small. It might be minor in Mexico, or insignificant in Siberia. But on the western flank of the Cumbre Vieja? A single quake that size could cause the entire mountainside—the fault block, geologists call it—to slip. If those quakes continue, the question is not *whether* the fault block will slide. It's *when*."

"Excuse me, Dr. Boyd," said Dawtry. "Let me play devil's advocate. What's the possibility of instrument error here? Isn't there a chance the seismometers set up by Dr. O'Malley are defective? Or could there be a glitch in the data transmission?" O'Malley knew he was asking a question that was on everyone's mind—and asking it more politely than one of the others might have asked. Even so, it felt like a minor betrayal, and her face burned.

"Most unlikely," Boyd said. "The three instruments are independent of one another. Three separate detectors, three channels of data, all highly consistent. As a scientist, I'd say this data set is quite robust."

"But isn't the global data more robust? That network has more sensors. Better ones, too, I assume." This, too, from Kincaid. O'Malley was beginning to dislike him. "Why trust O'Malley's data—a DIY project,

241

jury-rigged by an amateur—more than the data collected by real seismic stations all over the world?" Now she despised him, with a deep and implacable loathing.

"Because that data has been tampered with," Boyd said sharply. "It's been counterfeited. Plagiarized, in a manner of speaking—stolen from the network's own, earlier archives."

"What makes you sure?"

"Let me explain by way of an analogy." Boyd took a deep breath, and O'Malley sensed that he was trying to control his frustration. "If you took the complete works of Shakespeare and ran them through a document shredder, then dumped the shreds onto the floor, what are the odds that they would come back together, by random coincidence, in exactly the same arrangement they were in before—every page, every act, every scene, every line of dialogue identical?"

The Agency man gave a condescending smile. "Nice riff on the monkeys-at-typewriters meme, Doc. Obviously, it's not possible. But that's different."

"It's not," Boyd insisted. He retrieved a handful of printouts and gestured at the identical sets of squiggles. "The exact same data, month after month? That doesn't happen in nature. Only with counterfeit data."

"According to you. And Dr. O'Malley. That's it—just you two."

One of the MI6 men—O'Malley couldn't recall whether this one was Malcolm or Allen—cleared his throat. "Actually, we had a go at this ourselves," he said mildly, almost apologetically. "After Dr. Boyd finally got through to us. Our cryptography section. Oxbridge math whizzes, most of them." Kincaid turned to stare at him. "They agreed with Drs. Boyd and O'Malley—the Canary Islands data's dodgy. Worse than dodgy, matter of fact—it's as bent as a nine-bob note." Now everyone was looking at him dumbfounded—everyone except for his own colleague, who was nodding amiably.

"How could it be faked?" said Kincaid. "Who could pull off something that sophisticated?"

"Excellent question," the Brit replied. "We had a go at that, too, didn't we, Malcolm?"

"Right you are, Allen," said Malcolm. "Seems to be the handiwork of the same chaps who mucked about in your last presidential election, Preston. We've tracked it back to an outfit who work hand in glove with the FSB."

O'Malley raised a hand. "Sorry, what's the FSB?"

"Russian military intelligence," Dawtry interjected. "Used to be the KGB. Putin's alma mater. They could track your phone or hack your computer just like *that*." He snapped his fingers. "If *they're* involved—"

"Wait," said Kincaid coolly. "Hold your conspiracy-theory horses." His patrician face radiated condescension. "You can't just leap from a glitch in a database to a Russian plot without compelling corroborative evidence."

"That's what we thought, too," said Allen in his low-key, affable way. "So we asked some of our oil-and-gas friends to do a bit of monitoring on the QT." He reached into his pocket and pulled out a folded printout. "Stand-alone industrial seismometers in western Africa, not reporting to the Global Seismological Network. Their readings from the Canaries are spot-on with Dr. O'Malley's. Fainter, from a distance, but that's to be expected, right?"

"Right," seconded Malcolm.

Kincaid took the printout and studied it. He shrugged. "Okay," he conceded. "Someone—maybe independent hackers, maybe the FSB— could be trying to cover up evidence of seismic instability. In a dangerous fault zone. I get it."

"You *don't* get it, I'm afraid," Boyd said softly. "None of you except Dr. O'Malley fully gets it. This isn't just seismic instability. It's *induced seismicity*. Artificially triggered quakes. They have a distinct seismic signature." He riffled through the pile of papers, selecting two. "Here. See this earthquake pattern?" He held out the page and swung it in a slow arc so that everyone had a chance to see it. "This is from a recent earthquake in Oklahoma. Oklahoma had nearly a thousand earthquakes in 2015—the most of any state in the US. We now know that most of those quakes are the result of induced seismicity."

"From hydraulic fracturing—what the media chaps call 'fracking'?" asked MI6 Malcolm.

"From wastewater injection," Boyd said. "Wastewater injection pumps all sorts of liquids deep underground, most of them *not* from fracking. Brine from conventional oil extraction. Chemical and industrial wastes. Agricultural wastewater. Municipal wastewater." Seeing O'Malley's puzzled expression, he elaborated. "Wastewater injection is like flushing an immense loo down a sewer pipe two miles deep, under immense pressure. Eventually the earth literally breaks apart." He waved the printout again. "And this particular pattern of earthquake activity—again, *induced seismicity*—is exactly the seismic signature we're seeing on La Palma right now."

Dawtry leaned on the table. "And what do you make of that? What are the implications?"

"What I *make* of it, Mr. Dawtry, is that not only are people going to extreme and sophisticated lengths to *conceal* earthquakes on La Palma—"

"They're working hard to *cause* them," Dawtry finished.

"Exactly," said Boyd. "I think they're mounting a multipronged attack on the fault line. They seem to be using explosions—small ones so far, though perhaps they're gearing up for something bigger. But now . . ." He fished around in the pile of papers again; this time he extracted a photo—the photo of the apparatus O'Malley and Dawtry had spotted, just before *they* were spotted. "This photo is from La Palma. This is a slant drill rig, angling directly toward the base of the island's fault line. And *this*"—he showed the photo of the giant motor and large pipe located just below the rig—"is a high-pressure injection pump. Pumping seawater into a fault zone under intense pressure? It's like pumping machine oil into a rusty hinge. Pretty soon, it's going to move."

Malcolm nudged Allen, and Allen removed a sheaf of folded images from a coat pocket. "That's not the only one, I'm afraid," he said. "We've got satellite photos showing a dozen of these rigs. They're spaced at one-kilometer intervals along the flank of that entire ridge."

O'Malley said, "Sweet Jesus."

"Quite so," Boyd added.

Howell, the FBI legat, looked nervous. "We need to lean on the Spanish authorities. Get them to investigate, intervene. Shut the operation down if those are injection pumps that pose a hazard. That's the safest course of action."

"Or the riskiest," Malcolm said slowly. "If there's collusion at some level, we'd be tipping our hand."

"Give me a break," Kincaid scoffed. "You think *Spain* is colluding in a plot to kill millions of Americans?"

"*Somebody's* sure as hell colluding," Dawtry snapped. "I doubt that it's the government itself, but these people are clearly getting inside help. Dr. O'Malley's phone was being tracked with StingRay technology. At least two people at the observatory—which is administered by Spain—tried to kill us. And the authorities were looking for us at the airport. We have no way of knowing how high up the food chain these people have gotten."

Malcolm nodded. "If we tip our hand, the authorities might move slowly, whilst the terrorists go all out toward the tipping point."

Dawtry riffled through the maps and seismic graphs. "Dr. Boyd, what do you recommend?"

Boyd gave a vague shake of his head, and his eyes closed briefly. "As a lifelong academic, I'm *supposed* to say, 'Further research is required.' But as a human being who abhors mass murder? I say find the sons of bitches, gentlemen. And stop them straightaway. If it's not too late."

❖

They left a visibly drained Boyd and got back in the cars, the same seating arrangement as before. But they did not return to Regent's Park, as O'Malley had expected. "Where are we going?" she asked.

"The embassy," said Howell, the Bureau's legal eagle. "We've got an emergency briefing."

"With the ambassador?"

"Among others."

"What others?"

Howell twisted to look at Dawtry. "You weren't kidding—she *does* ask a lot of questions."

Dawtry winced at the elbow O'Malley jabbed into his ribs. "Good thing. If she didn't, we'd still have our heads up our asses on this. Like she said, what others?"

"Mainly the National Security Council. Our directors"—he nodded at Kincaid, the Agency man—"will both be there, of course. We'll also be looping in the ambassador to Spain, since this involves Spanish territory. Plus a scientific adviser of some sort, I'm told."

They turned south onto a busy thoroughfare and crossed a river—the Thames, O'Malley assumed—by way of what was labeled VAUXHALL BRIDGE. On the far bank, a brooding, hulking building loomed above the river. It rested, or, rather, bristled, on a sharp-cornered foundation that reminded O'Malley of a star-shaped fortress from some bygone century. Rising above the foundation was a structure whose muscular Art Deco turrets and towers might have served as a movie set: the fortress of Darth Vader or Lord Voldemort or a Batman supervillain. "That's creepy," O'Malley said, reaching between the front seats to point it out. "That might be the most sinister building I've ever seen."

Howell chuckled. "I'll tell them you said so. They'll appreciate that."

"Who?"

"MI6. That's their headquarters."

O'Malley felt a sense of relief when they turned parallel to the river and left the building behind. A half mile upriver, they came to a cube of glass, ten or twelve stories high, luminous in the twilight. It was set in what appeared to be a park, surrounded by lawns, trees, and a pond. The building radiated light, transparency, and a sort of friendly wholesomeness, on its own merits but also, especially, in contrast to the brooding building inhabited by British intelligence. "Welcome to US territory," announced Kincaid.

O'Malley gaped. "This is the embassy?"

"It is," Howell said. "Brand-spanking-new. We're still unpacking. Ignore the boxes and lack of furniture." The car angled down a ramp toward a security gate, armed guards, and an underground garage.

"It's gorgeous. Not menacing at all."

Kincaid turned and gave her a crocodile smile. "The perfect disguise."

O'Malley had been waiting for an hour—sitting, stewing, chafing—in a hallway outside a conference room while Dawtry, Howell, and Kincaid sat inside: *conferred* inside, she supposed, though conferring, in this case, seemed to be a word that meant "shouting." She tried to eavesdrop, but the words were muffled, protected against spying ears, including ears that were far sharper and more important than her own. She wondered if the Russian embassy was nearby; if it wasn't, the KGB—*no, the FSB,* she corrected herself—surely had listening posts in the neighborhood. Perhaps the FSB occupied several floors of the tall, missilelike skyscraper she'd glimpsed towering over the riverbank halfway between the US embassy and MI6. Perhaps someone somewhere in that tower had read her emails, listened to her phone calls, sent thugs to her apartment. She shuddered at the thought.

The door opened and Dawtry emerged, his face red and grim. "Well, *that* was fun," he muttered, beckoning to her. "If somebody asks you a question, answer. *Briefly.* Otherwise, keep quiet."

"Yes, sir."

The conference room was as big as O'Malley's entire apartment, and the wall at the far end was covered with large monitors showing maps, seismograms, and video feeds of other participants in the teleconference. One feed was captioned "Madrid—Local Time 8:17 p.m."; front and center amid a handful of people in the Madrid group was a distinguished sixtysomething man O'Malley assumed was the US ambassador to Spain. Another feed, captioned "NSC/Washington, DC—Local Time 2:17 p.m. EST," showed several men in military uniforms, along with a handful of civilians. O'Malley was both disappointed and relieved to see that the president was not among them, but she did recognize other VIPs, including the vice president, the secretary of state, the attorney general, and the FBI director.

A third video feed was labeled "Federal Emergency Management Agency" and registered eastern time as well. The fourth and final feed was captioned "UC Seismology Lab, Berkeley, CA—Local Time 11:17 a.m. PST." O'Malley gasped when she saw the face on that screen: David Solomon, her ex-husband. It took all her willpower—that, and the admonitory squeeze Dawtry was giving her forearm—to keep from shouting, "David, what the hell are *you* doing here?"

"Dr. Solomon," said one of the DC military brass, "you've written quite a bit about rising risks of earthquakes and tsunamis affecting the *Pacific* Coast. But you haven't written about the East Coast and La Palma. Is that because you think the risk is small?"

"Until recently—until today, in fact—I *did* believe the risk from La Palma was minor. Insignificant, even. But now? Frankly, I'm gravely concerned. Alarmed, in fact. La Palma shows signs of serious and rising instability. And the consequences for our Eastern Seaboard could be catastrophic. 'Apocalyptic' would not be an exaggeration."

"Explain," said the talking head identified as the director of FEMA.

David nodded. "On its own, La Palma is active, volcanically and seismically. The terrain is high, steep, and unstable. There's evidence,

248

historical and prehistorical, of major landslides and large tsunamis, some of them hundreds of feet high, in the Canary Islands. All that's indisputable, but not particularly worrisome. What's new and alarming is what we've learned only this week. There's been a deliberate and very sophisticated effort—a very *successful* effort—to hack into the Global Seismological Network. To manipulate the data in order to mask an increase in seismic activity on La Palma. This hacking was discovered and brought to our attention by Dr. Megan O'Malley, a respected Johns Hopkins scientist." O'Malley was pleased and grateful that he called her a "scientist" rather than an "astronomer," a term that would surely have undercut her credibility on seismic matters. "To be honest," David went on, "at first I was skeptical about Dr. O'Malley's findings. But my colleagues and I have combed through the data, and Dr. O'Malley is absolutely right. The hacking is real, it's irrefutable, and it's been going on for the past two years."

"Dr. Solomon, if I may," began another of the civilians in Washington. He paused, giving the video camera time to zoom in on him.

Dawtry leaned toward O'Malley and whispered, "CIA director." Her eyebrows shot up and she nodded, duly impressed.

"Yes?"

"Granted, the data hacking is cause for concern, and we do have our cybersecurity experts tracing the source. But if the data we have is flawed, it seems to me the only firm conclusion we can draw is that we don't really know what's happening on La Palma. Maybe La Palma poses a danger, maybe not. Isn't that correct?"

David nodded slightly, but his eyes flickered in a way that O'Malley recognized from prior, sometimes-painful experience. The nod acknowledged the question; the eye-flicker dismissed its validity and warned of a withering response. "Actually, that's not correct at all. La Palma is a ticking time bomb, and someone's doing their best to fast-forward the clock."

"What's your basis for that?" pressed the CIA director.

"Twofold. First, we've gone back and looked at other sources of data—oceanographic data and industrial seismology, oil and gas seismic readings that don't report to the global network. These provide independent indicators of seismic activity on La Palma—data strongly contradicting the hacker-modified database. What we see from these independent sources points to a dramatic increase in seismic activity on La Palma beginning eighteen months ago—an increase in both frequency *and* intensity. Second, we now have direct, reliable data—real-time data—from La Palma itself, thanks once more to Dr. O'Malley. Dr. O'Malley placed three seismometers on the island, and in the past thirty-six hours alone, they've recorded sixteen events, all of them centered near the fault line that bisects much of the island. This trio of seismometers reports four earthquakes and twelve sets of explosions." O'Malley noticed a flickering reflection from David's glasses, and he glanced down, peering at a corner of his screen. "This just in," he said. "Another quake occurred less than sixty seconds ago. Magnitude four, the strongest yet."

"Let me be sure I understand you," said the FBI director. "You're saying it's getting more dangerous by the minute? As we sit here talking to you?"

"Yes, sir, I'm afraid so. And the reason is that someone—I have no idea who—is working very, very hard to *make* it more dangerous."

"And if this trend continues?"

"It will be cataclysmic. Let me show you something." He looked down again, made a few keystrokes, and reduced the window showing his face to a small thumbnail image. Another window opened, this one showing a large three-dimensional map of La Palma. "This is an animation showing the landslide and the tsunami that could result from a major quake. Bear in mind, this model assumes worst-case conditions—the largest collapse, the fastest slide, and therefore the biggest tsunami. But the modeling is scientifically solid." He clicked the "Play" arrow, and the men in DC and London and Madrid saw what O'Malley had seen a few days before—Christ, had it been only days? It felt like a year, a lifetime—when she had gone down the rabbit hole of tsunami research. A huge portion of the island broke free, slid rapidly downward, and plunged into the ocean. The view widened, and color-coded waves radiated outward from La Palma toward other coastlines: northwest Africa, southwest Europe, the United Kingdom.

David had slowed the playback, and his voice accompanied the animation, tolling the height of the tsunami as it struck: "Casablanca, two hundred feet. Lisbon, one hundred fifty feet. France and the UK, thirty to sixty feet. Iceland, sixty to eighty feet. Maine, a hundred thirty feet. New York City, a hundred. District of Columbia, fifty." At the mention of the capital, the people in DC shot worried looks at one another. "Newport News, eighty." Now the uniformed men turned ashen. "Charleston, sixty. Jacksonville, sixty." More military bases, more military grimaces. "West Palm Beach, Fort Lauderdale, and Miami, sixty-five." The pulsing colors subsided. "Here's another animation," he continued. "This one superimposing the runup on the profile of lower Manhattan. The view is from New York Harbor, southeast of Battery Park." As they all watched, mesmerized—including O'Malley, who had not seen this animation—the base of the Statue of Liberty disappeared beneath the crest of a wave, and the buildings of the world's financial epicenter seemed to sink: one story, two stories, three, five, seven, nine, ten. Streets vanished, replaced by canals: New York was transformed into Venice. "This animation shows approximately how high the surge would go, within one to two minutes," David explained. "What it doesn't show is the force and the damage. Every window hit by the water would shatter; even windows way above the water level would blow out from the internal pressure. Buildings would collapse. Cars and trucks tossed around like corks." The image—New York under a hundred feet of water—disappeared, replaced once more by David's face. "If this happens on a weekday, when four million people are in Manhattan, the death toll there alone could be in the hundreds of thousands, with a million or more injured."

The FEMA director looked terrified. "Dr. Solomon, are you saying we should evacuate New York City? Are you saying we should evacuate the entire Eastern Seaboard?"

"Christ, Bob," said one of the civilians O'Malley didn't recognize, staring at the FEMA director as if he were an imbecile. "Evacuate to where? Where would they go, where would they stay, and for how long—forever? We can't evacuate the East Coast. The stock market would implode; the entire economy collapse. That's not an option."

"So what's your suggestion, Jim?" the FEMA guy shot back. "You're saying we just let millions of people die? Tens of millions? The population of the low-lying Atlantic Coast is over a hundred million. You think millions of deaths won't ding the damned *market*? Is that what you think?"

"*Stop* it," shouted O'Malley. Every head snapped in her direction. "Just *stop* it!"

"*Don't*, Megan," Dawtry hissed through clenched teeth. "Shut the hell up."

She did not. "Quit arguing about what to do about the damned disaster and just *stop* it. Keep it from happening!"

"Get that damn woman out of the room," said one of the White House guys.

Dawtry stood up and took hold of her arm. "Come on, Megan." He pulled her to her feet.

"No." She yanked her arm away. "*No!* You guys can't see the forest for the *bullshit*. Dr. Solomon, I can tell you who's doing this. It's the Russians, in league with al-Qaeda." She swept a pointing, accusatory finger across the faces on the screen. "You don't believe me, ask your friends at MI6. What you need to be talking about is not the fucking stock market. It's what else these assholes are doing to trigger Armageddon."

"Jesus H. Christ," muttered Kincaid, the embassy's CIA guy.

Dawtry put an arm around her shoulder and attempted to turn her toward the door. She shook him off again. "A *nuke*," she shouted. "What if the Russians have given a nuke to al-Qaeda? Any of you geniuses think of what *that* might do to the fault line, as weak and unstable as it already is?"

"Get that bitch *out!*" shouted the politician. "Now!"

The ambassador pushed back from the table and walked, with the air of an unruffled man in charge, toward O'Malley and Dawtry. "Dr. O'Malley. Special Agent Dawtry. Would you give us a moment, please." It wasn't a question; it was a command, but a calm and even courteous command. A diplomatic one.

Dawtry nodded, gripped both of her arms, and steered her—marched her—to the door. He opened it and propelled her out. Then, before following her out, he turned back toward the room and the video camera. "She's right, morons," he shouted. "She's the only one who's been right. The whole damn time, she's the only one. Quit covering your own asses and protect the American people."

He slammed the door. In the stunned silence his words had created, the slam boomed like an explosion.

CHAPTER 20

She was carrying the dragon bowl up the mountainside once again. This time it was heavier than before; she staggered beneath the weight, almost unable to bear the burden. Finally, she reached the rim of the caldera and set down the bowl, taking care not to jar the delicate mechanism. Then, exhausted from her labors, she lay down beside it to rest. She had been asleep for only a few moments when she was awakened by the shaking of the earth—gentle at first, then insistent, then violent. Slowly she opened her eyes. Directly in front of her was the immense dragon bowl, one of its dragons directly above her face. As the shaking continued, the dragon's eyes opened, too, and the head turned slightly, the eyes searching, until the dragon's gaze focused directly downward: directly on her. As she returned the stare, frozen with fear, the beast's mouth opened and a ball fell from it. The ball dropped toward her, plunging into her open mouth, and she could not breathe.

"Megan. *Megan!*" O'Malley's head jerked up and her eyes opened. The Osprey was bucking, and Dawtry's hand was squeezing her knee insistently. She was coughing violently, thrashing against the straps of the shoulder harness. "You okay?" She shook her head no, then yes. "You seemed to be in some real distress there."

"I guess that's what I get for going to sleep, huh?"

"Sorry to wake you up, but we're landing anyhow."

Now that he'd said it, she realized that the bucking and shaking that had awakened her was simply the Osprey slowing, changing direction, descending in the darkness. Craning forward and peering out the small round window, she saw the antennas and aquarium-like windows of the command bridge on the *Wasp*, then saw the deck, its landing zone outlined by green lights, just as it had been a few nights before. *No, not a few nights,* O'Malley realized with astonishment. *Last night. That was last night.*

When she and Dawtry staggered down the ramp, leaden with fatigue, they were met once more by Stark, who snapped a salute. "Welcome back," he said.

Dawtry nodded warily. "You fixing to lock us in the brig?"

"The brig? No, sir." The captain smiled. "Though I did hear you two caused quite a stir in London. Even more of a stir in DC."

"It got a bit intense," Dawtry said. "We didn't even see the worst of it. The shouting really ramped up after they kicked us out." He paused. "I was sure they'd stick us on the first flight back to the States. Any idea why they sent us back here instead?"

"Way I understand it," the captain said, looking from Dawtry to O'Malley and back again, "you two are the brains of the operation."

"Operation?" said O'Malley. "What operation?"

"*This* operation." He gave a sweep of the arm to encompass the flight deck, which was bustling with sailors and marines. O'Malley and Dawtry stared at him, then shot questioning glances at each other. "It's loud out here," the captain said. "Let's go inside."

He led them into the carrier's island and up a level, into a room jammed with sailors at computer stations and radar screens. "This is our CIC—Combat Information Center. Nerve center of the operation."

"You keep saying *operation*," Dawtry said. "An intel mission?"

"No, sir."

"Then what?" The captain's only response was a cryptic smile. Dawtry stared. "You're serious? A military operation?"

Stark nodded. "Operation Wave Goodbye. Gotta love the name, right?"

"But . . ." Dawtry searched for the right question to ask. "It seems clear that Russia's involved in this. What happens if the Russians escalate? If they *retaliate*?"

"They can't. Not directly, anyhow. They've boxed themselves in—categorically denied any involvement."

"Wait. *Wait*," O'Malley said. "They *deny* it? Does that mean somebody actually *asked* them? 'Hey, Comrade Putin, why you try to slaughter millions of US peoples?' What kind of asshat idiot would *ask* that?"

Stark's mouth might have twitched, almost imperceptibly, but the rest of his face remained carefully neutral. "The commander in chief."

"What?"

"The president felt it was 'necessary and appropriate'—his choice of words, I'm told. President Putin assured him that there's no nefarious plot—"

"Brilliant," O'Malley interrupted. "Let me guess. 'I give you pinkie promise, my friend'?"

Stark resisted taking the bait. "And the president believed him. Russia's not involved. That's the official White House position."

Dawtry was studying the captain's face, his eyes in the laser-beam mode O'Malley had seen on a few prior pivotal occasions. "And the president has authorized an invasion of Spanish territory?"

"No, sir, he has absolutely not authorized an invasion. He hasn't authorized anything."

Dawtry frowned and squinted. "Help me out here, Captain, because I'm confused as hell. The president doesn't think the Russians are involved, the president hasn't authorized an invasion, and yet we're launching a military invasion?"

The captain held up an index finger. "Not an invasion."

"What, then?"

"Technically, it's called a preemptive act of self-defense."

Dawtry chewed on this, then a look of comprehension dawned on his face, along with a slow smile. "So we're white, in this particular chess match."

Stark nodded.

"Huh?" said O'Malley. "You guys have lost me."

"Means we get first move," Dawtry said.

"Military Theory 101," Stark added. "The side that strikes first gains an overwhelming advantage."

"I get that," she said, "but I still don't get how you can do it without authorization."

"Standing Rules of Engagement," the captain said.

O'Malley held out her hands and shook her head.

"Sorry, I'll translate," Stark said. "I'll start with a question, Dr. O'Malley. If that fault line lets go and half the island drops into the ocean"—he pointed at the giant screen, filled with a 3-D map of La Palma—"what would the height of the tsunami be when it reaches us?"

"Depends. Where are we now?"

"Fifty nautical miles west."

"We're only fifty miles out? Due west?"

He nodded.

"Jesus, Mary, and Joseph. You got a death wish?" O'Malley mentally replayed the animation she'd watched on the screen in London less than eight hours before: the vivid bands of yellow, orange, red, fuchsia, purple, and blue radiating outward from La Palma, unfurling like some tropical blooming of the apocalypse. "I'm shooting from the hip here, but if I'm remembering right, we're talking a thousand-foot surge here. Plus or minus." She looked at Dawtry, who nodded in grim confirmation.

The captain's eyes glinted. "This ship can't survive that. Not a chance. Dr. O'Malley, I don't give a rat's ass who's trying to trigger that wave—Russian spies, al-Qaeda crazies, insane surfer dudes. What I care about is defending my ship and my men against hostile intent."

Dawtry looked thoughtful. "Hostile intent," he echoed. "And under the Rules of Engagement . . ."

"I have the right—the duty, in fact—to take preemptive action against any 'ship, aircraft, or ground site' that threatens my ship with hostile intent."

Dawtry was nodding now. "That was the basis for the navy's missile strikes against Yemen in 2016, right?"

"Exactly. The USS *Mason* took out three radar stations that were targeting our ships."

"There does seem to be a credible case that your ship and your men are threatened."

"*My* ship? *My* men? Hell's bells, Chip, from what I understand—not just from you and Dr. O'Malley, but from DOD intelligence now, too—this thing threatens every US warship in the Atlantic. Plus every vessel at port on the East Coast. Norfolk. Jacksonville. King's Bay. Key West. New London. We're absolutely within our rights to strike."

"The politicians and media pundits might not see it that way, Captain."

"The politicians and pundits can screw themselves," Stark said. "They've got no skin in the game. Hell, they're already running for higher ground. 'A planning retreat at Camp David,' they're saying. I don't know about the planning, but they got the 'retreat' part right; that's for damn sure."

"Figures." Dawtry locked eyes with the captain, looking grim. "Anything goes wrong here, you'll swing from the yardarm, you know."

He shrugged. "If I swing, it'll be with a clean conscience. And for what it's worth, I won't hang alone. The Sixth Fleet commander backs me on this."

"You're sure?" said Dawtry. "You've got that in writing?"

"I've got that in force. Task Force Sixty is heading this way."

Dawtry whistled. "That's huge."

"What's Task Force Sixty?" asked O'Malley.

"That's the cavalry," the captain said. "The big guns. The 'Mighty Ike'—the USS *Eisenhower*, the Sixth Fleet's supercarrier. The Ike comes with an air wing, four guided-missile cruisers, and two guided-missile frigates. The *Ohio*'s coming, too." She raised her eyebrows in question. "An attack submarine full of cruise missiles."

O'Malley's eyed widened. "Sounds like you could conquer the whole island with all that."

He smiled grimly. "With all that, ma'am, we could conquer almost any nation on earth."

A sailor approached and signaled to the captain. "Sir, you've got an urgent call on the secure frequency." Stark excused himself and stepped to a phone at one side of the room.

He returned several minutes later, ashen-faced. "Bad news," said Stark. "I hate to say it, but it appears that Dr. O'Malley was way ahead of us all. Again."

"What was she right about *this* time?"

"We've just gotten evidence that a nuclear device may have been smuggled into Santa Cruz harbor. There might be a loose nuke on La Palma."

CHAPTER 21

O'Malley stared at the captain, hoping she had misheard his words "A nuclear device? As in a nuclear *weapon*? How could that happen?" She herself had floated the idea in London, but it had been a bluff, or so she'd thought: a desperate attempt to get the bureaucrats to take the danger seriously. "Aren't there arms-control treaties and nuclear safeguards? Doesn't the government keep *track* of this shit?"

"Yes, ma'am," said Stark, "but it's a lot to keep track of. When the Soviet Union came apart, there were thirty-two hundred strategic warheads—big nukes, on ballistic missiles—scattered through sixteen republics. Since then, all of those have been removed. The weapons-grade uranium and plutonium from those bombs has all been recovered and downblended—diluted into low-grade fuel for power reactors."

"So what's the problem?" pressed O'Malley.

"The problem is the other devices."

"What other devices?"

"Tactical devices. Small warheads. Battlefield munitions. Twenty thousand or so, some small enough to fit in a duffel bag."

"Christ," she said. "You're saying there are *twenty thousand* nukes just floating around, God knows where?"

"No, ma'am, I'm not saying that. Moscow recovered all of those, too. Supposedly. But . . ."

"But what?"

"But twenty thousand's a big number, and Russia's a big place. Lots of corruption, lots of profiteering. Lose one out of a thousand, and that's twenty loose nukes."

"Shit," O'Malley said. "Who—"

"Sorry," Dawtry interrupted. "Can you back up, Captain? You said there's evidence that a weapon's been smuggled in. What kind of evidence? Intel intercepts? Human assets? What?"

"Multiple kinds of evidence," said Stark. "Human intel. Also radiological signatures."

"That's bad," said Dawtry. "Very bad."

"Signatures from decay products?" asked O'Malley.

"Yes, ma'am," Stark said. "The decay of the nuclear material is slow, and warheads are well shielded, but trace amounts get out. If you've got a good detector that's close enough, you can pick up the signature."

Dawtry nodded. "The detectors are getting better all the time. Until recently, you had to be within forty, fifty feet to pick up the gamma radiation from a warhead. Now, we've got detectors sensitive enough to read the signature from a drone."

She turned to Stark. "And there's a drone over La Palma?"

The captain nodded. "There is now. A Sea Avenger."

"Impressive," said Dawtry. "That's the new one, right? Like a Predator, but with a jet engine? Flies at, what, four hundred miles an hour?"

Stark nodded. "When there's a need for speed. But it can poke along at a hundred, once it's on station. Stays aloft for up to twenty hours."

Dawtry pressed. "Strictly surveillance? Or does it have strike capabilities, too?"

"Strike. Hellfire missiles on all six hardpoints."

"Wowzer," Dawtry said. "Good to have options. But can I circle back to the radiation detectors?"

Stark nodded. "We found traces of gamma in the vicinity of Santa Cruz harbor last night. A cargo ship docked yesterday. Came through the Strait of Gibraltar two days ago. Before that, it was in Istanbul. Before Istanbul, it was in Odessa and Sevastopol."

Dawtry frowned. "The Black Sea. Ukraine and Crimea. A nuke could've been loaded aboard in any of those places. Is it still on the ship?"

"Not sure," Stark said.

O'Malley shook her head. "It won't be. That nuke's long gone. Already headed for the fault zone."

"I'm afraid you're right," Stark said. "We're trying to pick up the trail, but that requires flying a grid search. Maybe you've got ideas that could help us narrow it down?"

"I'll try, Captain. Can I get on the Internet with one of these computers?"

"Sure. What do you need?"

"Professor Boyd created a secure website for the seismometer data. It updates automatically every time there's a seismic event. I want to look at the latest data."

The captain led her to a workstation; then he entered a password and offered O'Malley the chair. "Help yourself."

O'Malley typed a website address, then a password. A screen with dozens of columns of numbers popped open. "That's a fast connection."

"If you're at war," he said, "a second—a fraction of a second—can make all the difference."

Dawtry leaned over one of her shoulders, the captain over the other. "As you can see, it's a spreadsheet. Each column represents a distinct seismic event."

"That's a lot of events," Stark said.

"Unfortunately, they're happening with increasing frequency. There are three sets of rows, one set for each instrument. The first line in each row is the amplitude. Multiply amplitude by ten, and you'll get the approximate magnitude of the event."

The captain put on a pair of glasses and leaned closer, scrutinizing the figures. "So most of these are very small—magnitude less than one. We don't need to worry about those, right? Just these bigger ones, the threes and fours?"

"The big ones are the scary ones," she said, "but the tiny ones are the interesting ones. The informative ones."

"Come again, ma'am?"

"A big one is more likely to trigger the landslide. But if you look at these data cells"—she pointed, in quick succession, at three lines of data—"you can see that the bigger quakes are all over the map. Here a quake, there a quake, everywhere a quake quake. But if you focus on the little ones, which are ripple shots of explosives"—this time she pointed to several of the small, microsecond shocks, like the ones that had interfered with her search for Planet Nine—"what jumps out at you?"

"My God," said Dawtry. "They point to the same spot every time. Every explosion happens in exactly the same place as the one before."

"Almost," O'Malley corrected. "Not quite. Look at the last digit, the last fraction of a degree. It changes very slightly—and very consistently— every time."

"So the explosions are in multiple locations?" Dawtry said.

"Not just multiple locations. Steadily *moving* locations."

"Jacobson," the captain barked at a sailor a few workstations away. "Sir?"

"Triangulate these positions. Three compass bearings apiece."

"Ready, sir."

Stark rattled off ten sets, ten trios, of compass bearings. "Got it?"

"Yes, sir."

The captain pointed to the large relief map of the island. "Plot those points on the map. Not all at once, though. Sequentially. Add a position every half second, but don't erase the priors. Can you do that?"

"No problem, sir." The sailor's keyboard clattered. The 3-D relief map on the large wall-mounted screen shifted in perspective, to a straight-down view. "Eye altitude 30 mi," read a scale in the lower-right corner. A red dot flashed onto the screen, in a forested part in the southwest region, midway between the coastal highway and the crater-marked ridgeline. A half second later the dot grew brighter; another half second, brighter still. The process continued by intervals, the dot—only one dot—seeming to brighten and smear slightly, elongating into a small oval.

"Zoom in, Jake," Stark said. "What does that look like from five miles up?"

A cursor hovered over a slider on the screen, and the terrain rushed closer. For a moment O'Malley felt as if she were skydiving from thirty miles up. Then the dive stopped. "Eye altitude five miles, sir; here comes the sequence."

This time, the sequence produced not a smear but a string of ten distinct dots, their edges touching.

"Excuse me, uh . . . Jake," O'Malley said.

"Yes, ma'am?"

"Can you show us that from one mile up?"

"Skipper?"

"Whatever Dr. O'Malley wants."

Another dizzying drop, another five-second animation. This time the dots marched in a precise, steady, clearly separated advance from west to east, a line as straight as an arrow. "Son of a bitch," said O'Malley. "They must be close to the base of the fault line. How'd they get there so fast?" Something in her subconscious was nagging at her, tugging at the sleeve of her mind. *What?* she asked herself. *What is it?* It had something to do with the map. "Jake?"

"Ma'am?"

"Zoom back out, please. But slowly."

"Yes, ma'am."

Why? she thought. *What am I looking for?* It was driving her crazy. As the view slowly widened, Santa Cruz appeared on the east coast, Los Llanos on the west, linked by the highway that squiggled partway up the island's flanks, then burrowed through the central ridge in a pair of tunnels.

"Oh, and Jake," she added, surprising herself. "Can you hide the man-made features? The roads and towns? Show only the terrain?"

"Sure." A moment later, the roads and towns vanished, as if they'd never been there. The island looked pristine, the way it might have looked a thousand years before.

Slowly, steadily, the image continued zooming out. *"Stop,"* she said excitedly. "Stop—that's it!" Dawtry and the captain looked at her, puzzled. "I just remembered something. An old map I saw. In the 1800s, they decided to run a pipeline across the island. *Through* the island, actually."

Dawtry looked puzzled. "A pipeline? For oil?"

"No, for water. There's loads of water in the east, not much in the west. So they started tunneling through the mountains, working from both ends, aiming to meet in the middle. But they abandoned the project. The western end got too hot, and workers started dying from toxic fumes. Volcanic gas." She pointed at the line of dots on the map. "The tunnel was right here." She paused, giving them a moment to absorb the information. "These bastards are smart. That abandoned tunnel gave them a mile-long head start toward Armageddon. That's where they'll put the nuke."

The captain scrutinized the map. "And how close are they to the finish line—the fault line—by now?"

O'Malley picked up a laser pointer from the console. She pressed the button on the side, and a bright-green dot appeared on the screen, hovering and squiggling between two reddish-brown craters near the center of the island. "The fault line starts right around here," she said, "and runs due south along the ridgeline." Slowly she traced the ridge, then stopped, the pinpoint of light trembling where it intersected the most recent blasting site. It was directly beneath the ridge. "They're already there. With those injection wells putting pressure on the fault, that nuke is sure to break off the fault block. If the weapon's in place, they could hit the button any minute now."

"But they won't," Dawtry said. "Not yet." O'Malley and Stark both looked at him. "They want maximum casualties, and maximum media. Today's Sunday. They'll wait till tomorrow—a weekday—when Manhattan's full of workers, the media's searching for stories, and Wall Street's riding for one hell of a fall."

The captain glanced from Dawtry and O'Malley to the map, then excused himself. He stepped to the secure phone on the wall and placed a call. As they watched him confer, Dawtry leaned close to O'Malley. "One thing we haven't talked about," he said. "If the bad guys realize we're coming, what do you think they'll do?"

"They'll push the button, if they can. It might not be their dream scenario—might not be the ideal time on the ideal day to kill the maximum number of people in front of the most possible viewers, but still . . ."

"Agreed," he said. "Alternatively, if they're not ready to push the button, you think they might make a preemptive media strike? Announce that millions of Americans on the East Coast are about to die?" She cocked her head, puzzled, so he elaborated. "Even if we manage to prevent the disaster, they could still create mass hysteria and chaos."

"You mean like that Martian-invasion panic in the 1930s? *War of the Worlds*, right?"

"Right," he said. "That was a radio drama masquerading as news. If these guys did something similar with video, they'd scare the crap out of America. Gridlock up and down the whole East Coast. Maybe cause the stock market to crash, costing us trillions. No small accomplishment. How do we stop that?"

"We find the guy in charge," O'Malley said. "Or at least the guy the Russians are hiding behind. Who's that al-Qaeda mastermind you mentioned?"

"Al-Zawahiri?"

"Him. We find him and we keep him from making that broadcast."

"Find him *where*, Megan? In the caves of Tora Bora? In Yemen? In Moscow? He could be anywhere."

"But he's *not*." She was surprised to hear herself add, "He's *here*—on La Palma! I bet he came in on the ship that brought the nuke."

Dawtry blinked, processing the idea. "You think? So he can go out in a blaze of glory—a *wave* of glory? Martyr himself in style, so he gets seventy-two million virgins in heaven?"

"No. Not so he can die. So he can *watch*. If he's playing God, he'll want to see his handiwork unfold firsthand. But he's a survivor, right?" She snapped her fingers. "He'll be up at the observatory. A ringside seat." Dawtry looked unconvinced. "It's perfect," she insisted. "Like Moses on Mount Sinai. The observatory's way above the danger zone, and it's got video and uplink capabilities galore. He can film a message and broadcast it from there. If the mountainside breaks off and the ocean rears up, he's got Nat Geo–worthy video to show the world. If it doesn't break off, he can still scare the bejesus out of every American east of the Mississippi."

He nodded, tentatively at first, then with conviction. "For an academic egghead, you make a lot of sense." He borrowed the laser pointer from O'Malley. "Yo, Jake?"

The technician looked up. "Sir?"

Dawtry used the pointer to sketch the rim of the caldera. "You see these buildings? They're telescope domes. Can you zoom in on that complex and give us a high-res printout? Big as you can make it?"

O'Malley gave him a puzzled look. "What do you want that for?"

"To help us find our way around."

"We don't need that. I know that place inside out."

"That's great, but you're not going."

"Like hell I'm not going!"

"Megan, this is a military assault. You can't go."

"Bullshit. Reporters go with troops into battle all the time."

"You're not a reporter. You're an astronomer."

"I'm the astronomer who figured this shit *out*. Or did you forget that, Special Chauvinist Dawtry?"

Dawtry looked up at the ceiling, running his hands through his hair in frustration. "Of *course* I didn't forget it. I just chewed out the vice president, the joint chiefs, and the entire National Security Council for not taking you seriously. You're brilliant. Absolutely brilliant. But you're not a soldier, and you're not invulnerable. You could get hurt or killed."

"I've almost gotten killed a bunch of times already. What's one more?"

"This is different, Megan."

"*How* is it different?"

"There might be a lot of shooting, by a lot of people. There might be explosions. It's hugely dangerous."

"I have to be there, Chip. Our guy's gonna be at the observatory, and I'm the only one here who knows the observatory firsthand."

"The risk is too high."

"Screw the risk, Chip. If I don't go, and millions of Americans die because the troops don't know exactly where they're going? *That's* the risk I'm not willing to accept."

"Dammit, Megan . . ."

"Dammit, *Chip*. You heard what the captain said—when you're at war, a fraction of a second can make the difference between victory and defeat. I could provide that fraction of a second."

"Excuse me, folks." It was Stark. They hadn't noticed him approaching. He laid one hand on Dawtry's shoulder and the other on O'Malley's. "I couldn't help hearing some of that. I have to say, Chip, I think Dr. O'Malley's right." Dawtry glared, but the captain went on.

"Ma'am, if you're sure about this, I think you could be a real asset to a team at the observatory."

"Thank you, Captain. I'd be proud to help any way I can."

Dawtry looked away, his jaw muscles clenching.

The captain studied him for a moment. "Chip, you've spent time on the island recently. And you're obviously good in a crisis. Can we enlist you, too?"

Dawtry sighed, conceding defeat, then gave a tight smile. "Abso-damn-lutely."

"Great." The captain cocked his head slightly. "No offense, but can you keep your head in the game? Focused on the mission?" His eyes darted briefly toward O'Malley, then back to Dawtry. She felt herself flush, and she saw Dawtry redden as well.

"Fair enough, Captain," he said. "But, yes, I can."

"Excellent. Glad to have you both. You'll need to see the armorer for gear. We launch in one hour."

CHAPTER 22

O'Malley waddled toward the Osprey, encumbered by the tactical vest. She was strong and fit, so the vest's thirty pounds wasn't the issue; the issue was its bulk. The protective plates along her sides created a Michelin Man effect, forcing her arms to angle outward, and the groin guard—a triangular pocket and protective plate dangling in front of her crotch like some primitive tribal adornment—swung and flapped and threatened to wedge itself between her thighs at every step. She tapped Dawtry's arm, and he turned toward her, peering from beneath the brow of the combat helmet. "The groin guard," she shouted over the whine of turbine engines and the thud of rotors. "I might have to add it to my life list of partners. I just hope it'll respect me in the morning."

He gave a bulked-up shrug, which caused a twitch in the rifle slung across his chest—a stubby, menacing weapon that O'Malley instinctively feared. "Way I see it, better to have the groin guard and not need it than need it and not have it."

"Good point." They waddled up the ramp and into the cargo bay, threading their way between two rows of marines—O'Malley counted twenty-two of them—already strapped into their seats along either side. As they passed, the marines gave them looks ranging from blank neutrality to outright scorn.

Their seats, the last two on the aircraft, were directly behind the cockpit. "Hey, we've been upgraded to first class," Dawtry shouted, but neither O'Malley nor the marines within earshot cracked a smile, because they all knew that the she and Dawtry were the wild cards and the weak links. Unknown and unproven, they were more likely to be a liability than an asset—contributing little and requiring extra protection. Despite her loathing of guns, O'Malley couldn't help envying Dawtry the weapon; it helped him fit in, look less weak. Unarmed and a woman, she was doubly suspect. It was only as she was wiggling into the seat harness that she noticed the marine sitting directly across from her: a young woman, virtually indistinguishable, except by her smaller size, from the male warrior beside her. The woman's eyes—frank and confident—met O'Malley's, and she flashed a thumbs-up and a smile of solidarity as the rotors dug in and the Osprey took flight.

The aircraft flew low, skimming fifty feet above the waves. Eleven other Ospreys were in flight at the same time, O'Malley knew from the briefing—one flying alongside them, the other ten deploying to targets farther south. Two were headed for the opening of the abandoned water tunnel, which O'Malley and the seismometers had identified as the likely placement of the loose nuke. The other eight would fan out to the sites where high-resolution satellite photos showed massive pumps—US-made pumps, ironically—injecting seawater into the fault zone under intense pressure.

By loosening her shoulder straps and leaning forward, O'Malley discovered that she could see through the opening into the cockpit and out through the front windshield. At first, she saw nothing but sea and sky, but ten minutes into the flight, she caught sight of a familiar mountain surfacing from the sea, or so it seemed: an instant replay of the volcanic island's birth eons before, this time unfolding in minutes rather than millennia.

The Osprey aimed for an opening in the coastal cliffs, one that became a deep, jagged valley—the immense, canyonlike fissure piercing the caldera's western flank. O'Malley gasped as walls of rock reared above them, filling the windshield ahead and as far to either side as she could see. Reaching down and to the side, she felt for Dawtry's hand, which took hold of hers and held it tight as the aircraft hurtled toward the cliffs. O'Malley noticed that her lips seemed to be moving of their own accord, and after a moment she realized that she was murmuring a prayer she hadn't said in many years: "Hail Mary, full of grace . . ."

She closed her eyes, waiting for the Osprey's crash into the cliffs. It did not come, and when she looked again, in response to a squeeze from Dawtry, she saw that they had ascended into heaven—or at least sufficiently heavenward to clear the cliffs and emerge above the rim of the caldera.

The radio in her helmet clicked, and she heard a dispassionate voice announce, "Rifle rifle rifle. Missile away. Time of flight, thirty seconds." This, she knew from the briefing, was a Hellfire missile, fired from the unmanned drone. The missile's target was the nuke that was tucked— they *thought*—deep in the old water tunnel. If the Hellfire succeeded in destroying the warhead, some quantity of radioactive material would be released, true, but there would be no nuclear explosion—only a conventional explosion, with a tiny fraction of the nuke's force. A moment later, she heard a different voice say, "Tomahawks in three, two, one, *impact*." The Tomahawks—cruise missiles from the submarine—had a different target: the high-pressure injection pumps that were forcing water into the fault zone. O'Malley pictured the flashes as the missiles hit; pictured the injection pumps fragmenting, pictured geysers shooting from the mountainside as pressurized water gushed from the rock.

"Hellfire One is trashed," she heard the drone pilot's voice say. "Missed the opening by ten feet. Reacquiring target. Launch in three, two, one." O'Malley tensed. "Rifle rifle rifle. Missile away. Time of flight, thirty seconds." O'Malley waited, holding her breath, for what seemed an eternity, then heard, "Bull's-eye! Direct hit on target." O'Malley felt herself gasp. She turned to Dawtry, her eyes shining, and he flashed her a thumbs-up and a huge grin. Then another voice on the radio: "Mother ship here. Good shooting, Lieutenant, but we need deeper penetration in that tunnel."

O'Malley's face fell. Then she had a flash of insight: *He can't just* hit *the tunnel—he has to* thread *it. But he can't. Not from where he is.* She fumbled for the "Transmit" button on her shoulder. "This is O'Malley," she said. "Can you hear me?" Dawtry's head jerked toward her, his eyes wide with alarm. He mimed slashing motions across his throat—the universal signal for "cut!"—but she shook her head.

The frequency fell silent for several seconds. "Stark here," came a reply. "Go ahead, ma'am."

"The drone's too high. The angle's wrong. He has to shoot from the same altitude as the entrance. On the tunnel's exact east-west heading. A straight-in shot's the only way to thread that needle."

"Understood. Lieutenant, can you bring that bird down to . . . *Jake,*" she heard Stark shout. "What's the altitude of that opening, and the compass heading of the tunnel?" The channel went quiet for a few more seconds before the captain resumed. "Lieutenant, we need you at three thousand two hundred feet. Directly abeam that tunnel, on a heading of zero eight seven. We need you looking down its throat."

"Roger that. Copy altitude three thousand two hundred, heading zero eight seven. It'll take a few minutes to get that low, Captain."

"Understood. Don't break the plane, but boogie down as fast as you can. They know we're here now, and they're not sitting on their hands."

"Seven of the Tomahawks made direct hits," came an excited transmission. "Satellite imagery confirms targets destroyed!" The marines in the Osprey erupted in a volley of cheers. "Reacquiring remaining targets."

O'Malley felt a nudge in her ribs. Dawtry pointed toward the windshield and shouted, "Showtime."

Ahead, the great silver dome of the Gran Telescopio Canarias—the world's largest optical telescope—glinted in the sun. The Osprey skimmed low over the dome, angling for the Residencia, where the teleconference studio and satellite uplink were housed. Ahead and to the right, the twin exposed mirrors of the MAGIC telescopes—the Eyes of God—stared as they approached. *God, if you're watching,* O'Malley thought, *this would be a great time to pitch in.* She caught a glimpse of the helipad, but the helipad was too far away; their landing zone was the parking lot at the Residencia's front door.

The Osprey's rear ramp began opening even before they touched down—slammed down—and the marines were unbuckled and hustling out by the time the aircraft stopped lurching. They scurried down the ramp two by two, dangerous animals disembarking from their armored ark, then fanned out and dropped to one knee, aiming their rifles in a protective, outward-facing circle. The squad's leader beckoned, and O'Malley and Dawtry jogged awkwardly down the ramp.

Beside them, the second Osprey and its marines were completing the same unloading maneuver in near-perfect synchrony, and the two groups converged to form a flying wedge, O'Malley and Dawtry protected within it, and then charged across the parking lot toward the building's glass-walled entrance.

Just as they reached the front steps, two pickup trucks careered into the parking lot and screeched to a stop. Their cargo beds were jammed with armed men, and amid a din of shouting, O'Malley heard the rattle of gunfire and the clinking cascade of shattering glass.

The marines at the back of the wedge spun around, closing ranks around O'Malley and Dawtry, firing at the attackers as the group pressed on toward the entrance. As they charged inside—their entry sped by the absence of the shattered glass wall—O'Malley glanced toward the reception desk out of habit, or in an attempt to reclaim some shred of normalcy or familiarity, some memory of the quiet, orderly place that hosted bookish astronomers from around the globe.

And, indeed, she saw a familiar figure, Antonio, behind the counter. He was half-hidden, barely visible, but as O'Malley neared, she saw him rise and lift a hand, as if in greeting. But the hand was gripping a pistol, and the pistol swung directly toward her. The muzzle flashed and a fist slammed into her chest, knocking her sideways. As she fell, she saw Dawtry swing the stubby rifle to horizontal. She heard three quick shots, and Antonio crumpled. Then Dawtry was kneeling beside her, his face close to hers. "Megan, Jesus, can you hear me? Are you hurt?"

She was too dazed to reply—too dazed even to know if she was hurt—so he ran his eyes up and down her body quickly, and then again more slowly. "I don't see any blood," he said. "Do you feel pain anywhere?"

She blinked, shook her head to clear the fog, and took a quick inventory. "My right side. Middle of my rib cage. Feels like I got kicked by a mule."

He moved her arm so he could take a better look, then reached down and tugged at something. She grunted in pain. "You got kicked by a slug," he said, holding up a mushroom-shaped lump of copper and lead. "Thank God for the vest."

Her eyes widened. "Amen," she agreed. "Like you said, good to have it if you need it." She gathered her feet beneath her. "Help me up."

"You sure you're ready?"

"Gotta be." She grabbed his hands, and he hoisted her to her feet. "Ow, *shit*," she said. "They don't tell you about the pain when you sign up for astronomy." Outside, the gunfire was tailing off—no longer a hail of gunfire but intermittent volleys and individual shots instead. Inside, the Residencia was still and quiet, as if the place were deserted or holding its breath.

The marines' leader appeared in front of them, scrutinizing O'Malley closely. "You okay?"

"Feeling fine. Feeling lucky. Ready to go." She pointed. "The teleconference room's that way. Two doors down. The control booth, with the computers and video uplink, is behind door number three." He nodded and signaled his men, and they scurried down the hall at a half crouch.

Dawtry laid a restraining hand on O'Malley's arm. She turned to him and shook her head. "I gotta go, Chip. You coming?"

"Christ," he said. "Of course."

They followed the marines, who had taken up positions in the hallway outside the teleconference studio. Through a large window, O'Malley saw the profile of a man wearing a white robe, a white turban, and a white prayer shawl. A full gray beard extended below his collarbones, and for a moment O'Malley thought she was seeing the ghost of Osama bin Laden—an effect, she realized, that was almost certainly intentional. Dawtry tapped her to get her attention, then mouthed, "al-Zawahiri."

The man was looking into a camera lens and speaking, and a small speaker in the hallway relayed his words. ". . . and so I tell you that you are doomed. Your sins are an abomination, and the wrath of Allah has grown mighty." Behind him, O'Malley could see part of a backdrop—a projection screen—and with a start, she realized that what was projected on the screen was New York Harbor. "And in his wrath, Allah is sending a great wave of vengeance, a wave that will crash down upon you with all the force of your own wickedness." As O'Malley watched in horror, a gigantic tsunami reared up and smashed into the city, and the great skyscrapers shattered, some of them—including Freedom Tower—toppling like bowling pins. O'Malley cried out, "No!" and as if her cry were a signal, al-Zawahiri shouted, "*Allahu akbar*—Allah is great! Death to the West!" and the marines stormed the studio, and gunmen swarmed from the control booth, and the building erupted again in gunfire.

Once more O'Malley was knocked off her feet. This time, after the initial impact, she felt a great weight pressing down upon her, making it impossible to breathe. *Is this what dying feels like?* she wondered. Her limbs were losing sensation—one arm was wrapped around her head at an odd angle, across her mouth, but when she tried to move it, it did not respond, and when she thrashed her head against it, the arm registered no feeling.

Only then did she notice the dark, coarse hair on the back of the hand. Her mind spun, wildly disoriented, before the realization hit: *That's not my arm. That's someone else's arm. The arm of a dead guy on top of me.*

The dead guy moved suddenly, the arm unwinding from across her face; the two-hundred-pound deadweight pressing her down shifted and lightened. The dead guy was Dawtry, but he wasn't dead. His face swam into her field of view, close and out of focus. Even blurry, he looked worried. "You okay?"

"I might be shot," she said. "Something walloped me really hard."

"That was me. Sorry."

"You hit me?"

"Tackled, more like. I kept yelling, 'Get down,' but you kept standing up. Tackling seemed like the best option, under the circumstances."

She processed this. "And you laid on top of me to protect me?"

"I tried to hide underneath," he said, "but you were too heavy."

She smacked him in the chest. "Ow," she said. "That vest hurts."

"Serves you right. When will you learn? Use your words, not your fists."

"Can we get up now?"

"Let me see." He raised his head and peered around. The shooting had stopped, and an eerie silence had taken its place. "Sergeant? All clear?"

"Yes, sir. All clear."

"Help me up?" she said again, and again he hauled her to her feet. "So, help me figure out what we were seeing. I mean, obviously, the footage of the wave hitting New York was simulated, but the message—was that a live feed, or were they recording?"

"Good question. Sergeant? Can you ask Captain Stark if they're monitoring transmissions?"

The sergeant nodded, and they saw him talking into his mic, evidently on a different frequency from the one their headsets were receiving. A moment later he signaled to them. "Nothing. Must've been a taping session."

"Thank God," said Dawtry. "I'd hate to think that was going out live to the world. Imagine the panic in New York."

O'Malley nodded. "Awful." But something was nagging at her. She looked through the window—or, rather, the opening where a window had once been—into the studio. A half dozen bodies were strewn around the room, most of them crumpled on the floor, but two—al-Zawahiri and a guard—sprawled across the conference table in spreading puddles of bright red. *Carmine red. Only not.* The biting smell of cordite hung heavy in the air, overlaid with the metallic, coppery tang of blood. O'Malley moved slowly past the studio, still unsure what was tugging at the sleeve of her mind. Something in the control room. But what? A body lay across the doorway, the legs in the hall, the torso and arms and what remained of the head spilling into the control room. Averting her eyes, she stepped over the body and into the room.

Another body lay slumped on the control console, one hand still resting atop a computer mouse. A small hole and a large circle of blood marked the center of the dead man's back. Fighting back nausea, O'Malley leaned over the corpse and stared at the computer screen. What she saw made her blood run cold. "Chip!" she screamed.

Dawtry leaped through the doorway and reached her in a second. She pointed at the screen. "Upload in progress," the display read. A solid blue bar extended across much of the screen, expanding from left to right. Beneath the bar, fleeting numbers indicated the number of seconds remaining until the upload was complete: "30 seconds remaining"; "20 seconds remaining"; "10 seconds remaining." "Stop, stop, *stop*," she pleaded, frantically jabbing the escape key and control-Q and control-alt-delete. The upload bar grew wider: "5 seconds remaining." "No no *no*," she yelled at the screen. "Don't you *fucking* do it!" In desperation she reached behind the console. Her fingers found a cluster of cables, and with a final "No!" she clutched them and yanked with all her strength.

The bar stopped moving. O'Malley held her breath and silently counted: *One Mississippi. Two Mississippi. Three Mississippi. Four Mississippi*. When she reached *five Mississippi*, she closed her eyes. Dawtry's arms encircled her from behind, and when she heard his sharp intake of breath, her eyes flew open. "Upload Paused," the screen informed them. "Resume and Complete?"

"Over my dead body," she muttered. She lifted the dead man's hand off the mouse, moved the cursor to the "No" button, and clicked. "Take *that*, motherfucker."

The upload bar flickered, then vanished, replaced by a pair of flashing words: "Upload Aborted."

O'Malley sagged and would have fallen, but Dawtry held her up.

The radio crackled in her ear. "Now at three thousand three hundred and level," came the disembodied voice of the drone pilot. "Heading zero eight seven degrees. Distance to target, two miles. Laser is locked, weapon is active. Firing in three, two, one. Rifle rifle rifle—missile away. Flight time, seven seconds." Again O'Malley counted, and again she held her breath. At *seven Mississippi* she turned to Dawtry, searching his eyes for more information—or more hope—than she possessed. But his gaze mirrored her own uncertainty and fear.

"Contact lost," the pilot reported. "Repeat, contact lost. I guess that one was a dud."

"Shoot again," said Captain Stark.

"Roger, Captain, but I have to circle around and reposition. I'm getting a terrain warning."

"Shit," Dawtry muttered.

O'Malley wiggled free and hit her transmit button again. "It's O'Malley," she said urgently.

"Stark here. Go ahead, Doctor."

"Check the seismometers."

"Say again?"

"Check the seismometers. See if they're showing an event just now."

They heard background noise, then a whoop from the captain. *"Bingo,"* he said. "Five seconds after we lost contact, something rang that island like a bell. Coordinates put it at the site of the latest ripple shot. That Hellfire made it all the way in—it took out the nuke! That's good shooting, Lieutenant. *Damn* good shooting."

Dawtry grabbed O'Malley by the shoulders, his eyes wide. "We did it, Megan! By God, we did it!" He leaned down and kissed her on the mouth. All around them, marines cheered and whistled, perhaps because the mission had succeeded, perhaps because of the show Dawtry and O'Malley were putting on.

She pulled away, flushing from the attention or from the kiss—or from both. The sergeant gave them a nod, then stepped close. "Ma'am? Sir? There's something in the other room you might want to see."

O'Malley shot Dawtry a puzzled look; he responded with an equally puzzled shrug.

They followed him into the studio, picking their way around the fallen bodies and pools of blood. The sergeant nodded at the corpse of al-Zawahiri.

Dawtry leaned over the body and gave a low whistle. He straightened and shook his head. "I'll be damned."

"What?" O'Malley looked from Dawtry to the corpse and back again.

"Take a close look." He stepped aside to give her better access.

Overcoming repugnance and nausea, O'Malley forced herself to move closer, to look closer. When she saw it, she gasped. "The beard's a *fake*," she said.

"Five bucks says the prayer bump on his forehead's bogus, too," Dawtry said. "A wad of Silly Putty and some makeup."

"But why?"

Dawtry shrugged. "Wild-ass guess? A smoke screen for Putin. Let the jihadists take the credit and the blame, without putting al-Zawahiri—the real one—in harm's way."

Suddenly the radio clicked and crackled again. "Dr. O'Malley?" Stark's voice no longer sounded jubilant. His voice sounded urgent and grim.

"Yes, Captain?"

"Bad news. We've just picked up some radio intercepts. Best our analysts can tell, there's a plan B. A second device on the island."

"*What?* Where?"

"That's what we're hoping you can tell us. A hundred years ago, that water tunnel was being dug from both ends, east and west, right?"

"That's right, Captain. The plan was to meet in the middle."

"Could they have put a second device on the other side of the island? The other leg of the tunnel?

O'Malley struggled to conjure up the faded map she had seen on the wall in the Cosmological Society. She felt panic trying to take over her brain—trying to shut down her brain—and she fought it. "No," she said finally. "That leg of the tunnel doesn't come close to the fault line. And they weren't blasting on that side."

"Then where?" demanded Stark. "Where else could it be?"

"I . . . I don't *know*," she said. "Seems like they'd've put everything they had in that tunnel. A surface blast wouldn't shake hard enough to trigger the fault. The explosion needs to be deep underground. That's why the tunnel—" She broke off with a gasp. "Oh my God."

"What is it?"

"I'm so *stupid*," she said. "The water tunnel's near the center of the fault zone. But there's another tunnel near the *north* end of the fault zone. Ready-made—no drilling required. It's perfect."

"Explain," Stark said. "Fast."

"There's a highway tunnel through the ridge. The road from Santa Cruz to the west coast. To Los Llanos."

She heard Stark barking orders at Jacobson to find the highway and zoom in on the tunnel. "Got it. We'll take it from here."

"*Wait,*" she said, suddenly remembering a detail. "There are two tunnels, not one. One tunnel each way."

"Got it. Thank you, Doctor. Signing off—"

"*No,*" she shouted. "Listen. The tunnels aren't side by side. The eastbound tunnel's newer and bigger than the westbound. Longer. Deeper underground. That's the one they'll use—to get as close to the base of the fault as they can."

"And, Captain," Dawtry said. "If they can, they'll dynamite both ends first, to seal the tunnel before the nuke goes off. They'll want to contain the explosion, make sure the force goes up through the rock instead of just shooting out both ends. The marines have got to get there before that tunnel closes."

The radio went silent, and O'Malley wondered if she or Dawtry had offended the captain, or if perhaps her battery had gone dead. She shot a look at Dawtry. "He's gone to a different frequency," he told her, as if he'd read the question in her mind.

"Come on," she said. "Let's go."

"Go where? What are you talking about?"

"Outside."

"Why?"

She didn't answer; she was already running—sprinting into the hallway and toward the ravaged front of the building.

"Megan! Wait—it's not safe!" He tore after her, but she had a head start, and his injured leg slowed him down.

She took a scrambling shortcut up the hillside, then turned onto the road that snaked toward the rim of the caldera. Despite the altitude she was running hard, running on pure adrenaline. When she reached the precipice where Dawtry had sent the pickup cartwheeling into the abyss, she stopped. Leaning forward in a gasping half crouch, her hands on her knees, she scanned the ridge to the south of them, her gaze darting from the steep, wooded flank to the sloping farmland below.

Dawtry reached her two minutes later, his breath ragged and punctuated by grunts of pain, his wheezing stance mirroring hers. "Damnation, Megan, what the hell?"

"Hush," she said. "Help me watch."

She pointed. Miles away and far below them, a pair of dots angled toward the western flank of the mountainside. They might have been birds—gulls or ravens surfing the currents of wind coming off the ocean and curling up the mountainside. But O'Malley and Dawtry both knew that they were not birds—not gulls or ravens, at any rate—but Ospreys.

"Hurry," she prayed aloud, standing upright and shading her eyes with her hands. "Please, please hurry." Dawtry stood and shaded his eyes, too.

The dots settled to the ground, disappearing from view. A moment later, a fireball erupted from the spot where they'd landed. O'Malley gasped and reached for Dawtry's hand. "Oh God," she said. A plume of black smoke roiled skyward.

"Not good," Dawtry said. Forty seconds later, they heard the rumble of the explosion.

"But that wasn't the nuke, was it? Please tell me that wasn't the nuke."

"It wasn't the nuke," he said. "That's fuel burning. I think one of the Ospreys crashed. Or got hit by a Stinger or something. Looks bad for the troops on board."

"So there's fighting."

"Maybe. Probably."

Jon Jefferson

"Which means the nuke is there."

He nodded gravely.

"They have to stop it, Chip. They *have* to."

"I know. I know. They will." He moved behind her and wrapped his arms around her. They stood motionless, rooted to the ground, silent except for their breathing, which had settled, and their hearts, which had not.

Suddenly O'Malley stiffened. "No," she whispered. "Please, God, no."

"What?" said Dawtry. Then: "Oh shit."

The ground was shuddering beneath their feet.

CHAPTER 23

"Please, God, no," O'Malley repeated. Her prayer was not answered. Indeed, the shaking continued and intensified. She freed one of her arms from Dawtry's embrace and crossed herself. "Hail Mary, full of grace, the Lord is with thee; blessed art thou among women," she prayed, for the second time in the past hour. For the second time in decades.

"Megan, we have to get out of here," Dawtry said, but she paid no attention. "Megan, come on, we gotta go."

"Go where, Chip? And why?" Her gaze locked on the island's volcanic backbone. She stared, mesmerized and trembling—quaking as if she were an extension of the island itself.

Dawtry gave up trying to pull her away; he held her close and felt his own body begin to shudder as well, though he could not have said if it was from fear or empathy or simply in response to the vibrations from the ground and the woman.

And then they saw it. It was almost invisible at first, the merest hint of a shadow, but then it darkened and widened into a distinct line—a crack in the rock—and then the mountainside lurched visibly and a fissure opened, clearly visible even from eight miles away. O'Malley gasped. "Dear God in heaven," she whispered. "All those people. So many people. Why didn't we warn them, Chip? Why? We didn't even give them a chance."

The fissure widened, and the mountain's flank began dropping—twenty feet, fifty feet, a hundred—and O'Malley's broken sobs gave way to a rising, keening wail.

And then the mountainside lurched again—this time, to a halt. "Look! Megan, look—it's stopped!" Dawtry squeezed her tighter, and she reached up with both her hands, pressing them onto his. Beneath their feet, the ground steadied and gradually stilled. They continued to stare, as if their eyes alone were holding the mountainside in place.

She risked a breath. "Look," she said. "It's not the whole fault block that moved. Only half, maybe less. And it only slid a little." She gave his hands a squeeze. "Oh my God, Chip—maybe it's okay after all."

As if to mock her words, as if to punish her for her pride, the quaking began again. "No no no," she moaned.

"It's not as strong," he said. "Maybe it's just an aftershock."

"But an aftershock might be enough to finish the job."

As they watched, the mountainside jerked again, slid again, and O'Malley gasped again. "*Stop* it," she said fiercely—and it did.

And so it went, in fits and starts, in stillness and in aftershocks, for what seemed an eternity. In reality, it was no more than ten minutes.

And ten minutes was enough: enough to allow the mountainside to ease—to lurch, rather than to plunge—into the ocean, leaving behind a raw, sharp cliff, five miles long and nearly a mile high. O'Malley fought to conjure up a mental map of the island. How many farms, how many towns—God, how many *people*—had vanished into the water? Finally, the image crystallized in her mind, and she gasped with relief: miraculously, the slide had claimed one of the island's emptiest stretches of coastline.

Even more miraculously, the slide had created whirlpools and eddies and waves—waves that might overrun seawalls, wash out a few beachfront highways, smash the windows of foolishly placed condos in Florida—but there would be no apocalyptic wall of water. Not today.

Maybe not ever, now that the ticking geologic time bomb had been defused, or, rather, made to fizzle.

Suddenly the wind picked up; it grew stronger and stronger, buffeting them—deafening them—and an Osprey landed on the road behind them.

The rear ramp dropped open, and the marine sergeant stood in the doorway, beckoning to them. "Ma'am! Sir! Let's go—search and rescue time!"

They scrambled to their feet and ran to the Osprey, grateful for the chance to look for survivors.

Grateful to know that there would *be* survivors.

Millions upon millions of survivors, most of whom would never know what they had survived.

EPILOGUE

The *Washington Post* ran the story on the front page, but below the lead article about the president's latest feud with his critics. "US, Russia Launch Joint Quake-Relief Effort," trumpeted the headline. "Get a load of this," Dawtry said, flashing the headline at her.

O'Malley looked up from the latte she was sipping and gave a snort of disgust.

Dawtry began reading the story aloud.

> In a rare gesture of solidarity, Washington and Moscow have announced a cooperative earthquake-relief effort on the island of La Palma, which suffered a major earthquake two days ago. The temblor, magnitude 7.5, caused a landslide that destroyed several rural villages. Early reports indicate that as many as 50 people were killed, with dozens still missing. Initial search-and-rescue efforts were led by US sailors and marines from the USS *Wasp*, which was dispatched from the Mediterranean immediately after reports of the disaster. The Russian navy's lone aircraft carrier, en route from Russia to Syria, will join the *Wasp* as a "full and friendly

partner" in the effort, Moscow announced. A White House source described the joint operation as "a prime example of improved relations" between the US and Russia.

Dawtry tossed the paper onto the table. "Can you believe it?"

"Sadly, I can," she said.

Two older men were seated near them in the sunny, soaring atrium, at chairs that faced each other across a glass-topped coffee table. Between the men was a wooden chess board, its black and white armies decimated and in disarray. One of the men was wearing a navy-blue beret; the other sported a helmet covered in tinfoil. "Believe half of what you see and none of what you hear," advised the man in the helmet.

The man in the beret nodded sagely. "Good advice, Benny. Who said that—Benjamin Franklin?"

O'Malley laughed. "Herman, you should spend less time stargazing and more time listening to tunes. Marvin Gaye said that." O'Malley stood up and began singing "I Heard It Through the Grapevine" in a low voice, right there in the vast lobby of the Central Intelligence Agency. Her feet started a jive step that started out low-key, then got steadily more sassy, her arms and hips joining the party. When she reached the end of the chorus, two pairs of hands behind her began clapping in slow synchrony. O'Malley spun, carmine-faced, to see CIA Section Head Jim Vreeland and FBI Assistant Director Andrew Christenberry—freshly promoted from Acting Assistant Secretary—behind her, watching and smiling.

"Bravo, Dr. O'Malley," said Vreeland, far less snarkily than she would have expected, given what she'd heard about him from Dawtry. "Sorry to keep you folks waiting. These interagency operations do involve a bit of red tape."

"I'm shocked, shocked," O'Malley said.

"Shall we?" Vreeland led them out of the atrium and through the garden that housed the *Kryptos* sculpture. "Someday," he said, nodding at the encrypted message, "after you've found Planet Nine, perhaps you'll take a crack at solving our signature puzzle."

"It's not that hard," said Benny. Vreeland stopped and turned to look at the silver-helmeted visitor. "I could tell you what it says, but you wouldn't believe me. You guys think I'm crazy."

"Don't tell 'em, Benny," said Dawtry. "Make 'em work for it."

"Don't tell them, Benny," echoed Christenberry. "They'll have nothing to live for once their Great Mystery is solved."

"Very amusing," Vreeland said. He led them through the glass doors of the Bubble and into the auditorium, which was filled to capacity, just as it had been the one other time Dawtry had been inside it. This time, Dawtry was not there to audition for a posting to Langley. This time, he was there, as was O'Malley, to receive the CIA's Intelligence Medal of Merit and the FBI's Medal for Meritorious Achievement. They were the first people—the only people—to be awarded both medals. Not that anyone aside from Agency and Bureau personnel would ever know, beyond Benny and Herman, the quirky surrogate family members they'd been allowed to invite. The CIA medal was jokingly referred to as a "jockstrap medal," because recipients were required to keep it a secret.

But the medals were beside the point, they both knew. The point— the reward—was what they'd done on La Palma, not what anybody in DC or Langley decided to say about it afterward.

The accomplishment, not the ceremony, was what O'Malley meant when she said, "Thank you. I'm so very proud of this. So very grateful. What a remarkable and unexpected honor."

And O'Malley, not the assembled throng, was who Dawtry meant when he said, "I am so very honored to be in such heroic and distinguished company here today."

❖

Two hours later, sitting in the coffee shop just down the block from his condo, Dawtry looked up from another newspaper—this one DC's alternative weekly. "Hey, Star Lady."

"Yeah?"

"I know you think astrology's a load of crap, but I say there's actually something to it."

"And you're saying this why?"

He waved the paper at her. "Because my horoscope totally kicks ass."

She snorted. "No kidding? You actually check your horoscope? Because . . . ?"

"Because it's right next to the 'Savage Love' column, which is full of good sex tips."

She raised her eyebrows and smiled. "I hope you got some."

"I haven't gotten any lately."

"I meant tips, not sex. But tell me about your horoscope. Summarize, please."

"Why summarize when I can quote? It was so good I memorized it." She raised her eyebrows—a challenge—and picked up the paper that he slid across the table. Lifting an index finger, he struck a pose and recited, his tone dramatic. "The world is once again falling deeply in love with you," he intoned. "Let's hope that on this occasion—unlike what happened the last two times—you will accept its adoration in the spirit in which it's given." He paused, lowered his finger, and confided, in an aside, "Here comes the really swell part." He resumed the pose and the recitation: "Let's hope that if the world offers you the moon, the dawn, and the breeze, you won't reject these gifts and say that what you really wanted was a comet, the sunset, and a pie in the sky. There would be nothing sadder than to see the world suffer yet another case of unrequited love." He leaned toward her. "Pretty great, huh?"

"Pretty great," she agreed.

"It's *slightly* off the mark, though."

"How so?"

"The world seems to be offering me the moon, a comet, *and* a pie in the sky."

She laughed. "Hey, G-Man."

"Yes, miss?"

"Just for the record, I never said astrology's a load of crap." She, too, leaned forward. She kissed him, then pulled away, slightly breathless. "And, G-Man?"

"I'm right here, miss."

"About that pie in the sky." She stood up and turned toward the door. "You feeling hungry?"

"Oh yes, miss." He scrambled to his feet to follow. "Oh my, yes."

ACKNOWLEDGMENTS

To my literary agent, Giles Anderson, I'm grateful for the Job-like patience with my long delay in turning this idea into a book . . . and, once there *was* a book, for finding it a good home at Thomas & Mercer.

My acquisition editors at Thomas & Mercer—JoVon Sotak and Jessica Tribble—were also remarkably patient. Equally important, they were enthusiastic and encouraging, and I'm extremely grateful. In addition, Jessica offered many helpful suggestions on the first draft.

Development editor Caitlin Alexander did a masterful job of guiding the manuscript through successive revisions. Caitlin understood and liked the characters, and she appreciated the way the story unfolded; she also asked incisive, probing questions and suggested countless ways to tighten and strengthen the tale. And copyeditor Paul Zablocki read the manuscript closely, attentively, and respectfully, appreciating its various charms, correcting its sundry lapses, and polishing the whole to a higher sheen.

On the island of La Palma, location scout Conny Spelbrink of Active Connect offered a wealth of knowledge and (not surprisingly) connections. Local guide Wim Coen was a gracious, adventurous, and good-humored conductor to off-the-beaten-track places, as well as a skilled driver on steep, slippery volcanic sand. The director of the observatory complex, Juan Carlos Pérez Arencibia, was most gracious in allowing me to visit, as were the staff astronomers who allowed me to spend a fascinating evening at the world's (currently) largest optical telescope—a titan compared with the more modest one I allowed Megan O'Malley to use. Last but not least, Sheila Crosby's book *A Breathtaking Window on the Universe*—a fact-filled guide to La Palma's observatory complex, written by an astronomer—was a valuable reference for supplementing what I learned during my on-site visit and Internet research.

I owe a special thanks to one of the scientists who first called attention to the possibility that the flank of the Cumbre Vieja could collapse and unleash a devastating mega tsunami. Dr. Simon Day, of the Institute for Risk and Disaster Reduction at University College, London, was remarkably gracious, good-humored, and helpful in responding to a novelist's many, many questions. Motivated by a desire to increase public awareness, seismic monitoring, and emergency preparedness, Dr. Day offered countless insights and suggestions, which helped make the book's scientific underpinnings more accurate—and its nefarious plot more plausible. For the things I got right, I warmly thank him; for the things I managed to get wrong, I sincerely apologize.

As ever, I offer my heartfelt thanks to friends and family. The intrepid Colleen Baird accompanied me on my first research trip to La Palma in 2007; no doubt she is astonished to see it finally in print. JJ Rochelle was steadfastly encouraging but never a nag. And Dennis and Judy McCarthy kept faith in the project long after they could be forgiven for having given it up for dead. As for my family—Jane McPherson and our diverse and sundry offspring, Ben, Anna, Nathaniel, and Ursula— you are my bedrock, solid and unshakable. Much love to you all.

AUTHOR'S NOTE

The idea for this novel came to me some fifteen years ago, when I watched a BBC documentary exploring the possibility that an earthquake and landslide on a small island off northwest Africa could cause a massive tsunami, one that might devastate the entire Eastern Seaboard of the United States. The collapse of the World Trade Center towers was still fresh in my mind. *My God,* I thought, *if terrorists could find a way to trigger that tsunami, the death toll would be orders of magnitude worse than 9/11.*

I made a research trip to La Palma in 2007, intending to quit talking and start writing, but I got sidetracked for a decade, writing a series of other books, in a long and fascinating partnership with one of the world's greatest forensic scientists.

Meanwhile, unlike countless other story ideas that have come and gone, the La Palma plot wouldn't let me go. So in 2016, as soon as I'd finished writing the tenth Body Farm novel, I took another trip to La Palma. I revisited the immense Taburiente caldera, rehiked the Ruta de los Volcanes, and got an insider's view of the island's amazing, otherworldly observatory complex.

I've been asked, more than once as I've talked about this project, "Why would you want to give ideas to terrorists?" My answer always goes something like this: "Look, if I can think of this, so can plenty of highly motivated terrorists." Far better, in my opinion to acknowledge the possibility and minimize the risk—by guarding against it—than to pretend it doesn't exist . . . and blindly hope that no one's trying to make it happen. Crossed fingers are seldom an effective defense strategy.

Ironically, I'm writing this note just days after reading that the Trump Administration has proposed crippling budget cuts to a tsunami warning network—one that could save many, many lives if a large tsunami were heading for the East Coast. Eternal vigilance may be the price of liberty, but sophisticated monitoring is the price of disaster preparedness.

ABOUT THE AUTHOR

Photo © 2017 Grayson Holt

Jon Jefferson is a prolific author, veteran journalist, and seasoned documentary writer/producer. His two-part National Geographic documentary—*Biography of a Corpse* and *Anatomy of a Corpse*—took millions of viewers behind the razor-wire fence of the University of Tennessee's renowned Anthropological Research Facility, better known as the Body Farm.

Under the pen name Jefferson Bass—collaborating with forensic legend Bill Bass—he has written ten crime novels in the *New York Times* bestselling Body Farm series. He has also written two true-crime books about Bass's career and cases.

A runner, cyclist, and pilot, Jefferson lives and writes in Athens, Georgia.